A TRACE OF BLOOD

by

Bill Rogers

C A T O N

Published in 2011 by Caton Books

Published by Caton Books 2011

www.catonbooks.com

ISBN: 978-0-9564220-4-0

Cover Design by Dragonfruit
Design & Layout by Commercial Campaigns

"The wran, the wran
The king of all Birds
On St. Stephen's Day
It was caught in the furze,
Although he was little,
His honour was great,
So jump up me lads,
And give him a trate,
Up with the kettle
And down with the pan
Give me a penny
To bury the wran."

A traditional song
Sung by
The Wren Boys of County Kerry,
On St Stephen's Day

Acknowledgements

One of the most enjoyable aspects of writing a novel such as this is the research involved. In this case it was deeply fascinating – not least because of the parallels with my own family history. I would therefore like to gratefully acknowledge the following for their assistance in the writing of this novel:

Staff at Manchester City Library, New Hampshire, USA; Walter Hickey, National Archives – North East Region, Boston; The Irish American Post; Nicky at Alléchante Artisan Bakery, Vermont; The Statue of Liberty-Ellis Island Foundation staff; David Biggins, Anglo-BoerWar.com; Staff at Listowel Library – especially Patti-Ann O'Leary; Adrian Corcoran, Office of Public Works, Eire; Heritage Ireland; Johno Hegarty at Kerry Fire and Rescue, Tralee; Staff at the Preston Family History Centre, Chorley England Stake – The Church of the Latter-Day Saints; Staff at the London Metropolitan Archives and the Family Records Centre; www.norwayheritage.com for the background to the voyage of *The Erin*; And former Chief Superintendent Brian Wroe. Any mistakes that remain are entirely my own.

For my wife, and best friend, Joan.

1

Miriam Caton was late. The fact that she had left her rosary beads on the dining room table, and had to go back, only served to increase her anxiety. She closed the door, and hurried down the path. There would only be a handful of people waiting in the church, but they would be relying on her. It meant a lot to them, the prayer meeting, especially those, like herself, of advancing years. She slowed as she approached the end of the block, paused for a moment to check for traffic, and stepped onto the crosswalk.

He watched her hover, in the way that older people do, looking repeatedly left, right, then over her shoulder. The streets were empty. She would want to be sure in the failing light of early evening, and a steady drizzle out of a cloud filled sky. He let her cross. There were too many windows lit in the houses on either side. Several had the blinds up. Through one of them he could see a television flickering, and a woman clearing the dinner table in another. He had chosen his spot. No reason to change it now.

As she turned the corner he counted to ten, and started the engine. He checked in his mirrors and, without switching on the lights, eased away from the curb. He rolled up to the intersection, saw that the street he was entering was empty, and turned left. She was sixty metres or so ahead of him, moving faster than usual. The clock on the in-car computer said eight ten pm. He smiled to himself. She was late for her meeting.

Miriam wished that she had brought her umbrella. The rain was pooling in the rim of her hat, and the sideways motion of her hips caused it to slop over onto the shoulders of her coat. She could feel it beginning to seep through to her blouse. Not far to go, just one block. Less than two minutes. She began to rehearse her apology.

He waited for her to reach the section where the houses were set back from the road, down substantial drives, curtained by trees and shrubbery. A few more steps and she would be past the only fire hydrant on this section of sidewalk. He slipped up a gear, and gently pressed the accelerator.

Miriam heard a car approaching, and the sound of spray from tyres. Someone in even more of a hurry than herself. That was all she needed right now, to be soaked by the bow wave of a thoughtless driver. Without shortening her stride she moved as far from the road as possible. She heard the change in pitch as the car accelerated, and the bump as it mounted the curb.

Niamh was on her computer when the apartment entry phone buzzed. She looked at her desk clock. Nine thirty seven pm. She wasn't expecting anyone tonight. Nobody called this late, not that she couldn't do with the company. She crossed to the door and pressed the button.

'Hello?'

It was a man's voice. 'Ms Caton?'

'Who is this?'

'This is Patrol Officers Casson, and Bukovitz. Manchester Police Department. Can we have a word please Ma'am?'

She stood by the door waiting for them, wracking her brains. There had been the scratches down the side of the car in the City Hall car park, but that was months ago. Nothing spotted on the CCTV. The claim settled immediately by the insurance company. A perfect paint job. A couple of weeks ago she had reported the late night drummer in the apartment above her to the noise abatement officers in environmental health, just down the corridor from her office. He had moved out before anyone had a chance to come out and check. A West Coast tour with a band she had never heard of. Other than that...

There was knock on the door. Niamh peered through the spy hole. Two officers in uniform, a man and a woman. The man held up his ID for her to see. It looked right, but with the distortion of the fish eye lens it was impossible to be sure. She opened the door on the chain, checked it again, and let them in.

'Sorry to keep you,' she said. 'You know how it is. A woman living alone. You'd better come in.'

The female police officer – Bukovitz according to her name tag – nodded. 'Quite right Ma'am. Can't be too careful.'

Niamh closed the door and turned to find them standing awkwardly, side by side, in the centre of the tiny lounge. 'Please sit down,' she said, pointing to the sofa.

'If it's alright with you Ma'am we'll stand,' said Officer Casson. It struck her how young and embarrassed he looked, fiddling with the cap in his hands, unsure how to proceed.

'I think you ought to sit Ms Caton,' said Bukowitz.

Niamh's blood ran cold. She had been here before. The very same words. In this very room. Not eighteen months ago.

'Please Ma'am.' Officer Bukowitz pointed towards the sofa.

Niamh remained standing. 'Just tell me,' she said.

Bukowitz looked expectantly at her colleague. He took a deep breath. 'I'm afraid there's been an accident Ms Caton.'

Suddenly it came to her. 'Miriam!'

He nodded. 'Yes Ma'am. Miriam Caton. An accident involving a car.'

'I'll get my coat. Which hospital is she in? Is she alright?' It came out in a rush. Before they could stop her she had pushed past them, and headed into her bedroom. She emerged seconds later wrestling with a three quarter length coat, her car keys and purse in her left hand. Officer Bukowitz blocked her path. When she spoke her voice was steel in a gloved hand.

'I'm sorry Ma'am, but there's no other way to say this. Your aunt is dead. We need you to identify her body.'

Father Mercier got up as the nurse led her into the relatives' room. 'Niamh, I'm so sorry,' he said, taking her hands in his.

She noticed that his hair was wet, his face drawn,

and his hands uncomfortably hot. Or perhaps it was just that hers were as cold as ice.

'I was over at the Catholic Medical Center,' he said. 'I came as soon as I heard.'

'Is it alright if I leave you with Father now?' The nurse asked her. 'There's a police officer who needs a word with you. I can arrange for someone else to sit in with you if you'd like that?'

Niamh shook her head. 'No, I'll be fine. And thank you. You've been very kind.' The nurse smiled, and hurried out in response to her pager's insistent bleep.

Father Mercier sat, and drew her down with him. His hands felt oppressive, but she couldn't bring herself to pull them free. 'It's a shocking thing,' he said. 'Do you know what happened?'

'Only that there was an accident. She was struck by a car. When the ambulance got there she was already dead. There was nothing they could do.'

'And the driver? Was he drunk?'

'They don't know. The driver left the scene. Left her lying there in the middle of the road. Alone. Dying.'

'Dear God!' He let go of her hands, and crossed himself. She withdrew her own, and sat with them folded in her lap. 'Poor Miriam,' he continued. 'If any soul on this earth did not deserve to die like that it was Miriam. She was on her way to lead the prayer group in my absence you know. If only I hadn't asked her to stand in…'

'She would have been going anyway.' Niamh reminded him.

'That's true.' He acknowledged.

She thought she detected a sense of relief in his voice. This isn't about you, she wanted to scream.

'And what about you?' he said. 'You don't deserve this either. First your parents, and now Miriam. I can't begin to understand how you must be feeling. And here's me feeling sorry for myself. Some priest I am.'

'Don't worry Father,' she said. 'It's enough that you're here. Just don't start telling me how this is all some part of God's mysterious plan.' Before he had a chance to reply the door opened, and in walked a police officer.

'I am sorry to intrude Miss Caton,' he said. 'My name is Sergeant Michael Johnston, I'm with the Traffic Division, and I am involved in the investigation into your Aunt's death. May I sit down?'

'Of course.' It came out like a whisper. As he folded his six foot four frame into the sofa opposite, Niamh found herself wondering how he managed to fit into a traffic car. Determined to concentrate, she cleared her throat and squeezed her hands together.

'Please accept my condolences for Ms Caton's untimely death,' he said. 'And those of the entire department. I assure you we're going to do everything possible to establish what happened here tonight.'

'Someone ran my aunt down in cold blood and then drove away, leaving her to bleed to death in the street. That's what happened here tonight.' She knew the words were hers, but it didn't sound like her.

'On the face of it, that's how it looks,' he agreed. 'But my job is to establish the facts, the circumstances...'

'And arrest the bastard that did it!'

'Niamh, please.' Father's Mercier's hand was on her knee. 'Officer Johnston is only doing his job.'

When she didn't respond the Sergeant took it as an invitation to continue. 'I understand that Ms Caton was on her way to a meeting at the Church?'

Father Mercier nodded. 'That's right. A prayer meeting in the church hall to be precise. She was going to lead it. Deputising for me.'

'Was this a regular meeting?'

'Yes.'

'And did she always attend?'

'Never missed a single one.'

'What time was the meeting due to start?'

'At eight o'clock on the dot.'

Johnston consulted his notes. 'The first witness on the scene dialled 911 at twelve minutes past eight. Neighbours reported hearing a car accelerating, and a squeal of tyres, a minute or two before that.'

'That can't be.' The priest said, as much to himself as to the police officer.

'Why not?'

'Because Miriam was never late.'

'She was tonight. Maybe she was hurrying. Perhaps that's why she crossed where she did…why she never saw, or heard, the car coming…'

Niamh sat bolt upright. 'What do you mean… crossed where she did?'

Johnston checked his notes again, deliberately giving her time to compose herself. 'Your aunt was found in the middle of the road, sixty yards from the nearest crosswalk.'

'That's impossible!' Niamh protested. 'Miriam's hearing was perfect, and so was her eyesight. Even more to the point, for over forty years she taught road safety in her Civics classes. It was a passion of hers. Almost an obsession. There was no way she would have crossed mid block.'

Johnston looked sceptical. 'It was evening, getting dark, and raining. The street was not particularly well lit. She might not have seen or heard the car until it was too late. If the driver wasn't concentrating,' he shrugged his shoulders. 'It shouldn't, happen, but I'm afraid it does.'

'You're not listening to me,' she said. 'My aunt always used the crosswalk. Always!'

Sergeant Johnston started writing in his notebook. 'I am listening,' he said. 'And I'm also writing everything down.' When he had finished he closed the notebook, put it back in his pocket, and hauled himself to his feet. 'Ms Caton. I can only begin to imagine how hard this is for you. I want you to understand that in order to get to the truth we have to consider every possibility. But I also want you to know that whatever the circumstances, I and my colleagues will do everything in our power to bring the person responsible before the courts.'

Niamh stared up at him for what seemed an age. 'I believe you,' she said.

2

Clods of earth drummed on the coffin lid, like rain on a corrugated iron roof. Niamh stood with her back towards the grave, her gaze on the thickly wooded sides of Beards Hill. Already the leaves would be turning in the Great North Woods. The colours rippling slowly southwards into the White Mountains, down through the Lakes, over Vermont, and along the seacoast regions until, finally, they arrived here, in the Merrimack valley. By mid October these slopes would be a riot of red and gold, copper and bronze. She took some comfort in the knowledge that Miriam would have appreciated this resting place, with its uninterrupted views across the hills towards Mason's Drive where she had loved to walk. She smiled wistfully; half turned, and walked towards the huddle of mourners waiting patiently on the New St Joseph's Cemetery car park.

There were three of them in the limousine; Niamh, Mary Donaghue - Miriam's neighbour and lifelong friend from their kindergarten days - and Grace Hammond, a former teaching colleague. They travelled north on Donald Street, into Milford Street, left onto South Main Street, and across Granite Bridge beneath which the Merrimack flowed serene, reflecting a blue and cloudless sky. Only when the car dropped down to turn left onto Elm Street was the respectful silence broken.

'It's a lovely spot you chose Niamh.'

It was a tentative statement, Mary Donahue testing the waters. Niamh nodded, her head against the window, watching the early lunchers crowding into Greg's Place. It was here on match days, the diner full to bursting, that Miriam, Niamh and her parents met up to watch the baseball and ice hockey at the adjacent Verizon Arena. Emboldened, Mary pressed on.

'Thoughtful too, right next to her brother and sister-in-law.'

She nodded again, this time half-heartedly. She needed no reminder of her deepest loss. The service and committal had all but reopened those wounds still raw after barely a year. They passed Veteran's Park, and eased through the busy Merrimack junction, before pulling in beside the impressive frontage of 614 Elm Street. Niamh glanced at her watch.

Notwithstanding the driver's reverential pace, the two and a half mile journey had taken precisely six minutes. It had felt like forever.

As a one man practice, William S Fitzgerald, Attorney at Law, had one of the smallest suites in the building. It hardly merited the term. Just an office, and an executive toilet, tucked away at the rear of the fourth floor. But it was perfectly appointed. Every piece of furniture, from the desk, the table and chairs, to the bookcase and filing cabinets, rich, traditional, New England cherry wood, sourced right here in Manchester, New Hampshire. On the walls hung double matt finished, gold embossed certificates replete with twenty four carat gold plated medallions confirming his status as notary public, and attorney at law. He was justifiably proud of the way in which, against the odds, he had hauled himself out of the life of poverty, and unremitting toil, into which he had been born, and had risen to the dizzy heights of professional respectability. And he loved his job. Not just the status and the material comfort it brought, but the people he met, and the part he believed he played in the resolution of their problems. There were those who considered all lawyers to be leeches. Sucking the life blood from people at their most vulnerable. William S Fitzgerald was not such a man. Whenever possible he charged no more than a client could afford, and did more pro bono work than any other attorney he knew. That was why he had one of the smallest offices, and a thirty inch waist.

He glanced at the grandfather clock, strategically placed where he could see it without alerting his clients. One minute to midday. He picked up the manilla folder from his desk and crossed the room to place it at the head of the table. He moved it across the highly polished surface with his index finger, centring it on an imaginary meridian. He was not obsessive compulsive, merely nervous. He had seen Niamh arrive at the church. Had observed her throughout the service. Had watched as she followed the coffin down the steps of St Anne's, and departed for the cemetery. He more than anyone could tell that Miriam's death, coming hard on the heels of that of her parents, had affected her more than she realised. Not only that, but the manner of those deaths would have tested the strongest of folk. A cautious double rap on the door told him they had arrived. There would be no authoritative pose at the head of the table, or officious invitation to come in. Not for Niamh Caton. He straightened his tie, took a deep breath, walked over to the door, and opened it.

'Come in Niamh...come in ladies,' he said. 'Sit yourselves down, you must be exhausted.'

He placed a hand softly on Niamh's shoulder as she lingered by the door. She placed her hand over his, and looked up at him. He was the kindest, thinnest, gentlest giant she had ever met. At six feet seven he should have been on the college basketball team, but her father, who had roomed with him in their sophomore year, confided that Bill Fitzgerald had always had problems with his balance. In any case, the slightest on court contact would, she felt sure, have shattered his body into a thousand pieces. But as far she was concerned whatever he lacked in the physical presence was more than compensated for by his kindness, understanding, and integrity. There was no need for words between them. They had all been used up in the month since Miriam was killed. He nodded his head. She smiled, and patted his hand.

He waited for her to sit before taking his own place at the head of the table. She could see the photograph behind him on his desk, angled away from her towards the windows. It was, she knew, of her mother and father on their wedding day. Towering above them, his arms encircling them, was William S Fitzgerald. The best man, her father used to say, in every respect. It suddenly occurred to her that he was now the nearest thing to family that she had left. He cleared his throat.

'Niamh, ladies,' he began. 'I want to keep this as informal as possible, but I hope you'll forgive me for beginning by saying how sorry I am for your loss... for our loss. Every one of us in this room dearly loved Miriam Caton, though none as much as Niamh. The number of people in church today was a testimony to her work in this community, the many lives she touched, and the regard in which she was held. She'll be greatly missed, but always in our prayers. As will you Niamh.'

'Thank you Bill,' she said returning his gaze with a self control that surprised her. If anything, his were the eyes that threatened to mist over. I'm all cried out she decided. So why do I feel like a dam waiting to burst?

Hastily he picked up the file on his desk.

'I have here,' he said. 'The last will and testament of Miriam Bridget Caton. I have a copy for each of you as beneficiaries under the terms of this will. I would like to propose that you allow me to tell you the main terms of the will, and how it affects each of you, and then leave you to take away your copy to read at your leisure. Then if you have any questions you can either ring me or come in, and I'll be happy to answer them. I generally find that works well. What do you think?'

The others looked to Niamh for a lead, and seeing that she was content nodded in unison. Fitzgerald opened the folder and consulted the summary he had placed on the top.

'Niamh, you are named as the first beneficiary. Your aunt has left you her house, which is free of mortgage, its contents, and the sum of one hundred and seventy five thousand dollars.'

He inclined his head towards Mary Donaghue sitting primly in the smart black trouser suit bought less than a year since for the joint funeral of Miriam's brother and his wife.

'Mrs Donaghue...to you Miriam has left the sum of fifty thousand dollars. She earnestly hopes that you'll now get your porch fixed, and take that holiday to Ireland you have been promising yourself since you were nine years old.'

That brought smiles from the four of them. The gentle humour was so typical of Miriam.

'And you, Mrs Hammond, have been left the sum of twenty five thousand dollars as a token of your support and friendship.The residue of the estate, some two hundred and thirty thousand dollars, less taxes, the costs of the funeral, and the probate process, Miriam has left to charity. Thirty thousand to the charity for the homeless here in Manchester for whom she worked tirelessly as a volunteer in recent years – and one hundred and fifty thousand dollars to the US Coast Guard Station at Portsmouth Harbour, to support their work with education partnerships, and kids.'

He paused and looked up. 'I don't think that will come as a great surprise to any of you. I don't need to remind of you of the heroic efforts made by crews from that station to save the lives of Patrick and Teresa in the face of Hurricane Florence last September. The fact that they were able to bring them back to us for burial was a miracle in itself. But what I doubt that any of us knew – unless perhaps you do Niamh – is that on the 21st of July 1944 Miriam's father, your grandfather Niamh, was, with the Third US Marine Division, delivered safely by the US Coast Guard through heavy surf and treacherous fire onto the island of Guam. It was a debt that he never forgot, and that Miriam has now repaid.'

He set the summary on one side, and handed each of them in turn a white envelope containing a copy of the will.

'Given the circumstances of Miriam's death, and the time which has therefore elapsed, I have been able to complete a great deal of the probate process. Unless there any appeals against this will – which I think unlikely – I should be in a position to send each of you a cheque with the next few weeks.' He placed both hands palm down on the table top and leaned back in his chair. 'Are there any questions?'

There were none. Neither Mary nor Grace had expected to benefit, beyond a token piece of china perhaps, or a painting admired over the years. As for Niamh, she thought it a good and generous resolution, and a final demonstration of the wisdom and compassion, of her aunt. She neither needed, nor had expected, any money, and the house and its contents were the best gift she could possibly imagine. She had never been able to consider moving back into her parents' home and had sold it straight away, before the subprime scandal depressed the market for real estate. But Miriam's house held different, less sensitive, memories. She could see herself living there for a while at least. The only ghost would be a comfortable, comforting one. Part of her roots.

'Niamh?'

The lawyer's voice brought her out of her reverie. They were staring at her with a mixture of concern and surprise. Lost in her reverie she had been smiling to herself, and had missed whatever it was that had been said.

'I was saying,' Fitzgerald told her, 'That I would happily offer you all a drink but I gather that there's a table waiting for you over the road?'

She looked at her watch. 'You're right,' she said. Thank you for everything. For being a friend to Miriam, and for the way you've supported me through the past few weeks. I don't know how I would have managed.'

They pushed back their chairs and stood.

'Perhaps I could have a quick word with you Niamh?' he said. 'Alone.'

'We'll go ahead,' Mary Donaghue said. 'You take as long as you need.'

Fitzgerald waited until the door had closed behind him. He sat on the edge of the table to lessen the difference in height between them.

'Miriam was more than just an aunt to you Niamh,' he said. 'She was a friend on whom you could rely for advice, for wisdom, for encouragement. Someone to lift you up when you were down, and to slow you down when you were getting ahead of yourself. And someone you could turn to at times like this. She was taken away from you at just the time when you needed her most. I know that I could never replace her, but I'll always be here for you. Not just as a lawyer but as a friend.'

This time she thought the tears were going to come. Somehow she managed to choke them back. It took a moment or two before she was sufficiently composed to reply.

'I know that Bill. You were always the brother that

Dad never had, and a surrogate uncle to me. As far as I'm concerned you always will be. I'll never ever be able to repay the kindness you've shown to me, and to my family.'

'You already have,' he replied. 'Yours was the family I never made for myself, and you were the daughter I never had. So we're quits. You never need to thank me again.'

'At least come and join us this afternoon.'

'I'd love to, but I've a stack of appointments this afternoon, and anyway, the memories you and I share of Miriam we can chew over whenever we need.'

She stepped close to him, kissed him tenderly on his cheek, turned without a word, and closed the door softly behind her. Only then did their tears begin to flow.

Across the road the red awning was up over the cluster of tables outside the restaurant, jam-packed with folk taking advantage of the Indian summer that had settled over Manchester for almost a fortnight now. Niamh walked back down to the single crosswalk on Merrimack and crossed to the other side of Elm Street. The others were waiting for her at theirs, and Miriam's, favourite corner table.

When they had chosen their meals the talk turned to Miriam.

'She was a wonderful woman your aunt,' began Mary. 'Did you know she was instrumental in finding a home for the soup kitchen in St Anne's Community Centre?'

'And for the past few years,' added Grace not to be outdone. 'Not only has she supported the Women's

Refuge, but she's been active as a Deaconess since the parish lost its priest.'

Mary nodded enthusiastically. 'It looks certain that St Anne's, St Augustine's and St Hedwig's will now become a single parish. I wonder what your aunt would have said about that.'

'She would probably have seen it as a step forward,' Grace replied. 'St Augustine's has always been seen as the French church. St Hedwig's has been predominantly Polish. St Anne's – especially with its growing Hispanic population – has been the most multicultural. That has to be a good thing surely? A universal parish for a universal church?'

Niamh let them burble on, freeing her mind to wander through more personal recollections. It was only when the dishes had been cleared away that she really joined in the conversation. Not that they gave her much of an option.

'What will you do now Niamh?' asked Rosaleen.

'I don't know,' she replied. 'I guess this has shaken me up more than I knew – coming so close on the death of my parents.'

'How long has it been dear?'

'Eighteen months – although it feels like only yesterday. My bosses at City Hall have been great – they've given me a fortnight's compassionate leave. I think I'm going to ask them to let me run that into an unpaid sabbatical.'

'So they should,' Mary said firmly. 'Especially given how hard you worked canvassing for the Mayor, and all in your spare time.'

'It'll give me time to take stock. To work out what I want to do with the rest of my life.'

'Unpaid? But how will you manage?'

'Well, I've got my inheritance from Mom and Dad, and now the money Aunt Miriam has left me. And I think I might lease my apartment, and move into her house. The way the market is at the moment, with all the subprime fall out, I'd never be able to sell either of them at anything like their true market value. But my apartment will be an attractive rental for a young single professional. I doubt I'd have any problem getting a good tenant. One of the university students perhaps.'

Mary lowered her voice almost to a whisper. 'Well be careful,' she said. 'A woman of independent means, and at your age, you'll be a great catch for someone. There are a lot of young men out there with very few scruples.'

Niamh shook her head and smiled. It was last thing on her mind.

3

Her heart sunk as she drew up outside her apartment block. Parked out front was the now familiar white saloon with three blue stripes down the side. As she got out onto the pavement Sergeant Johnston, and another man in a beige lightweight suit, emerged from the car, slammed the doors in unison, and waited for her beside the path.

'Let's go inside,' Niamh said. 'There's a breeze getting up.'

'Do you have some news for me?' Niamh asked as she ushered them into the kitchen diner.

Officer Johnston shook his head. 'If you mean have we arrested anyone, I'm afraid not. This is Detective Supervisor Lieutenant Madera. His division has lead responsibility for the investigation.'

Niamh studied him closely. Just short of six feet tall. Thick black hair, blue eyes, a strong confident face. He looked awkward perched on the stool she used for her breakfast bar. This was a final confirmation that this apartment was too small, even for her.

You were in church...at the requiem mass,' she said. 'Sitting near the back. I noticed you as I was leaving.'

'You're very observant Ms Caton.' he replied.

'I always notice the strangers at weddings and funerals.'

'Did you notice any more besides me?'

She thought about it. 'No, I can't say I did. That's probably why you stood out.'

He smiled. It was a nice smile she thought, neither polite nor professional. Just genuine. 'Not good for a detective…standing out.' He said.

She smiled back. 'I suppose not.'

'I've a few questions I need to ask if you don't mind.'

'Go ahead,' she said.

He got straight to the point. 'You've seen the Medical Officer's final report. You know that we now view this as more than just a normal hit and skip accident?'

'Normal? What would you count as normal detective?' As soon as she'd said the words she wanted to take them back. Even to her they sounded unnecessarily combative. He was only doing his job. It didn't faze him. His cool blue eyes held her gaze.

'I apologise Ms Caton if that sounded unfeeling in any way. But believe me there is a difference. Nearly twenty percent of all pedestrian deaths in the USA are down to hit and skip. Officer Johnston here could give you any number of categories: a driver momentarily distracted, by a child or a dog in the car perhaps; lighting a cigarette, changing a compact disc; a juvenile behind the wheel; an elderly driver on the border of senility who shouldn't be driving at all; then there's driving impaired - a drunken driver, someone high on drugs, or spaced out on a legal prescription;

an unlicensed or uninsured driver, either because they're an illegal, or their licence has been revoked or suspended. Any one of these people might panic when they feel the bump, look in the rear mirror, realise what they've just done. Shock, shame, fear of the consequences...who's to know how any of us would react? Sadly, that's what we mean by normal.'

Niamh nodded her understanding. 'I'm sorry I snapped at you.'

He smiled. 'Forget it.'

She was grateful that he'd made no attempt to patronise her. To refer to the funeral, or everything she had been through.

'Because your aunt was found lying in the road,' he continued. 'Some distance from the nearest cross walk, it was not an unreasonable assumption that she had been knocked down while crossing the road.'

'I never believed that.'

'Well, you were right. Further investigation by Officer Johnston and his team suggests that your aunt was on the sidewalk at the time that she was struck. We believe that the vehicle mounted the pavement, hit her from behind, scooped her up onto the bonnet, and drove back onto the road, where it carried her for some way before braking sharply, and throwing her forward to the spot where she was found.'

'What at first sight appeared to be the marks of tyres braking on impact were made when the car finally came to a halt some fifty yards further on,' added Officer Johnston.

Niamh looked from one to the other, the realisation sinking in. 'So you're telling me that my aunt was murdered?'

Detective Madera leaned forward. 'There was no evidence that the vehicle had swerved, or skidded. There were no marks on the street, prior to the point where we believe it crossed the curb. Your aunt would almost certainly have heard such a manoeuvre, and turned before she was struck. That did not happen.' He paused, choosing his words carefully. 'And I'm afraid that the autopsy has revealed that the vehicle not only drove over your aunt as she lay in the road, but reversed and drove over her a second time before leaving the scene. That alone would make it homicide.'

Niamh was silent. Trying hard not to let the scene form in her mind's eye. Finding it impossible. 'But who would do such a thing...and why?'

'That, Ms Caton,' said Lieutenant Madera. 'Is what we were hoping you might be able to tell us.'

Two cups of coffee later they were no nearer to finding the answer, and it was like her head was full of cotton wool. Miriam had led a blameless life. For reasons unclear to everyone who knew her she had remained a spinster. But she was never lonely, simply happy with her own company. The majority of her adult life had been spent helping others, as a teacher, and as a volunteer church worker. She had never had a bad word to say about anyone. The notion that she might have made an enemy was unthinkable. They had urged Niamh to see if she could remember any strangers at the funeral. She could not.

'Was there anyone who might have benefited from her will?' the detective asked.

Niamh fetched her copy of the will, and gave it to

him to read. 'As you can see, aside from me, the major beneficiary was the Coast Guard station at Plymouth Harbour, and even then the purpose for which it can be used is clearly set down. In any case, nobody knew the contents of her will apart from Mr Fitzgerald.'

'And the witnesses.' Johnston pointed out.

'I think you'll find that Mr Fitzgerald – who was not only our family attorney but also a friend to us all - and his secretary, witnessed the will.'

He handed it back to her and waited until she had placed it back in her bureau.

'I understand that your parents died in an accident last year?' he said.

She wondered why it was being raised now. His face was a mask. 'That's right. A year ago last Saturday.'

'At sea?'

'They were out in their yacht. Coming back from Rockport to Portsmouth Harbour.'

'That's what…thirty miles or so?'

'Twenty four nautical miles. I'd done that journey with them many times over the years. There was a hurricane on its way. They wanted to be sure to get back before it arrived. So that they wouldn't have to stay over. Unfortunately, it suddenly picked up speed, and although it didn't make landfall, there were still winds in excess of ninety miles an hour along the coast.'

'That was hurricane Florence, right? There were a lot of call out's that night, even here. Trees down, telegraph wires down, alarms set off.'

'They were hit by a massive wave,' Niamh said. 'It smashed the mast, and tore off the rudder. Even with the auxiliary engine they couldn't steer. My father managed to send out a Mayday, but before the coastguard could get there they were blown onto the rocks south of White Island. The yacht capsized. They were both flung clear. My father must have known they were going to end up in the water. They were lashed together in their lifejackets.' She paused for a moment. 'The lifeboat nearly came to grief trying to reach them. But it did manage to recover their bodies not far from the wreck.' She paused again, her fists clenched on top of her thighs, the knuckles white as she fought to control the tremor in her voice. 'They must have been thrown against the upturned hull, or the rocks. Both their skulls had been fractured.'

'Was the boat recovered Ms Caton?' he asked gently.

Niamh shook her head. 'Not intact. But parts of the hull were washed up on the shore several days later.'

'So no one was able to determine exactly what happened?'

She had no idea where this was leading, but now she was angry. 'My father told the coastguard what had happened. He was in contact until just before they were swept against the rocks. What reason could he possibly have had to lie?'

He held up both hands defensively. 'I wasn't implying anything, I promise you Ms Caton. I just needed to know if there was any possibility that the engine might have been tampered with.'

'It was only a 20 horse power diesel but as tough as old boots. I never knew it to fail. And if my father said it was still working, then it was!'

The detective nodded to his colleague. The two of

them stood. 'I'm sorry Ms Caton,' he said. 'To have intruded on your grief in this way, and I am personally sorry to have raised doubts about the tragic accident that took your parents from you. I hope that you understand that I have to eliminate any possibilities so we don't set off down blind alleys. I assure you we'll do everything in our power to find the person who killed your aunt.'

Her composure regained, Niamh regretted her outburst. She got to her feet and held out her hand. 'I understand detective,' she said. 'And I hope you'll accept my apology for snapping at you. It can't be easy bringing people bad news, and then having to ask them questions that you know will upset them further.'

'Thank you Ma'am,' he said. 'It isn't. But you've made it a lot easier than most.' They started to leave but he paused in the doorway, and turned. 'Either I, or Officer Johnston, will be in contact when we have any news for you. Thank you again. We'll let ourselves out. You take care now.'

She watched them walk down the steps, heads together comparing notes. As he stooped to get into the car Lieutenant Madera turned, and looked up at the window as though he had known that she would be there. He nodded briefly, and ducked out of sight.

When the car had gone she cleared away the cups and saucers, loaded them in the dish washer, and sat down on the sofa, emotionally drained. She knew that she ought to feel something as result of the news the officers had brought, but she did not. Not unless numbness counted. Perhaps they would catch whoever had been responsible for Miriam's death.

34

She doubted it. Not after all this time. The vehicle would have been destroyed by now. Burnt out, or more likely crushed. A cube of metal on its way across the Pacific to feed the Chinese economic miracle. And it was pointless them looking for a motive. Miriam had simply been in the wrong place at the wrong time. The victim of a mindless psychopath. Not strictly mindless, simply lacking in empathy, devoid of even the slightest inkling of conscience. The absolute opposite of his victim. Always supposing that it was a him. These days you could never be certain. Either way, nothing would bring her back. She suddenly realised that her thoughts were running away with themselves, tumbling over and over in her head. She made a decision, stood up, picked up the phone, and dialled. It was answered immediately, well within the three ring corporate standard.

'Kerry Grant, Neighbourhood Regeneration Team. How may I help you?'

'Hi Kerry. It's me, Niamh.'

'Niamh! We didn't expect to hear from you today. How are you holding up?'

'I'm O.K. I just need a word with Marcia, is she there?'

'Sure. If you hang on I'll put you through. You look after yourself, you hear?'

'I'll do that.'

In the background she could hear her colleagues talking. No doubt sharing their thoughts about the catalogue of misfortunes that had befallen her. It was partly this misplaced concern for her that had finally helped to make up her mind. Better to be remembered fondly, missed even, than pitied.

'Niamh...we didn't expect to be hearing from you today. How are you?'

'Hi Marcia. I'm fine thanks. But I need to talk with you if that's OK?'

'Of course.'

'You remember we discussed the possibility of my taking some time off..?'

'The sabbatical? Of course. Another six months, you'll automatically qualify...you know that.'

'Yes. But If I wanted a break right now? I don't mind if it's unpaid.'

There was silence at the end of the phone. When Marcia spoke her voice confirmed the hesitation Niamh had sensed.

'That might not be necessary. I'll have a word with the Mayor. But are you sure that's wise? At least at work there will plenty to take your mind off everything that's happened this past year.'

Niamh stood tall, wanting to sound positive, in control. To communicate that this was a decision she had thought through. Not a cop-out.

'I know that if I come back to work it might take my mind off it, but I'll just get into the same old rut. The reason I need a break is to get my life back on track. You know how I've been. No boyfriend, no outside interests. Just work, work, work.'

'So what will you do? Play, play, play?'

She laughed at that. 'Not exactly. But it'll give me time to think. To work out what it is I do want to do with the rest of my life.'

'Well,' Marcia said, lightening up. 'While I don't envy you the circumstances that led you to make the decision, I have to say I wouldn't mind a chance to get off the conveyor belt, to step back and take stock.'

'Better not let Harry know you feel that like,' Niamh told her. 'He might think you plan to change him for a newer model.'

She laughed. 'No problem, I've already told him that.'

'So you'll let me know? About the sabbatical?'

'Soon as. But you can consider it sorted. We're really going to miss you. Niamh.'

'And me you Marcia. And everyone there. But I'll keep in touch.'

'Make sure you do. And good luck. You sure deserve it.'

'Thanks Marcia, for everything.'

'You're welcome. You've earned it. And Niamh...'

'Uhhu?'

'You take care.'

She placed the phone back on its charger. That was the third time in as many minutes someone had told her to take care. It made her feel like an invalid. Like a victim. No way was that going to happen. Not to her, Niamh Caton. No way.

She put the mug of coffee down on the desk mat, and stared at the blank page. All her professional life she had been involved in the development of plans for other people. Now it was time to make one for herself. How to start? The same way she always did. With a mind shower. Don't think about it, she told herself. Just do it. Her fingers flew across the keys.

Make a list of things I want to do before I die: - places to see; people to meet; things to do; Sort out Miriam's stuff; Sort out Mum & Dad's furniture, & let go of the pieces I'll never use; Do up Miriam's House; Let out the apartment; Move; Learn another language; Write a book; Finish My Roots; Find a guy; Get Married; Have babies...

She stopped typing. Have babies! Where did that come from? It wasn't something she had thought about in over a year. Nor had she been actively looking for romance. If anything she had shied away from it. And now here was her subconscious giving her a nudge. She allowed herself a smile. Well at least I get to marry first. She decided to put them in some sort of order, if only to get started on something. Filling in the detail and sorting out a timeline could wait a day or two. In any case, the one thing she had learned about planning for the future was that it never worked out the way you intended. "If you want to make God laugh," her father once told her. "Tell him your plans." Tragically, prophetic though that had proved, she doubted that God was laughing when the Rose of Tralee foundered off White Island.

The dream wish list was probably better done, she decided, with her feet up, and a glass of chilled Anderson Valley Brut in her hand. As for sorting through Miriam's possessions, there was no way she could face it right now. At least, not today. And as for redecorating and moving in, that was a medium term project. But she would definitely contact the realtor in the morning. Once the signboard went up outside the apartment it would force her to think seriously about what to take with her, and what to buy new. The language learning, and the novel, would have to wait. Maybe in the spring when the sap was rising. Speaking of which, there was no way she was going to pursue romance. Better to let it come to her. At least she would have some time to prepare. To think about how she would play it when it did. There you go, she chided herself, thinking you can plan for it. That left just one action she could get on with right now. Unfinished business. She decided the term action plan was far too grand, saved the document as My To Do, and closed it down. Then she clicked Open under the file command, and searched for the folder Roots that she had created back in May; four months before Miriam had been killed, since when she had felt unable to continue with it. Now she had an urge to get it finished, and a reason.

There were just four files: one containing a list of web site links; the second, a working document; the third, a sort of diary of observations as she worked through the project; and the fourth - the one which she now selected - a chart showing the current state of the family tree she was building. She picked up her mug, sipped her coffee, and waited patiently for the virus scan to do its work.

4

Niamh moved the cursor to the words Miriam Clare Caton, Born March 7 1945, Manchester New Hampshire, and added Died August 16th 2008. The starkness of that phrase had about it an even greater sense of finality than the lowering of the coffin into the grave. It felt as though she had written the final words in the Book of Caton. The cursor blinked in time with the beating of her heart, reminding her that this was not the final chapter; the penultimate perhaps. There's still me, she pondered, as her eyes slid across to the left of this chart that depicted as much of the Caton ancestry as she had managed to trace so far. And there's Tom.

Niamh had begun this enterprise shortly after her parents' funeral. Among the books in her father's study she had found an aged pocket edition of the Holy Bible, with copious marginal readings between parallel texts. Printed in Coldstream, Scotland, for the Free Bible Press, it was dated MDCCCXLVI. She had worked that out to be 1846. The cover appeared to be of black embossed leather. The pages were edged in fading gold. The spine was damaged, and the first few pages were yellow and brittle. She had been about to toss it on the reject pile when something prompted her to first flick through the pages. She was amazed and delighted to discover that the two end sheets at the very back had been used to record births and marriages on her father's side, for seven generations, right back to her great, great, great, great grandfather, Joseph Padraig Caton, born in Listowel, County Kerry, in Ireland, in 1818. Three different sets of handwriting told her that this bible had been handed down over the years. The most recent entry was in her father's neat hand; starting with his own parent's details, and finishing with Niamh Alicia Caton. Born August 1st 1977. She had immediately resolved to complete the family tree as best she could.

By midsummer she had filled in some of the gaps, and discovered new routes she had yet to explore. She had started with that birth in 1818. The paucity of Church and State records in Ireland – particularly of Catholic families – was immediately evident. Many of the clergy were illiterate. Some failed to record anything other than baptisms. Of those that were kept, the vast majority had been lost or destroyed. Without visiting the country for herself, and scouring graveyards and miscellaneous abstracts of documents painstakingly compiled by genealogists such as the famous Gertrude Thrift, it was clear that she had no chance of tracing ancestors back into the eighteenth century. Instead she concentrated on fleshing out the information that she already had.

It was recorded in the family bible - although no date had been given, nor subsequently found – that Joseph Padraig Caton had a younger brother, Michael, who became a priest. She knew this because the date of his consecration was also there in the bible. She opened another file, and reminded herself of the article she had downloaded from the archives of the Diocesan Newsletter. It was a copy of the eulogy that remembered his selfless work as a parish priest visiting the sick and dying at the height of the Potato Famine.

"Never minding the ever present threat of fatal infection, Father Michael Caton went from hovel to louse ridden hovel, tending to the wretched victims of the black fever, sharing with the hollow cheeked children what little food he had for himself, and blessing the wretched corpses as they were tipped into the communal graves on the barren hillside, and the quick lime shovelled on top of them."

At the time of his death, in 1899, he had risen to the rank of Monsignor, and was still working as an assistant to the Bishop of Kerry. Niamh had written to the Diocese asking if any of Monsignor Caton's correspondence or diaries were perhaps held in the diocesan library, or archives. She hoped that it might provide some additional information, and family connections, for her to pursue. Much to her surprise, she was informed that all of her great, great, great uncle's private correspondence, and effects, had been sent to America – to his nephew Joseph. Since they were not among her father's effects she assumed that they had long since disappeared.

Joseph's wife, Brighid McMahon, had given birth to just four children: the first, another Brighid, in 1840; then Padraig in 1842; Joseph in 1846 – the year the Great Famine began to reach its peak – and Colum, in 1847. Both Colum and his mother had died in that same year. Whether as the result of the birth, or the famine, was not recorded. Niamh had failed to find any later reference to Padraig, and suspected that he may have emigrated from Ireland to America. It was one of the lines of enquiry she had yet to follow. However, the fate of Brighid Caton, their only daughter, was simple to ascertain. A note had been written in the margin beside her name.

Brighid had been one of thousands of Catholic immigrants from the Old World, sponsored by the Queensland Emigration Society to help populate this newly founded State. She had emigrated with the QES on board the Queen of the Colonies, and died, of a fall, on the evening of 27th December 1867.

Brighid's brother Joseph had fared better, and Niamh had been able to build up a full account of his procreation. In 1869 he had married Mary McCarthy – an only child born in 1849, and living in a neighbouring street in Listowel. They in turn had seven children. The youngest, Mary, born in 1870, was - according to the story Aunt Miriam had told her – engaged to a fine young officer in the Royal Dublin Fusiliers. They were due to marry as soon as his battalion returned from fighting in the Boer War. In November 1899 he was killed by a shell fired from Long Tom, the Boer's ancient and infamous artillery piece. The gun was manned - through a cruel trick of fate – by MacBride's Brigade, a group of Irishmen working in the South African mines who had lined up alongside the Boers to fight the British. Mary's heart was broken. She travelled to Europe, and joined a community of Irish and Belgian Benedictine nuns in Ypres. When the abbey was destroyed during the First Wold War the nuns took refuge in London, and many years later, they moved in search of a permanent home to County Wexford. Mary had ended her days at Kylemore Abbey in Connemara. As a child Niamh had thought the story romantic, but now she saw it as rather sad, and cheerless. Like Miss Havisham in Dicken's Great Expectations.

The next child, Joseph John, born in 1871 just a year after Mary, by a remarkable coincidence also died in the Boer War. Niamh had written to the War Office, the Imperial War Museum in London, and finally, to the Connaught Ranger's Association, hoping to find a hero in the family. Her persistence was rewarded with a letter stating that Joseph John Caton had been awarded two commendations for bravery, one of them posthumously. Niamh found herself learning more about history from her painstaking research into her family tree than she had ever done at school. In fact, she was beginning to think that for her this was the most satisfying part. It was as though, through her ancestors, she was connected at a strong emotional level to the history of the previous two centuries.

Elizabeth was born in 1873. A year later she was dead. No cause was given, but Niamh knew from her research that any number of infantile and adult epidemics rampant at that time could have carried her away. Eighteen months later Mary had given birth to twins Frederick and Clare. Clare died at birth, but her brother thrived and went on to have two children of his own, a grandson, and a great grandson, Tom Caton, the only living relative of whom Niamh was aware.

That left just two more children born to Joseph and Mary. She smiled to herself at the religious significance of those names. A holy family. Is that, how they saw themselves? Colum was born in 1875, the other was her own great grandfather, Patrick Caton, who had emigrated in 1878, and settled right here in Manchester, New England. Their first two children – Joseph and Maggie born in 1900 and 1902 respectively, had died together on October 10th 1918. The cause of death was given as influenza. Niamh had seen Robert Kenner's film *Influenza 1918,* part of the American Experience Season at the Library - and knew that Spanish Flu had killed over forty million people worldwide, including over six hundred thousand Americans, and that Boston, Philadelphia, and New York had borne the brunt of this terrible pandemic. Now she knew for certain that it had touched her family in the cruellest way possible. But at least Patrick Joseph, her grandfather, despite being only one year old, had miraculously survived. He had married Jane Enright, herself a second generation Irish American, and through them Miriam born in 1945, and Patrick, born in 1947, had entered the world. At this point, she had a wealth of oral family history on which to draw.

Twenty five years later, her parents had told her, Patrick, her father, met Teresa Jameson, a third generation Scottish American on a Master in Education course at Lynch School of Education, Boston College. Within a year, the two were married. After an increasingly stressful four years of trying for a baby their only child was born. When they saw her bright eyes, and golden locks, they named her Niamh, after Niamh of The Golden Hair, Princess of the Land of Promise, in the legends of the Fenian Cycle.

Niamh instinctively ran her fingers through her hair. By the time she was three years old that gold had reddened to strawberry blond. "The rarest of natural hair colours in the world," her mother had told her. "Just like you." She wondered sometimes if her own children would inherit that colour, and if there were any other Catons with such a striking shade out there. Her eyes slid across the screen and rested on the name of Frederick Caton's great, great grandson, Tom Caton, her fourth cousin twice removed. Born in Manchester, England, on the 27th of April 1970, he would now be thirty eight years of age. A shrewd inquiry to the international operator had established that there were just two T. Catons in the Manchester postal district. Both of them were ex-directory. She had contemplated writing a letter to both of them, but could not decide how to start, or what exactly to say. Then, by a stroke of luck, or genius she preferred to think, a simple Google UK search had thrown up an archived article in Brief, the Greater Manchester Police in-house newspaper. It reported the appointment of a Tom Caton to the rank of Detective Chief Inspector, and Head of the newly created Special Detection Group within the Force Major Incident Team. He was, the article stated, thirty eight years old. An email to the GMP headquarters had provided a work email address, and a telephone number. At that point, back in August, Niamh had just plucked up enough courage to make the call when the door bell rang, and she had found Officer Johnston outside her apartment, with the news that Miriam was dead.

Niamh stared at the screen until the words began to dissolve into each other. She shook her head, rubbed her eyes, and stood up. Time for a cup of a coffee. Then, she promised herself, she would make that call.

Three thousand, one hundred, and forty four miles, west-northwest as the crow flies, in the heart of Manchester, popularly regarded as England's second city, Caton ducked beneath the boundary tape, straightened up, and slowly scanned the scene before him.

This was a seminal place in European urban history. Ten years before he was born the bulldozers had rolled in. The close community of extended families, in Victorian terraced streets, had been dispersed. Their homes replaced by grey high rise, deck access, concrete blocks in homage to Bath's Georgian Crescent. In less than ten years they had deteriorated into slums where the old, infirm, and vulnerable hid behind plywood doors, and grey net curtains. For over thirty years, burglary, street robbery, and drugs, made it a notorious no-go area for all but the brave and foolhardy. And then the city's second regeneration plan had taken hold. This part of south central Manchester had been transformed.

Where dealers dealt, and stolen goods were passed from hand to hand, where scores were settled, and prostitutes and rent boys plied their trade, were now two acres of green field park, whose primary aim had been to design out crime, and attract in the community. Seventy metres at its widest point, surrounded by angled horizontal railings above a metre high brick wall, everyone, and everything, was visible. No hiding places. A podium and canopied performance area, a basketball court, football pitch, BMX jump track, and a sensory garden. Steel bollards and grills to stop the motor bikes and joy riders. Walkways connected directly to the City Centre less than a mile away. High rise blocks had been replaced by superior two storey flats, and brand new houses. Over by the children's Treasure Island playground, with its dunes and shipwrecks, dolphins, sharks and monsters, the trees were losing a canopy of golden leaves that drifted idly over the royal blue rectangles of impact cushioning surfaces. To universal surprise, crime had plummeted, awards had followed. Right now, at seven o'clock in the evening, it was cold, damp, and gloomy. All but deserted. Cleared by the cordon of community support officers lining the perimeter. Forlorn pools of light heightened Caton's sense of alienation as he set off towards the huddle of people at the southern end of the playground.

Detective Inspector Gordon Holmes saw him approach, detached himself from the group, and came to meet him.

'They've got a name for the victim Boss,' he said, plucking at his chin with a latex glove. 'Marvin Brown, amateur gunsmith. And they've got a probable motive.'

'Does that mean they know who the perpetrators are?' Caton asked, more in hope than expectation.

'DI Tyldesley says she's got a pretty good idea who did it.'

DI Tyldesley, the female deputy on the Xcalibre Task Force, the longstanding initiative that had broken the stranglehold of gun crime in the city. If anybody was likely to know, she would. Caton followed Holmes towards the others. A pool of bright white light appeared at the centre of the group, casting them into shadow and sending spears of light through the gaps between them.

'Duty pathologist is on her way,' Gordon told him. 'Not that there's any doubt about the cause of death.' He turned and headed towards the others. They parted as Caton reached them.

The victim lay sprawled in the harsh glare of twin LED flood lamps, face up, across the children's roundabout. A mixed race male in his late forties. The head, torso, and legs, were squeezed between the central struts, the arms flung wide between the gaps on either side. Blood had spread from an ugly hole at the base of his neck, fanlike, across the front of his leather jacket. Identical holes had been torn through both thighs above the knee.

'Those are exit wounds?' Caton asked. Their size and shape, and the way the jagged edges of the cloth splayed outwards, left little room for doubt.

'Yes Sir,' replied the lead crime scene investigator. 'It looks as though he was shot from behind in both legs over there,' she pointed back towards a climbing frame. 'Then he was shot through the base of his neck, close up, execution style.'

Caton could see a dark patch where blood had pooled, and three parallel tracks that smeared the limestone pathway. 'Then his body was dragged over here, and displayed like this.'

'Yes Sir. Then it looks like the roundabout must have been spun really fast. That's why we're standing this far back.' She pointed to the ground ahead of them. In the harsh light he could make out a star burst of crimson that had sprayed in a two metre radius circle from the victim's head, across the blue composition surface. 'You can even see,' she added. 'Where it spirals ever closer as the roundabout slowed down, and his heart stopped pumping.'

It was obvious, now that she'd pointed it out. The action played in his mind like a video nasty. The victim fleeing in desperation, his heart thumping in his chest. Hoping against hope that they wouldn't take him down out here, in full view. Knowing that he wasn't going to make it. Swift confirmation from the twin shards of pain slashing through his thighs. Cold steel against his neck, and then oblivion. It wasn't hard to imagine, but it would be some time before Caton would be able to stop the images returning. Much longer for anyone who might have seen it for real.

'Were there any witnesses?' he asked.

'A woman walking her dog over by the Zion Centre, two youths on the BMX area, and another five having a kick around on the pitch,' Holmes told him. 'Plus anyone in the flats who might have been out on their balconies. We won't know till we get the results of the door to door.'

'Presumably the ones we do know about would have been alerted by the initial shots, and had a really good sight of the rest of it. Including which direction the gun man went in?'

'Gunmen,' Holmes corrected him. 'Two of them, on mountain bikes. They went off in the direction of Castlefield. But I doubt if anyone is going to be able to ID them. Hoods up...the light was failing...didn't get a clear view...all happened so fast. You know how it is Boss. Self preservation.'

Gordon's natural cynicism had been honed by years of experience, and Caton knew that he was right. No one was going to stand up and be counted. And he couldn't say he blamed them. And that was why these two had been able to take their time. Dump the body like that. Spin it round. It was their way of sticking up two fingers to the police, and to their own community. *This is our turf. We do what we want. And there's not a damn thing you can do about it.*

'We think we know who did,' said DI Jean Tyldesley. 'The problem is going to be proving it.'

'Then the sooner you track them down,' Caton said. 'The better. They must be covered in blood from that little stunt they pulled with the roundabout. Not to mention the blowback residue from the gun.'

'My team are already onto it,' she told him 'We know their home addresses, and bolt holes, and most of their associates.'

Caton nodded. 'Sounds like you've got a head start on this one,' he said. He paused, and stepped deliberately away from the tight knit circle. 'Can I have a word?' She followed him until they were out of hearing range. Even so, he dropped his voice, knowing that it would carry on the still night air. 'Jean,' he said. 'The only reason that I'm here at all is because this is your first murder as the senior investigating officer. And believe me, I know how that feels. So I have no intention of breathing down your neck.'

'Thank you Sir,' she replied, the relief showing on her face in the near darkness.

'Don't thank me,' he said. 'I've a week's leave due

before I join the Serious and Organised Crime Agency on a week's training course. I'm leaving you DI Holmes instead.'

She had difficulty hiding her disappointment. 'Gordon Holmes?!'

'Don't let his physical presence or his manner fool you.' Caton told her. 'Beneath that bluff exterior and self deprecating manner, he's a hell of a lot brighter than people think. It's what makes him a good detective...taking people by surprise. And he's been where you are right now, so he knows how it feels. He won't get in your way, and he won't throw his weight around. He has more connections in the Force Major Incident Team than I have. Give him a chance. And if it doesn't look as though it's working out, call me.' He led her back towards the others. 'Anyway,' he said, raising his voice on purpose. 'Looks like you'll have this sorted in no time.'

Niamh looked at her watch. It was 2.30 pm. In England it would be 7.30 in the evening. Too late to catch him at work. Change of plan. She sat down, opened her mailbox, and selected Compose. Having already rehearsed what she was going to say, her fingers flew over the keyboard. She read it over and, before she could change her mind, pressed Send. It was done. Now all she had to do was wait.

He could see the clouds rolling in from the North West, across Kilbaha Bay. There was rain in the offing. But then there was always rain in the offing in this part of County Kerry. The woman sensed it too. He watched as she stopped on the track below him, and turned to look up at the darkening sky, and out towards the sea. She called to the dog, turned, and strode purposefully back the way she had come, down the path that led off the mountain. The dog bounded into view, swiftly overtook his mistress, and disappeared around a bend.

He cursed, and climbed out of the natural hollow in the rocks in which he had waited so patiently from the moment he saw her leave the house to head out across the fields. He hefted his rucksack onto his back, made sure that he had left nothing behind to betray his presence here, and set off. Behind him he sensed the looming bulk of the summit of Stack's Mountain, ahead the long descent. He set off at a steady jog, conscious that he had to catch her before the mountain side flattened out on the lower slopes of Beennagheeha Mountain.

Ten minutes later he saw her up ahead, picking her way confidently down the stony path. The wind had picked up, and a soft warm rain was falling. Her head was down, and the hood of her anorak, like his, was up. Steadily, he narrowed the distance between them. Suddenly the dog raced past her, and up the track towards him. There was barely room for the two of them but the great dog bounced lightly past him, then ran ahead of him again, just keeping pace, its tail wagging enthusiastically, spraying water. He heard her call, and watched as the dog bounded off again, past his mistress, and out of sight.

When he and the woman were ten yards apart he hung back, maintaining the distance between them. He moved carefully now, so as not to disturb the stones beneath his feet. Around the next bend he saw the perfect place, and hurried to catch her. He was almost at her shoulder when she sensed his presence, and began to turn. He grasped her shoulders and swung her body sideways, off balance, and over the side of the precipice. She fell without a sound, bounced several times on the exposed rocks, and came to rest in the ravine below.

The dog appeared ahead of him. It stood for a moment, confused, looking first up, and then down, the track. It loped towards him, stopped a yard away, and looked over the precipice to where his mistress lay smashed and broken, like a rag doll, the bulk of her body on the bank of the river, her head and one arm floating just below the surface as the fast flowing water eddied around them. The dog began to whine. It looked up at him with appealing eyes half hidden beneath the long grey hair matted by rain. It moved closer to the edge, and began to bark. He took one step towards it, and launched a vicious kick into its side, sending it over the edge, and down the mountainside. Then he turned on his heels, and set off back up the mountain the way he had come. It would be a stiff climb, and an extra three miles to travel, but less chance of being observed, save for the harriers, and kites that bossed this barren mountainside.

5

It was twenty after midnight when Caton closed the door of his office, and headed for the exit. There would a mountain of work built up when he got back from his two weeks away, without having the current back log to contend with. At least now his in-tray was empty. The monthly report completed. Appraisals filed. The only one of his cases awaiting trial was wrapped up to the satisfaction of the Crown Prosecution Service. The remainder were in safe hands until his return. One week preparing for the big move, and then another closeted in a state-of-the-art simulation centre courtesy of the National Police Improvement Agency. In truth, this was a break he could do without.

Ten minutes later he entered his apartment, and keyed the cancel code into his alarm. Just one more week of doing this, he reflected, then life will never be the same again. Buying an apartment with Kate was the biggest step he had taken in thirteen years. When you get divorced that young it knocks the stuffing out of you. At least it had for him. When Kate had come into his life it had been the second chance he had thought had passed him by. Not that he was too old, simply that he had ceased to believe that there was someone out there he could make happy, and who would be prepared to put up with him. With his job. Her part time role as a Home Office accredited profiler, when she wasn't busy lecturing and teaching at the University, meant that she had a better insight into what his job entailed. In every sense, practically and emotionally. The way the Bojangles case had panned out, and the horrific situation it had placed her in, had left them both in no doubt about that. And now she had agreed to become part of his life forever.

Both he and Kate had agreed that it would have been better if they could have moved into either his apartment or her flat. At least then there wouldn't have been the mess of selling up and dividing the spoils if things didn't turn out. But neither place was big enough. And anyway, as Kate had been quick to point out, wasn't that like setting up a pre-nup? Expecting to fail before you'd even given it a go?

He walked through to the lounge, and stared at the clock on the plasma TV hard drive. It was exactly 1am. He knew from experience that it would be pointless getting straight into bed. He would just lie there waiting for the alarm. Instead he fixed himself a hot chocolate, and took it across to the computer. Before he had left work there had been an email he had forwarded to his personal mail box. He sat down, placed the mug on a desk mat as far from the keyboard as possible, and clicked on Mail.

There it was. *Caton to Caton from across the Big Pond. NiamhcatonNH@aol.com.* The address was not one he recognised. Intrigued, he opened it up.

'Hi Tom,

I'll apologise right now in case I've got this wrong but, well, here goes. My name is Niamh Caton, and I live in Manchester New Hampshire, USA. Hey that's a coincidence in itself don't you think? Well it is if you turn out to be who I think you are. I'm rambling here. Nerves I guess. The thing is, I'm researching my family tree – the Caton side at any rate – and I believe we may share great, great, grandparents. Joseph Caton and Mary McCarthy. Patrick emigrated from Ireland – Kerry to be precise - in 1878, and settled here in New Hampshire. If I'm right, then you are the son of Francis Frederick Caton and Beatrice Roberts. And if so, that makes us fourth cousins once removed...I think! I've attached a file showing who I've traced so far. If you really are Tom...of course you are! I mean the right Tom. Well I wondered if you might be able to help me with the next step. You see I'm kind of stuck. So if you are, please email me back. And if you're not, please disregard the ramblings of a throw back from a distant clan!

Best wishes Tom,

Hopefully,

Niamh Caton

NiamhcatonNH@aol.com

(603) 6247-6460

Caton read it over again. This didn't look, or feel, like a scam. The tone was too straightforward for that. And the details had a ring of honesty about them. Certainly he had been led to believe that his father's family had hailed from Kerry, although he'd only known of a Grandfather who had died when he was six. Without hesitation he opened the attachment.

After a four second delay a rudimentary family tree appeared.

Joseph Padraig Caton b 1818 m Brighid McMahon Padraig b 1842?
Joseph b 1846   Brighid b 1840 [Emg Australia – d. crossing] Michael [Priest]

Joseph Caton b 1846 m Mary McCarthy b 1849
1876 Frederick & Clare(d76) Mary b70 Colum b75 Patrick b73
Elizabeth b73 d74 Joseph John b78 d 1900

Frederick Caton b1915 m Selina Renihan 1935   Joseph b 1900 d. 1917

Patrick b1917 [GF]   Maggie b 03 d1918

Francis Frederick Caton b 1939 Jennifer Jane b41 d 44]
Patrick Joseph b 1947 Miriam Clare b 1945 d   Aug 2008

Francis Frederick m Beatrice Roberts 1968
Tom Caton b 1971   Patrick Joseph [F] m Teresa Jameson both died 2006

Niamh Caton b 1978

He studied it with amazement. She was right. They were related. But there was something else that that they had in common which she had presumably not yet discovered. His parents had both died in the same year, as had hers. All four of them were in their sixties when they died. It was uncanny. More than that, he found it unnerving. After thirteen years in the police force he didn't believe in coincidence. And, he noticed, her aunt had only just died. He wondered if that explained Niamh's sudden interest in her ancestry, now that she was the last of the line. As, for the time being at least, was he. Tracing his ancestors was not something that had ever interested him. Not even when his parents had passed away. Perhaps that would change when…if…he corrected himself, he had children of his own. They would probably want to know. In fact, although he hated to admit it, presented with five generations like this he found his curiosity had been stirred. Not least about this distant relative. Niamh was possibly his only remaining connection to his father's genetic pool. To a line of Homo sapiens stretching back two hundred and fifty thousand years. Looked at like that, it was a sobering thought.

He clicked on Reply, and sat there staring the screen, his fingers poised over the keyboard. Caton was not one for digitised conversation, for blogs, and chat rooms. The majority of his emails were functional, crisp, to the point. Any that were personal - agreeing arrangements, promising to phone - tended to be one-liners. He flicked back to her email and read it again. Then he typed world time zones into his search bar, and looked for Manchester New Hampshire. The difference was exactly five hours. It would be eight twenty in the evening over there. For the second time in as many minutes he acted instinctively, and dialled the number.

Niamh was eating supper in the kitchen, with the television on, when her phone rang. An International number. Another automated cold call.. With her finger poised to cancel, something prompted her to pick up.

'Hello,' she said. 'This is 6460.'

'Hello 6460,' came the reply. A cultured voice, English, with a smile in it. Her heart skipped a beat. 'This is Tom Caton.'

The twist of spaghetti slipped from her fork, splashing a smear of tomato sauce down the front of her blouse.

'Oh my God!' she exclaimed.

'No, just Tom Caton,' She could hear the smile widening. 'I take it that you're Niamh?'

'Yes...yes,' she replied, frantically trying to wipe the stain with her serviette. 'I'm so sorry. You took me by surprise. It never occurred that you'd ring back this late. It must be after midnight your time?'

'One twenty three to be precise. I just got in, saw your email, and thought I'd give you a bell.'

'Give me a bell?' Not certain that she had heard correctly, she reached out and turned down the television.

He laughed. 'Sorry – it's just an expression we use. It means phone you. I've got a feeling it's not the only time I'm going to have to translate.'

'Me neither.' He sensed her lightening up. 'You gave me such a start,' she said. 'I've just slopped pasta down my front. I'm mopping it up right now with something I think you call a napkin. To us, that would be a diaper.'

Caton had this bizarre image of warm gloopy pasta, a heaving bosom, and babies' nappies. He tapped his forehead with the phone.

'Are you still there?' she asked, concerned that he may have slipped away as suddenly as he came.

'I'm here,' he said. 'If I gave you a surprise Niamh, you certainly gave me a bigger one. I had no idea that you existed, nor had I much idea of anyone beyond my grandparents.'

'Nor I,' she said. 'Not until I started doing this

earlier in the year. Now I've got to admit I'm really hooked.'

'I was sorry to see that you've only recently lost your aunt,' he said tentatively, wondering if now was the best time to mention it, to get it out of the way.

'Thank you.' Tom heard a catch in her voice. 'In fact, we buried her just this morning,'

'God, I'm sorry. If I'd known, of course I would never have called you.'

'No, it's fine. Really it is. Even though we don't know each other at all, in a strange sort of way, it's comforting. After all...we are family.' He could tell that she meant it.

'Blood thicker than water?' he replied, for want of something better to say.

'I guess so,'

'It must be hard, coming so soon after you lost your parents?'

She felt the usual prick of pain in her chest that came every time someone mentioned them. Yet she was glad that he had. She sensed that Tom had the direct, intuitive, concern she had always imagined of the brother that she had never had.

'It was,' she said. 'Miriam and I were really close.' It was too soon, she decided, to tell him how her aunt had died. 'Enough about me. How about you Tom? How are your parents keeping?'

The awkward silence filled her with foreboding.

'The thing is,' he said at last. 'My parents died when I was thirteen. In a car accident.'

Her hand flew to her mouth. Now it was her turn to feel bad. 'Oh Tom, I'm sorry. If I'd known...'

'It's OK.' he reassured her. 'It was twenty four

years ago. I'm over it.' Even as the words came out he knew them for a lie. The flashbacks – rare though they had become – were all the evidence he needed.

'My parents were killed in an accident too,' she said as much to herself. Making the same connection that Tom had done a half an hour before. 'They were out at sea in a storm.'

There was a pause while Tom processed it. 'By the look of it, we haven't had a lot of luck we Caton's,' he said, hoping to take the edge off it.

She laughed, awkwardly. 'You're right. Not just our generation either. When you have a closer look at my website, you'll see what I mean.'

'Website?'

'I've started a Caton family website where I'm posting the results of all the research I've done. I'm inviting other people to contribute. No one has so far, but I live in hope. I'll email you the link.'

'I'll be sure to check it out.'

'There's something else you can do,' she told him. It's the reason I contacted you. That, and hoping to make contact, of course' she added hastily. 'I've got stuck on the only two of our paternal ancestors whose descendants I haven't been able to trace. Our great, great grandfather Padraig, born in 1872, I'm pretty sure emigrated from Ireland to America. I'm about to start working on him. But the other one – our great grandfather Colum - who I think was born in 1875 – I can't find any record other than his birth. I wondered if you could see what you might dig up.'

'Not literally I hope?' He instantly regretted his murder detective's graveyard humour. He needn't have worried. There was a giggle of amusement down the phone. Not the childish kind, but mature, sophisticated. Not words he would normally have attributed to a giggle. He realised that he was warming to this woman he had never met, had not known existed a half an hour ago. Feeling protective in ways that he had hitherto only felt for Kate.

'That's up to you Tom,' she said. 'You do whatever you have to do, just so long as you bring home the bacon.'

'You have bacon over there?'

She laughed again. Whatever clouds their depressing personal histories may have formed dispersed. 'Listen Tom. Much as I'm enjoying talking with you, I'm conscious that it's long past your bedtime. And your phone bill must be going through the roof. Do you have Skype?'

'I don't even have a web cam,' he told her. 'And don't you worry about my bills, I reserve that for my own masochistic pleasure.'

'Well, why don't you go out and get yourself one? Then in future we can do this face to face without spending a fortune.'

'I might just do that,' he said. 'In the meantime I'll check out your website, and see what I can do. Then I'll get back to you. It'll be a couple of days at least I'm afraid.'

'That's fine. As long as it takes. And Tom. Thanks for "giving me a bell". It's been lovely talking with you.'

'The pleasure was all mine,' he replied. 'Good night Niamh.'

'Goodnight Tom.'

Niamh placed the phone on the table top. She felt the tide of emotion that had been dammed up inside her leach away, and another sensation take its place. Like a hot tub on a winter's night. It had been a long shot but it had paid off big time. Her project was alive and well, and now she had found somebody to help her with it. Not just any old body either. A cousin. OK, a fourth cousin, but family none the less. The pasta had gone cold but it didn't matter. She recognised a sensation to which she had been a stranger for too long. Not quite happiness, nor contentment, nor excitement. More a pleasurable anticipation. She filled her glass with wine, picked it up, and headed for her computer.

It was gone two in the morning when Caton switched out the light. He lay in the darkness trying to form a picture of her in his mind. A wild raven haired Irish American beauty perhaps, with bright green eyes, like Kate's? Or a black haired blue eyed Kerry girl, the double of his grandmother in the photo his father had shown him once, since lost. The images began to form and fade. An ever changing kaleidoscope, that swirled around the body sprawled across the roundabout in Hulme Park playground until, mercifully, sleep crept up, and took him.

6

The phone woke him. The digital display said eight forty three. It was Kate. Bright and breezy.

'Hey handsome. Where are you up to?'

'It's Saturday,' he groaned. 'I was catching up on my beauty sleep.'

'You don't need it,' she said, more cheerfully than he could cope with. 'In any case you've a whole week to do that you lucky devil.'

'You should worry. What is it university lecturers get, four and a half months' holiday a year?'

'It's not like that, and you know it.' Now she was bristling.

He smiled, turned over, drew his knees up to his chest, and closed his eyes. 'I know,' he mumbled. 'Papers to mark, lectures to prepare, books to write. My heart bleeds.'

Kate refused to rise to the bait. It was a game they had played too many times to have any mileage in it. 'So what have you got planned?' she asked.

'City have a home game this afternoon – I thought I might go. Then The Alternatives are meeting on Monday evening. I've missed the last two discussions so I'd better go to this one. John Le Carre's *The Mission Song*, right up my street. And I've got a stack of books to read…DVDs to watch.'

'Stop it Tom Caton,' she interrupted. 'You know very well what I mean. What have you got planned for us?'

'Funny' he said. 'I thought *us* planning was your domain.'

'Fair enough. In which case, this morning we're going shopping for curtains.'

He groaned, and pulled the duvet up over his head in the vain hope that it would somehow protect him.

'We can start in town and then, if we don't find what we're looking for, nip down to the Trafford Centre.'

He could think of nothing worse. Trawling around the city from store to store. Retracing steps to double check. Then battling through the traffic to circle the car park at the shopping mall, jostling with the masses, then back into Manchester to the very first store they'd visited to make a purchase that could have been made at ten in the morning instead of five o'clock in the afternoon.

'Tom. Are you still there?'

'Yes, I'm still here.'

'What are you doing? You're voice is all muffled. It sounds like you're under water.'

'Close. I'm under the duvet, but it feels like I'm drowning.'

'And then this evening, how do you fancy the Royal Exchange? There's an Oscar Wilde play on. We could have something to eat at San Carlo first. But you'll have to decide now if I'm going to book the banquettes. They'll be gone within five minutes of the booking office opening.'

He gave it serious consideration. An Italian meal, followed by the theatre. Lounging on the banquettes where he could stretch his feet out as much as he liked. Enticing, but a whole day shopping was too high a price to pay. He came out from under the duvet, and eased himself up until his head was propped up against the headboard.

'Sounds great to me,' he said. 'There's just one thing.'

'Go on.'

He could tell from her tone that she was way ahead of him. That was the trouble with psychologists, too damn smart.

'Well, it's just that there's something I need to do this morning that could carry over into the afternoon. I'll be able to make San Carlo though.'

'You want to go to the match.'

'I was just winding you up. They're playing Arsenal away.'

'So what's more important than choosing the décor for our first home together?'

This had clearly assumed an importance in Kate's mind way beyond what Caton had envisaged. He saw it now as a challenge and an opportunity. If he got this right it would become a precedent. But then if he got it wrong the same would be true.

'Something to do with the family has come up. I've got some research to do at the Family History Centre in Chorley.'

'Family history?'

It's a bit complicated, but I'll explain this evening. And let's face it, I'm no good at interior design. You on the other hand are brilliant at it. I trust you implicitly.'

'You hate shopping more like,' her voice softened. 'And you think flattery will get you get you off the hook. As it happens, it has. Just this once.'

He knew that she had a soft spot for anything to do with his family. Chiefly because in that respect he had been so unlucky.

'Leave your mobile on, and I'll ring to confirm that I've managed to book the tickets, and the restaurant.'

Caton smiled, and punched the air. 'Brilliant. You have a great day, and I'll see you this evening.'

'You needn't look so smug,' she said. 'You owe me.'

He replaced the phone and snuggled down. She was smart, and beautiful, and moving in.

Caton left the apartment and walked out onto Liverpool Road. On the opposite side, a stream of children, with sundry adults, meandered towards the Museum of Science and Industry. Shafts of morning sunlight reflected by the huge glass windows forced him to shade his eyes. He checked his watch. Twenty five to ten. Plenty of time. Beyond Quay Street he cut through The Square in Spinningfields, and came out onto Deansgate by the side of the red sandstone faux gothic John Rylands Library. A little further down on the other side he could see Katsouris. The best breakfast in town.

It was ten thirty precisely when he wiped the tomato sauce from the side of his mouth with a paper serviette, collected the spicy chorizo ciabbata sandwich he had ordered for lunch, paid, and headed back to Woolam Place by the same route. Kate would be in Harvey Nick's or Selfridges by now but it wasn't worth the risk of being spotted. He understood why all this mattered so much to her. It wasn't just about playing doll's house, or nest building; for both of them it was far more important than that. This was his first serious commitment since the divorce. Thirteen years. It seemed like only yesterday, and he still felt twenty five years old. If only. He was determined that it would work this time, and so was Kate, if anything, even more so. She had never mentioned biological clocks ticking. She hadn't needed to. And now they were due to exchange on the brand new apartment in the New Islington Wharf complex in just a week's time. Her apartment had been sold, his was in the process. No going back.

Thirteen miles North West of Manchester the M61 motorway dipped down between green hills as it threaded its way through the Lancashire countryside. To his right, Winter Hill marked the furthest edge of the West Pennine moors. On the opposite side of the motorway, stark in the autumn sunshine, loomed the white granite walls of the Preston Temple of the Church of Latter Day Saints. Atop the narrow steeple the statue of the Angel Moroni - prophet warrior, guardian of the golden plates – clothed in gold leaf, stood guard. Caton turned off onto the slip road, left at the first roundabout, right at the second, and first left down the driveway onto the thirty acre site. The Family History Centre was located away from the temple, beside a cluster of seminar and meeting rooms, and a residential block. He parked, picked up his notebook containing the downloads from Niamh's web site, and went inside.

The room was unremarkable. There was an information desk beside the door, eight sets of filing cabinets, four rows of study carrels, readers for the micro film and micro fiche records, computers for search online, and space to study documents, to write, and think. Mrs Standish the librarian - a local retired teacher, and part-time volunteer - told Caton that she was still engaged in building up her own Genealogy. A fourth generation descendant from two Irish families, she had already waded through the mire of nineteenth century Irish records, and was only too happy to help.

By the time she had explained some of the difficulties, not least the reliance on parish and county level records, and illiterate or lazy priests who had rarely bothered to complete the records anyway, and even if they did were more likely to record baptisms than births, he was already regretting having agreed to help his distant cousin.

'One thousand one hundred and fifty three parishes, two thousand nine hundred and ninety two sets of records – not records mind you – sets of records,' she told him. 'And many of those incomplete. Well…you get some idea of what you're up against.'

But when he showed her what he had from Niamh's web site, her eyes lit up. 'Why didn't you say?' She said. 'You've broken the back of it. And the late nineteenth century is a good place to start if you're tracing forwards not backwards. Come on, I'll show you.'

Ten minutes later his head was whirling. He had

a list of records to search, and knew exactly where they were located in the room. He already knew that his, and Niamh's, great, great, grandparents - Joseph Caton and Mary McCarthy - had married in Listowel in the County of Kerry in 1864, and their son, whose descendants, if any, Niamh had yet to trace, had been born in 1875, also in Listowel. He began with the record of marriages which from eighteen seventy six were split up quarterly. It was ten to one in the afternoon when he had his first break.

Colum had married a Margaret Ryan in 1903. He immediately switched his attention to the index of births beginning in that year. Twenty minutes later he was rewarded with an entry for a Colum Patrick, born to Colum and Margaret Ryan on September 8th 1905. He felt the same sense of satisfaction in this single victory that he did with a breakthrough on a murder case. He copied down the details, closed his notebook, went out to the car, and retrieved his sandwich from the glove box. Spicy chorizo had never felt as good, or so deserved. His mouth was full when the mobile vibrated.

'Hi Kate, how are you getting on?' he spluttered. Rose stained breadcrumbs spattered the dashboard.

'I'm having a great time,' she told him. 'I hadn't realised how much it takes the pressure off doing this alone.'

'That's true of a lot of things,' he said. 'Not just shopping.'

'Tom Caton, you've got a one track mind,' she said before she'd had time to figure it out. By the time she did, he was already holding the phone a respectable distance from his ear. 'Hang on,' she said. 'Are you saying I put you under pressure to perform?'

'Perform? Who said anything about performing? For me it comes naturally.'

That set them both off laughing. He wasn't sure if she was laughing with or at him. He thought it best not to enquire.

'So what have you chosen?' he asked, wiping the dashboard with his free hand.

'Don't be silly. I haven't actually decided yet, but I've a better idea of what I want.'

This was not the time, he decided, for quips about women being from Venus. 'Did you get the banquettes?'

'Yep. And San Carlo is booked for twenty past five. We have to pick the tickets up by quarter past seven, so don't be late.'

'I won't. But I'm going to have to get a move on.'

'Make sure you do.'

I will. And Kate...'

'Yes?'

'I love you.'

'I should hope you do, or what am I going to all this trouble for?'

She blew him a kiss, and ended the call. At least he hoped that's what it was. Not a raspberry. God, he thought. One second I'm whispering endearments, the next I'm paranoid that she doesn't really love me. I've finally reached adolescence. At thirty eight years of age.

He no longer had time for the brisk walk around the campus he'd promised himself, and pitched straight back into the records. By a quarter to four he had finished. He sat back in his chair, and stared at the notes in front of him. A combination of marriages, births, and census records – and some incisive interventions by Mrs Standish - had enabled him to unearth Colum Patrick's marriage to Joan Marshall in 1936, the birth of their son Padraig in 1937, of their daughter Oona, in 1940, and Joan's death in 1944. In 1960, at the age of twenty three, Padraig had married Shelagh Murphy. Their son Patrick Michael was born in the same year – five months after their marriage he noticed – and his brother Matthew was born two years later. Patrick's death was recorded in 1980 when he would have been just twenty years of age. Matthew however, went on to marry one Jennifer Lloyd in 1990, and in the following year she gave birth to a son whom they christened William. If he was right, this branch of the family had never strayed from the town of Listowel – or to be precise - a village called Lixnaw within the administrative district. And, most important of all, it looked as though Oona, Matthew, and William were still alive - a second cousin, and two third cousins.

He gathered together his notes, thanked the redoubtable Mrs Standish, and walked to his car. Niamh would be delighted. Come to that he was feeling pretty pleased with himself. First class detection and not a body in sight. At least, none that he need bother about.

Driving against the traffic flowing out of the city, he was back in Manchester in half an hour. Shaved, showered, and changed he found he even had enough time to dash off an email to Niamh with the salient names and dates. He hoped she would make sense of it. He arrived breathless on the steps outside San Carlo at five twenty precisely, just as Kate came around the corner of Deansgate. She waved and ran to meet him.

'You're looking pretty pleased with yourself,' she said, taking his arm. 'And on time for once.'

'Early actually, by five minutes,' he said smugly.

She squeezed his arm a little harder than necessary.

'Don't push your luck. You owe me, remember?'

7

Niamh had spent much of the morning in the library using the computer link to the Ellis Island emigration site to flesh out her great grandfather Patrick's journey from the West coast of Ireland to the States. As she was leaving she found herself enticed into the adjoining room. Kathy Brodsky was reading from her wonderful children's book My Bent Tree. Niamh had come across this story herself and knew it to be about overcoming disability, about the power of friendship, and the importance of protecting the environment. She had loved the rhythm of the verse in which it was told, the charming illustrations, and above all the humour, compassion, and insight that it had into the joy's frustrations, and sadness that women experience. Hearing it read by the author gave it another dimension entirely. By the end, she felt an inexplicable sensation of being both uplifted and emotionally drained.

She paused at the intricately wrought black iron window grill in the corridor, and stared out at the tall and slender trees uniformly crowding Victory Park. No room for bent ones here, she reflected. She paused by the Pine Road entrance to capture the smell of autumn on the North Easterly breeze. In her childhood memory bank were pine needles, sage, and musty leaves, split wood, and apples baking on the stove. In the here and now she was presented with a hint of ozone, mixed with traffic fumes.

Niamh opened the door to her apartment, and stepped into the tiny hallway. Where once this had been a welcoming place, it now felt cold and cheerless. With everything packed, and ready to go, devoid of personal possessions, this place was suddenly soulless. She made her decision right there and then. She would leave by the end of the week regardless of what the real estate agent had come up with.

As she walked into the kitchen diner she heard the unmistakeable ping. She had mail. Email to be precise. When she saw that mail was from Tom her spirit lifted. She read the contents and the attachment with amazement. He had achieved in two days what she had expected might take her a month. And here were three more living relatives. Oona would be sixty eight years of age she calculated, Matthew thirty six, and William seventeen. She sat down and typed a reply.

Tom
You are a GENIUS!!! I have no idea how you managed to pull this off so fast. You didn't fly out there did you?? No of course you didn't! I'm just being stupid. Again!!! I'm going to see what I can find out about them. I think I might contact the Diocese and find out who the PP is. They seem to know everything about everybody by all accounts. Something to do with the confessional perhaps?! Anyway, I'll be in touch as soon as I find out anything. In the meantime, you have a great weekend. You deserve it!!
Best Wishes

Niamh

Already an expert on the time zone difference between the two cities she had no expectation that he would reply immediately. Nor did she need him to. He had given her just the boost she needed. She spent the next fifteen minutes updating her website. Then she sat back, and began to formulate a plan. If these three relatives had been living in America, she asked herself, what would she do? Try Yellow Pages, or one of the other subscription based services. But that would cost. Not a lot in all probability. She had no idea if there was a similar service for Ireland. She typed it into the search bar anyway,

The very first site on the list not only gave her instant access to a free search for numbers, but a link to three genealogical sites specific to Ireland she had not previously come across. For neither Matthew nor William Caton did the site return a listed number when their names were entered, together with the place name Lixnaw but, much to her surprise, Oona did. She glanced at the digital clock on her desk. It would be early evening in Ireland. Before she had a chance to change her mind she picked up the phone and dialled. It rang, and rang, and then clicked through to an answer message. The voice was unmistakeably Irish. A soft lit, yet cultured. Confident and mature. Sounding younger than she had expected. The kind of voice you immediately warmed to.

'Hello there. It's Oona you've reached. I can't take your call right now, but if you'd be so good as to leave a message after the tone, I'll get right back to you as soon as maybe. Until then...may the good saints protect you.'

Niamh was so busy listening to the message that

the tone caught her by surprise.

'Oh, Err...' she began. 'Hi Oona, my name is Niamh...Niamh Caton. You don't know me, but I think we may be related. Look...don't bother to return the call, I'm phoning from America. I'll try again...if that's alright? Bye then...'

She put the phone down heavily. It wasn't the impression she had been hoping to make. She decided to make herself a decaff coffee while she pondered what to do next. She had just switched on the kettle when her phone rang. She picked up, hoping that it was Oona. It was a man's voice. Irish. Older than Oona's. Tentative.

'Hello...have I reached a Niamh Caton?'

'Yes,' she said. 'You have.'

'Did you ring just a moment ago?'

'Yes, I was hoping to speak with Oona.'

'And you say you think you might be a relative of hers?'

'Yes. I believe we are cousins. Third cousins. On my father's side. Although I've just traced her...today as it happens. And her nephews too.'

There was a long pause. She could almost hear the man thinking.

'Ah. That'll be Matty and Billy,' he said.

'That's right.' This time it was Niamh that paused. This was a strangely dislocated conversation. It wasn't just that this man might be gate keeping for Oona Caton, filtering out her callers, verifying their authenticity. There was something else. She decided to press him. 'I was hoping to speak with Oona.'

'So you said. Well I'm very sorry, but I'm afraid that won't be possible...' She was about to ask him why, when it dawned on her that he hadn't finished what he was trying to tell her. '...you see,' he continued. 'I am sorry to have to tell you that Oona passed away just yesterday.' He waited for her to reply. When none came he said. 'Niamh...are you still there?'

She stared at the phone, half hearing the disembodied voice, hardly registering the shift in tone from compassion to concern.

'Miss Caton. Are you alright?'

Oona had died yesterday. It wasn't fair. She recalled her father's favourite saying.

'Niamh...life is not fair. If you can accept that, you'll become a stranger to self pity, and be better placed to make your way in this world.'

'Niamh! Are you there?'

'I'm sorry,' she said. 'I'm alright. It's just such a shock.'

'Well I'm sorry for springing it on you like that. That's why I had to ask you those questions. To find out how close you were to Oona. If I'd realised it would affect you so much, well...'

'Please, don't apologise. You did the right thing. I'm OK, really I am. It's just that...well I've only just buried my aunt.'

There was an intake of breath. 'Holy Mother of God,' he said. 'No wonder it hit you hard.' He recovered his composure. 'I'm sorry for your loss Niamh.'

'Thank you.'

'Perhaps I should explain. My name is Father Patrick Keenan. Oona was one of my Eucharistic Ministers. The Garda asked if I'd be willing to tidy the place up after they'd finished with it. Matty and Billy couldn't bring themselves to do it. Though...' he added rather uncharitably she thought. '...I've no doubt they'll be happy to sell it soon enough.'

'How did she die Father? Was it expected? Had she been ill for a while?'

'Not at all Niamh. It came right out of the blue. That's why the Garda were here. They just wanted to be sure that there was nothing untoward. I told them it was out of the question, but you know how it is with the police.'

'I'm sorry, Father,' she said. 'But I'm not following this.'

'And why should you? Isn't it me that's rambling? Oona went missing the night before last. Mrs Mangan, her neighbour, became suspicious when Donal came back on his own. She found him on her porch, soaking wet, and miserable.'

'Donal?'

'Oona's dog. He's an Irish wolfhound crossed with a lurcher. A beautiful great animal. Sure, she was never without him. He even went with her when she was taking the Sacrament round the parish to the elderly, and infirm. That's what alerted Mrs Mangan. She rang the Garda. They rang the Mountain Rescue. But they said it wasn't really a matter for them, and to call out the Civil Guard. And it was them that found her.'

'On a mountain?' Niamh found it difficult to imagine what a sixty eight year old woman would be doing alone on a mountain in late September, albeit with her dog. He sensed her disbelief.

'Beenagheea,' he said. 'Sure it's only a spit above six hundred feet, but it's the nearest we've got to a mountain till you get to McGillycuddy Reeks.' He paused for a moment as though suddenly aware that none of this meant anything to her. 'It was the fall that killed her...God rest her soul.'

Niamh needed none of the details. She had had enough of those to last a lifetime. 'You mentioned the police,' she said. 'Something about them wanting to be sure?'

'Ah, yes.' She sensed him trying to work out how to put it sensitively. In the end he gave up trying. 'That it wasn't suicide. She lost her husband Jimmy a couple of years ago.'

'Husband?'

Tom had obviously not come across their marriage. Niamh wondered if there were any children.

'They were inseparable, the pair of them,' the priest was saying. 'And always up and down the mountains together. He was a great loss to her.' His voice softened. 'And with no children to comfort her. She bore her grief well, and immersed herself in serving others. She was a great woman. I told them there was no chance she was thinking of giving God a nudge. And so it proved.'

'You said that Oona died the day before yesterday?'

'I did.'

'When is the funeral Father?'

'This coming Thursday. I'm conducting the requiem myself.'

'I should like to be there,' she said, without even thinking about it. It was an instinctive need. Something she felt she had to do. She realised that there was neither rhyme nor reason to it. Some would say, her friends Mary and Grace among them, that it was the last thing she needed right now.

'Are you sure that's a good idea Niamh. It's such a long way. And for someone you've never met.'

'I'm sure Father. And at least I'll get a chance to meet my cousins.'

There was silence at the end of the phone. When he did speak it was with an air of resignation. 'There is that I suppose. But then we don't always get the relations we deserve.'

'And those costumes...weren't they breathtaking?' Kate walked down the hallway and into the lounge. 'Especially Mrs Chively's – that turquoise and orange one. And that one of Mrs Chiltern's at the end – the cream one.'

Caton shrugged his jacket off, and let it fall over the arm of the sofa.

'Breathtaking. As in squeezing the breath from their bodies,' he replied. 'When did you last see waists that tiny on such voluptuous women?'

She pouted her lips, and feigned jealousy.

'Philistine! Trust you to disregard the dresses in favour of what lies beneath.'

'That is what all men do,' he said aping Noel Coward's exaggerated diction. 'It is just that women hope to snare us with the layers of falsehood with which they clothe themselves, in the vain hope that we will only discover too late what lies beneath.'

She was genuinely surprised. 'That's not Oscar Wide is it? I don't remember it.'

'No,' he said, picking up a cushion with which to defend himself. 'It's me.'

She launched herself at him, delivering blows into the cushion as he moved it from side to side against the onslaught.

'Coward!' she managed between laughs.

'No, it's not him either,' he said, releasing the cushion, grasping her wrists and pinioning them together. 'I told you...I made it up. Clever aren't I?' He swivelled to his left, pulled her down onto the sofa, and kissed her. As she relaxed he let go of her arms, and she placed them around his neck, pulling him into her, her rich auburn hair cascading over both their faces. Just as he was about to lift her up, and carry her into the bedroom, Kate placed the palms of her hands on his chest and pushed him away. She sat up, took a deep breath, and began to wriggle.

'I'm sorry,' she said. 'All that coffee, not to mention the Amarone.' She leapt up, and disappeared in the direction of the bathroom.

Caton used it as an opportunity to sneak a quick look at his emails. There was just the one, from Niamh. He opened it.

'Hi Tom,

Just to let you know. I rang Ireland. Oona died the day before yesterday. Can you believe it? A tragic accident. I'm going over there for the funeral. It's on Thursday. Hope to meet Matthew and William while I'm there. I know it's a rush...but any chance we might meet up? I'll ring when I land.

Niamh. X

He read it through again. She was right. Another coincidence. As for meeting up, with the move in the offing Kate would have something to say about that.

It was too late to reply, and she clearly didn't expect him to.

He only became aware that Kate had entered the room when he felt her breath on the nape of his neck, and her hair brushing his cheeks. He closed his mail down, and turned to face her.

'I wish I knew how you manage to suddenly appear like that,' he said.

'Ah, *the strength of women comes from the fact that psychology cannot explain us. Men can be analysed, women . . . merely adored,*' she said, quoting directly from the play. 'Anyway, what was in that email that is more important than finishing what we'd started?'

'*Questions are never indiscreet. Answers sometimes are,*' he said, playing her at her own game.

He took her hand and led her towards the bedroom.

8

Niamh arrived at Logan International Airport for check in with forty minutes to spare. For the first time in her life she was being impetuous. No grand plan, just going for it. It felt good.

They took off on time, at 19.15. At the airport she'd bought a copy of The Deposition of Father McGreevy by Brian O'Dogherty, because it was set in Ireland, and had been short listed for the Booker Prize back in 2000. It was only when she settled back on the plane to read it, armed with a gin and tonic, that she discovered from the flysheet that it was about the demise of a remote village in the mountains of Kerry. A village where all of the women die suddenly, and inexplicably. Where the parish priest is left struggling to cope with the almost preternatural elements, the anguish, misery, and superstition of his remaining parishioners, and the suspicions of those in the nearest town. The photo on the cover, she realised, should have been clue enough. A man in a cloth cap sat on top of a stone wall; beside him a priest wearing a black felt hat, leant on a bicycle. The two of them faced away, past a Celtic cross by a grave, over fields, towards a purple haze of distant hills. She opened the book, and began to read.

Shannon Airport at six in the morning. Niamh had slept for seven hours, and had a coffee and croissant for breakfast. Clear of customs and immigration, she collected the hire car, paid for an optional satellite navigation system, and entered the address of the Listowel Arms where Father O'Leary had reserved a room for her.

'It's the Harvest Festival Week,' he'd told her. 'What with the Races, and the National Wren Boys Band Competition, you could be on the phone all week, and never get a bed. Leave it to me.'

Driving on the left turned out to be anything but the nightmare she had envisaged. By the time she reached the River Shannon crossing point on the outskirts of Limerick, the rush hour traffic was only just building up. Limerick, the Shannon…these were names and places that had always held a romantic pull for her. Her parents, both the third generation of an immigrant family, and her aunt Miriam, had kept the old traditions alive. Her Aunt at least had visited Ireland, and beguiled her with accounts of the countryside, the people, the music, and the Craic. Perhaps when the funeral was over she would have a look around and do the tourist things.

The N69 took her straight into the Town Square. It was so much larger and grander than she had expected, bordered on all four sides by Georgian houses and shops, with blue slate roofs, and pastel coloured walls in pink and yellow, maroon, and blue, some with ornamental plaster paintings over the door. In the centre stood a grand Gothic church, blue grey in the morning sun. The prim and proper voice of her satellite navigator led her past the tree lined pavements to the south west corner of the square.

Large red letters across the white façade of the three storied building proclaimed *The Listowel Arms Hotel.* She took her bag from the boot, and trundled it up the red carpet into the hotel.

'You don't know how lucky you are,' said the receptionist. 'It's mad, what with the races, and the bands. We wouldn't have had this room for you at all, only we had a jockey who took a terrible fall. They helicoptered him off to The North West Regional Hospital in Limerick, and now he's in St Nessan's at Croom. He's fine, thank God, but from what I hear he'll be having no need of a room for some time to come.' She looked around, and lowered her voice, although Niamh could see no one in ear shot. 'It's the second best room we've got,' she confided. 'They've all slept in there. Daniel O'Connell, James Thackeray, Charles Stewart Parnell himself…the uncrowned King of Ireland. If Father O'Leary had left it a moment longer you'd have missed it. They were queuing up for it like rooks at a road kill.'

The O'Connell Suite boasted a king sized iron bedstead covered in what looked like an Egyptian cotton duvet and sheets. There was a huge antique white and gold bath on legs in the centre of the ensuite bathroom; a separate sitting area with sofas; and a balcony with a spectacular view across the wide bend of the River Feale, to the Racecourse on the far side. She stepped out onto the balcony, and stared at the crowds milling around. A race was underway, and shouts of encouragement drifted over the water. The sun was shining, the sky was blue, and Manchester

New Hampshire was a million miles away. She could hardly believe that she was here. Let alone that she had come for a funeral.

By half past ten she had unpacked and driven out on the Lixnaw road. At Finuge Cross she slowed as she passed a low white cottage with a thatched roof, and a green half-door. It reminded her of a scene from her mother's favourite film, *The Quiet American*, with John Wayne and Maureen O'Hara. This was a moment she would dearly love to have shared with her parents. *Spilt milk Niamh*, she could hear her mother saying, *spilt milk*.

Oona Caton was laid out in the funeral parlour. All those who had arranged to pay their respects had come and gone except for the neighbour, Mrs Mangan, who was expected.

'Would you like to go in on your own, Miss Caton, or would you prefer to wait, and go in together?' The funeral director asked her.

Niamh had no idea how she was going to react, and decided it would avoid any embarrassment if she went in on her own. The director showed her into parlour, lifted the lid of the coffin, and pulled up two chairs.

'I'll be out in the front when you're ready,' he said.

Niamh stepped forward, and gripped the side of the coffin. Her immediate, and overwhelming, feeling was one of relief. This was a stranger. Oona Caton bore little resemblance to anyone in Niamh's immediate family. She looked a little older than the five years she had on Aunt Miriam. Perhaps there was a hint of Miriam's cheek bones, but that was all. Her face had an almost translucent glow about it. Traces of ginger in her long grey hair suggested a flame haired beauty in years gone by. Wrinkles had been smoothed away – either by death, or the skill of the mortician. They had done a good job. There was no trace of the injuries that had led to her death. Her lips curled upwards slightly at either end giving the impression of a pleasant dream. Or perhaps a scene fondly remembered.

Niamh sat down on the chair and folded her hands in her lap. When her parents had died she had found it impossible to cry. For the six months following the funeral she had drifted through life in a dream, a half world where she was numb, and where nothing seemed to matter. She had lost her appetite, had trouble sleeping, and had begun to despair. The doctor explained that this was a depression beyond grief. More a kind of self imposed mourning for the loss of the relationship she had had with her parents. He warned her that she would have to find a way of letting them go. That if she didn't, then she would in all probability lapse into a kind of melancholia where part of her would die with them, leaving her emotionally crippled, unable to function normally. It was the shock she had needed. From that point on she had made a concerted effort.

'It won't be easy,' he had told her. 'But there will be signs that you're getting there. For instance…you may find yourself crying when you least expect it. In response to a film, or the reported death of someone you barely know. If so, don't be embarrassed. Embrace it. Think of it like the valve on a pressure cooker releasing all that pent up emotion. And, above all, as confirmation that your feelings are alive and well.'

And so it had proved. It was almost as though she had been given permission to feel. Watching films, listening to music, arranging flowers in a vase, all of these had been a trigger for tears. Then came the blow of Miriam's death. This time she had wept. For Miriam, her parents, and herself. And now as she sat here she realised that at last she had reached some kind of equilibrium. She could distinguish between personal grief, and mourning, and empathy for the bereavement of others. She had acquired the strength to move on with her life. Sitting here all she felt was disappointment that she had never had the opportunity to get to know this woman, to find out a little about her own heritage. That, and compassion that her cousin had ended her life alone on a bleak mountainside. Lost in her thoughts she failed to hear the door open.

'You must be Niamh.'

She turned, a little startled. A small woman with a large round face framed by a shock of curly black hair, greying at the temple, advanced with one hand extended. From her other hand hung a voluminous black handbag, incongruous against the bright red coat she wore.

'I'm Mary Mangan,' she said, clasping Niamh's hand, and squeezing it. 'Isn't she the lucky one to have you come all this way to be with her? Don't you be getting up,' she said as Niamh started to rise. 'I'll join you down there.'

She pulled up the other chair, placed her handbag beneath it, and sat down beside Niamh.

'Now, let's have a look at you,' she said, staring straight into Niamh's face, then at the corpse in the coffin, and then back at Niamh again. 'Well, you're nothing like her at all,' she declared. 'But I can see her brother Padraig in your eyes, and the tilt of your nose. What a shame we lost him to his lungs back in two thousand and three. He'd have been delighted to meet you, as would poor Oona here.'

She turned her attention back to the coffin, and sat quietly for a minute or two, her lips moving in silent prayer. For want of something to do Niamh began a decade of the rosary herself only to find it interrupted half way through.

'Have you been here long Niamh?' Mrs Mangan asked.

'About twenty minutes.'

'Sure that's long enough isn't it?' Mrs Mangan said, reaching down for her bag. 'Will we be away?'

Niamh nodded, and stood up. Mrs Mangan joined her, leant over the side of the coffin, and touched the rosary wrapped around Oona's hands.

'May the Irish Angels welcome you into Heaven Oona, and may the Lord enfold you in the mantle of his love,' she said, with a warmth and reverence that threatened to bring a tear to Niamh's eyes.

Mrs Mangan's house was a neat two bedroomed bungalow with a small wooden decking at the back, on a yard full of gravel the colour of the limestone hills towards which it faced across boggy fields, and coarse mountain pasture.

'Your cousin Oona's is just a spit around the corner,' Niamh's host told her. 'Matty's got the key, but I've one myself if you'd like a peek?'

Niamh had been preparing for this on the short journey from Lixnaw to Kilfeighny. Initially she had wanted to, but since leaving the funeral parlour it no longer seemed appropriate. 'Thank you, but I feel it would be an intrusion,' she said. 'Apart from the fact that I've no right to do so... to be honest, I think I'd feel a bit like a voyeur.'

'Perhaps you're right.' Mary Mangan said, though Niamh could see she was secretly disappointed. 'But you'll have something to eat I hope? They'll not have stinted on your breakfast, so I've just prepared a little taste of Kerry.'

Before Niamh could reply she scurried into the kitchen, and returned with a large plate piled high. 'There's some soda bread, some barm brack, and a nice piece of yeasty fruit loaf Mrs Shanahan brought across.' She set it down on the table. 'She'll be joining us shortly. She knew your grandfather better than I did, and she met your Aunt Miriam when she crossed the water.'

Right on cue there was a ring of the bell. Mrs Manghan hurried out into the tiny hallway. She came back with a woman much the same age as herself. Siobhan Shanahan was a head taller than either of them. Her hair was silver, tied in a bun. She held herself erect in the manner Niamh associated with models, and members of old Bostonian families who prided themselves on their lineage. When she spoke, it was with exactly the precise and cultured tone Niamh would have predicted.

'Niamh Caton,' she said. 'It's a pleasure to meet you, despite the circumstances that made it possible.'

She advanced and surprised Niamh by giving her a hug. Then she stepped back. 'Why, you're the double of your Grandfather when he was a boy – not that I remember that far back,' she added with a smile. 'But I saw the photos in his mother's parlour.' She took in the plate of cakes, and slipped off her coat. 'Are you brewing some breakfast tea Mary?' she asked. 'I don't know about you Niamh, but I'm famished.'

An hour later the plate was littered with crumbs, and Niamh's head was spinning. She had heard tales of the Grandfather she had never known. And much of Oona's life – including the time just the previous year when she had narrowly missed being crushed when the bridge at Ballinagar had collapsed under the weight of a truck of pigs - and had been entertained with vivid descriptions of traditional wakes, including a demonstration of keening by Mary Manghan that set her hair on end. Only once – in direct response to her own questions – had Matty and Billy been mentioned.

'Sure, those two are a queer couple…' Mrs Manghan had begun, but a look and a shake of the head from Mrs Shanahan – so slight that Niamh almost missed it – stopped her straight in her tracks. In the awkward silence that followed they could hear an animal whining. Mrs Manghan shook her head.

'Poor Donal,' she said. 'He's been like that since yesterday morning. Mourning his mistress I suppose.'

'Are you sure that's all it is Mary?' Mrs Shanahan asked. 'It sounds like he's in pain to me.'

'I was thinking that myself,' Niamh said. 'Perhaps we should take a look?'

Mary Manghan led them out through the kitchen

onto the decking. A large dog with a thick coat of grey hair was curled up beside the wooden guard rails. His breathing was laboured, and he looked up at them with sad and cloudy eyes. Niamh knelt down and stroked him gently on the top of his head, and beneath the short white beard on his chin. As she moved her hand down along his flank he yelped with pain, and drew his front legs up protectively. Niamh stroked his head again to reassure him.

'There's a definite swelling here,' she said. 'And some traces of blood in his fur. I wouldn't be surprised if he's bruised or broken some ribs.'

'I'd no idea at all,' Mary Manghan said. 'But that's it then. I can barely afford to feed him, and I certainly can't pay for the vet. He'll have to be put down. Poor Oona. She loved him to death.'

'Oh you can't do that,' Niamh had blurted out before she could stop herself. 'I'll happily pay for the vet to have a look at him.'

'There'll be no need for that.'Mrs Shanahan said, in a sharp and imperious tone that brooked no disagreement. 'Oona was my friend, and I'll see to it. And I'll make sure that he finds a decent home, even if I have to take him in myself.'

Niamh sensed that she had been rebuked, and it was obvious that Mary Manghan felt a little humiliated that she alone had not been able to find a better solution. Niamh decided that it was time to thank them for their kindness and hospitality. She made her apologies, and left with a promise to see them at the funeral the following afternoon.

On the way back to Listowel she made a detour to

have a look at the cottage where she had been told Matthew and William Caton lived. She came across it just a hundred yards from the road, up a narrow track, beside dark brown fields scarred by the cutting of peat. It was a single storey cottage, almost hidden behind a mass of nettles and brambles. Stone walls, white with a limestone wash, a blue slate roof, and a faded wooden door with a large window on either side. The windows and the door were edged with mouldering red bricks. Vertical wooden planks held together with four thin strips of wood served as shutters, or security, or both. Half a dozen of the tiles were missing from the roof, and double that number were broken. A wisp of blue grey smoke rose from one of two chimneys. She had no idea why she had come and no sense that she might be welcome. A bout of coughing began somewhere inside the cottage. She seized the opportunity to slip the car into gear, and reverse slowly down the lane.

As she got out of the car in front of the hotel, she realised that her phone was still off from when she was on the plane. She took it out, and switched it back on. There was just one voice message, from Tom.

'Hello Niamh. I'm sorry to have missed you…and to hear about Oona. I would have loved to have come across and meet you but it's impossible at the moment. Kate and I are moving to a new apartment at the end of the week. Just a thought…perhaps you might come across to Manchester for a few days after the funeral? Anyway….let me know. Bye for now.'

A few days in Manchester was not out of the question. But if Tom was moving, would he really want her in the way? Deciding to sleep on it, she left the phone on, and slipped it back into her coat pocket.

After dinner, the noise of music and laughter drew Niamh into the hotel Writer's Bar. It was heaving. The area around the polished mahogany bar was packed three deep. The counter itself was stacked with patient rows of rich black Guinness waiting for the creamy clouds swirling through them to settle. Whisky chasers were passing from hand to hand over the heads of those waiting. In the window bay a band consisting of a fiddle player, a guitarist, a flautist, and a young man playing the traditional bodhran drum, was in full flow. As far as she could tell, every seat was taken.

'You'll never get near the bar in a month of Sundays,' a young man standing beside her confided. 'Will you hang on a minute?' He reached over the shoulders of the man in front of him, and poked in the back another man, at the front of the bar. 'Make it another one Michael…a double!' He shouted. Then he turned to Niamh. 'What's your name if you don't mind me asking?'

'It's Niamh,' she told him.

'Well I'm Sean,' he said grinning. 'So now we've been properly introduced, you better come and sit with us. It's either that, or stand up all night.'

He led her, through the crush, around the tables, to a group of seats his colleagues were guarding beside a blazing fire in the ancient black iron fireplace. A few minutes later she knew all their names, was reassured that this was just the famous Irish hospitality, no strings attached, and settled back to sip her whisky, and listen to the music of the Wren Boys

Bands.

It was several sets later that the MC for the evening stood up and made an announcement.

'And now,' he said. 'Noel Carmody will share with us his remembrance of St Stephen's Day 1913.'

An old man – in his nineties at least – with a lifetime etched on his face, was helped to a seat in front of the band. They brought him a large glass of whisky, and a tumbler of water. He took a sip of each, and began. From the moment he opened his mouth it was obvious that he was a practised story teller. His voice was rich and strong, not reedy and tremulous as she had expected.

'We heard them coming,' he began. 'From way over the other side of the hill. The flute, the tin whistle, and the throbbing sound of the bodhran as they beat their way to our door. With us being the furthest from the village, it was late when they came. We children had been waiting all day, and were excited and frightened at the very same time. As was our mother, a God fearing woman who thought all of this a terrible heathen practice, which of course it was, but who was caught up in the tradition like the rest of us.'

He cleared his throat, and took a sip of whisky.

"Will they really have caught and killed a wren, Dada?" My little sister Caitlin asked. "Sure I doubt it," my father replied. "There was a time when they did, but even then they would have kept it alive, and carried it around in a wicker cage for all to see." She wasn't for letting him off that easy. "And then would they have set it free Dada?" My father caught our mother's eye. He patted our Caitlin on the head. "Sure they would," he said, though none of us boys believed him. We knew that the whole point was to sacrifice the wren, to drive out the winter, bring back the sun, and hasten the spring. "That," he had once confided to us boys. "And to get as much money out of the terrified old biddies as possible."

He took another sip, letting the tension mount.

'By now the noise was upon us, and the dogs were howling in the yard. "You'd best call the dogs off before they beat them with their cudgels," our mother told him. Father upped and opened the door, yelling at the dogs until one after the other they slunk inside, and took their favourite positions either side of the fire. I plucked up my courage, and went and stood beside my father.'

He paused, and stared right through us.

'I remember seeing them appear, like ghosts, through a curtain of snow that fell in silent feathery flakes. There were seven of them. Their hats and coats were made of oat straw. What little could be seen of their faces was painted white. The noise they made was deafening. Those not playing the instruments held shillelagh in their hands to beat off the dogs, and discourage the competition. Their leader held a pole aloft, from the end of which dangled a wretched wren. Dead as a door nail. My father immediately blocked the doorway. "If you want to come in, you'll set that down out here," he commanded. "You'll not frighten my children." I was worried that some of them would remember this, and that I would have to face their taunts in the village. As it happened, they were more frightened of my brothers than they were eager to enjoy my discomfort. One by one they trooped into the house until the room was full. We stood at the margins, and watched as they danced, and whirled, and sang their songs. One of them grabbed my arm, dragged me into the midst of them, twirling until my feet left the floor, and my head was dizzy. Our mother brought each of them a buttermilk scone, a thimble of hedgerow wine mulled in the pot over the fire, and a farthing.'

He smiled to himself, and shook his head gently from side to side.

'She said it was for the entertainment they'd given us, but we knew it was for luck. For all her great faith, the old superstitions held sway at times like this.'

He smiled, and looked around the room.

'Sure, it's a rare man can say he's never bet each way at the races.'

He poured a little water into his tumbler of whisky, took a sip, and continued.

'The snow had picked up by now, and there was a wind that threatened to pile it in drifts where a donkey could fall in a ditch, and never get out again. They made their goodbyes, and trooped out into the yard. Their leader took up his pole, and headed for the gate with the rest behind him. The flute kicked off, and then the whistles, and then the boy with the bodhran beat the hell out of the goatskin, and set the jingles jangling, till those of us inside were dancing again. I stood at the door, with the dogs at my heels, and watched as they disappeared, wraithlike, into the night.'

This time he paused for a good half a minute, staring out beyond the audience as though he could see them still. The room was hushed; nobody moved.

'It wasn't many years before I was one of them

myself,' he said. 'And it was a tradition I was proud to be part of. But it was that first sight of them that I remember best. '

He took up the tumbler of water, drank a little, and placed it carefully back down on the table. He wiped his lips with a handkerchief he was clutching in his left hand, and then continued.

'Of the boys that came that night six of them joined the Royal Munster Fusiliers …and perished together on the battlefields of Europe. Barry Monaghan, the one that led them to our door, charged a machine gun emplacement that had pinned down his platoon, and died a hero. One made a life for himself over the water. One became a priest...and the other a farmer like his father before him.'

With some difficulty, he stretched himself to his full height...

'So I'd like you to join me in a toast.' He raised his tumbler of whisky. 'To the Wren Boys. May the Lord keep them in his hand, and never close his fist too tight!'

Niamh joined in as everyone present rose to their feet. The sweet, smooth, amber spirit sent a warm glow through her body. The old man was not quite finished. He had saved a measure in the bottom of his glass.

'And I've a toast from me, to you,' he said. 'May you never resent growing old, for there's many denied the privilege.'

He drained his glass, to a standing ovation, and slammed it down on the table top. Another glass, with a double measure, appeared as if by magic, and was placed in front of him. The band struck up, the crowd began to clap and sing.

'The Wran, the wran, the king of all Birds, on St. Stephen's Day, it was caught in the furze,

Although he was little, his honour was great, so jump up me lads, and give him a trate,

Up with the kettle, and down with the pan, give us a penny, to bury the wran.'

Niamh discovered her feet had a mind of their own, tapping out the tune like she'd known it forever. It was close to midnight when she finally made her way to her room. She read a few pages of her book, then switched out the light, and drifted off to sleep lulled by muffled sounds from the bar of the fiddle, the flute and the bodhran.

9

The funeral was not until midday. Niamh set the best part of the morning aside in the light and airy Listowel County Library doing some more research into the Catons. Despite the fact that they were run off their feet this particular morning with a children's reading group, and a creative writing session, the librarians bent over backwards to help.

'The Catons is it?' Said the one called Mary-Ann O'Leahy, with a broad smile. 'Well if I remember rightly I think you'll find a fair bit in our newspaper archives. We've got them on microfilm. You might like to start with *The Kerryman*. I'll be surprised if that doesn't throw up a thing or two.'

She paused for a moment, and lowered her voice to a whisper.

'And when you've finished here, you might want to have look at the court records in the Courthouse next door,' she said. Niamh felt sure there was a twinkle in the bright brown eyes behind the spectacles.

In the space of an hour Niamh had found a number of articles relating to Oona's grandfather Colum Patrick, and to his grandson Paddy, Matty's brother. The most illuminating and comprehensive were the reports of their deaths. What had united the two of them in life, or would have done had the grandfather lived long enough, united them in death. Both had been fervent supporters of Irish Nationalism, and both had paid for it with their lives. Colum Patrick had been killed by the Irish Special Branch in October 1943 in an ambush near the border town of Clones. According to the article he had been attempting to smuggle an undisclosed quantity of .303 rifles, ammunition, and explosives, over the border into Fermanagh to supply a commando unit of forty men operating there as part of the Northern Campaign. His grandson Paddy's exploit was less cut and dried. It was alleged by the Garda that he had been killed in a gun fight with cross border smugglers from whom the IRA cell, of which he was believed to be a part, were trying to extort money. Taxing was the term they used at the time. The date was March the twenty second, 1980. Paddy was just twenty two years of age. Although Niamh found a letter to the editor from Paddy's father, vigorously denying the accusations, this was somewhat undermined by the fact that a week later there was a photograph, and an account, of Paddy's Sinn Fein burial, and a year further on, the unveiling of a memorial stone in his honour, paid for and erected by the local Sinn Fein Cumann, or Society.

Niamh recollected that her own parents had always supported the Nationalist cause, and the Civil Rights movement in particular. But had been horrified, as had she, by the bombings and the shootings in Ulster. She had been twenty years old almost to the day, when the Omagh bomb went off. She could still remember how she felt. And the words of a fellow student, Gerry Flaherty, as they came out of church together that Sunday morning.

'Casualties of war,' he'd told her in response to her protestations. 'There's a war over there. Do you think they'll get a peace that changes anything just by talking?'

Now there was peace, and another go at power sharing. She hoped that this time it would stick. That some of the Irish Republic's prosperity might brush off on the North and that a unification of hearts and minds might come about through economic necessity, and cultural osmosis, where force of arms and political attempts had failed.

Oona's name came up in the papers a half a dozen times. Most of them related to her work in school. She had clearly been an inspirational teacher, much loved by her pupils. There was also a brief mention of her being inducted as an extraordinary minister for the purpose of taking the Eucharist to the sick, elderly, and infirm. And finally, when Niamh entered her name, and Lixnaw, into the internet search engine, it produced a photograph of her with a party of pilgrims setting off for Lourdes in 1997.

It was only when she turned her attention to Matthew and William Caton that she began to understand the reluctance of Mrs Manghan and Mrs Shanahan to pursue that topic. It also explained the gleam in Mary-Ann's eye. *The Kerryman, The Kerry's Eye* and the online version of *The Kingdom*, all carried accounts of their court appearances. Together, and severally, they had notched up more than a dozen in the past ten years, most of them for drunken behaviour, brawling, and petty theft. The most recent

– just a month previously, had an eye catching heading, and a report that left nothing to the imagination.

Final Warning for Father & Son.

At Listowel District Court this morning Matty Caton from Kilfeighny North, and his son Billy, were warned in no uncertain terms that, if they appeared before the court again, they would go to prison.

"On Thursday last, they were observed in Church Street by Sergeant Cairanne Kelly, and Garda Patrick O'Shaughnessy, wrestling a man to the ground, and laying into him with their boots. When they were told to stop, they responded by hurling abuse at the Gardai and redoubling their efforts to render the poor man senseless.

'It took us several minutes to apprehend them,' claimed Sergeant Kelly. 'And in the course of subduing them I was bitten on the hand, and Garda O'Shaughnessy received multiples bruise to his shins. The object of their anger – one Damien Power – required hospital treatment including an overnight stay. Had we not come upon them there was, in my opinion, a likelihood that he would have suffered grievous, and possibly fatal, injuries."

In answer to the judge's questions it was confirmed that both men were heavily intoxicated, and had refused to co-operate with the Garda throughout their arrest, and subsequent incarceration in the Bride.

The court heard that the men had a long record of offences for drunken and abusive behaviour, assault, affray, and causing public nuisance. They were both currently on probation for the theft of a car from Listowel Town centre which they had used to get home after a night's drinking.

Judge Michael Marshall, fined the pair six hundred euros and sentenced them to six months in prison, suspended for one year on the understanding that they would submit to a medical assessment, and co-operate with whatever treatment was prescribed to deal with their drinking, and help manage their tempers.

"I am sick and tired of seeing the two of you before this court," he said. "If either of you appear before this court again in the space of one year, your custodial sentence will immediately commence, together with whatever additional time is determined for your subsequent offence."

Father O'Leary's words rang in Niamh's ears.

"We don't always get the relatives we deserve."

She logged off, gathered up her notes, and made her way to the exit.

'Did you find what you were after?' Mary-Ann asked her.

'Thanks to you I did,' Niamh replied. 'But it was not quite what I'd expected.'

'The librarian smiled ruefully. 'When it comes to relations,' she said. 'It rarely is.'

Niamh returned the smile. 'So it would seem,' she said. 'Thank you anyway, you've been really helpful. In fact, there is just one other thing …is there a florist in Listowel?'

'There is indeed. It's called the Centred Centre. Go straight to the bottom of Courthouse Road, turn right into Church Street, and you can't miss it. Have a great day now.'

Niamh found the shop with ease. The florist helped her to choose a spray of green carnations, white wax flowers. Bells of Ireland, and Queen Anne's lace, perfect for a funeral, and not too pretentious. Deciding what to write on the card proved more problematic. In the end she settled for: *To Cousin Oona, from Niamh Caton. Rest in Peace.* She was tempted to add, Give My Love to Miriam, but decided that would raise questions from among the mourners that she would rather not face.

She was held up on the road first by a tractor, and then by a slow moving coach full of tourists. The Angelus bell was ringing as she parked beyond the line of cars on the main road. St Bernard's Church was already full. She slipped in at the back, prepared to stand. A woman on the end of the back row spotted her, and made her son offer up his seat. Niamh accepted gratefully, caught her breath, and looked around.

A series of steel and timber portals forming the roof concentrated the light on the main altar behind which rose a stunning modern stained glass window in yellows, blues, and greens. At the altar steps the coffin rested on wooden stands. A cross and a bible rested on the lid. The priest was in the process of blessing the coffin with holy water.

For Niamh, the Requiem Mass had become an all too familiar ritual. It passed in a blur except for the eulogy, presented by a fellow Eucharistic Minister of Oona's, which confirmed the fond and high regard in which she had been held.

The coffin was carried out of the church, followed by the entire congregation, row by row, starting from the front. The hearse set off slowly, the congregation walked behind it on foot. At the cross roads a woman

Garda held up the traffic while the procession passed.

'How far is the cemetery?' Niamh asked the woman closest to her. The woman, in her mid sixties, smiled at Niamh, and eyed with open curiosity the spray of flowers.

'Kyrie Eleison?' she said. 'Why it's only a half a mile or so. Do you think we'd be walking it otherwise?' Then she turned back to her companion, and picked up the conversation they had been having.

'It was the strangest thing,' Niamh heard her say. 'Her being found like that, don't you think? And her knowing the hills so well.'

I know what you mean,' her younger companion replied. 'Doesn't it put you in mind of Fionn MacCumhaill?' She caught sight of Niamh, saw the bemused expression on her face, and nudged her friend. 'I don't think this young woman has the faintest idea what we're talking about,' she said. 'Don't you think we should enlighten her?'

'I'm sorry,' Niamh blurted, and began to blush, embarrassed at having been caught out listening in to their conversation.

'No need for that,' the older woman told her. 'It's us that should apologise. Talking among ourselves, and you the stranger.' She took Niamh by the arm and drew her between the two of them. 'Did you know how poor Oona was found?' she asked.

Niamh nodded. 'I think so. Didn't she fall somewhere up in the hills, and hit her head on a rock?'

'That's right,' said the younger one. 'But she was actually found in the bed of the river just as the great Fionn MacCumhaill was found. Fionn was the chief of the Fianna Eireann. A great athlete, and a great warrior. When Daire Donn, the King of the Underworld, landed at Ventry Harbour out there on the Dingle with his warriors, to conquer Ireland, it was Fionn and the Fianna who defeated him...'

'And after the battle,' interrupted her companion, eager not to be excluded. 'They pitched their tents in the foothills of Stack's Mountain, and had a great time hunting the stag, and fishing the rivers. Only Fionn, on his way back from chasing a stag, decided to show off by jumping backwards over a glen, and fell to his death in the river below.'

'I can't imagine Oona attempting that,' Niamh said.

The older woman nodded her head vigorously. 'Exactly what we were saying.'

'Oona could have walked in those mountains blindfolded, and never miss a step,' her friend confided. It's more believable that Fionn Mac Cumhail really slew the King of the World than that Oona slipped on that path. It's nothing short of a mystery I tell you,' she said, shaking her head, and crossing herself. 'Nothing short of a mystery.'

After a third of a mile the procession turned right up a metalled road, and proceeded gently uphill until they reached the cemetery. It stood among green fields, within the low stone wall surrounding the remains of the Cistercian Abbey of Abbeydorney. All that remained was the West tower, part of the great North wall, and the end wall of the chancel, with its Gothic stone window frame miraculously intact. Lichen had stained some of the stones brown, out of others sprouted small shrubs and grasses. The plot prepared for Oona was in the far Eastern corner, beyond the Chancel.

As Niamh approached Mary Mangan detached herself from the group beside the coffin and hurried towards her.

'We've been looking for you everywhere Niamh,' she said breathlessly. 'Did you not make it to the church?'

'I did, but the church was full,' Niamh told her. 'I sat at the back.'

'That's not right. You should have been up at the front where you belonged. Anyway, you're here now.' She took her arm. 'Come on, Father's waiting to start.'

Niamh was guided past the enquiring looks of the other mourners until she was near the head of the coffin, within a few metres of the priest and his acolytes. Siobhan Shanahan stood on her left, Mary Mangan on her right. Immediately opposite, two men were staring directly at her, one in his late fifties, the other in his mid twenties. They wore ill fitting woollen suits, with crumpled open necked shirts. The elder of the two had a beige anorak over the top of his jacket, and held a light grey cap in his hands. It had to be Matty and Billy, Niamh decided, except they should have been younger. Niamh attempted a smile, but their gaze was so unwelcoming that it froze on her lips. She turned away, and tried to follow the service.

A light wind crept up out of nowhere, and dark grey clouds began to scud across the sky. Niamh shivered involuntarily at the sudden chill in the air. It came as a relief when the coffin was lowered into the grave

Niamh laid her spray of flowers beside the others

waiting for the grave to be filled. As she straightened up Mary Manghan took her arm.

'Come on Niamh,' she said. 'I'll introduce you to Father, and there are loads of people dying to meet you.' No sooner had the words come out than she realised their inappropriateness at this time and place, though it could just as easily have been the dig with her elbow that Siobhan Shanahan gave her. Her hand flew to her mouth. Before she could apologise, Niamh had placed her hand over hers, and given her a perfect smile.

'Don't worry,' she said. 'I'm thicker skinned than that.'

'Then you're clearly a Caton,' Siobhan Shanahan chuckled. Leaving Niamh to wonder yet again if this was a compliment, or not.

Father Keenan's words proved fitting for the occasion, assuring Niamh of Oona's virtue in life, and certainty of reward in heaven. He was sensitive to the fact that she had never met her cousin, and that the accident had come at a difficult time for her. Then, out of the corner of his eye, he caught sight of the two men Niamh had noticed earlier. They were lurking beside another grave with a great granite tombstone at its head, muttering to each other, their eyes directed towards Niamh. Indecision was written on their faces, and in their body language.

'Have you not met your cousins yet?' the priest asked her.

'Niamh gave them a fleeting look, and shook her head. 'No,' she said. 'We've not been introduced.'

'Then it's time that you were,' the priest said firmly. 'Matty, Billy,' he called out. 'Will you come over here, and meet your cousin?'

It was more a command than question. The two men shuffled forward reluctantly, until they were less than a yard away. Niamh could see now that her first impression of their ages had been out by a good few years. A combination of hard weathering, and alcohol, had added almost a decade at least to both father and son. They stood there in silence, their heads bowed a little. The father fiddled with the cap in his hands. The son had his hands in his pockets.

Father Keenan knew it was down to him. 'Matty, Billy,' he said. 'This is your cousin Niamh. All the way from America for your Aunt Oona's funeral. Have you nothing to say to her?'

Niamh held out her hand. The father reached out and took it in his. His grubby hand was rough with calluses. When he lifted his head to look at her Niamh could see that his eyes were glassy, not with tears, or emotion.

'How are Yeh?' His speech was slurred, his breath stank of whisky.

'I'm fine thank you. And you?' Niamh replied, resisting the temptation to flinch.

'I'm fine,' he said, and drew back his hand.

'Billy?' Said the priest with a trace of irritation in his voice.

The son took his left hand from his pocket and turned it awkwardly in the air to shake Niamh's. She was instantly reminded that her father, and his father before him, had been left handed. Bill Fitzgerald had teased her father about it at her eighteen birthday party. 'A left footer, and a cack hander,' he'd said. 'Don't tell me God hasn't a sense of humour!'

'I'm Billy,' the young man said as though he had just discovered the fact. 'How are Yeh?'

His hand was rough like his father's. His eyes a little clearer, but still bleary. The smell of alcohol masked by a stronger reek of diesel fumes that seemed to come from his hands and boots. He glanced at her, lowered his eyes, and shuffled his feet.

'I'm fine thank you Billy,' Niamh said, trying to put him at his ease. 'It's great to meet you both at last.'

The young man squeezed her hand ever so slightly, then pulled it away, and stuck it back in his pocket. Neither of them spoke. Niamh had another try.

'I was so sorry to hear of your Aunt's death,' she said. 'I felt I had to come to the funeral.' She waited to see if that would get a response. When nothing came she said gamely, 'Perhaps I might see you again before I have to fly back?'

'Maybe you will…and maybe you won't.' Matty replied gruffly. He nudged his son's arm with his elbow, and turned to go. Billy raised his head slowly, and looked Niamh in the eyes with a steady gaze. She thought she detected a hint of a smile, then he nodded his head ever so briefly, and turned to follow his father.

Niamh watched them thread their way between the graves, heads bowed as if the weight of the world was upon them. She sensed that their offhand manner, and sudden departure, owed more to shyness, and embarrassment, rather than any intended discourtesy. Mary Manghan had a different opinion entirely.

'They probably think you're after a share of Oona's house,' she said.

Niamh was taken aback. It had never occurred to

her for a moment. Surely Oona had not even been aware that she existed, let alone likely to leave her something in her will. And there was no way that Niamh would ever have contested a will, if there was one. For a start she had no need, and secondly, it was not in her nature. Then she remembered that Miriam had visited Listowel, and presumably Lixnaw and Kilfeighny. Of course they would know. In a community as tight knit and family oriented as this. Why, there was even a map just inside the door of St Bernard's Church showing the location of every family in the parish.

'I hope not,' Niamh said. 'Nothing was further from my mind. Perhaps I should go after them? Set their minds at rest?'

'I wouldn't if I were you,' Siobhan Shanahan told her. 'That might only make it worse. I'd leave them to themselves. It's how they like it.'

Niamh doubted that was true of young Billy.

'You're coming back to the parish hall I hope?' Mary Manghan asked. 'A few of us have laid out a little spread for those who knew Oona well.'

'If you don't mind, I won't.' Niamh replied. 'I'd like a little time on my own. To sit up here, and to have look around.'

'Well if you're sure. And if you change your mind we'll be there for an hour or two. Just ask anyone where it is. You can't miss it.'

'And if you don't, at least make sure you come and say goodbye before you fly back to America.' Mrs Shanahan told her. 'Or we'll never forgive you.'

The two women began to walk away, arm in arm. Siobhan Shanahan stopped and turned. 'I almost forgot,' she said. 'You were right about Donal. He has three broken ribs, and is lucky that none of them punctured his lung. The vet says it looks like someone gave him a good kicking. Can you believe it?'

'Who in God's name would do such a thing?' Mary Manghan added. 'Anyway, the vet's hanging on to him until he's mended. He says he knows someone who'll give him a good home thanks be to God. So at least its ended better than it began.'

Niamh followed them down to the roadway. She leaned against the dry stonewall, and stared across the fields and hills, over the village, to the mountains beyond where Oona had died. With the exception of those with stubble, the fields were a lush emerald green like the trees and hedges that spotted the rolling hills. On the lower slopes of the nearest mountain, perhaps three miles away, there was a sudden flash of light. The sun reflected on a camera lens. Or perhaps from a spinning blade at the wind farm in the Stacks Mountains. In the middle distance a pair of red kites soared effortlessly on thermals, waiting to steal another predator's kill. To the South West the towering McGillycuddy Reeks were tinged with purple. For Niamh this was a kind of magical place. A place of contrasts, wild and grand, beautiful and bleak. A slight drizzle slanted out of the darkening sky. She hurried out onto the lane, and headed back towards the cross roads.

Out on the hillside he turned his back to the rain, wiped the lenses of his field glasses with a soft cloth, and placed them back in their carry bag. To anyone watching, he might be a walker getting his bearings, or one of the hundreds of naturalists that flocked over these hills like starlings, in search of the elusive hen harrier. He slipped the bag over his shoulder, pulled up the hood of his anorak, and set off on the path to the road below.

10

Kate shoved the TV guide under the coffee table to make some space, and flipped open the catalogue at the page marked with a post-it-note.

'What do you think of these?'

Tom stopped fiddling with his mobile phone, and stared at the photographs of two stainless steel objects. One conical, the other like a mushroom, the head of which was cut with concentric circles. He turned to the cover, and read the title.

Kitchen furniture?' he said sceptically. 'They're just door knobs.'

'They're actually door handles…for the units in the kitchen,' she told him. 'So stop playing for time, and answer the question.'

'Which was?'

'Which do you prefer?'

He grinned. 'I think you'll find it was actually, what did I think of them.'

'Well you've forfeited that option. The question is which do you prefer?'

He pursed his lips.

'Mmm…hard to say really. Which do you prefer?'

'Tom Caton!'

'Look,' he said. 'Is this a real question, or is it one of those trick ones, like which of these dresses shall I wear tonight?' Or, does my bum look big in this?'

She dug her elbow into this ribs.

'It's a real one. We don't eat until you've answered it. Which one do you prefer?'

'All right,' he said, moving as far from her as the sofa would allow. 'To tell you the truth, I don't like either of them. They're too like the units. No contrast. Boring.' He drew his elbows in to his sides, and held his palms out in front of his face ready to repel the assault. It never came.

'Thank God for that,' she said. 'I knew there was something about them, but I just couldn't put my finger on it.' She turned the page over, and pointed to a slim rectangular handle, with stainless steel sides, and a wooden inlay along the front.

'What about this one?'

'So it was a trick question?'

'Never mind that,' she said. 'What do you think?'

'That one is perfect,' he said, switching his attention back to his mobile.

Kate pulled off the first of the post it notes, scrunched it up, and closed the catalogue. She reached under the coffee table, and pulled out another.

'These are the blinds I've chosen for the kitchen,' she said.

'Good,' he said, continuing to search his address book.

'Well are you going to have a look at them or not?' she persisted.

'If you've already chosen them,' he said. 'There's not much point is there?'

The catalogue caught him on the side of his head, and his phone flew out of his hand.

He listened intently while she told him about the injuries to Donal, and the conversation she had had with the two women mourners on the way to the cemetery. He made her go over it a second time.

'So all you have is a dog that's been kicked, and the suspicions of a couple of elderly women based on Oona's familiarity with the mountains?' he said.

'Isn't that enough to at least get the police to look into it? she asked.

'I doubt it. In any case, the Garda will already have considered the possibility of foul play. If there had been any, the post mortem would have thrown up something.'

'But what if they weren't looking for it?'

Tom wasn't sure if she wanted to believe that her aunt had been murdered or needed reassurance that she had not.

'However experienced Oona was,' he said. 'Accidents do happen. Especially on mountainsides, and when there's a dog involved. She was in her sixties. She could have lost her footing momentarily, or had a dizzy spell. The dog could even have caused her to lose her balance by jumping up at her.'

'But what about Donal? The vet said someone kicked him.'

'The vet could be wrong. What if Donal had fallen down a slope and smashed his ribs on a rock. Oona might have tried to reach him, and fallen herself. Equally, he might have pitched up at someone else's house before he turned up at Mrs Manghan's. Matty and Billy's for example. Anyone could have kicked him to shoo him away.'

'When you put it that way...' she said.

'So what will you do now?' he asked.

'I was thinking of exploring a bit. I'm definitely going to drive around the Dingle peninsular, and the Ring of Kerry. Go into Tralee. Then there's Limerick, and Killarney. I might even drive across to Dublin.'

'Dublin? That some drive you know.'

'It's only a hundred and fifty miles or so.'

'Only?'

Niamh laughed. 'Don't forget you're talking to an American here. I've got friends who do that as a round trip to the mall.'

'Well take care,' he said. 'There's a depression coming in from the Atlantic, and most of it is going to fall on you. Where do you think all those emerald green fields come from?'

She laughed again. 'I've gone native; I bought an umbrella.'

'I meant when you're driving. From what I've heard the roads can flood when you least expect it.'

'I'll be all right,' she said. 'When you've driven through a twister, you can cope with pretty much anything. Is it alright if I ring tomorrow to let you know how I'm getting on?'

'Feel free, I'm on leave.'

'Kate won't mind?'

'Why would she? You are my cousin.'

'That sounds nice,' she said. 'My cousin.'

Kate appeared in the doorway with a tumbler in each hand, head to one side, eyebrows arched. Tom smiled at her reassuringly.

'Look, I've got to go Niamh.'

'OK Tom. Nice speaking with you again. Bye for now.'

'Speak to you soon...bye.'

Kate advanced towards him arm outstretched. As he reached for the glass she drew it back out of reach.

'Not too soon, I hope,' she said.

After dinner Niamh felt restless. On impulse she decided to drive out to Kilfeighny. She had no plan, other than to drive past the house where Matty and Billy lived. She didn't expect to be invited in. In fact she wasn't sure that she'd have the courage to knock on the door. It would be dark. No one would see her. She would take her time, and be back by ten. She just wanted to see again the place where more than six generations of Catons had lived. It wasn't asking a lot.

As she reached the car it started to rain; a light drizzle that was only visible where it passed through the beams of the street lights, and speckled the windscreen. Just behind the Square, to her right, the floodlit ancient tower of Listowel Castle glowed like a pale pink beacon. She stood there for a second or two wondering whether to turn back, chided herself for her indecision, opened the door, and got in.

At first the roads were well lit, and relatively quiet. The rain had discouraged the street artists - the tumblers and jugglers, the mummers and musicians that had entertained the festival goers on the previous evening. Small groups scurried along the pavements, hoods up, heads down, from pub to pub. By the time she'd crossed the River Feale over the five stone arches of the Big Bridge, as the locals referred to it, hers was the only car on road. She was surprised how familiar this route had become. Within five minutes she had a passed through the hamlet of Finuge shrouded in darkness, just the odd light in a window or two. Five minutes later, on the outskirts of Lixnaw, she turned left off the N69 onto the minor road to Kilfeighny North.

Now the road was dark and narrow. She drove past the forbidding bulk of a conifer plantation. Beyond the walls and hedges she knew there were fields of rough pasture, and bog land scarred by the cutting of peat. There were no lights here and she drove slowly, wary of animals crossing her path. Suddenly there was a warning flash on the wall ahead. Almost immediately she was blinded by a pair of headlights. She broke sharply, shielded her eyes with her hand, and waited for the other vehicle to dip its lights, and back up. When it was obvious this wasn't going to happen she put the car into reverse, and drove slowly and nervously back the way she had come. Beams of light from the other car crept steadily forward, matching her progress.

Finally she was able to reverse up the track of a disused limestone quarry. Relieved to have made it she waited with headlights dipped expecting a wave of thanks.

As the other car drew level with the entry to the lane it stopped for a moment. The driver wore a mask across the top half of his face. A bird mask, with a long pointed beak like ones she had seen the mummers wearing on the streets of Listowel. The lower half of his face was deathly white. He turned his head, stared at her for a moment with eyes as black as coal, smiled thinly, and accelerated away. Niamh shivered involuntarily, listening as the sound of the car's exhaust faded into the distance. She took a deep breath, exhaled slowly, slipped into gear, and drove back onto the road.

Even before she reached the track up to the house she knew something was wrong. There was a red glow above the limestone wall, and as she turned off the road she could see flames leaping into the air. Oblivious to the fact that this was a hire car she drove at speed over the sodden ruts. Stones ricocheted off the underside as she lurched from side to side to avoid the deepest hollows. Twenty yards from the house she pulled up, and leapt from the car. The house was engulfed. Black acrid smoke billowed through the gaping windows where wooden shutters had already been consumed. Gold and crimson flames licked around the door jamb, and burst through the roof where the slates had gone, and roofing timbers were ablaze. There was a noise like a great wind. The fire seemed to have a life of its own, crackling and spitting at her. Without thinking she ran forward until the heat forced her back. She reached into her anorak pocket and pulled out her cell phone. She was about to dial 911 when it hit her that that wouldn't work. Her head was like mush. What the hell was the number? Something must have kicked in because she found herself dialling 112. After a short delay the operator put her through to Kerry Fire and Rescue headquarters in Tralee.

'Now try to calm down,' the controller told her. 'First of all, what's your name?'

'Niamh Caton,' she told him stepping back from the flames licking at the brambles in front of her.

'There's a fire you say Niamh. What's on fire exactly?'

'It's a house, my cousins' house...Oh God, it's terrible.'

'Where is it exactly?'

'Kilfeighny North. I turned left off the road from Listowel just before Lixnaw. It's about a mile from the main road.'

'Do you know if there's anybody in the house?'

'No…but I think my cousins might be.'

'How many cousins Niamh?'

'Two, Matty and Billy…they're father and son.'

'How many storeys has it? Is it a house or a bungalow?'

'One, it's a cottage I think.'

'Have you an address for this cottage?' he asked her calmly.

'No, I'm sorry…no.'

'Are there any landmarks…did you pass any pubs, houses, phone boxes..?'

'No…please hurry…Oh God.' She began to cough as the wind blew smoke into her face.

'Niamh…It sounds like you're standing too close. Can you move back, away from the fire?'

She did as he told her, her left hand over her nose and mouth, tears streaming from the irritation to her eyes.

'Have you a satellite navigation system in your car?' the controller was asking.

'Yes,' she managed to get out.

'Is it on?'

'I think so.'

'Well that's great; it'll be quicker than trying to triangulate your phone. I want you to go back to your car. Make sure it's switched on, and read me the co-ordinates.'

She looked back at the house. Her feet were rooted

to the spot. 'But what about Matty and Billy?' she said.

'Believe me, this is the best thing you can do for them. The appliance is on its way, but the sooner you do as I ask, the sooner they'll reach you.'

She tore herself away, and stumbled back to the car. Her door was still open. She leaned inside. The display was still lit up.

'What do I do?' she asked.

He guided her through the menu options, until she reached the correct screen.

'Look for two sets of numbers,' he said. 'One with an N after it, the other with a W. They'll start with 52 degrees, and 9 degrees, respectively.'

'I've got them!' she shouted.

'Well done. Read them out to me, slowly now.'

When she'd finished, he said. 'You've done brilliant Niamh. We've got two appliances on their way to you, one from Listowel and one from Tralee. They'll be with you any minute now. You've done everything you can, and we don't even know for certain that there's anyone in there at all. So please don't do anything silly. Just stay well back, and wait for the Fire and Rescue to arrive. Will you do that?'

'Yes I will.' She straightened up, and stepped away from the car, staring in disbelief at the wall of flames against the night sky. In the distance she thought she could hear the sound of sirens getting closer.

'And keep your phone on. I'll stay on the line until they arrive. Alright?'

Before she could reply there was flash of white light, a deafening boom, and a blast that flung her backwards into the ditch at the side of the lane.

11

Her ears were ringing, her head felt like a truck had hit it, and her right shoulder hurt like hell. She was vaguely aware that her clothes were soaked, and it was raining hard. Rivulets of water streamed down her face from sodden hair. There was a hand behind her neck, cushioning it.

'Don't move now Niamh. You're all right...just don't move.' The voice was strong, and reassuring, with an Irish lilt to it.

She opened her eyes. To her right the cottage was still blazing. Trees and shrubs were crackling, throwing sparks into the air. Dark shapes darted to and fro. Luminous stripes on their arms, and around their chests, danced like fire flies. The light from the fire illuminated the white helmet of the man kneeling over her, and cast a yellow glow across one side of his face. It was a strong face, rugged, with high cheek bones.

'I'm Station Officer Gerry Hogan,' he said. 'I take it you're Niamh?'

She made the mistake of trying to nod her head. Pain shot from her shoulder up the right side of her neck.

He felt the muscles spasm beneath his hand, and saw her wince. 'No, don't move,' he said. 'And especially don't try to nod your head.' She felt him take hold of her left hand. 'If you don't want to talk just squeeze my hand,' he said. 'Once for yes, twice for no. Try it now.'

She squeezed it once. 'It's alright,' she said, 'I can talk.'

'Good. But whatever you do keep your head still. Can you wiggle your toes?'

She was relieved to find that she could. 'Yes I can.'

'That's great. Do you have any pain anywhere?'

'My right shoulder is worst. Like a dull ache, with shooting pains when I try to move. And my head is throbbing.'

'What about your back, and your legs?'

'No, just sore I think.'

She felt him let go of her hand.

'I'm going to feel your shoulder and your head now, is that OK?'

'Go ahead,' she said.

His hand moved gently but firmly over and around her shoulder, then over her head.

'Ouch,' she said.

'That's a bump you've got there,' he said. 'You probably banged your head on one of these stones. You were lucky. A few more feet and it would have been against the wall behind you.'

'I don't feel lucky,' Niamh said. Looking past him she realised that her car was no longer there. 'My car....it's gone,' she said, panic beginning to take hold.

'Don't worry,' he said. 'We moved it back down

to the road so we could get the pump up here. It'll be fine. And your shoulder...it's not dislocated, and I'll be surprised if there's anything broken.'

Two more figures appeared at his shoulder. 'Ah the paramedics are here,' he said. 'I'll leave you in their capable hands.'

One of them knelt, and took over, supporting her neck. 'My name's Marie,' she said. 'This is Shaun. What's your name?'

'Niamh.'

'Well now Niamh, you're going to be just fine. I'm going to shine a light in your eyes. Keep them open for me will you? And then I'm going to put a brace around your neck, just as a precaution.'

With the brace in place she expertly strapped Niamh's right arm across her chest with a triangular bandage.

Station Officer Hogan turned to join his colleagues fighting the fire.

'Mr Hogan. My cousins...have you found them?' she called after him.

He looked back at her, his face in shadow, the fading fire a halo around his head.

'No Niamh, we haven't. Let's pray they were away when it started.'

The paramedics pronounced her fit to stand, and helped her back down the track, past a red and silver Volvo appliance, over the snaking hoses, to the end of the lane. A silver SUV with red and white chequered squares down its flank, and Kerry Fire & Rescue on the window, a second appliance, a white Mondeo with GARDA in blue across its bonnet, her own hire car, and an ambulance, lined the roadside. Their emergency lights flashed in syncopated rhythm. She was helped up the steps into the ambulance, and told to sit down on the bed.

'We are going to take you to hospital for a check up,' said the paramedic called Marie Murphy. She attached a blood pressure cuff to Niamh's left arm. 'We're just going to wait here for a while to see if there's anyone else needs our help.'

Niamh prayed that there wouldn't be. That the two of them were in a pub somewhere, getting steadily drunk. Her hands began to shake uncontrollably. She felt she was going to be sick. The paramedic placed a blanket over her shoulders while her colleague made his way to the cab. She made her lie down on the bed, and placed a pillow under her feet. 'You're suffering mild shock,' she said. 'Hardly surprising after what you've been through. But don't worry Niamh; you're going to be fine.' She turned, and stepped down onto the road to speak with Station Officer Hogan who had just appeared around the side of the ambulance. She lowered her voice, but Niamh could still make out what they were saying.'

'I'd like to get to her off to hospital as soon as possible. Get her checked over, just in case,' said the paramedic.

'Well if there is anyone inside that cottage, they'll be way beyond anything you could do for them,' he replied. 'But I'll still need some back up here, just in case any of my team gets into difficulty.'

'Shaun's already called for a replacement ambulance,' she said. 'We'll be off as soon as it gets here.'

A yellow helmeted fireman joined the two of them. Niamh raised herself up onto her elbows. She could only see him in profile, but she knew instantly from the droop of his shoulders, and the fact that his voice was inaudible, that he was bringing bad news. She saw him nod his head in response to a question from his superior, then shake it slowly, and finally raise his hand, two fingers extended. If she needed confirmation, it came when he turned his head to look into the ambulance, and saw her staring back at him. Even in the half dark, the red and blue flashes from the emergency lights turning his face into a ghoulish mask, she could read the disappointment and pity etched across it. He turned back, and spoke to his colleagues. Marie Murphy immediately climbed back into the ambulance, and closed the doors.

'You should be lying down, Niamh,' she said firmly. 'We'll be on our way now.' She walked to the front of the ambulance, knocked on the window, and spoke to her colleague. The engine started up. She returned, and busied herself securing straps across Niamh's lower chest, and legs. 'We wouldn't want you to fall out now, would we?' she said brightly. 'Some of the bends on these roads are awful tight.'

Ignoring the pain in her shoulder, Niamh grasped the woman's hand, and hung on until the eyes that had been avoiding hers capitulated.

'Matty and Billy, they're dead aren't they?' she said.

'I am so sorry Niamh,' she replied. 'But I'm afraid they are.' She took hold of Niamh's hand, and held it lightly. 'They're in God's hands now,' she said gently. 'Let's concentrate on getting you right.'

Niamh began to feel dizzy again. She laid her head back on the pillow. Her ears were still ringing, and her head ached. She closed her eyes, and waited for the darkness to swallow her up.

When she awoke, it was light. A policeman was seated beside the bed. A male nurse was adjusting a drip on a stand, from which snaked a thin white tube strapped above her left wrist, where the canola entered a vein. Her mouth was dry, her lips parched.

'Where am I?' she croaked.

'Kerry General Hospital, in Tralee,' the nurse told her as she cheerfully poured water from a flask into a tumbler. 'And you're doing fine Niamh.'

He helped her to raise her head, plumped a pillow behind it, and held the glass to her lips. While she sipped, he had a good look at her eyes, checked the monitor on the wall behind the bed, and nodded to the Garda, who immediately got up from his chair, and left the room.

'My name is Benny,' said the nurse putting the glass back down on the locker. 'And I'll be looking after you until the doctor discharges you, which shouldn't be long at all.' He saw the bemused expression on her face. 'You were suffering from mild shock, but because you'd passed out a couple of times the doctor decided we'd better keep you in for observation. We gave you something to help you sleep by the way.'

Niamh could tell that her shoulder was still strapped, and judging by the cold, and weight, there was an ice pack on it. She tried to move a little and was relieved to find that it only ached.

'You were lucky there too,' Benny told her. 'It's not a dislocation, it's a just a type one shoulder separation.'

'That sounds a hell of a lot worse,' she said grimacing.

He smiled. 'Well it's not. Pain relief for a week or so then a bit of physio', and you'll be as right as rain.'

The Garda appeared in the doorway. He had woman colleague with him.

'The police want a word with you,' Benny told her. 'I'll be back when they've finished. Then it's breakfast. The doctor will be round by eleven, and I wouldn't be surprised if you're out of here by midday.' He headed for the doorway, pausing to address the Gardai. 'Don't be too hard on her,' he said. 'She'll be fine, but she's had a hell of a shock.' He turned back, gave her a reassuring smile, and left.

The female officer pulled up the chair on which her colleague had been sitting, and sat down. She had serious eyes, and a firm chin. Her hair was short and black, with a bit of a curl to it. Thirty three at the most. There were streaks of grey that belied her years. The result of wearing that cap all the time, Niamh decided, her mind wandering.

'My name is Sergeant Cairanne Kelly of the Garda Siochana,' the officer said. 'And this is Garda Eugene Byrne. If you're up to it Ms Caton, we'd like to ask you a few questions?'

Niamh thought she recognised the names, but had no idea where from. She forced herself to concentrate.

'Go ahead,' she said. 'I've got some questions of my own.'

'You don't mind me calling you Niamh?' said Kelly.

'No. Please do.'

'Good. Well first of all I'd like to offer you our condolences. I understand that you buried your cousin Oona yesterday, and less than ten hours later you witnessed the fire in which your cousins Matthew and William Caton died?'

Niamh nodded. 'That's what I wanted to talk to you about.'

'All in good time Niamh, all in good time,' said the sergeant. 'But let's get my questions out of the way first. I understand you flew in the day before yesterday. Was that specifically for Oona's funeral?'

'Yes. It was.' she replied. She told them about her research into the family tree, Aunt Miriam's death, and her conversation with Father O'Leary.

Cairanne Kelly listened intently. Her male colleague made notes in a small notebook.

'So tell me what you've been doing from when you arrived,' she said. 'Up until yesterday evening.'

When Niamh had finished there was a long silence while the Garda sergeant reflected on what she had heard.

'So that was only the conversation you had with Matty and Billy?' she asked.

Niamh sighed, and tried to adjust her position to take the weight off her neck.

'If you could call it a conversation.'

'And did you notice anyone strange hanging around when you drove past the house that first time, or at the funeral?'

Niamh pressed down on the bed with her left hand, and her heels, and hitched herself up into a semi-sitting position. Her pulse began to race.

'So you think it was arson?' she said.

'I'm not saying that at all,' Kelly said firmly. 'I'm just following a routine line of enquiry in cases such as this. Please answer the question Niamh. Did you notice anyone strange hanging around at the funeral, or the cottage?'

'I wouldn't know a stranger if I saw one. But there was something really odd that happened…someone who gave me a real fright. Just before I arrived at the cottage.'

The officers leant forward in unison. Garda Byrne's biro poised expectantly.

'Go on,' said Kelly.

Niamh watched for their reactions as she described her confrontation with the car on the narrow lane, and the man in birdlike mask.

The Garda sergeant's expression gave nothing away. Eugene Byrne nodded sagely.

'That'll be one of the Wren Boys,' he said, earning a warning glance from his superior.

'It's too much of a coincidence though surely?' said Niamh.

'We'll certainly look into,' Cairanne Kelly replied. 'But Garda Byrne's right, the district is full of mummers and supporters of the Wren Boys Bands this week…with the Races and the competition in Listowel. Sure, if you're staying at the Listowel Arms you can't have missed them?'

'But this is a country lane seven miles away, at nine thirty in the evening,' said Niamh, pressing her point.

Kelly pursed her lips. 'Plenty of time to get to the town, and two or three hours of drinking time left.'

'So how did the fire start then?'

'Look, if it's any consolation,' the sergeant said. 'It seems Matty and Billy were dead before the flames got to them. It was the smoke that killed them. As for the cause, we won't know for certain till later on today. The fire investigation team will be taking their time. The building's unsafe, with what's left of the roof likely to cave in at the slightest excuse.'

'But you must have some idea?'

Kelly sucked her lower lip as she considered her response. It was the kind of reaction that her detective colleagues, and the poker school back at the station, would have described as a "tell".

'The most likely cause is a chimney fire,' she said. 'I'm afraid they still account for the majority of call outs in Kerry, and the majority of house fires.'

'A chimney fire?' The incredulity in Niamh's voice was almost a challenge.

'You've got to remember,' the sergeant continued. 'That there is still a hell of a lot of old houses where peat, or wood, and sometimes coal, has been burnt for nigh on two centuries. If they're not cleaned regularly the build up of carbon and dust in the chimney can be ignited by just one spark. And if the flue itself has broken down the fire will spread to the rest of the house in an instant.'

'We had a fire in the chimney in our house every couple of years when I was a lad,' added Garda Byrne. 'And I know a couple of people who've died in them. Why, I was called to one only last...'

Cairanne Kelly held up her hand imperiously.

'Thank you Garda Byrne,' she said, cutting him off mid sentence.

'What about the explosion?' Niamh asked. 'That

wasn't a chimney, surely?'

The Gardai looked at each other, and then at Niamh. 'Explosion? What explosion?' said Kelly.

Niamh told them.

'It's not unusual,' the sergeant told her. 'Probably a gas canister, in which case you're lucky to be alive. And since the fire was still underway, we know that it wasn't the cause of the fire don't we?'

Defeated by the logic, Niamh sank back against the pillow. She knew this wasn't right. That there had to be more to it. Sergeant Kelly stood up. Behind her, Garda Byrne closed his notebook and clipped his biro carefully back into his pocket.

'I think that's about it for now Niamh,' said Kelly. 'You've been very helpful. We'll be in touch when we hear from the boys at the Fire and Rescue. Until then, I think it's time you had a bit of a rest, don't you?'

Niamh didn't have a response. She simply nodded her head, and watched them go. Cairanne Kelly had been right. She was tired. She closed her eyes hoping to doze for a while. The images kept playing through her mind, like a surreal video film, jumbled up, at half speed. Running through it, insistent and repetitive like a lost chord rediscovered, was a recurring shot of that light flashing from the hillside above Kilfeighny. She still had no idea what it meant.

12

They discharged her that afternoon, with a sheet of do's and don'ts, and a reminder that she needed to arrange for a series of physiotherapy sessions for her shoulder, starting in a week's time. The senior registrar explained that whilst there was no evidence that she had suffered concussion, there was still a possibility that she might experience some of the post concussion symptoms such as headache, dizziness, disturbances to her vision, memory problems, emotional disturbance, and unexplained depression. Niamh thought that she would have no problem explaining any emotional disturbance or depression that might happen along, but decided to keep that to herself.

A very nice woman from the Department of Social and Family Affairs called in to assess her need for counselling, be it post traumatic or bereavement, or both. Apart from the ache in her shoulder, and the bruise on her head, Niamh felt fine. The only emotion she had right now was one of anger, but she wasn't going to admit to that either. All she wanted to do was get out of there.

There was no way that she could drive, and in any case the police had taken her car back to Listowel. A place had been booked for her on the Kerry Flyer, along with a number of outpatients and hospital visitors, until they realised that she wasn't going to Lixnaw, but all the way through to Listowel. After a flurry of phone calls a taxi was booked. By 4pm she was back at the Listowel Arms.

The concern from the staff was almost overwhelming. With the door finally closed, the Do Not Disturb sign on the door, and a pot of tea and a plate of pastries on the table beside her, Niamh sunk back into the arm chair, and switched on her cell phone. There were just two phone calls. Both from Mary Manghan.

'Niamh. Are you there? ...You're not? Well I was hoping to tell you face to face. But you'd better know. There's been a terrible fire over at Matty and Billy's. The pumps and the Garda are still there, but they're giving nothing away. Can you give me a ring when you get this?' At which point she ran out of message time. The second was even more frantic. 'Niamh. Are you there? Oh God, she's not there...' Addressed to someone else at her end. 'Niamh, when you get this... for the love of God... ring me!'

Benny, the charge nurse, had fielded a call from Mary Manghan the night it had happened, and had told her that Niamh was recovering well, and not to be disturbed. Niamh had spoken to Mary shortly before she was discharged so there was no need to do it now. She deleted the messages. The last thing she needed right now was an interrogation. Instead she tried to ring Tom, but his phone was switched off. She was about to leave a message when she remembered that he would be in the middle of moving, so she rang Bill Fitzgerald instead. He picked up straight away.

His voice was calm, and reassuring. It made her wish she was back in New Hampshire. That she could pretend none of this had happened. He sounded surprised, and pleased at the same time.

'Niamh, it's great to hear from you. You were lucky to get me. I'm just off to lunch with a client...but how's it going over there?'

'In that case, it'll keep,' she said, 'I can ring you later if that's OK?'

He picked up on the tension she was trying so hard to keep out of her voice.

'What's the matter Niamh?'

'No, it's nothing really. I'm fine. I'll ring you back.'

'You'll do nothing of the sort,' he said firmly. 'My client will wait.

He listened patiently while she told him everything. His response was succinct, and immediate.

'Come home.'

'I can't do that,' she began, 'Not until...'

He cut her off. 'Right now Niamh. The first plane you can get on. You are fit to fly I take it?'

'Yes but...'

'Then just do it.'

'I can't.'

'Why not?'

'Because the police want to talk to me again. When they've got the results of the Fire Department investigation.' It wasn't what she'd been told, but it was a reasonable assumption.

'Then I'm coming over there.'

'No Bill. That's silly,' she said. 'I'm fine...really I am.'

'You have no idea how this is going to affect you... on top of everything else.'

She bristled. 'Right now, apart from stiffness in my shoulder, I am perfectly fine. And if you're thinking of my emotional state, if anything this has got me feeling more alive than I have in a long time. And very, very angry.'

There was a long pause as he weighed his words.

'Anger is one of the symptoms of post traumatic stress Niamh.'

'It is also a perfectly normal response to having your aunt, and three cousins – however removed they might be – murdered in the space of two months.'

'You don't know that's what happened to Oona, and Matty and Billy.'

'You're a lawyer Uncle Bill,' she said. 'Give it to me straight. No bullshitting. Are these reasonable grounds for suspicion, or what?'

He had never heard her swear before. And there was something other than anger about the way she sounded. She was determined...in control.

'Grounds for suspicion, I admit,' he said. 'But that's all it is, suspicion. Leave it to the police, and get out of there. Please Niamh.'

'Not till they've told me what's going on.'

'Then I'm coming over.'

'No you're not!'

In the long silence that followed the two of them regretted the gulf that was growing between them. Niamh was the first to bridge it.

'I'm sorry Bill,' she said. 'I know you're only trying to help, and if the positions were reversed I'd be saying the same. As soon as I know they're taking this seriously, I'll come home. I promise.'

'I believe you, but I'm still not happy about it,' he

said. 'If you are right, then you may well be at risk. Why don't you ring your cousin...Tom is it? Didn't you say he's a detective? He may be able to help. At the very least, he has a right to know what's happened'

'I will. So stop worrying.'

'That's easier said than done. I'll stop worrying when you're back here, safe and sound.'

'Thanks Bill,' she said.

'You're welcome,' he replied. 'Though I haven't the faintest idea what for. Call me.'

It was nearly seven o'clock. Empty packing cases, stacked one inside the other, lined the hall. The two of them were exhausted. Caton slumped across the sofa, his head on a cushion.

'I suppose that leaves me to brew the tea...again,' Kate said pointedly, staring down at him.

'No. it's alright. You sit down and I'll do it.' Tom allowed one foot to slide unconvincingly in the general direction of the floor.

'And pigs will fly.' She turned her back on him, and disappeared behind the half partition wall that led to the kitchen area.

'I hope you're not maligning my profession,' he called after her as he reached under the cushion for his mobile phone.

'Is that what you call it?' she replied. 'Don't forget I do sometimes work with you lot. I'll let you know the day the word professional begins to apply.'

'Come in here and say that,' he told her. 'See what you get.'

'Promises, promises.'

He flipped open his phone. 'You should be so lucky.'

'Actually,' she said, with the seductive tone in her voice that even at this distance he found irresistible. 'I was thinking we might try out the shower, get a Chinese take away delivered...open that bottle of champagne, and then see how lucky we both get?'

Suddenly his exhaustion was merely a minor impediment. 'Sounds good to me.'

There was one message on his phone from his DI, Gordon Holmes, and a missed call. Gordon sounded upbeat.

'Hi Boss. Hope the move's gone to plan...you lucky sod. Plush pad, minutes from the office, views out to the Pennines, and all the advantages of marriage without any of the disadvantages – like screaming kids, and a lifetime sentence. Anyway – the Marvin Brown shooting...DI Tyldesley's doing OK...surprise, surprise. Couple of new leads...arrests in the offing. Sad to say, we're managing without you. You don't need to ring me back. Have a good time on the course...not that that's likely is it? Anyway, see you when I see you Boss. Bye.'

The missed call was from Niamh's mobile. Kate was still in the kitchen. He returned the call. After all, it was only going to be a short one.

Ten minutes later he was still on the phone, the mug of tea going cold on the coffee table, Kate on the balcony looking out across the canal, listening to his side of the conversation and impatient for it to end.

'I know what you're saying Niamh,' he said. 'But it's far too soon to be jumping to conclusions. Look, you know it's not in my jurisdiction, but I'll see if I can find someone to talk to in the Garda. Find out where they're up to. Make sure they're taking it seriously. Then I'll ring you back straight away.'

'Tom that would be great. It'll stop me dwelling on it all the time if I know you're involved.'

'Hardly involved,' he said. 'But I promise I'll do what I can.'

'I'll wait for you to call.'

'It might not be until tomorrow.

'I know.'

'Goodnight then Niamh. And take care.'

'Goodnight Tom. And thanks.'

Kate turned and came back into the room. Only to find that he was already dialling again.

'What on earth's going on Tom?' she asked.

'Those cousins of ours I tracked down – Matthew and William – their house was burnt down last night with both of them in it. Niamh got there too late, was rocked by an explosion, and ended up in hospital.' He put the phone to his ear.

Kate's hand went to her mouth. 'Oh my God,' she said coming and sitting beside him. 'Is she alright?'

He nodded.

'Helen? It's Tom…Tom Caton.'

'DS Gates?' Kate whispered.

Tom nodded again.

'Tom, I thought you were supposed to be on leave?' said Detective Superintendent Gates. 'Moving into that new gaff of yours.'

'I am,' he said. 'And I'm really sorry to bother you, but I've a got favour to ask. When you were in Dublin this summer, at that Europol Conference, did you make

145

any contacts in their criminal investigation branch?'

'As it happens, I did. Detective Chief Super-intendent Eamon McCarthy. He's the Head of the National Bureau of Criminal Investigation, based in Dublin. And don't repeat this, but he tried his charm on me late in the evening in the Hotel bar. Not surprising since I was one of only a handful of women in the place.'

'I'm sure it wasn't just that,' Tom said, knowing it was what she wanted to hear.

'And don't you come the charm offensive as well, Tom Caton.' she said, just a little too officiously to have meant it. 'Anyway, why do you ask?'

It took him half the time to tell her that it had taken Niamh. He left nothing out. She was far too smart for that.

'Well, ordinarily I'd think twice about bothering him with this on the basis of little more than suspicion,' she said. 'But if there does turn out to be anything in it, well it means that one of my own officers could be at risk.'

Smart indeed. She had already made the connection that Caton had made, and not shared with Niamh.

'If it's alright with you,' she said. 'I'll give him your mobile number, and he can come straight through to you. If he's prepared to. That's the best I can do.'

'It's more than I could have hoped for,' Tom told her. 'I really appreciate it.'

'You're welcome,' she said. 'And I hope Tom, that this relation of yours turns out to be wrong. For all your sakes. The last thing we need is a transatlantic serial killer on the loose. We've got enough of our own. '

The remains of the Chinese meal had dried to a

semi glutinous paste. The champagne bottle was only half empty. It had not turned out to be the celebration either of them had hoped for. Kate was about to clear it away, leaving Tom to top up their glasses, when his mobile went off. It began to vibrate its way ominously across the shiny surface of the table. She stopped in her tracks and stared at it, hoping that he would not pick up, knowing that he had to.

Tom flipped it open and repeated his number. He never gave his name unless he recognised the caller.

'Is that Tom Caton?' asked the caller. A rich Irish brogue. Authoritative and equally cautious.

'Yes,' replied Tom. 'It is.'

'My name is Eugene McCarthy. Do you know who gave me your number?'

'Detective Superintendent Gates.'

'Right then,' he said. 'I looked into that business your boss told me about. It's not as straight forward as they were thinking.'

'I see,' said Caton.

'An accelerant was used. On the front and back doors, and on the shutters of the windows. Bastards knew what they were doing. Apart from getting the place ablaze before the occupants would realise it, they it made impossible for them to get out.'

'So they think there was more than one person?'

'I'm not sure about that. They may be getting ahead of themselves on that one. It's just that there's a line of enquiry they'll be following that might involve a number of people.'

'Can you tell me what that is?' Caton said, knowing full well that he had no right to expect it.

'Look Detective Chief Inspector, I know this is

personal rather than professional, but there's a limit to what they know, and even less that I can tell you.'

'I understand that. I'll just be grateful for what you can tell me.'

'Right, well just between the two of us, the two that died…'

'Matthew and William Caton.'

'Matty and Billy…there was a suspicion that they were selling green diesel on the black market. Undercutting a local syndicate. Reason enough to be taught a lesson.'

'Some lesson!'

'Mr Caton. You know what these scum are like. They wouldn't know subtlety if it bit them on the arse.'

'So you don't think there's any connection with the death of their Aunt – Oona Caton?'

'I'm a hundred and fifty odd miles away from Tralee,' he sounded weary. Probably calling from home. 'I haven't seen the file. All I've got to go on is what I've been told about how she was found, and the post mortem findings. No suspicious circumstances. If I were you, I'd put your cousin's mind to rest, and get a good night's sleep yourself. We've assigned a detective inspector to the case, and he's to keep me informed, personally. If anything comes up I'll make sure and tell you. Is that good enough for you?'

It was more than Caton could have reasonably expected.

'I'm very grateful, Chief Superintendent,' he said. 'And I'm sorry you've been put to all this trouble on a Saturday night.'

There was a chuckle at the end of the phone. 'No

problem Tom, Just tell your boss that next time I see her, she owes me one.'

Caton sat there with the phone in his hand. Kate came and sat beside him.

'Well?' she said. 'What did he say?'

'That it was arson.'

'Oh my God!' she put her hand on his arm. 'Do they have any leads?'

'They think it may be thieves falling out.'

'And that other cousin...Oona?'

He shook his head. 'He doesn't know, but there's no evidence to suggest it was anything other than an accident.'

'Well that's something, surely?'

'It doesn't mean a thing. A remote mountainside, a fall, a fractured skull, and hypothermia. All it would take is a nudge. What evidence would there be?'

'I don't know. Footprints? Disturbed soil at the point where she went over?'

'The path would be covered with boot prints, scuffs in the soil. A walker's paradise, not to mention the locals like Oona who use it on a regular basis. And if the rescue team went down from the same spot that would have made even harder to decipher.' He went into his address book.

'What are you doing Tom?'

'Ringing Niamh,' he said. 'To tell her I'm coming out there.'

She let go of his arm, and placed her hand over the phone. 'No Tom, please...think about it?'

'What's to think about?'

'Well for a start, we've just moved in here in case you hadn't noticed. And secondly, if they're right, it has nothing to do with Niamh, and thirdly, it's not your patch…it's not even your country. There's nothing you can do except get in their way.'

The fact that she was making sense didn't help. It made him feel even more impotent.

'She's thousands of miles away from home, for God's sake! Just witnessed a double murder. Just got out of hospital. And she's my flesh and blood. I can't just hope she'll be all right, I've got to make sure that she is.'

'Come on Tom, get this into perspective.' Kate persisted. 'You only found out she existed a couple of weeks ago. And what is she? A fourth or fifth cousin?'

For a second he felt his anger might get the better of him. Instead he took a deep breath, and stood up.

'Has it not occurred to you that if there is something going on…I could be as much at as risk as she is?' He stormed out of the room, and into the bedroom, taking the phone with him

Alone on the couch Kate clenched her fists.

'Of course it bloody well has,' she said to the empty room, her nails biting into her palms. 'Why do you think I don't want you to go?'

13

As it turned out Niamh wouldn't hear of it.

'If the police are wrong, about who started the fire... and about Oona...then the answer must lie back home,' she said. 'That's where this started...whatever it is. I'm going to go back, and find out what the hell is going on. You'd be better staying there with Kate. I know if I was her, I'd be spitting turkey feathers.'

'The police may not let you leave.' Tom told her.

'Why ever not?'

'Because you are a witness to arson? The only person found at the scene?'

'That's ridiculous,' she said. 'What possible motive would I have?'

'How would they know until they've checked you out? Even now there will be emails flying back and forth across the Atlantic. That's what I would be doing. For all they know you may be an arsonist.'

'Is that what you're wondering Tom? After all, you know nothing about me either. I might not even be who I say I am.'

'True. But it would have to be a pretty elaborate hoax. And why draw a Detective Chief Inspector into it? It wouldn't make sense.'

She sounded genuinely disappointed. 'That's not the answer I was hoping for.'

'OK,' he said, trying to redeem himself. 'In all of our conversations I've sensed an absolute honesty in everything you've said.'

'Only sensed?'

'Come on Niamh,' he said, trying not to let his exasperation show. 'I'm a policeman. I've learnt from bitter experience that people, and things, are rarely as they seem, me included.'

'That's a shame,' she said, hoping to inject a little humour. 'Just as you were growing on me.'

He smiled at that. 'Seriously though, they'll be checking you out, and I doubt they'll want you to leave the country just yet.'

'Well nobody's told me that, and my passport is still here. So if they do want me to stay they'll have to be quick about it.'

'If they do, I want you to tell me straight away. Then I will come out. I'm not having you hanging around there on your own, an easy target for whoever set that fire. Don't forget you may well have seen one of them.'

'In a mask, with the rest of his face painted white. That's hardly going to convict anyone.'

'He's not to know that is he?'

'If it was a he. I couldn't even swear to that.'

'Stop being evasive Niamh. Just promise you'll tell me.'

'Alright,' she said. 'I will.'

And until you do leave, don't go anywhere on your own. Stick around the hotel.'

'I promise.'

'And ring me when you hear anything. If I haven't heard from you, I'm going to ring you every morning and evening to find out where you're up to. Right?'

'Tom Caton,' she said affecting a husky flirtatious tone, 'I didn't know you could be so masterful.'

He laughed. 'There's not much wrong with you then.'

'That's what I keep telling you,' she said. 'Now don't you think you should get back to Kate before she dumps you?'

He could hear Kate in the kitchen, loading the dishwasher. Banging the pots as she did so. The champagne bottle, and the two glasses, were gone; the table had been cleared. He put his phone down on the sofa, and walked through to join her.

'What time are you leaving?' she asked, with her back to him.

'I'm not.'

She paused for a moment, and then ferreted in the soap box for a tablet. She placed it in the compartment, closed the lid, switched on the machine, pushed the door too, and turned to face him.

'Your decision, or hers?'

'Mutual,' he said.

She searched his face. It was sufficiently true for him to get away with it.

'Right then,' she said, wiping her hands on her apron, and starting to turn away. He reached out and gently took hold of her arm

'I'm sorry Kate. I behaved like a complete plonker.'

The corner of her lips curled up as she tried to resist a smile.

'Yes, you did,' she said.

He pulled her towards him, put both arms around

her waist, and kissed her, tentatively at first, and then with passion. ,

'That champagne,' he said when they finally came up for air. 'I hope you didn't pour it in the sink?'

She shook her head.

'It's in the fridge.'

'Why don't you fetch it, and I'll get another couple of glasses,' he said. 'We've got an apartment to christen.'

She placed both hands on his chest and pushed him away.

'Better hurry then,' she said. 'There's a bedroom to christen first.'

Niamh spent the whole of Sunday in the hotel, apart from a brief tour of The Square. The rest of the time she sat in the lounge, and read The Deposition of Father McGreevy. She went up to her room to freshen up before dinner, and sat on the bed looking out across the water to the race course. The view reminded her of one of Brian O'Doherty's lines about street lights scribbling on the surface of the river. There were so many ways in which the story had touched her. It left her feeling deeply connected to this part of Ireland, in ways she would never have imagined: spellbound by the lyrical nature of the language, fascinated by the way in which pagan superstition and religious observance coexisted in uneasy symbiosis, saddened by the harshness of the life eked out on the mountainside, horrified by the way in which gossip, tittle tattle, ignorance and prejudice had brought down an entire community. Above all, she was disturbed by the similarities to her recent experience: the fire that razed the mountain village, the inexplicable deaths of all of the womenfolk. Not identical events, but close enough to leave her wondering.

It was the last night of the races, and the festival that went with them. After dinner she spent a pleasant evening in the lively ambience of the Writer's Bar with her acquaintances from the night she arrived. When they enquired about her shoulder, – impossible to hide with the strapping still in place - the whole story came out. They insisted on buying her drinks, and were genuinely disappointed when she finally pleaded tiredness, and retired to her room. Mercifully, her dreams were of Father McGreevy's mythical mountain village, and the beautiful mythical creature, an aisling, with a fleece of golden hair.

Detective Inspector Sean Foley was waiting for her when she came out from breakfast. He was a pleasant surprise. Mid thirties, six foot two tall, athletic build, with a strong jaw, high forehead, an unruly head of black curly hair, and bright blue eyes with early crows' feet beside them that told her he smiled more often than he frowned. The hotel manager made sure they had the lounge to themselves. They pushed their chairs back out of range of the roaring fire in the hearth.

'I'm sorry for your loss Ms Caton.' he said with sincerity beyond the requirements of duty.

'Thank you Inspector,' she said. 'I understand you have the results of the fire investigation?'

He looked at her quizzically for a moment, and then smiled as it dawned on him.

'Of course, Detective Chief Superintendent McCarthy will have told your contact. I should have realised.'

'I'm sorry,' she said. 'It's just that Tom is family, and with him being in the police...' Her voice trailed off.

'Don't worry about it,' he said. 'In his place I'd have done the same. So, do you want to tell me what you've been told, or do you want to hear it from the horse's mouth.'

'I'd rather hear it from yours,' she said, provoking a smile.

'The fire was started deliberately with the intention of killing whoever was inside. Most arsonists would have broken in, or poured petrol through the shutters. No way would they have gone to the trouble of soaking every door and window. That tells us that whoever did it must have known that Matty and Billy were inside. Either because they'd been watching the place, or had called at some point to check. If it was the latter, that suggests the perpetrator, or perpetrators, were known to them. Are you with me so far?'

'Yes I am.'

'Good. This brings us to motive. I'm afraid those two had a sight more enemies than friends. They were bully boys when the drink was inside them, especially the father. There's many a man between here and Tralee bears them a grudge. But to be honest, it's unlikely that any of them would think it reason enough to commit murder. Not that we're discounting the possibility.'

'What about their links to the IRA?'

His raised his eyebrows. 'You know about that too do you?'

'From newspaper reports, and the internet,' she said.

'How long have you been over here?'

'Since Thursday.'

'My, you've been busy then,' he said, his voice full of respect. 'Well that was all in the past, Billy's grandfather and his father before him. Both of them heroes as far as the organisation was concerned. But neither the Real and Continuity IRA nor the PIRA would have wanted anything to do with Matty and Billy. Those two would have been more of a hindrance than a help. No, we think it more likely that this was to do with them dabbling in the illegal supply of green diesel.'

'Green diesel. What is that?' Niamh asked. 'I'd have thought it was a good thing. Environmentally friendly…something like that?'

He grinned. 'Ah well, that's our sense of humour I guess. Everyone else calls it red diesel, because of the dye that's put in it. Ours would have to be green wouldn't it?' He could see from her expression that she was still none the wiser. 'It's Marked Gas Oil - or fuel if you like - where the tax is rebated to make it cheaper for diggers, and tractors, central heating, fishing boats, and the like. It could save a motorist a euro or more per litre, but it's illegal to run an ordinary vehicle or a lorry on it. Last year alone it cost the country millions in lost tax. There's a big crackdown just started. The Revenue are dipping the tanks of cars at petrol stations, and in supermarket car parks. Anyone caught using the stuff stands to lose their car unless they cough up a mighty big fine.'

'How were Matty and Billy involved?'

'We've good reason to suspect that they were middlemen, between an oil laundry, and a couple of garages selling the stuff on to owners of leisure craft, and to private motorists. Plenty of room there to make real enemies, hiking the price up, creaming off the top, diluting the product to make it go further. Then there's rival gangs. Or even someone with connections who didn't know what he was being sold, and ended up getting his prize Mercedes, or his motor yacht, confiscated.'

'They didn't look like they were making a lot of money.'Niamh said, thinking back to their appearance at Oona's graveside.

'Well if they were hoarding it, it's gone up in smoke for sure,' he said. 'But from what I've been told it's more likely they…' He was about to say "pissed it away" but in deference to Niamh he said '…drank it away.'

'So you don't think it had anything to do with Oona's death, or my being here?'

'Niamh…Can I call you that?'

She nodded.

'I understand you've been through a hell of a lot recently, but I assure you I don't think that your judgement's impaired. I don't believe in coincidences any more than you do. If there's one thing I've learned as a detective, it's that they're more likely to be suspicious than not.'

She sat up, and leaned forward. 'So you do think there's a connection?'

He held up his hand. 'Now hold on a minute. I'm not saying that. What I'm saying is that I'm going to explore the possibility. Go back over the report, have a look at the sight of the accident, take a few statements. Then we'll see.'

'Thank you Inspector,' she said. 'Thank you so much.'

'But there's something I need you to do in return,' he said solemnly.

'Anything.'

'I want you to go over your statement with me again, to look at a few faces I've got on my lap top – just to see if any of them have been hanging around this hotel, or at the funeral, and then...' he paused, knowing full well what her reaction would be. 'I want you to go back home, to America.'

She felt suddenly deflated.

'You just want me out of the way,' she said.

'Not at all. I want you somewhere safe, a long way from here. I think it unlikely you're in danger at all, but as long as you're here I'll have to worry about you. That's going to take up time and resources I don't have.'

Despite her disappointment she could see his point. She reminded herself that it had been her intention to go back anyway.

'So I'm not a suspect then?' she said.

He smiled. 'Hardly. Oona died before you even entered the country. As for Matty and Billy, the accelerant had to be carried in some kind of container. There were no traces in your car, and nothing found at the scene. Let's face it, when you were found, you were in no state to be able to dispose of it.'

'But you checked my car?'

'Oh yes. Like I said. I have to consider every possibility, however unlikely. More than anything else, this job is about elimination. Ask your friend in Manchester. He'll tell you.'

There was nothing new in her statement. She recognised none of the digital photographs he showed

159

her. In the final analysis she could see that he was right, just as both Bill Fitzgerald and Tom had been. She would be safer back home. And in any case, she decided, if there is a connection, that's where it started. So that's where I'm going to find it. Her only regret - well not the only one if she was honest, but the main one - was that she wouldn't be seeing Detective Inspector Sean Foley again. Or not any time soon.

Courtesy of the Shannon Stopover Agreement which dictated that every other flight from Ireland to Canada, or the USA, had to stop at Shannon, Niamh was able to book a seat for the following day. The plane took off at 11.25 in the morning. As it began to climb, she looked out of window on the portside. She thought she could make out around the loop in a river, across the wide ribbon of the Shannon Estuary, amid the green fields and bog lands, the brown patches of peat, and lines of plough share, the cluster of buildings that was Listowel. Further south, and west, white dots marked the wind farm on the Stacks Mountains above Lixnaw and Kilfeighny.

She lost sight of the land for a moment as the plane began to bank. When it straightened out all she could see were Atlantic rollers crashing white against the steel grey cliffs below the Loop Head lighthouse. And then there was nothing but the wide open sea, and a clear blue sky dotted with cotton wool clouds. She made herself a promise, that come what may, she would be back.

14

First thing on Wednesday morning Niamh rang the Manchester Police Department, gave her name, and asked to be put through to the Detective Supervisor.

'We have three of those Ma'am,' she was told. 'The captain, two lieutenants, and two sergeants. Which one did you want?'

So much had happened since the day of Miriam's funeral. Niamh could not remember his name.

'Perhaps if you gave me the names of the two lieutenants,' she said. 'I might recall it.'

There was an ill-disguised sigh at the other end of the line.

'Well, we have Lieutenant Madera, and Lieu...'

'That's him,' Niamh interrupted. 'Detective Supervisor Lieutenant Madera. He's in charge of the case.'

'And you said your name is...?'

Got you! Thought Niamh. And I only told you a moment ago. So it's not just me. It was childish she knew, but right now she needed all the confirmation of her sanity she could get.

'Niamh. Niamh Caton, and it's in respect of the murder of my aunt, Miriam Caton.'

The word murder had the desired effect. Niamh detected an awakening of interest in the creak of a chair, a straightening of the spine perhaps.

'Just a moment Ms Caton, I'm sure he's still here, I'll see if I can you put through.'

The next voice she heard was his, friendly yet wary.

'Ms Caton. It's good to hear from you. When did you get back?'

'Yesterday,' she said.

'Did you have a good trip?'

'Good is not the word I would choose to describe it,' she said, rubbing her shoulder to ease the ache. 'That's what I wanted to talk to you about. And to find out if you've made any progress.'

'I'm afraid I haven't a lot of news for you yet. We're still working hard on the case. Our strongest lead is from the paint and glass from the vehicle. We've narrowed it down to a black Ford Explorer XL, models 1998 through to 2002. You don't want to know how many of those there were. But we'll get there. It's a simple, if time consuming, process of elimination.'

Exactly what Detective Inspector Sean Foley had said. Different car, different country, same result. Time consuming.

Niamh told him about the fire, Matty and Billy, and her suspicions regarding Oona's supposed accident. He listened patiently, without interruption. When she finished, he whistled.'

'Wow, Ms Caton, you've surely been through the mill. Puts a whole different complexion on our investigation.'

'So you think there's a connection?'

'I have a healthy mistrust of coincidence. Lightning

has been known to strike the same person twice – usually when he's been dumb enough to keep playing golf in storms – but three times? I don't buy it.'

'So what will you do?'

'Keep an open mind on this. Liaise with this Irish detective when you've given me his name and contact details. Run a search on people flying out of the US into Ireland in the period since your Aunt Miriam's death. When we get a list of the owners of those Ford Explorers I'll run a cross match. You never know, we might get lucky. It's a long shot...and to tell you the truth I hope you're wrong.'

'Me too,' she told him.

'In the meantime, I suggest you get on with your life, but take sensible precautions.'

'Like keeping off the sidewalk. Not going out. Having sprinklers installed in the house?'

'I realise this is tough for you Ms Caton,' he said. 'And I don't blame you for feeling spooked, but there's not enough here to warrant protection. Like I say, you're just going to have take care.'

Spooked. Niamh thought that a classic piece of understatement.

'And don't hesitate to call me straight away,' he added. 'If you see or hear anything out of the ordinary.'

'I will,'

'Make sure you do now. I'll be in touch.'

Never had Niamh had so many men worrying over her. She had arrived home to find emails from Tom and from DI Foley, both checking that she had arrived safely, and a phone call from Bill Fitzgerald.

And now she had another guardian angel at Police headquarters, right here in Manchester New Hampshire. Far from reassuring her it simply confirmed her worst suspicions. She decided she had to keep herself busy.

There were now just three things on her to-do-list. The rest could wait. The first - moving into Miriam's house - would take no time at all. After all, the apartment was so small there was hardly anything to move. But not until she'd had a proper alarm system installed. That was something she would see to straight away. Then there was arranging some physio sessions for her shoulder. Not that it was proving that troublesome, but she hated being under par. And last, but certainly not least, researching the remaining branch in the Caton family tree. This was where the key to the mystery must lie.

By one o'clock in the afternoon Niamh was once again in the City Library at 405 Pine Street, on the Eastside. Her focus was on Padraig, born in 1842. The only one of her great, great, great, grandfather Joseph Padraig Caton's children whose details had so far eluded her. She explained her problem to Morgan Page, the librarian who was a leading member of the New Hampshire Genealogy Society, and had already been a great help to her.

'After the record of Padraig's baptism, in the same year he was born, he seems to have disappeared from the records. There was no sign in the records, or on the Kerry gravestones lists, of a marriage or his death, nor does he appear in the 1901 census of households, by which time he would have still have been only

164

fifty nine.'

'And you've tried all the online Caton websites?' Morgan asked her.

'There aren't many,' Niamh told her, 'I exhausted them before I left for Ireland.'

'Then, it's reasonable to assume that he emigrated. That might be where your own great grandfather got the idea from - following in his father's footsteps.'

'So you think I should go on the Ellis Island site and search the immigration records?'

'When did you say he was born?'

'According to the family bible, 1842.'

Morgan shook her head. Ellis Island didn't open as the centre for immigration from Europe until 1892. I'd start on the Castle Garden site. Come on, I'll show you.'

There were a hundred and thirty eight entries for Caton. To Niamh's amazement, of the first ten names, eight were from France, one from Sweden, and one from Germany. They were not in date order. She was ploughing through them, when Morgan Page peeked over her shoulder, and pointed out that she could enter the first as well as the surname. Within seconds, a single entry with the name Padraig Caton appeared.

His age was given as twenty two, and his occupation, "Laborer." He had sailed on the Erin, from Liverpool via Queenstown where he had presumably embarked, and had arrived on the thirtieth of April 1866. His destination was given as 7328. His future plans and passage were unknown. The dates matched. It had to be him. Niamh selected the page, and sent it to the library printer.

On her way to the bank of printers she met Morgan

coming towards her with the sheet in her hand.

'I think this is for you,' she said. 'Looks like you've struck lucky.'

'But what does this number mean under destination?' said Niamh.

'To be honest, I have no idea,' the librarian confided. 'But the majority seem to have that number so it could mean New York, or even America. I'm sure I can find out. Is it important?'

'I don't think so, but it would have been helpful to know where he went next.'

Morgan smiled. 'Follow me,' she said.

An hour and a half later Niamh had become expert at using the library's HeritageQuest Genealogy Online database. She had searched the US Census from 1870 right through to 1920, without finding a single Padraig Caton, or even a Patrick Caton come to that. Just as she was thinking of calling it a day, Morgan came to the rescue yet again.

'It's perfectly possible that he changed his name,' she said.

'Why would he do that?' Niamh asked.

'It was a lot more common than you'd think. The main reason was to overcome ignorance and prejudice that might stop them from getting a job, or even accommodation. There was a lot of prejudice against the Irish and the Jews. As the century moved on so did the prejudice. Next it was the Italians and Russians. Immigrants regularly gave false names on the ships manifests so they already had a different identity before they were processed on Ellis Island. But the Italians stuck to their guns. They became padrones – labor contractors - controlling employment from construction to entertainment, clubs and bars and restaurants. They kept their name and their pride.'

Seeing a cloud pass over Niamh's already disconsolate face she quickly added. 'But if your ancestor did change his name, that's not necessarily a problem. That's one set of records that's a hundred percent intact.'

It didn't turn out as Niamh had expected. By five o'clock, just a half an hour before the library was due to close, she'd managed to establish that if he'd applied to become an American citizen, it was not recorded in the US National Archives, and had not therefore taken place after 1906. Which left the archives of the fifty individual states in existence prior to that date to trawl. Daunted by the task, she gave up, and went home to her empty apartment, surrounded by packing cases.

The following morning, buoyed up by the knowledge that the security system was being installed in Miriam's house, and an email exchange with Tom in which she brought him up to date with her discovery, she set off for the library. Despite the sun and the clear skies, there was a distinct chill in the air. The leaves fluttered on the breeze as she walked across Victory Park, and crossed over Pine Street. There was lightness in her step. It was Morgan Page's day off, but it didn't matter. Niamh had a plan.

She knew that the majority of immigrants – unless they had relatives sponsoring them – initially settled in reasonably close proximity to their port of landing.

It helped to explain the phenomenal growth of New York in the nineteenth and early twentieth centuries. So she started with the New York State Archives and worked outwards. By lunchtime she had begun on the New England Archives serving Connecticut, Maine, Massachusetts, New Hampshire, Rhode Island, and Vermont. Almost immediately she found a match. There were no details, just the name Padraig Caton, associated with a petition for naturalisation. She could send for the record, but the quickest way was to drive over and see it for herself. Her heart began to flutter as she checked the address of the archives, 380 Trapelo Road, Waltham.

She clicked on Google Earth, waited impatiently for it to load, entered the address, and sat back marvelling at the speed with which she was zoomed to her destination. There it was, just to the West of Boston. She used the ruler tool to get the distance. A little over forty two miles as the crow flies. Maybe fifty by road. Straight down The Everett Turnpike, or down on Route 93, and across on 95. She decided to let the sat nav decide. Either way, no more than an hour and thirty, including jogging back to her apartment for the car. She closed down the sites, logged off, and headed for the exit.

15

The North East Region Headquarters of the National Archives - a massive, low, white stone building with a dramatic pyramid topped portico and Old Glory fluttering proudly on the flag pole - looked as though it belonged at the Pentagon. .

'You're lucky,' the receptionist told her. 'Thursday is late night closing, 9pm. But we don't pull any original records after 4pm. You can leave your bag in the lockers over there. And please remember to switch off your phone. Do you know what you're looking for?'

Niamh told her.

'Right, then you'll have to fill in an application for a researcher identification card, and a reference service slip, at the Reference Desk. Have a nice day.'

At the reception desk Niamh was asked for some photo ID. She showed them her driver's licence. It was explained that she could take her lap top, and a notebook, with her, but no food or drink. It was only then that it hit her that she'd skipped lunch altogether. Too late now. By the time she was seated in the secure reference room, it was nearly two pm. Her hands shook a little as she began to read the five by eight inch photographic copy of Padraig Caton's naturalization document.

He gave his date of birth as the 27th of January 1842, his nationality as Irish, and his place of birth as Kerry, Ireland. His place of residence was 47 West First Street, Boston, Massachusetts, and his occupation was a longshoreman. He stated that he had a wife who was a citizen of the United States of America, born in Boston. He had no children. There followed the declaration in which, in addition to confirming his desire to be admitted to citizenship, he renounced his former allegiances, and confirmed that he was neither an anarchist, nor a polygamist. The document ended with the Oath of Allegiance, his signature, and those of a witness, and the Clerk of Common Pleas, neither of which could Niamh decipher.

There was a note on the Petition that had been smudged. She showed it to the archivist, who studied it carefully, and smiled.

'This states that prior to this Petition, a Declaration of Intention was filed in the United States District Court for the District of New Hampshire,' she said. 'In which case we'll have a copy of it here. Would you like to see it?'

'Oh yes please,' said Niamh. The excitement in her voice triggered a note of caution.

'Don't get your hopes too high,' the archivist responded. 'Often the information will be identical to that on the Petition. You never know though, you might strike lucky.'

Niamh filled out a second request and waited nervously. It turned out that the archivist had been ninety percent correct and that much of the information was the same. But for Niamh the ten percent was gold. This time, as well as affirming his intention to become an American citizen, and to change his name, his place of birth was given as Lixnaw, County Kerry, Ireland. And he confirmed that he had entered the United States of America from Queenstown, Ireland, and that his lawful entry for permanent residence was New York, under the name Padraig Caton, on the thirtieth day of April 1866. It was a complete match with the information she had garnered from the Castle Garden Immigration site. This was the Padraig Caton who had sailed from Ireland on the Erin

She sat back and took it all in. He had applied for naturalization, just four years after his arrival. And where he had given his name, and confirmed that he had never previously been known by any other name, he stated that from heretofore he wished to be known as Peter Clark. It looked as though Morgan Page had been right. An attempt to avoid the stigma of his Irishness? To anglicize his name? Fit better into Boston Society perhaps? She wondered how his parents would have felt. If they even knew. She doubted it, given the absence of any mention of him in the family bible beyond the simple record of his birth.

She pictured him in a tiny boarding house near the waterfront, loading and unloading cargo from the clippers and early steamships. She recalled the Scorsese film *Gangs of New York*, and the bloody and horrific gang fight between the WASP Bowery Boys, and Irish immigrant Dead Rabbits, that her father had told her really took place in 1857, and was followed by an even more dramatic riot in 1863 against the Draft Laws. Just three years prior to Padraig Caton's arrival in America, she reflected. No wonder he'd changed his name. And still five years of the Civil War to go. She wondered if he'd been drafted, and if so, if he had survived. There was only one way to find out. She paid for copies of the documents, and asked where next to turn.

She was advised to start with the Census Returns, and then track back for births and deaths. Armed with so much, the information came thick and fast. In the 1870 Census – under his new name Peter Clark - Padraig had risen in the world. His occupation was given as a stevedore. A quick Google revealed that this typically meant that he would have owned machinery or equipment for loading and unloading cargo, and hire longshoreman to do the work. His rise in status was matched by a move upmarket, to a house on the other side of the tracks – quite literally – on Harrison Avenue. He now had a wife Jane, and two children - Jane, and Moira. A son, Patrick, appeared in the 1880 Census having been born in 1871.

By half past eight Niamh had reached the 1900 Census, and uncovered four grandchildren: Patrick James, Mary, Brigid, and James, all children of Patrick. Jane had died five years previously of a fever, and Moira was still a spinster living in her father's house. Having exhausted her supply of records, and unable to access any fresh ones until morning, she collected her printed copies, and her notebook, and retrieved her coat and bag from the lockers.

As she loaded her bag it struck her that there was little point in driving back home to an empty apartment and then coming back in heavy traffic the next morning.

'Is there anywhere nearby I could stay for the night?' she asked at Reception.

The receptionist gave her a perfect smile. Her answer, rehearsed a thousand, times tripped off her tongue.

'Lord yes. There are several lodges and holiday lets less than a half mile from here that do stopovers, but I doubt they'd suit. If you'd like something a little smarter, I can recommend a host of possibilities down on the Business Park.'

'Sounds fine,' Niamh told her.

The smile grew wider. 'In which case, take a left back out of here, up to Hardy's Pond - that's the first main intersection - take a left there onto Lexington. In a mile and a half go left onto Totten Pond Road. In another mile you'll hit the Business Park. You can't miss it. They're all down there. The Holiday Inn, Best Western, Hilton Garden...'

'How far is that?' Niamh asked.

'Four miles at most. You'll be there before you've left.'

Niamh had to smile. It seemed a very Irish thing to say. And the woman's name badge read Anya Antonovna.

Apart from the fact that it was six stories high, the Hilton Garden Inn was not dissimilar in style to the Archive building. Right down to an almost identical portico, with an extra canopy on top. The room was more than adequate. A king bed, a large bathroom with separate shower, flat screen TV, a refrigerator, microwave, high speed internet with remote printing, and even an ergonomic work chair. She threw her bag on the bed, sat down beside it, switched on her cell phone, and checked for messages. There was a missed call from Bill Fitzgerald, and a text message from Tom.

Just checking Ur OK. Give me a call wen U can. Tom.

She smiled at his hybrid texting technique, not that her own was much better. It would be too late to ring him now, so she sent a quick reply.

I'm fine. Lot's 2 tell. Will call U. Niamh. X

She had added the X without thinking about it, and wondered briefly what Kate might think if she saw it. She sent it anyway. She couldn't face eating alone in the Grill Restaurant so she picked up a microwaveable ready meal, and a half a bottle of wine, from the Hotel's Pavilion Pantry, took them back to her room, and put them in the fridge while she had a shower.

It was incredible the difference a power shower made. The needle jets of water left her feeling clean, wholesome, and relaxed. She studied herself in the bathroom mirror. Size eight. Well toned. Surprising given how much she had recently neglected her normal exercise regime. No lines on her face. Her breasts still firm, her stomach not slack from child bearing. The bruising around her shoulder had paled to brownish yellow, with a little purple at the edges. There was a slight step where the collar bone had slipped outwards, just as the doctor had predicted. She grinned ruefully; it was not enough to stop bag straps slipping off her shoulder. Hopefully that would disappear when the physio's had worked their magic. Not bad for my age. Then why am still single? She had no idea, other than that she hadn't met the right person yet. She worried that she was getting too fussy. It she didn't start shaping up she would end up on the shelf. Like Moira. Perhaps it ran in the family? She flicked her reflection with the towel, put on the white cotton bathrobe, and went through into the bedroom.

She put the meal in the microwave, opened the wine, and took a bottle of sparkling water from the fridge. Ordinarily she might have questioned the wisdom of drinking water that had required another eleven litres just to extract, bottle and transport it. But tonight it never occurred to her. While the meal turned slowly and inexorably on its plate she checked the TV listings. *Entrapment* was just about to start on HBO. Nine till eleven pm. Sean Connery and Catherine Zeta Jones in a rework of *The Thomas Crown Affair*. She had seen neither of them. She sat on the bed propped up against the pillows with the tray on her lap, and her glass on the bedside table, and switched on.

Niamh woke with a start. The tray was on the floor where she had put it earlier. On the screen was a medieval make-believe land with a swashbuckling hero, and a beautiful damsel in distress. She checked the time. It was twenty after eleven. According to the listings she had dozed through the end of *Entrapment*, and the beginning of something called *The Princess Bride*. She decided to listen to her body for change, turned off the TV, got under the covers, switched off the light, and went back to sleep.

She awoke early, and after another shower, set up the lap top, and entered on her website the details for Padraig, and those of his son and grandchildren. It was just possible that someone out there would have the missing piece of the jigsaw. After breakfast, knowing that he would be worried, she rang Bill Fitzgerald.

'Niamh, where are you?' he said, clearly more anxious than she had anticipated.

'Calm down,' she said. 'I'm fine. I'm at the Hilton Garden Inn just out of Waltham.'

'Waltham? What on earth are you doing there?'

'Your not hearing me Bill, I said I'm OK. I came down to do some stuff at the National Archives.'

'On Trapleo Road? The North East Region?' She could hear the relief in his voice.

'That's the one,' she said.

'Why did you stay over?'

'Because it was a late finish, and I didn't fancy driving back down this morning. Anyway, the flat's cold and empty. What would you have done?'

'You're supposed to be taking care...watching your back.'

'What makes you think I can't do that just as easily here as there?'

'Because at least up here you know the territory. You're on home ground.'

'Look Bill,' she began, her irritation coming through in the way she gave the words undue emphasis. 'I really appreciate your concern, but you're beginning to make me nervous. I can't live my life like this. Looking over my shoulder everywhere I go.'

He was tempted to tell her that that was exactly what she should do.

'I'm sorry Niamh. It must be so hard, and I don't mean to make you feel worse than you already do.'

'Then let's change the subject. Do you want to know what I found out yesterday?'

'You bet I do.'

She told him.

'Right here...in New Hampshire?' he said. 'But that's amazing. How come your father didn't know about it...or Miriam?'

'Presumably because of the change of name...and if Padraig fell out with the family...'

'I don't suppose that changing his name, becoming a US citizen, and renouncing his allegiance to Ireland would have helped in that regard?'

'I reckon not.'

'So what are you doing today?'

'Seeing where this takes me. For all we know I could have relatives in Manchester, within a block of where I live.'

Neither of them spoke as they thought it through. If that was the case, and Niamh turned out not to be paranoid but actually correct in her suspicions, they too would be at risk. Finding them would have a greater imperative than joining up the dots, completing the family tree. Niamh rehearsed that opening conversation in her head.

'Hi, I'm Niamh. Niamh Caton. You don't know me, but I have reason to believe that we are cousins. Fourth Cousins actually... Yes, it is isn't it? Amazing. Look, I don't know any other way to say this but... the reason I'm contacting you... well... it's a little difficult... but I thought you ought to know. I don't know why exactly, but I think someone is out to kill you.'

As an introduction, that would sure take some beating. Bill Fitzgerald broke the silence.

'I'd better let you get on with it then,' he said, leaving the rest unspoken.

'I will.'

'Ring me when you get back,' he said. This time he had the sense not to add *take care*.

Back at the Archive Niamh was quickly into her stride. Before lunch she worked on the period up to the end of the First World War. In 1919 Patrick James Clark was still alive, but his brother James, and his sisters Mary and Brigid, had all died of typhoid within weeks of each other in 1907, the year that Mary Mallon, she discovered, became the first typhoid carrier to be identified. Typhoid Mary, as she came to be known, survived. The three Clark children did not.

Niamh went to the lunch room. This time she had taken the precaution of picking up a single-decker clubhouse sandwich, and a juice, from the Pantry to eat out front when she got peckish. She ate her sandwich, and pondered the fortunes of the Caton clan. Too many, it seemed to her, had died young or childless. She recalled having seen in a TV documentary that Genghis Khan had sixteen million descendants living today. So what did he have, she wondered, that the Catons did not apart from concubines, an inordinate capacity to reproduce, and a propensity among the dynasties he spawned to inter marry? She preferred not to think about it.

Ten minutes into her afternoon session Niamh reached the Census of 1930. It was here that she made an astounding discovery. Patrick James Clark, and his wife, had been blessed with a son, John James Clark, born in July 1921. She stared at the screen transfixed. She recognised that name. Few people living in New Hampshire could put their hands on their hearts and say they did not. John James Clark. Reclusive billionaire. Almost as famous as Howard Hughes in his day. She shook her head in disbelief. It had to be a coincidence. It couldn't possibly be him. She wondered if he was still alive. There was an easy way to find out.

Over at the Research desk she asked if she could use one of the computers with internet access. Online, she typed in his name, plus billionaire. There were seven pages of entries. She clicked on the one that looked most like a biography and that had a recent date. Up came one page with a short resume, and several embedded hyperlinks. She speed read the first and last paragraphs. There was no doubt about it. John James Clark, the great, great, grandson of the Padraig Caton - immigrant and longshoreman - was a billionaire. According to the article, he was still alive, and living in Vermont.

She clicked on the first of the hyper links which took her straight to a Forbes 400 article. And there he was. A head and shoulders shot of an elderly man in a black suit jacket, and white shirt, with a red tie. His face was wrinkled and fleshy, his hair white and wispy. And yet she could see in the shape of his head, the set of the jaw, and the black eyes staring out from red rimmed lids, the image of her own grandfather. His net worth was shown as $5.1 billion, which meant that he just crept into the top fifty on the Forbes 400 richest Americans list. The major source of his self-made fortune was given as *Gambling, Entertainment* and *Leisure*. His age was shown as eighty seven, his hometown as Boston, and his place of residence as Vermont. Against *Education*, it said simply *High School Diploma*. He was divorced, with no children.

The son of a stevedore working the docks, he had dropped out of school in ninth grade. During WWII he flew Mustangs and Warhawks, and trained US and British pilots. After the war he flew surplus Air Force planes into South America, and built up a charter flights company coast to coast. He sold the company in 1964 for $80 million profit, and bought his first casino in Atlantic City. Over the next thirty six years he built, bought, developed and sold casinos and hotels, building his fortune along the way. Despite several flurries in Vegas, and New York, the majority of his holdings remained in and around Atlantic City.

There were allegations – unproven – that he had deliberately asset stripped, and then bankrupted, some of his acquisitions, at the expense of the shareholders while turning a nice profit for himself. In the manner of the uber richer he had dabbled in philanthropy, if to a lesser extent than most. Several New England Colleges had scholarships funded by him. He had founded two refuges for homeless people, one in Boston and one in Atlantic City. There was only one entry after the year 2000.

Niamh sent a copy to the printer, and began to trawl through some of the other sites. None of them shed much light on the man, beyond that which she had already read, except for a 1997 Time Magazine article. It portrayed an obsessive, driven, and lonely man, on the cusp of old age. In the interview he had revealed his regret that his single minded determination to increase his wealth had cost him his marriage to a wealthy and educated Boston socialite, and that he felt he was on a treadmill that he could no longer get off.

There was just one other article – the most recent - that caught her eye. It was a speculative piece in the financial section of the New York Times. It repeated a story in a rival newspaper that two nurses had recently been employed to live in, full time, at the home of billionaire John James Clark in Vermont. The writer went on to reminded readers that the billionaire recluse had not be seen in public for over seven years, and wondered if – given his age, implied infirmity, and absence of offspring – he had made a will. This piece would have had little merit as a rehash of someone else's article had the journalist not found a new source, a former personal assistant to Clark. This source claimed that Clark had not to his knowledge written a will despite him and his employer's solicitor trying to persuade him to do so. John James Clark, he claimed, had never wanted to contemplate his own mortality. A parallel was drawn with Howard Hughes, whose estate had become the focus for wild speculation, and even forgery. The date of the article was April 2007.

It took a moment or two for the enormity of it to hit her. She sat there staring at the screen. She read the article again, and then a third time. Now it all made sense, if sense could ever be applied to the murder of four perfectly innocent people. More like insanity. But here at least was a motive. Five billion dollars worth of motive. What she didn't understand was that since John James Clark had neither siblings nor children, and she and Tom were the only surviving members of the Caton family tree, who else stood to gain? At last she had found the key. The trouble was she had no idea what lock it fitted. Come to that, she had not the faintest idea where to begin to look.

Niamh made a note of the web addresses for the three articles, printed each of them, paid for the copies, and hurried out to her car.

16

There was a storm brewing. The North West wind drove darkening clouds diagonally across the Appalachian Mountains, and the gentle curve of the lofty Berkshire Hills. Rolling over Mount Monadnock, thirty five miles away, they descended on the northern outskirts of the city. As Niamh opened the car door the rain came. Great globes of liquid hammered on the roof like bullets. She clambered inside, and slammed the door shut. The windscreen was a waterfall. The sky was as black as pitch, as though night had come early. No way was she going to set off in this. She opened her bag, and took out her phone.

Bill Fitzgerald didn't pick up, probably in court or with a client. She left a message for him to call her back when he was free. Tom's number rang and rang. Just as she was about to end the call he answered, breathlessly.

'It's me,' she told him. 'Niamh.'

'I'm glad you rang,' he said. 'I left a message earlier. Just wondered how you were.'

'I'm fine. I was in the National Archives…I had to switch it off.'

'Listen,' he said. 'I'm hanging blinds. Can you give me a minute, and I'll ring back?'

'Why don't I call you back,' she countered. 'I've such a lot to tell you. It wouldn't be fair to rack it up on your phone bill.'

'If you're on your mobile, that's going to cost you a fortune.'

'I don't care,' she said. 'I have to tell someone.'

'OK. Give me two minutes,' he said. 'Just to be on the safe side.'

He listened in silence. When she had finished he said, 'Where are you right now?'

'In my car...in the car park...outside the NARA.'

'Have you locked it?'

'Tom, you're making me nervous,' she said.

'You haven't answered the question Niamh. Is the car locked?'

She pressed the button beside the handbrake.

'It is now.'

'Good. I don't mean to scare you Niamh, but five billion dollars! That's what, about two thousand five hundred and forty million pounds at current rates? We both know there are people that would sell their soul for less.'

'That's why I had to tell someone,' she said. 'But I don't want to feel like a victim, sitting around waiting for this bastard to catch up with me.'

Tom had never heard her like this before.

'You don't have to,' he said. 'We still don't know that there's a connection between the deaths of Miriam, Oona, Billy, and Matthew, only that what you've discovered makes it more likely.'

'Much more likely, Tom. You're the one who doesn't believe in coincidence remember'

'Alright,' he conceded. 'Much more likely. But now we have a motive, that's eighty per cent of the way to finding the perpetrator…assuming there is one.'

'I'm not sure eighty per cent sounds that encouraging,' she said. 'Not when my life is at stake.'

'*Our* lives, Niamh,' he reminded her.

She realised that she had been so focused on her own vulnerability that she had forgotten that he was just as much a target.

'You're right,' she said. 'I'm sorry, it's just that I have no idea where to go from here.'

'There are three things you need to commit a murder,' he told her. 'Or any crime come to that: motive; means; and opportunity. We've a pretty good idea what the motive may be. The means was available to anyone who can drive a car, fill a can with petrol, and push a woman down a mountainside.'

'That narrows it down.' She observed wryly.

He chose to ignore it. 'We need to do two things,' he continued. 'Firstly to find out who, apart from ourselves, will stand to gain if our cousin dies intestate. And secondly, to establish that that person had the opportunity to commit the murders, because he or she was in the vicinity at the time of each murder.'

'Won't the cross match between the lists Detectives Madera and Foley are compiling give us the name we're looking for?' she asked.

'What name are we looking for?'

'Caton, or Clarke presumably,' she said.

'Not necessarily. Padraig Caton proved that by changing his name to Clark. It only needs for the perpetrator to have done the same, either by deed poll or identity theft, and it will be like looking for a needle in a hay stack. And frankly, I'll be very surprised if he hasn't done so. I know I would.'

She felt completely deflated. It was the one thread of hope to which she had been clinging. She slumped back into the soft leather driving seat.

'Then I've no idea where to go from here,' she said.

'We have to find out who, apart from ourselves, will stand to gain if John James Clark were to die intestate.'

'But there's no one left but us. Surely that's the point of all this?'

'There's the perpetrator. The one who's doing all this.'

'But I've gone down every branch, and reached dead ends except for the two of us.'

Dead ends indeed, Tom reflected. 'Well I hesitate to propose it,' he said. 'But we are going to have to go back over every one. It's what I'd do if I was running this as an investigation. There must be something you've missed. But when I say we I mean detectives Madera and Foley. As soon as you present them with this new information they're bound to step up their efforts, including double checking your research. They'll have far more resources at their disposal. If you like, I'll talk to my contact in Dublin, and you can go in and see Madera. The police at your end should be able to find out if there is a will or not, and if the lawyers are aware of any likely claimants. I have a feeling we two are going to come as something as a shock to them.'

The rain had slackened to a constant drizzle as Niamh pulled out of the parking lot. It had been a roller coaster of a conversation. Starting on a high, plummeting, then coming out up the other side. She felt better knowing that Tom was on the case, and that there were practical things to be done. He had also pointed out that Bill Fitzgerald should be able to help as well. That he was bound to have connections with lawyers upstate where John James Clark was living.

It was twilight, and still dark beneath the cloud cover. The wipers clacked back and forth, clearing a path that was instantly inundated again. She concentrated hard on the road ahead, glancing only periodically in her rear view mirror. It was only when she reached the Richardson's Pond interchange between the Yankee State Highway, and Route 93, that it dawned on her that the same black sedan had cruised a steady twenty metres behind her all the way from Waltham. She told herself that it had been only eleven miles or so. That this was a popular route. That her eyes could have been deceived by the rain, and the poor visibility. But when it stayed on her tail as she made the left onto the 93, her heart skipped a beat.

She considered speeding up to see what would happen, but she was already doing fifty. Equally, there was no way she was going to pull over; not in this rain. Even if she did she doubted that anyone would stop, except perhaps her pursuer.

She thought about calling 911 on her hands free, but had no idea what she would say to them. In the end she decided to wait a little longer. There was plenty of traffic on the road. If the car was still there when she got to Manchester she resolved to drive straight to the police headquarters where there was bound to be CCTV covering the approaches. The cameras would surely capture the registration. She recalled an episode of CSI Miami where the cameras recorded not only the licence plate, but the disc, the nodding dog on the rear parcel shelf, and the little green scented pine tree hanging from the driver's mirror.

It was another eleven troubled miles before Niamh saw the flashing right hand indicator, and watched in her mirror as the sedan turned off at the interchange with Route 495, and headed off towards North Andover, and the Lawrence Municipal Airport. Relief flooded her body like a reverse shot of adrenalin. Twenty five miles to go. She turned on the radio, and relaxed into her driving.

Niamh closed the door to her apartment, punched in the code to cancel the alarm, and stooped to pick up the note on the mat. It was from the security firm working on Miriam's place.

Ms. Caton. All done. Please find invoice attached. 28 days to pay. We appreciate your custom. Have a Nice Day.

The phone began to ring. She picked up her bag, and hurried through to the lounge. It was Bill Fitzgerald returning her call.

'Sorry about that Niamh,' he said. 'I was in court, and then I had two urgent consultations with clients. I didn't even have time to have lunch.'

'I guessed as much,' she said. 'Look, I've so much to tell you. But I don't want to have to do it over the phone. Why don't you come over when you've finished there? I can make us both some dinner?'

There was barely a pause.

'I could be with you by eight.'

Niamh smiled. It had never been in doubt. A confirmed bachelor who had never really taught himself to cook, he was a sucker for home cooking.

'So what do you think?' she asked, as she handed him his cup of regular filter coffee, and sat down on the sofa beside him.

'Butternut squash and nutmeg risotto, with Barolo wine and Castelmagno cheese…what's not to like?'

He blew across the surface of his coffee.

She would have punched him but for the danger that it would spill. 'You know very well what I mean!' she said. 'So stop fooling around, and give me a straight answer, or you can forget your Jim Beam White Label.'

He feigned hurt and disappointment. 'Come on Niamh…you know you only got that in for me. If I can't have it who the heck else are you going to serve it to?'

'I'll pour it down the drain before I let you make light of this,' she said.

He heard the catch in her voice, and turned to see that she was fighting back tears. He put the cup down on the coffee table, and put his arm around her shoulders.

'Hell, I'm sorry Niamh,' he said. 'I didn't mean to upset you. I suppose I was trying to take some of the heat out if it. And if I'm honest, to give myself time to think. Stupid of me.'

'Yes it was.' She snuffled. 'I reckon I've held it together pretty well until now, but I can't pretend this isn't happening. The only way I'm going to keep going is if I know that everybody else is taking it seriously. That we're making progress. That I've got some control over this.'

'You're right,' he said. 'And I do think it's serious. I should have known better than to patronise you Niamh. I'm sorry.'

'Yes you should. Now can we put that behind us? Get back to my question? Like I said...what do you think?'

He looked her straight in the eyes so that she could see that he was holding nothing back.

'I think it's about as serious as it can get. I agree with your cousin Tom, and with the detectives here in Manchester, and in Ireland. There are too many coincidences. And now that we know about John James Clark...well it doesn't take a lot of imagination to see how that could spark someone off.'

'But how could they expect to get away with it?'

'They have so far.'

'But if they ever got to the point of claiming against the estate they would have to come out of the woodwork...expose themselves.'

'So?'

'Then they would come under suspicion for all the murders surely?'

'Suspicion is one thing...proof another. I'm a lawyer Niamh, and I can tell you that unless there is more than vaguely circumstantial evidence to link a person with those deaths, there is no court in this land that will be able to disregard the merits of his or her claim.'

'But that can't be right.'

He shook his head. 'Right or wrong that's how it will be. Unless some hard evidence is found there is

She shrugged her shoulders. 'I don't know. But I'm sure you do.'

'Well I suppose if you both swore on oath, and I lodged it with the State Probate Court.'

'Then we could do interviews on WMUR-TV, the Radio News stations, the Manchester Daily Express.' Suddenly she could see a way out of this. She paced around the room as her excitement grew. 'Maybe even some of the nationals.' We could post it on the web.'

'I'm sorry Niamh,' he said, 'I'm not sure that that would work.'

'Why on earth not?'

'Because it would be obvious to everyone – and especially the perpetrator – that you were both doing it under duress. Probable to flush him or her out. Those oaths wouldn't be worth the paper they were written on. When the time came you could revoke them on the basis that you'd only done it because you had good reason to suspect your lives were at risk.'

'But we wouldn't'

That's not the point. I'm sorry. The point is that you could.'

She stood there letting it sink in.

'Is it alright if I carry on?' he said.

She slumped down on a stool. 'Why not.'

He turned back to the screen. 'OK. Assuming that there are no skeletons in the cupboard, he has no descendants. Neither are his parents alive. So the next in line will be his parents' descendants.'

'All dead.'

He looked across at her. 'All of them? You're sure'

She nodded disconsolately. 'Mary, Brigid, James. Typhoid Fever.'

He turned back. 'Grandparents?'

'No.'

'Grandparent's descendants... his great aunts and uncles and their descendants? Half of the estate will go to each side.'

She shook her head. 'No. Not unless I've missed something.'

'Not a lucky dynasty is it?' he observed.

'Tell me about it,' she said.

'Well that just leaves the next available kin related to the deceased, up to and including the fourth degree of kinship, which is where you and Tom come in.'

'And after that?'

'Well if there are no takers, then the entire estate passes to the State of New Hampshire.'

'How are the State's finances at the moment?' she asked with a wry smile.

'I don't know,' he said. 'But I wouldn't have thought they were so bad they had to resort to this.' He paused for a moment trying to decide whether to mention the other thing or not. There was only one chance in a million that it might become relevant. He hoped to God that it would not. In any case, if she did what she'd said she would do, and looked up the page for herself, she would find out. 'Niamh, there is something else,' he said.

She picked up on his tone, and steeled herself. 'Go on.'

'When this law was drawn up someone must have taken a lot of care. Thought about the kinds of things that might happen to challenge it. Maybe there was even a precedent, or a test case. Either way, there is a special clause.'

He had her full attention. 'Which is?'

'Unless it can be established beyond all reasonable doubt that a claimant survived the decedent by one hundred and twenty hours, then that person is deemed to have predeceased the decedent, and is therefore no longer entitled to a share of the estate.'

'In other words...?'

'If you, or Tom, or anyone else with a claim were to die within one hundred and twenty hours - effectively five days — of the demise of John James Clark, then you wouldn't get a cent.'

'I'm not sure I'm following that,' she said. 'If we were dead anyway, what would it matter?'

'Not to you it wouldn't, but it would to any one of your children, or anyone you had chosen to name as a beneficiary in your will.'

'But I haven't any children,' Niamh said. 'I haven't even written a will.'

'Maybe not,' said Bill Fitzgerald. 'But how is our perpetrator expected to know that?'

17

First thing in the morning Niamh was outside the City Police Headquarters, 351 Chestnut Street, one block east of Bill Fitzgerald's Office. The two storey beige brick building, with its narrow perpendicular windows, and triple bands of concrete cladding, had always struck her as a kind of modern day equivalent of a frontier fort. It sat uneasily among the stately Victorian houses along the tree lined boulevards.

Detective Lieutenant Supervisor Madera was expecting her.

'It was good of you to see me, at such short notice,' she said as he led her down a corridor.

'No problem,' he replied. 'I told you...anytime, just call me.' He opened a door and ushered her into a room just big enough for a desk, computer, and several plastic chairs. 'Sit down, Niamh,' he said. 'Can I get you a drink? Coffee, tea?'

'Just water would be fine.'

'Sure thing,' he said. 'There's a bubbler in the squad room. And so long as there are none of my people around you can call me Max. It's not as though you're a suspect or anything.' He flashed a smile, and left the room.

Max, she thought to herself. A big guy, with a big

personality. Max by name, and Max by nature.

He returned with two plastic beakers of ice cold water. He handed her one, put the other on the desk, and sat down next to her.

'So Niamh,' he said, getting right down to it, 'What's this about?'

He listened patiently, without interruption, and then made her repeat it all again while he made notes. Then he put the notebook down on his desk, and looked at her with something approaching admiration.

'I could do with you on my team,' he said. 'You've given me something to work with here. I won't pretend that my boss wasn't sceptical about all of this, but now…he's going to have to take it seriously. Not that we've been sitting on our hands here.' He added quickly.

'So have you made any progress at all?'

'It depends on your definition of progress. In terms of the way most investigations go, yes…I'd say we've made progress. We finally got the list of all the Ford Explorers matching that batch of paint, and the glass from the headlights. I've got people checking them out. Odds are it will have been registered stolen which is going to speed up the search, but make it harder to connect to our perpetrator. As for the lists of names from immigration and the airlines, I reckon that's going to take a couple more days. By the end of the week we should have a shortlist to cross reference with Detective Foley in Tralee.'

'I suppose you'll start with the names Caton and Clark?' she said.

'You bet, but I doubt somehow we're going to get that lucky. Then...you never can tell.' He looked at her closely, noting the lack of makeup, the dark rings beneath her eyes, and the hint of worry lines on her forehead where he had noticed none before. 'How have you been sleeping Niamh?' he asked.

'Not too bad,' she replied unconvincingly. 'I suppose I've been working pretty hard at this, if that's what you mean.'

He took a slow, deep, breath. 'I want you to hear me out on this Niamh,' he said. 'I think you should let us provide you with some surveillance.'

'There's no need,' she replied brightly. 'I've already seen to that. They finished installing a brand new system over at Miriam's house only yesterday. Heat and motion sensors, panic alarms, CCTV, why there's even a video link to the TV screen so I can see who's at the door without opening the porch. I'm moving in just as soon as I leave here.'

He shook his head. 'I meant *personal* surveillance.'

'You mean have someone tailing me? Following me everywhere I go?'

'Just till we can be sure that no one else is following you. It's all we can afford right now, and there's no way I could get you on a witness protection programme based on what we have so far.'

'Witness protection?! No way. How am I going to help you with this hidden away somewhere?'

'You're not. You're going to leave this to us, and to DI Foley over in Ireland. You're going to keep your head down so we don't have to worry about you.'

Niamh could tell that it was pointless arguing. She also sensed that underlying his professional concern was a more personal one. It made her feel angry, flattered, frustrated, and confused. Somehow she managed not to show any of it. 'Very well,' she said, smiling demurely, as though giving in gracefully. 'Though I can't say I'm happy about it, I can see it makes sense.'

Madera was surprised, but relieved. 'I'm glad,' he said. 'You've made the right decision believe me. You'll be able to stop worrying for a change, and I'll be able to concentrate on the investigation.'

'You'll keep me up to date though?' she said.

'Of course. And don't worry about the surveillance. I'll get onto it straight away. See if we can't start later today. You'll never be aware of our people. Let's face it, if you are, so will our perpetrator, and we wouldn't want that to happen would we?'

Niamh drove straight from Chestnut Street to Miriam's house. I'll have to stop calling it that, she told herself as she drew up outside. Better start calling it my house instead. The removal van was blocking the bottom of the drive, so she locked the car and started up the path. Mary Donaghue called out from over the picket fence dividing the two houses.

'Hi Niamh! Why don't you come over as soon as you've checked on those guys, and I'll put some coffee on, and dig out some cookies.'

It was the last thing Niamh wanted right now. Mary was bound to want to know what the security men had been doing, and why. No doubt she would have already brought them coffee, and plied them with questions. And she would want to bring her up to date with all the gossip. Unlike the historic City Hall Bell Tower up coast, in Gloucester, Niamh had neither the time, nor the inclination.

'Can I take a rain check on that Mary?' she said. 'I'm up to my eyes at the moment.'

'All the more reason to take time out,' Mary replied.

Niamh smiled sweetly for the second time that morning. 'Well I would, but I'm going to have to go straight out again. I'll catch up with you later, I promise.' She hurried on up to the front porch, and in through the open door.

There were packing cases everywhere. Thanks to her meticulous planning they were at least in the correct rooms. She found a workman in the kitchen plumbing in her white goods.

'I'm afraid I've found a problem with the water tank,' he told her crawling out from under the cupboards, and sitting up. 'I don't know when the previous owner last had it checked, but it's going to have to be replaced. D'you want to come up to the loft and see for yourself?'

'No, if you say so, that's fine by me,' she told him. 'Can you fix it today?'

'Sure thing. It'll have to wait till I'm done here, then I've got to go and fetch a new one. Be finished by four, four thirty, this afternoon I reckon.'

'OK. Go for it,' she said. Just then her phone rang. It was Bill Fitzgerald.

'I've been busy,' he said. 'Are you free to talk?'

She walked through from the kitchen into the hall, and sat on a packing case.

'Absolutely.'

'The word among the legal fraternity is that no one seems to know of a will having been registered. Not that that means a thing. There is no reason why such information would be in the public domain until after his death. In fact if it was, given his influence, the firm into whose care it had been entrusted would be asking for trouble.'

'He could sue them?'

'In a word. Yes.'

'So that's it?' She was as disappointed as she sounded.

'Not entirely'' he said, trying to appear upbeat. 'I've also managed to establish that JJC is on a ventilator and under twenty four hour care. Two nurses on continuous shifts. Eight hours on, eight hours off. There's also a doctor. Prognosis is not good.'

'What about the diagnosis?'

'That's not so clear. It's rumoured that he had a succession of strokes about four months ago. The last of them left him unable to speak or breathe for himself. His excessive weight, and general lack of exercise over the years, means that he's not in a position to do any of the remedial work that might get him back on his feet. The longer he lays there, the greater the morbidity of his organs. But like I say, that's mainly rumour and conjecture.'

'That's not good is it?'

'It's not how I would want to end my days.'

'That's not what I meant. It's not good for me, or for Tom. If he's likely to die at any time it puts the pressure on whoever killed the others to take us down. The sooner the better from his point of view.'

Bill Fitzgerald had no answer to that. He didn't like

her using those words "take us down". It sounded cold and clinical. Like you'd apply to a professional hit man. That was something he didn't want to contemplate. 'I've got his address,' he said, changing direction. John James Clark's address. I know where he lives.'

'You do! Where?'

She sounded far too eager. 'Up near Montpelier,' he said, keeping it deliberately vague.

'Where near Montpelier?'

'Outside a place called Waterbury.' He heard her suck in her breath.

Bill,' she said forcefully, 'Are you going to keep playing this game of question and answer, like when I was a kid, and you came out on picnics with us? Or are you going to cut to the chase, and just plain tell me the damn address?'

There was a long pause. 'I'm sorry Niamh,' he said. 'But no, I'm not.'

Now she was angry. She got up from the packing case as though standing would somehow add authority to her words. 'Come on Bill! Why the hell not? This is my cousin we're talking about. My life, or death, come to that.'

'Because I know you too well Niamh. If I tell you you'll be up there like a jack rabbit.'

'Damn true I will. Why wouldn't I?' She began to pace up and down, making it impossible for the removal men who had suddenly appeared holding a sofa. 'In there,' she told them pointing fiercely with her free hand towards the front parlour.

'I beg your pardon?' said Bill Fitzgerald.

'But it says rear parlour on here, Miss Caton' said

the older of the men.

'I know,' she said. 'But please...just for now, put it in there.'

'Are you alright Niamh?' It was Fitzgerald again. 'You seem to be rambling?'

'I'll be fine when you give me that address,' she told him.

'You go up there on your own, and you've no idea what you'll be walking into. If you really are being followed he'll know exactly what you're doing. There are long stretches of open road. Miles and miles of forests, and woods, and ravines, and lakes. You'll be a sitting duck.'

'The address please Bill,' she said, suddenly appearing in control, sounding ice calm.

'They probably won't even let you in,' he said desperately. 'Leave it to the police....to Detective Madera.'

'Last time Bill. Are you going to give me the address?'

'Niamh, listen...be reasonable...'

He heard the click, and the tone that signalled that she had ended the call. He cursed himself for his stupidity.

She was ten miles out of Manchester, heading North on Route 89, before she finally calmed down. According to the sat nav she had ninety seven miles to go before hitting Montpelier, and another ten and a half to Waterbury. It was now 9.37, so another hour and twenty minutes, and she would be there or thereabouts. Plenty of time to find the house, talk to someone, and get back before the plumber was due to go. In any case, she'd taken the precaution of leaving the keys and code to the alarm with Mary Donaghue, just in case she was delayed. William Fitzgerald – she always called him William when she was mad with him – how could he do it? Treat her like a spoilt child? She switched on the CD player, and filled the car with the hooky melodies and strings of Alicia Keys' *As I Am*.

Passing through Lebanon she became aware of a black saloon two cars behind her. Her mind had been on the music, the scenery, and the road ahead. Everything but her rear view mirror. She turned off the CD, and sat up straight, her nerves jangling. She had no idea how long the car had been there. Only that it was keeping its distance. But then why should it not? With just a few exceptions everybody was cruising on the limit. As she approached the next major intersection, at Hartford, she left it late, and then took the right that led onto Route 91. She watched in her mirror, saw the indicator light come on the black sedan, and caught a glimpse of it turning off to follow her. She lost sight of it on the long curving bend.

On the straight, heading up alongside the broad Connecticut River, the car came into view again. The sat nav was advising her, in a voice infuriatingly calm and matron like, to make a U turn at the next intersection in precisely five point two miles. She wondered if it could be the tail that Max Madera had promised to provide, the one she had deliberately sought to avoid by leaving before it was in place, knowing full well that he would try to stop her coming up here.

She studied the map on the sat nav, and made a

decision. At the next intersection she ignored the signs to Dartmouth College on the opposite bank of the river, and turned off onto the minor road to Norwich, slowing deliberately as she did so. She looked over her shoulder and watched the sedan cruise straight on up the 91. There was a balding man in the driving seat, in his early fifties, wearing tinted glasses. He didn't look in her direction, but stared fixedly at the road in front of him. Niamh heaved a sigh of relief, and kept her speed down for the half a mile it took to the next junction, where she stopped. On the corner of Main and Elm, next to the Episcopalian church of St Barnabas, was Alléchante, a bakery café according to the sign. She pulled in, and stopped the car.

The seductive smells of new baked artisan bread, and fresh ground coffee, pervaded the café. Niamh sat in the window where she could eat her pastry, and sip her coffee, with one eye on the road. When twenty minutes had passed she felt sufficiently calm, and confident, to set off again. Before she left she bought one of the specialities of the house, a gourmet sandwich of pacific prawn and guacamole. She backed the car out, hung a right, and headed back the way she had come until she hit Route 89 again.

She headed north towards Montpelier along the White River valley. In gaps between the trees she caught glimpses of children, and their supervisors, floating downstream in the characteristic red and purple tubes, like massive inflated tyres. It reminded her of the summers she had spent up here tubing with her mom and dad. Was it only twenty years ago?

The remainder of the journey was uneventful as the road climbed steadily through the rolling hills, the mountains, and forests. In an hour and ten she was dropping down to Montpelier. Fifteen minutes later she was entering Waterbury. The hills and the mountains crowded in on either side. Away to her right the snow covered peak of Mount Hunger, just visible through a stand of conifers, seemed close enough to touch.

The town was bigger than she had expected. There were a host of signs, including the Vermont State Hospital mental health facility, the office of the Vice Chancellor of Vermont State Colleges, Green Mountain Coffee Roasters, the cemetery, banks, churches, cafes, and restaurants. Niamh had no idea where to start. She pulled over, parked the car, got out and entered the nearest café on Park Row.

They were busy serving lunch. The waitress, a plate of soup in each hand, told her above the hubbub that she would be with her in a moment. Hands free she wiped them on her apron, and came over.

'Hi there. Table for one is it?'

'Actually, sorry, but no. I'm looking for my cousin's place, I wondered if you might know it? John James Clark?'

'I know the name, but I can't say where from.' She turned and raised her voice above the chatter. 'Anybody know where John James Clark might live?'

A few heads turned to look at her, the majority just shook their heads, and carried on.

'*The* John James Clark?'

Niamh turned. He was sitting at a table by the door. In his seventies, a full head of silver hair, weather beaten, a kindly smile, and watery blue eyes that had seen it all. He wore a faded brown oil cloth utility jacket, over a blue tartan shirt, and centuries old Levis.

'The billionaire? Mr Casino?'

'That's right,' she said, hoping she'd hit the jackpot.

'I heard tell he'd moved up here. Somewhere off Route 100, but I couldn't rightly say where.'

The waitress moved away, and left them to it.

'Route 100?'

'That's the one,' he said. 'Bottom of Main Street, hang a right, and you're on it. All the way down to Moreton, and Mad River. Somewhere off that stretch I reckon. Not as far down as Waitsfield though.'

'Thank you sir,' she said.

'Thank *you*,' he replied, with a broad grin. 'Been a while since I was called sir by a pretty young woman.'

She stepped out onto the sidewalk, and shivered involuntarily. She'd forgotten how much colder it would be up here. She walked to her car, popped the trunk, and put on the cagoule she kept for emergencies. She took the road atlas from her side door compartment, and opened it out on the hood. There were sixteen turnings off the 100 along that stretch. Several of those had branches going off them. It would take her all day, and into the evening, to cover them all. She looked at her watch. Twenty past twelve. That left two hours at most before she had to set off back. It had been a mistake to come up here like this. But now that she was here she was going to give it her best shot.

She tried the Chittenden Bank, Vincent's Drug and

Variety store, and the Fire Department - where she was convinced that they knew the address but were less than convinced by her reasons for wanting it. She finally hit lucky at the Service Station.

'Not a lot of people know this,' the part time attendant wiping the windscreens confided. 'But the driver who chauffeurs the old guy's personal assistant gets his petrol here, and so does his doctor. Don't get much out of the doctor, but the chauffeur's no way as discrete as he ought to be. Not after a few drinks over at the Legion'

Niamh waited him out.

'You have no idea what that place is like,' he said. 'Full size swimming pool in the basement, a gymnasium and a spa – not that he's in any state to enjoy them. There's a forty seat cinema, all the lights and the temperature are controlled by computers. Twenty bedrooms, separate quarters for the servants – every one of them sworn to secrecy. And the security. Did I tell you about the security?'

Niamh shook her head. 'No you didn't'

'Six foot high wall all the way round, an electric fence ten metres inside that, laser sensors on the lawns, and dogs patrolling the patios. What's he afraid of I ask myself?'

'Where exactly did you say this is?' she asked in as offhand a manner as she could muster.

'Didn't I tell you?'

'No,' she said.'

Finally, he did.

18

Five miles south of town, on Route 100, Niamh turned right onto the unnamed tarmac road that snaked up into the hills above the road. The red and white sign nailed to a post above the boundary wall was unequivocal. "Private Road. Strictly No Entry. Trespassers WILL be prosecuted." Someone had added with a nervous hand, in black spray paint, "If they survive the dogs."

Undaunted, she drove on through a landscape populated with sugar maple, beech and yellow birch, whose leaves had just begun to show the tell tale signs of autumn. The track flattened out beside a luscious pasture, then a flower filled meadow, before plunging back into the trees. Niamh had to change down to second gear. Glancing at the sat nav she was not surprised to learn that she had climbed two hundred and fifty metres in less than three minutes. Now there was a dramatic change in the surrounding terrain. The trees thinned out. The hardwoods were replaced by scrub, and clusters of common pine. The ground was littered with boulders formed, smoothed, and dragged by glaciers ten thousand years ago, scouring out the land as they advanced. Just as she'd convinced herself that she'd turned off too soon she crested a rise, and stopped the car in amazement.

Ahead, and below her, a U shaped valley had been carved out between the hills and the mountains beyond. Surrounded by hundreds of acres of deciduous forest was an area perhaps the size of twenty football fields, the majority of which consisted of the kind of parkland she had always associated with an English country house. Specimen cedars, and spruce, vied for pride of place with giant maple, and groups of soaring redwood. Closest to her was an orchard of apples. There was an empty paddock. A dozen horses grazed in nearby fields. She thought she could make out a large walled garden, beside which a distinct white cross marked out a helicopter pad. Beyond it, a gazebo looked out across a large expanse of blue grey water, glinting in the sun, fed by a ribbon of water that disappeared through the trees towards the mountains above. At the centre of it all stood a massive stone brick house with blue tiled roof, numerous clapboard barns, and outbuildings. Niamh took a deep breath, and set off down the road that snaked into the valley.

Into the six foot high stone wall was set a pair of ornate wrought iron gates. Set back, inside the perimeter, was a smoked glass globe high on an aluminium pole. She guessed that the cameras would already have warned of her coming, identified the plates on her car, and even now be zooming in as she parked the car, got out, and approached the stainless steel plate set into the right hand side of the wall. There was a round black circle a centimetre in diameter at the top of the plate, and three buttons to press, marked Call, Cancel, and Trades. The absence of alphanumeric options told her this was a twenty four seven monitored system. Someone would be watching right now. She pressed the button marked Call, and waited. The only sounds were the soft warble of eastern bluebirds preparing to migrate, and the hum of wasps among rotting fruit. There was a scent of pine resin, and the unmistakable smell of wood smoke in the air. She pressed the button again. It seemed an age until she heard the disembodied voice of a man with an accent that her father would have described as West Point.

'Yes Ma'am?'

'My name is Niamh Caton,' she said. 'I've come all the way from Manchester New Hampshire in the hope of speaking with Mr Clark. I believe that we are cousins.'

There was a short pause, then he said, 'What is your address in Manchester Ma'am?'

Definitely ex-military she decided. She gave him her address. There was another, longer, pause that could only mean that they were checking it – against her licence plate perhaps. This time it was another voice, older, even more cultured, polite, and in no way dismissive, but as unambiguous as the sign at the bottom of the road had been.

'I am afraid Miss Caton,' he said. 'That Mr Clark is indisposed. You should have phoned, it would have saved you a wasted journey.'

'I didn't have a number.'

'Even so, Mr Clark is indisposed.'

Niamh could see it slipping away from her. 'But it's really, really important that I speak with him. It's a matter of life and death.'

'In which case I am very sorry Miss Caton, but even if Mr Clark wished to speak with you he would, quite literally, be unable to do so.'

She could sense his patience running out, and decided she had no option but to explain, no matter how ridiculous it sounded. Either that, or let him end the call, and stand there like an idiot until they sent for the police, or the dogs.

'I understand that Mr Clark is ill,' she said. 'But I have to speak with someone. There are people close to me who have been murdered simply because they are related to him. I don't intend to be the next victim.'

She hoped he could hear the sincerity in her voice, see beyond the desperation.

'Murdered?'

'That's right...murdered. My aunt right here in New Hampshire, and three cousins in Ireland.'

'Excuse me,' he said, his tone suddenly brittle. 'But I find this conversation bizarre in the extreme Miss Caton. I think you should leave right now.'

She knew how crazy it must sound. That far from convincing him she had just ruined whatever chance she might have had. She played her final card.

'Has the New Hampshire Police Department in Manchester contacted you yet?'

'The police?' Now he sounded wary.

'That's right, the police,' she said, pressing her advantage. 'Detective Supervisor Lieutenant Max Madera is in charge of the investigation. He told me just this morning that you would be getting a visit.'

'Lieutenant Madera?' now there was note of scepticism in his voice. Niamh seized on it.

211

'That's right,' she said. 'If you give me a moment I can get you his number off my cell phone.' Even as she said it she realised that she had left it in the car. She was torn between running back to get it, and staying right there.

'Why don't you give *me* a moment Miss Caton,' he said.

She had no idea if he was checking with someone else, or ringing the Manchester Police Department. Nearly a minute went by. Niamh was near to screaming point. When the voice finally erupted from the speaker it made her jump. It was the younger man again, Mr West Point Academy,

'Kindly go back to your car Miss Caton,' he said. 'Do not start the engine until the gates have opened fully. Then you may start the engine, and drive forward towards the house. Please keep your doors locked. Please do not exceed five miles per hour. Please do not leave the car until you are invited to do so. Do you understand?'

'Perfectly,' she said. Her heart was racing as she walked back to the car and climbed inside.

The tree lined drive wound through the parkland, past the orchard and paddock. She glimpsed a flock of bluebirds among a copse of trees. There was no sign of the fabled wire fence, or the dogs. As the drive approached the house, it split left, and right, into entry and exit routes, culminating in a broad circular driveway below a patio, beyond which stood the house. At the foot of the steps stood a man in his early forties, crew cut, wearing a dark suit and red tie, and a woman of a similar age, in an identical suit, worn over a cream blouse with a red cravat. They watched her arrive with the eagle eye, and bland expression, of bodyguards.

The man stepped forward, and opened the door. His companion moved in to face him, boxing Niamh between them as she climbed out of the car.

'Leave the keys in the ignition please Ma'am,' the young man said. It sounded like a command you disobeyed on pain of death.

'This way please, Miss Caton.' The woman said.

The three of them set off across the drive, up the steps, between the huge stone pillars supporting the blue slate roof of the porch, through the double doorway, and into the hall. It was huge, with a chestnut floor on which stood a pair of antique chairs, and a matching chest. Reflected in a large gold framed mirror that might have graced the court of Louis XIII of France was one of the grandest chandeliers she had ever seen. A custom oak staircase, with intricately moulded spindles, led gracefully up to her right.

'I'm surprised you haven't frisked me.' Niamh said to break the tension she was feeling.

She thought she saw, on the face of the man, the beginnings of a smile cut short. 'It's not necessary Ma'am,' he said. He crossed to a door on the left, and opened it. 'In here if you please Ma'am.'

It was a study. Two of the walls were lined from the floor to the high ceiling with solid cherry wood shelving, and panels in the same material finished in crown mouldings. The shelves were packed with books. On the opposite wall was a stately marble fireplace in front of which two easy chairs and a coffee table had been arranged. A huge bay window looked out over the patio, parkland, and a forest that swept across the hills towards the distant Green Mountains. In the bay stood a cherry wood desk supporting a flat computer screen and keyboard, a leather blotter, and a wrought iron desk top book holder, like the one in the kitchen that Niamh used for her recipe books. Every surface gleamed with polish. The smaller crystal chandelier painted rainbow colours on the ceiling. Far from lived in, this felt like a room preserved, waiting more in hope than expectation.

'Take a seat please Ma'am,' the man told her pointing towards the easy chairs. 'Mr Hollister will be with you shortly.'

They left her on her own, closing the doors quietly behind them. Niamh listened as their footsteps retreated. She crossed to the window, and stared out at the breathtaking view. It was exactly eleven days since she had stood by Miriam's grave and looked up at the wooded sides of Beards Hill. So much had happened since then. Another grave, another set of hills. The fire and all that followed. She felt suddenly weary, and alone. Her shoulder ached. She turned her attention to the wall that held the book shelves.

A section had been reserved for photographs. She thought it strange that they were all of Clark himself, a conclusion she based only on their resemblance to one that she had found on the internet. Most of them spanned the last forty years of his life, but she was drawn to a faded photograph towards the bottom of the wall. A serious looking young man stared out at her. He had what could best be described as a square head, with a strong jaw, and a thick head of unruly hair. His eyes were large, beneath heavy brows.

Search as she might, she could see no resemblance to her father, other than the hair. Perhaps he had taken after his maternal line. She switched her attention to the rows of books.

There were sets of the classics – English, French and American - spanning five centuries. A shelf devoted to art and classical music, another on modern architecture. Two of the remaining shelves were devoted to Biographies and Histories – including several histories of Ireland. The final shelf was entirely given over to things Irish: three histories, books of myths and legends, of poetry and culture. There were travel books, and books on the geography and geology of Ireland. One book in particular grabbed Niamh's attention. It was called Myths of British ancestry, by Stephen Openheimer. As she took it from the shelf the door opened.

The man who entered was exactly as she had imagined he would be. Mid fifties, tall, dapper, in a Saville Row soft tailored suit, bespoke shirt, and Harvard tie. His jet black hair had silver flecks that gave him gravitas. When he spoke his voice was strong yet mellow, above all, it oozed confidence.

'Please sit down Miss Caton,' he said holding his hand out for the book. She passed it to him. He glanced at it, smiled, and returned it to the shelf. Once she was seated he sat down opposite her. 'My name is Roger Hollister. I am Mr Clark's factotum...his personal assistant. Mr Clark has been in a coma for the past eight months. I am the closest you are going to get to him, so if you have something to say, or that you think you need to know, this is your one opportunity.' He glanced at the ormolu clock on the mantelpiece. 'I can give you twenty minutes. And then I'm afraid you will have to leave.'

Niamh had already decided to tell him everything. She thought it unlikely that he could be involved. And even if he was, she wouldn't be telling him anything he didn't already know. He sat back, and listened intently. He took no notes, asked no questions, his body language gave nothing away. She had no idea if he believed her or not.

'All this must have been very distressing for you,' he said when she'd finished.

'*Is* very distressing for me,' she reminded him.

He acknowledged her rebuke with a slight inclination of his head. 'So what was it exactly that you were hoping to find out by coming here?'

Niamh leant forward eagerly, recognising this as her big opportunity, anxious not to blow it. 'If Mr Clark knew of any relatives other than those I've uncovered,' she said. 'People who might have a motive for all these deaths.'

'Or think they might have a motive,' he corrected her.

'Or think they might have a motive,' Niamh agreed. 'With all his wealth and influence I can't believe that he never made any attempt to trace his roots.'

Hollister surprised her. 'As a matter of fact he did. I know, because I helped him with it.'

'He did?!...You did?' Now she was excited.

'Unfortunately that was all he did. When I say he traced his roots I mean that he had me track back four generations to his great, great, grandfather Joseph Padraig Caton. He never took it any further than that.'

Niamh was not sure that she understood. 'Do you

mean that he made no attempt to trace any of his other relatives...living or dead?'

Hollister nodded. 'That's exactly what I'm saying. I'm afraid that his divorce, and the fact that he had no children, left him embittered. He had no interest in finding out how the rest of the family had fared.'

Niamh managed to hide her disappointment, and decided to press on. 'But he did find out that his grandfather had changed his name from Caton to Clark? That he was of Irish descent?'

'Oh yes. He took a sudden interest, bordering on obsession, in matters Irish,' he waved his hand towards the bookshelves. 'The history, culture, geography. He even had me take him to Ireland about ten years back.' He saw the surprise register on her face. 'He insisted on travelling incognito. We were there for four weeks.'

'Did you visit Listowel?' she asked.

'Yes we did. And we visited Lixnaw, and the Abbey. Not Kilfeighny though. Because of course you went further down the road with your research than me.' He glanced at the clock again, and uncrossed his legs. 'It became like an obsession for a while. And then he seemed to lose interest in it. That's all I can tell you I'm afraid.' He put his hands on the arms of his chair as though about to lever himself up.

'Has he made a will?' Niamh asked, desperate to cling on to this one opportunity.

Hollister got to his feet. 'I am not at liberty to tell you that,' he said.

Niamh remained seated. 'But surely you can see how important this is?'

'I am still not at liberty to tell you. Even had I been

a witness to Mr Clark's will, assuming he ever made one, I would not be at liberty to disclose the contents. Nobody would. Not even his solicitor.'

'Perhaps you'll tell the police?' she said defiantly.

He shook his head. 'Not even them.'

'What if I were to send you a copy of all the research I've done?' Niamh said clutching at straws.

'I'm sorry. It's really none of my business. Ultimately all this will be a matter for the courts to decide. Now I really must insist that you leave.'

'It won't be any consolation to me if it's a murder court, and I'm the victim,' she said, getting reluctantly to her feet.

He seemed not to hear, walked over to the study door, and held it open. 'Did you bring a bag with you?' he asked.

Niamh shook her head. As she reached the doorway she looked up at him.

'What made you decide to see me?'

'To tell you the truth, I was intrigued. Murder and mayhem, a connection with my employer. I think you'll agree that it wouldn't have been very professional to simply ignore it? In any case, if the police are really going to call I thought it best to find out why. I recognised the relevance of the name Caton of course. We confirmed that you were who you said you were – your website was especially helpful in that respect - that there is a Detective Madera in New Hampshire, and that I had twenty minutes to spare. ' He opened the door. 'I am truly sorry that I could not assist you further. Goodbye Miss Caton...and good luck.'

West Point and his female colleague stood by the doors holding them open. As she approached them

Niamh spotted for the first time the gunmetal sensors set into the door frame on either side. The man and woman followed her gaze, waited for her to look up at them, and nodded ever so slightly. The nearest they would ever get she decided to sharing a joke with anyone who called. They let her to go down the steps on her own. The car was waiting at the bottom with the keys in the ignition. Her bag was on the passenger seat. She could have sworn that she had left it in the floor well. She turned, and looked back at the house. The doors were already closed.

The drive back to Manchester was miserable and uneventful. The weather had turned. A moderate wind gave an edge to the drizzle that began to fall. Niamh kept a closer watch this time on the rear view mirror, but saw nothing suspicious. She knew that she had left it tight to get back before the plumber was due to leave, and hovered close to the limit all the way back. A blue and white pulled alongside just outside Lebanon. The driver, and the officer in the passenger seat, both looked across at her, and then it pulled away until she lost sight of it. Ten miles north of Manchester she became uneasy about an SRV that stayed a consistent couple of car lengths behind her, no matter how many vehicles moved in and out of the lane. Two blocks from Miriam's house, it turned off, and she relaxed. As she walked up the drive she could see that the plumber was waiting for her on the porch. He was talking to someone with his back to her. The man turned as the car pulled up. It was Lieutenant Max Madera. He seemed far from happy.

She let him cool his heels on the porch while the

plumber took her through what he'd done, and waited while she wrote him out a cheque. As soon as they were alone in the hallway Max exploded.

'What the hell did you think you were doing?' he said. 'I've had people out looking for you since midday. You went up there didn't you? To his place in Vermont? What the hell were you thinking about?'

Niamh felt like the child on the beach whose father thought she must have drowned, and showed his relief by shouting, and slapping her legs.

'I'm sorry,' she said. 'I just needed to do something. I couldn't just sit around here and wait to be murdered.'

'But I told you I wouldn't let that happen. That's why I arranged for you to be followed, for your house to be watched. What was I supposed to think when my guy turned up, and you were gone?'

'Like I said. I'm sorry.' Seeing him like this she was genuinely contrite. He was still furious, but she could see that he was on the verge of softening, off the ceiling, and half way down the walls.

'Don't you realise you could have got yourself killed?' he said, a hint of concern creeping in. 'If this guy had followed you…if he was watching the Clark place…then he would know by now that you're putting it all together. Don't you realise how much more vulnerable that makes you?'

'Much more?' Tears began to well in Niamh's eyes.

'God, that was stupid of me,' he said, reaching out instinctively to grasp her shoulders, pulling her protectively towards him. She winced with pain, but tried hard not to show it. Then she allowed herself to relax into his arms, her head against his chest. It felt right, and warm, and safe.

19

It was gone seven when Tom Caton arrived back at the apartment. Despite having to go into work Kate had managed to make the finishing touches. The packing crates had gone. The curtains were hung, the furniture arranged, the table set for their first dinner together, in this their first home together. The place was spotless. She had even managed to have a shower, and change into an emerald green silk blouse, and black silk trousers.

'I'm knackered,' he said, dropping his briefcase onto the virgin sofa.'

'Poor you.'

The irony in her voice was lost on him. He walked over, gave her a hug, and kissed her on the cheek. 'Eight hours nonstop, and another one and a half on the motorway,' he said.

'So what do you think?' she asked.

He looked perplexed. 'Of what?'

She pushed him away. 'You had better be joking Tom, or your dinner goes in the bin.' She stepped back to give him a better view.

He smiled, and said with as much conviction as he could muster, 'Of course I was. It looks fantastic. Amazing,' he saw her pupils contract and added hastily. 'And so do you…fantastic. It must have taken you all day.'

'To look fantastic?'

He grinned nervously. 'You know what I meant, this place. I thought you were supposed to be at the University?'

'I was. Until three o'clock this afternoon.'

'You must be knackered too.'

'I'm a woman,' she said. '*We* don't get knackered. We're not supposed to.'

He took her in his arms, and kissed her again, properly.

'Don't think you can get round me that easily,' she said when they came up for air. 'Go and have a shower, and put on something comfortable. Dinner will be ready in ten minutes.'

Tom picked up his briefcase, and took it through to the second bedroom that they'd set up as a study. His and hers desks back to back, a flat screen computer and a printer on one, and wireless connection for a lap top on the other. He put his briefcase down beside the desk, and opened the broadband link. He was waiting for it to load when she popped her head around the door.

'What are you doing Tom?'

'Just checking my email.'

'To see if there's one from Niamh?'

She was trying, he thought, just a little too hard to sound disinterested. 'Not especially.'

'Well can't it wait? This meal is going to spoil.'

'Fair enough,' he said, clicking *Cancel*. 'I'll check it later.'

They had champagne with the starter – Parma ham, and peaches, with shavings of parmesan, and a few green leaves – and a bottle of Cairanne Cote Du Rhone Villages with the fillet steak

They concentrated on the food until the plates were bare. Tom poured them both some more wine. 'That was fantastic,' he said raising his glass to her. 'Thank you.'

'You're welcome,' she said raising her own glass. 'By the way, did you know that *fantastic* is turning out to be your favourite word?'

'Alright,' he said. 'Delicious, scrumptious, luscious, delectable, yummy...just like you.'

She laughed. 'Enough already, you're going to put me off dessert.'

'What were you up to at Uni?' he asked.

'I had some assignments to mark, and a tutorial before lunch,' Kate said spearing a roasted vine tomato with her fork.' And then I had a lecture to deliver to the graduate students.'

'How did it go?'

'Not bad considering how little time I'd had to prepare with everything this move has entailed.'

Tom swirled a slurp of wine around his mouth, extracting every trace of fruit.

'What was it on?'

He waited patiently while she finished chewing.

'Promise not to laugh,' she said. '*Psychological Causes of Death, nature versus nurture.*'

He sat back in his chair. 'So what conclusion did you come to then?'

'How do you mean?'

'Rapists, multiple murders, serial killers - nature or nurture?'

She put down her glass, and adopted the serious

expression that he knew so well. 'Come on Tom, after twenty years in the Police Service, you know it's not as simple as that.'

'I'm not asking you to come up with a definitive answer, simply to share your conclusions with me. What impression do you think your students went away with?'

'That's the question I always ask myself. I don't usually find out until I get their assignments in.'

'OK, so what impression did you want them to go away with?'

'That it is complicated, but, that we know a whole lot more than we used to do.'

'For example?'

'That when it comes to the five most important personality traits they are almost entirely down to genetic disposition. That fifty percent of our IQ in childhood is accounted for by our genes, and that rises to eighty percent by the time we reach mature adulthood.'

'That doesn't leave a lot of room for family life, and schooling, to make a difference,' he said gloomily. 'Perhaps we shouldn't bother?'

'That's just defeatist talk,' she said. 'And I know that you don't mean it. Besides, with our genes they're going to be angels.'

It struck them both at the same time that this was the first time in their relationship that either of them had mentioned children. A short silence ensued while they drank their wine, both acknowledging the fact, neither of them believing it the right moment to explore it.

'So are you really saying that Gordon's right? These people are born evil?' Tom asked.

She shook her head vigorously, spilling a drop of wine from her glass onto the table mat. 'Not at all. There are plenty of other traits that are open to life shaping influences like our home, our parents, our friends, and our experiences. And when it comes down to it, genetic predisposition to pathological traits does not inevitably result in pathological behaviours...'

'Pathological?' he interrupted. 'How are you using that in this context?'

'Behaviour which is extreme, socially unacceptable, habitual, and compulsive.'

'Like lying, theft, flashing, rape, child abuse, murder?'

'Exactly. And even if there is a genetic predisposition towards such traits, nurture may well stop them from developing into actual behaviours.'

'Or provide the trigger that sets them off?'

'Precisely. But you know all this,' she said. 'You're just trying to test me.'

'Not at all. I love listening to you when you talk about your work. You get so excited, so serious. There's a fire in your eyes.'

She grinned. 'There'll be a fire in yours if you don't stop teasing.' She stood up and stacked the plates. 'Bring the desserts over would you, while I put these in the dish washer? It's only fresh fruit salad and crème frèche, I'm afraid, but there's a limit to what even I can put together in thirty minutes.'

They sat on their brand new sofa with the lights turned down low, looking out across the Ashton Canal towards Sports City, and the spot-lit Etihad Stadium.

'You haven't told me about your day,' she said. 'How has the course gone?'

'Not too bad,' he said. 'A load of seminars, simulations, and case studies, involving inter agency co-operation.'

'In relation to?'

'The trafficking of children and young persons for slavery and exploitation.'

'Wow. That's heavy stuff.'

'You're right. There wasn't a lot I didn't already know, but it wasn't comfortable being reminded about it. You forget how many different ways people have found to make a child's life unbearable: forced labour, bonded labour, early and forced marriage, trafficking for sexual exploitation, begging, work slavery. It's bad enough when it's in their own country, but when they've been taken thousands of miles away from their family it's sickening.' He went quiet.

She looked up at him. 'You're thinking of the Chinatown Case, and Wu Ling, the girl from Fujian?' she said.

He nodded. 'It was one of the case studies. I had to give a presentation. It brought it all back.' He went quiet again.

'There's something else on your mind isn't there?' she said.

He told her about the conversation he had had with Niamh the evening before, while she had been out getting the pizzas.

'Why didn't you tell me last night?' she said. 'Something as important as this?'

'Because you'd been working hard all day. You

were so excited about the apartment. I didn't want to spoil it.'

'But you were going to tell me?'

'I just have,' he said. 'You're the profiler Kate. I'm just a simple policeman. What I want to know is, do you think it's possible?'

She sat up.

'Someone going around killing off his blood relatives for the sake of a mere five point one billion dollars? Why are you even asking the question?'

'I know it's possible,' he said. 'Insane, ludicrous, but possible. I was hoping you could put together a profile. I just didn't want to spoil this week. Settling into our first home together; it's not something we'll ever do again.'

'I appreciate that, but this is far too scary not to take seriously. Whoever it is could be here right now, in England.'

'So you'll put a profile together?'

'Of course I will.' She got up and walked over to the floor-to-ceiling picture window. She stared out across the canal at the shadowy shape of the building site on the far bank. She stood with her back to him, her words tumbling out in free fall.

'We talked about this when you were investigating the murder of Sir Roger Standing. I told you at the time that it's not unknown for children – siblings – to murder their own parents, so how much easier must it be to kill relatives they've never met? Interestingly, in this case the methods – hit and run, and arson – I would classify as non-personal. By which I mean with no physical contact between the perpetrator and the victim. That suggests someone trying to avoid any possible emotional threat to their decision to act. The exception of course would be the way the aunt in Ireland fell – although that could still have been an accident, or perhaps the perpetrator rigged some kind of trip wire?'

Tom went over, and put his arm around her shoulder. 'I didn't expect you to do it right now,' he said gently. 'Tomorrow will be fine.'

She turned to face him. 'But I'm scared for you Tom. For us. Everything was going so well…and now this.'

'I know,' he said. 'But I can take care of myself, and of you. Between us we're going to crack this before it gets any worse.'

'In that case,' she said. 'Don't you think we'd better see if Niamh has been in touch?'

In the darkness, crouching beside a pallet of bricks, he saw them turn away from the windows, and disappear from sight. He had already worked out which floor the apartment was on, and its position. He wondered when they would use their balcony. That was one obvious possibility, less risky than the other options, but far less certain. He waited for another half hour, knowing from experience how important it was to establish routines. The woman - he had yet to discover her name - returned and drew the curtains. Only then did he stand and stretch his cramped limbs. He unscrewed the zoom lens from his camera and placed it carefully in the carry bag. He looked at his watch. It was only ten forty pm. The security patrol would check the site at eleven. By then, he would be long gone.

20

Niamh woke early on Friday morning to the sound of birdsong. All those years in the apartment the rumble of traffic, and the shriek of sirens, had been her dawn chorus. She lay there luxuriating in the ringing trills and cheerful chatter, and her recollection of the previous evening.

She had made Max a coffee. They had talked for almost an hour, more about themselves than the investigation. She recognised the signs. Her cheeks had flushed, her heart was racing, and her hands had been so clammy that at one point she had to make a pretext of washing up simply to run them under the cold faucet, and wipe them dry. True there had not been so much as a kiss, but she felt sure that he had wanted to. Surely the only thing holding him back had been his need to remain objective? Not to blur the relationship between investigating officer and...and what exactly? Witness, informant, victim in waiting? There was that word victim again, the one she'd promised herself she would avoid. She pushed back the duvet, swung her legs sideways, and sat on the edge of the bed. She wasn't going to let this one go.

The attic seemed smaller than Niamh remembered. She had been through all the boxes up here when she'd first sorted through Miriam's possessions. She thought it unlikely that she'd missed anything of significance, but it was worth one last try. She ignored the flat pack cardboard boxes full of bed linen, curtains, and ancient clothes that could only have been intended for fancy dress. It was the wooden tea chests, full of books and papers, to which she turned her attention. They were already earmarked, with different coloured stickers, for the charity shop, or for the city's new Yard Waste recycling collection. They were too heavy to take down the ladder, so she sat on one of the cardboard boxes beneath the eaves, using the weak illumination of the single bulb attached to the beam above. It took two hours to work her way through them. There was just one remaining chest against the brick end gable wall. It was only when she came to empty it that she realised that it was hiding a gap in the wall less than two foot square. She had no idea how she'd missed it before. With difficulty she managed to heave the chest aside. On bended knee she peered through the gap. The bulb was too dim, too far away. Her body masked what little light there was. Niamh crawled back to the ladder to fetch a torch.

The beam sliced through the darkness revealing a space as large again as that within which she knelt. There was a partition wall dividing the attic in two. Unlike the section nearest the ladder this one was devoid of boarding. Fibre insulation had been compressed between the floor joists. Spider webs festooned the exposed brick work of the chimney. Attached to a single roof support she could see the unmistakeable shape of a white, papery, wasps nest. The shaft of light settled on two boxes, each of them no more than a foot square, covered with a piece of carpet. They appeared to have been shoved in here against the partition wall, and long forgotten. Niamh squeezed her body as far as possible through the gap until she could grasp the nearest. Slowly, carefully, ever mindful of the wasps, she edged it towards her.

She sat with the contents of the first box spread out on the pine kitchen table. There was a chocolate box full of photographs, ones that Niamh had never seen, of Miriam and her brother - Niamh's father – and of both of her parents. Niamh sifted through them. These images were even more poignant now that all of them were dead. Next came Miriam's reports from kindergarten through to junior high. Then the Year Books for her senior high, and Mount St Mary's University in Maryland. There was always something fascinating Niamh thought about other people's lives. The way they had developed, the things that shaped them. She found it hard to remind herself that, interesting though it was, none of this was relevant to her search. Finally she tore herself away. She brewed a coffee, made a three bean salad, and opened up the second box. On the top were two layers of old newspapers, yellow and faded, already cracked along the folds. She lifted them out carefully and set them aside. She noted the dates. October and November 1903 respectively. Beneath them lay a bundle of oilcloth, wrapped round with a piece of ancient ribbon.

With trembling fingers she untied the ribbon, and unwrapped the covering. She was astonished to discover what looked like a diary bound in leather. Gently, she blew off the film of dust. On the cover, embossed in gold that had flaked and faded in places, was the name Patrick Caton Senior, and the date 1903. Beneath the diary, also tied with yellowing ribbon, she discovered a small bundle of envelopes each containing a letter, their edges brown, cracked, and fragile. Carefully, she set them aside, and turned her attention to the diary.

The ink was black but faded, the handwriting strong, clean and formalised. The letters leaned uniformly forward at forty five degrees. It gave the impression of confidence despite the virtual absence of loops and flourishes. It was immediately evident that this was not a diary at all, but a memoir. An account of a seminal period in his life. A title had been printed and underlined. Niamh took a sip of coffee, settled back, and began to read.

A MEMOIR OF MY VOYAGE TO AMERICA IN 1893.

I have taken the trouble of writing down this account of my voyage to America, that which compelled me to undertake it, and my earliest experience of the adopted country of which I am now proud be a citizen, in the hope that it might both interest and instruct my children, and their children's children. In particular, that they may come to understand that not only did I leave my beloved Ireland with a heavy heart, but that I left a part of my heart behind. It is no easy matter for a man to become an exile from his native land. Every day I pray that my sacrifice will be rewarded in the life that I am endeavouring to build for my beloved wife and children.   And every day I marvel at the patience and fortitude with which they continue to endure my occasional bouts of melancholia, and endless recollections of the Old Country.

The First Part.   My Earliest Recollections.
It would not be unreasonable for you to conclude, that if I loved the country of my birth so much, for me to take the momentous step of leaving her forever, life must have been impossible to endure. Well I must tell you that it was, and it was not. My father was born at the height of one of the most terrible periods in our history. They called it the Great Famine. There was nothing great about it at all.   It was monstrous, wicked, and evil. All the more so because it could have been avoided. America had grain aplenty, and sent as much as she was allowed, which was never enough, in the face of England's Protectionism.

Between the Whigs, the Landlords, and the Merchants, our people were betrayed. Dysentery and typhoid fever swept like a scythe through a land ravaged by malnutrition.   It was something my parents never forgot. It seemed to me as though it had seeped into the marrow of their bones and settled there, like a heavy weight they could never shake off. I often think that it must account for the way in which they encouraged us children to seek our fortunes abroad, though it broke their hearts to let us go.

There was never as fearsome a famine again, yet

times were hard as we grew up. My beautiful little sister Lizzie was taken from us first, in her second year. It was a simple cold that became a fever which her weak little body was unable to shake off. Next it was Clare, my brother Frederick's twin, who died as she entered this cruel world. My father baptised her with water from the yard in the hope that she would fly straight to Heaven, and be spared the uncertain fate of eternity in the Limbo of the Infants. Every night I pray for them both. When I am gone I hope that you too will continue to remember them in your prayers.

For those of us who survived, the early years were not without joy. Until we were old enough to attend the National School we played with abandon in the woods and fields, and on the hills above the village. It seemed that every month there was a feast day with music, and songs, and dancing. At the National School, my brother Colum and I loved to play the hurling, football, and handball. Joseph, ever wild, was a demon at throwing the weights, and in the races. Frederick and Mary were the serious ones, she always with her head in a book. Looking back, I think she was destined to become a nun. Although when I heard that she had joined the Benedictines I assumed at the time that it was the death of her soldier boy that had broken her heart, and sent her there.

While we passed the days in blissful ignorance our parents worked themselves to the bone to keep a roof over our heads, shirts on our backs, and boots on our feet. There was never enough work, and even when there was it produced barely enough money to feed us all. Colum was the first to be taken out of school. He was the strongest, but the slowest when it came to learning. The extra pair of hands, and the fact he could turn his hand to anything, anywhere, was enough to keep us afloat as my father would often say.

I will not bore you - since you have heard it enough - with recounting my first experiences of labour. Suffice it to say that neither Frederick, nor Joseph, nor I took easily to working the land. Tending sheep, repairing walls, digging ditches, cutting and carting the peat seemed second nature to Colum. To us it was nothing short of an ordeal such as that endured by Sisyphus in the Greek legend, pushing his rock to the top of the mountain only to see it come crashing down again, then having to push it up the mountain again, and so on for eternity. Between us we earned less than it cost to put food upon the table. I was the first to leave. Within two years Frederick had followed my example, only across a different sheet of water, to England. And as for Joseph? He was driven from an early age by romantic dreams of excitement, adventure and heroism. It was a surprise to none of us when he joined the Connaught Rangers, and set off to fight in Africa.

The Second Part. The Leaving. August 1893

I begged my parents not to come to Queenstown with me. It was hard enough for us all to say goodbye *in our own home. How much harder to wave goodbye as the ship steamed out of the harbour. We had a great party the day before I left. It was more like a wake, with friends and neighbours calling in throughout the afternoon and evening to wish me well, and press a coin or two upon me. It fair cracked me up that they should be giving me what they could plainly not afford to give. To me, who was leaving them behind, and my family, and the land that bore me. I felt like a traitor. Had it not been for the hopes and dreams that it seemed I carried for them, and the promise I had made to send back to my parents some of the fruits of my labour in the New World, I tell you I should have changed my mind there and then. And I almost did. My mother was unable to sleep, and neither was I. We stayed up all night, and stared together at the embers of the fire in the grate. Just before the first rays of the sun sent weakling shafts of light through the shutters she got up, and brought a loaf of bread and some cheese wrapped in paper to put in my bag. Then with the rest of the household fast asleep behind us, we held each other tight, our tears drenching the floor beneath our feet. With a final kiss on the cheek, she opened the door, and I stole out like a thief into the night. I never saw my mother, or any of them, again.*

The wharf in Queenstown was smaller than I had imagined and packed with all manner of people. The first class passengers in their finery were shown directly into a lounge inside the buildings. The rest of us – travelling steerage – managed as best we could, jostling for a place to sit and wait while the men from the National Line Steamship Company came to check our tickets and our fitness to travel. Some passengers sat on the chests in which they had brought their possessions. Others on wicker baskets or bundles of clothes. Tinkers and peddlers moved among us selling their wares. At times the noise was all but unbearable. I witnessed many a tearful parting, and was glad that I had come alone.

I had been there no more than an hour or so when there was a strange occurrence. I was approached by a mother and her daughter. The latter I took to be of sixteen or seventeen years of age. They had a most unusual proposal to put to me. The girl was travelling to America alone to join her uncle and aunt. Both mother and daughter were greatly agitated, having been disturbed by rumours circulating among the assembled that it was not uncommon for the Master and Officers of these vessels to prey on unprotected and vulnerable young women, using all manner of inducements to lure them to their quarters, have their way with them, and then disown them at the journey's end. I had heard such tales myself, and whilst I gave little credence to them I secretly acknowledged that she was indeed a most becoming, and shy young woman, and were such rumours to prove true I could see how her virtue might well be in peril. Naturally I kept such thoughts to myself, and sought to reassure them. The mother pleaded that I might make the pretence that her daughter and I were cousins, and

237

keep an eye out for her throughout the voyage. She assured me that, were I to agree to do so, her brother would repay my kindness as soon as we landed in New York. I was surprised, and flattered, that they should feel that I – a complete stranger – could be trusted with such a precious undertaking. And so I readily agreed. It was, after all, a task that I did not expect to find unrewarding, and so it proved.

The vessel on which we sailed was the SS Erin. I thought it a wonderful omen. "Éirinn go breá...Éirinn go Brágh" - Ireland the Beautiful...Ireland Forever! A reminder to never forget what I had left behind. And what a fine ship she was. Three hundred and seventy feet long, forty foot wide. Four thousand tonnes, - give or take a few – of iron and steel and wood. With her two main sails, fore and amidships, and a smaller one at the stern, she had something of the appearance of a clipper. But it was the single silver funnel, capped with a ring of black that explained the speed with which she sliced through the waves, and sped us to our destination.

We sailed on the 4th of August amid scenes of flag waving and more tears shed than I have known in a lifetime. Not least, I must confess, my own. As to the conditions on board, by all account the staterooms and the salons were elegantly furnished and spacious. It was confided to me by an officer that they were as fine as any hotel. There was a library and a smoking room,

bathrooms and ladies boudoirs. *The sixty first class
passengers were waited on hand and foot by stewards
and stewardesses, and should any fall ill then there was
a surgeon in residence. But Mary, for such was the
name of the young woman with whose protection I had
been charged, and I, were among the nine hundred
souls in steerage. No such luxury was afforded us,
though it was pleasant enough. The married couples
and those with families were berthed together. Single
persons of the opposite sex were berthed at opposite
ends of the ship, men in the bows and women in the
stern. Mary and I were only able to meet therefore in
the steerage dining saloon and on the deck. There was
ample fresh drinking water, though what it must have
been like on the sailing ships that took three times as
long to cross the Atlantic, I cannot imagine. Meals
were served three times a day, and there was always
plentiful soup, and bread. At thirteen pounds a ticket
I would not have expected less!*

*It took those of us who had embarked at Queenstown
several days and nights to find what the seamen called
our sea legs. It was an apt expression since I could
barely stand much of the time, and was nauseous in
the extreme. I shall spare the details, though I am sure
you can imagine them for yourselves! In the evenings,
and on those few days when the weather kept us below
decks, people would amuse themselves by telling
stories and singing songs about the lands they were
leaving. There were people of many nations*

represented there. Apart from the English and Irish, there were a large number of Swedes, and Russians, Italians and Poles. And numerous religions also. The captain permitted services to be held and it was both remarkable and instructive to observe the Rabbis conducting services in the very place where the following day our own Roman Catholic priests would say Holy Mass, and Lutherans and Quakers hold their prayer meetings – if such they were. Truth to tell, I could never be sure.

On our third day at sea whilst waiting for Mary to join me, I entered into conversation with a man – a farm labourer from Cork - who confided that he had lied when his details were entered on the ship's manifest. He had given, he said, a false name and claimed that he was a carpenter, when in truth he was a labourer like me. "And why would you do that?" I asked him? "Because they tell me the Irish are looked down upon," he said. "It's a devil of a job getting employment at the best of times, but it'll be a damn sight easier this way." "And don't you think your accent will give you away." I asked. "Sure I'm a hell of an actor." He said confidently, and walked off grinning to himself. I must tell you that I was glad that I had not stooped to such means. Nor would I ever. Not if it entailed disowning my country, and my family name.

On the fifth day there was a funeral at sea of an elderly Lithuanian woman whom it was rumoured had died of tuberculosis. Mary told me that the poor unfortunate woman's bedding had been taken away and burned, and her mattress also. Nor was it the only such sombre event. Over the next five days there were four more bodies consigned to the waves. One man, one woman, and two children, God rest their souls. This time two rumours circulated at the same time. It was measles claimed one. Cholera the other. Since both involved rashes, and high fever, there was no telling. And neither was the ship's Surgeon. There were two other persons, it transpired, confined in the infirmary. We were told that there was nothing with which to concern's ourselves, but with so many close confined, and nowhere to go, it was difficult not so to do.

The Third Part. The Arrival August 14th 1893
On the morning of the eleventh day, I went up on deck to find it as crowded as when we departed. Only this time there was shouting and cheering, and the tears were tears of joy. So many people had crowded to the port side that the ship was listing sharply, and I was genuinely afraid that we might sink. There were so many between me and the side that I could not see the object of their joy. I made my way towards the bows in the hope of finding a better vantage point. In so doing I met Mary. Together we climbed onto a ledge beside one of the lifeboats. All around us people were praying; the Hebrews in their prayer shawls, others on their knees. Mary had her rosary in her hands, and was reciting it with an alacrity prompted more by

excitement than religious fervour.

Suddenly all became clear. We had, it seemed, hove to during the night at the entrance to Upper New York Bay, and were now steaming proudly past Liberty Island. Like some fiery beacon the Statue of Liberty raised her torch skywards, reflecting golden rays of summer sun into the sky. Below and ahead of us, standing in the bows, a distinguished looking gentleman in his middle age, held his hat aloft and cried out with a resounding voice, basso profundo, the words of a poem which I did not recognise then, but which I now know to have been some verses from the sonnet about this Great Colossus.

"Keep, ancient lands, your storied pomp! Give me your tired, your poor, your huddled masses yearning to breathe free, the wretched refuse of your teeming shore; send these, the homeless, tempest-tossed to me, I lift my lamp beside the golden door!"

I should note that it was a report earlier this very year, in the New Hampshire Union Leader, that the entire sonnet had been engraved upon a bronze plaque, and mounted inside the statue, that decided me to set down this account of my experiences. I hope that one day, my children, you will visit the statue and read it for yourselves. Perhaps then you may feel something of the elation, gratitude and boundless expectation that filled the ship that day, and my heart close to bursting with the emotion of it all.

Almost as soon as we had rounded Liberty Island

the immigration station came into view. A huge wooden building clad in blue slate, it covered the entire island. With a tower at each of its four corners, and a vaulted roof, it had the appearance of a fort, or a cathedral, or perhaps a railway station. In truth, any one of those descriptions would have been an apt metaphor for the services provided beneath its roof.

A barge came alongside us, and the first class passengers in hats and boaters, their luggage carried by porters, disembarked, and were taken to the island. Then came the second class steerage in their bonnets, carrying their own luggage. Then the third class steerage families and married couples. Finally it was our own turn. A motley crew in caps, and shawls, and some bare headed, all of us carrying our pathetic possessions in parcels, or bundles, tied with twine.

On the barge the customs inspector pinned two numbers on our clothing, representing the page and line numbers on the ship's manifest on which our names were recorded. On dry land we shuffled forward in line through the medical examination room where I was passed fit in less time than it took to say a few words to the first examiner, and have the second peer into my eyes. The man ahead of me had an H — for heart - pinned on his chest, and was taken off for further examination. I have often wondered what became of him.

I met up again with Mary in the Great Hall where we were asked a number of simple questions to check our identities against the manifest. Then we were free to leave, just three hours after we had set foot on the island. Her brother was there to meet her, and when he heard how I had agreed to watch out for Mary, and her mother's promise to me, he shook my hand firmly, clapped me on the back, and pronounced that he was ever in my debt. To my great good fortune he promised to introduce me to his employer. The rest, as they say, is history.

I have set this down so that you will appreciate the sacrifice we made to make a better life for ourselves, and above all, for you. Never forget how hard it was won, nor how fortunate you are to live in a land of opportunity where a man, or woman, may make of themselves what they may, unhindered by notions of class or race or religion. Not that that was always true in the early days. Nonetheless, it is truer now. I urge you to make the most of the freedom you have, and never to forget the debt your mother and I owe to our forebears, and to the land of our birth. To Ireland!

Patrick Caton Senior
October 9th 1903

And there it ended. Signed with a flourish, just two months, Niamh reflected, after the birth of his second child Maggie. She thought it incredibly sad that almost fifteen years to the day this memoir was completed Maggie, and her brother Joseph, would be snatched away by the Spanish Flu. She wondered if this was when, heartbroken, he had wrapped it up in oil cloth, tied the ribbon, and placed it in the bottom of the chest.

Her lunch had gone uneaten, and the coffee was cold. Moving though this account had been, she felt it had taken her no further forward. She made a fresh mug of coffee, ate her salad, and turned her attention to the bundle of letters.

21

There were five letters in all. Three from Joseph John to his elder brother Patrick, and two from the Army. Enclosed with the second of the letters was a photograph. It showed three rows of soldiers. The rear row standing, those on the middle row seated on benches, and four at the front, legs crossed on the ground, their pith helmets in front of them. There were eighteen in total. The three in the centre of the middle row bore the triple stripes of sergeant on their sleeves. Niamh turned it over but there was nothing written on the back. She set it aside, picked up the first of the letters, and began to read.

4th of November 1899
Duke of York's Barracks,
London.
Dear Paddy,

I am sorry it's been so long since I wrote you. You know I am not one for the writing, so I am sure you will forgive me. We are going to see some action at last! I cannot tell you the details, but it is probably enough to say that it involves a very hot place in the colonies! With the Second Battalion already abroad we left Renmore barracks in Galway and now we're here in our barracks in London waiting to join up with the other regiments leaving with us. I had a bit of leave while we were waiting, and I met a wonderful girl. She has black hair and brown eyes, and skin like a peach. You would never guess she was English! I am in love. I know you will be thinking I have been many times in love. but this is love like I never knew it. Her name is Charlotte Roberts. Charlotte! Tis a wonderful name is it not? Leaving her behind is taking the edge off the prospect of a good fight. I have asked her to marry me when I get back, and she said yes! Please don't tell Mammy and Daddy. I will get round to that in due course. For now we are busy doing parade ground drills. I often wonder how it is with you Paddy in the land of milk and honey? One day maybe I'll bring Charlotte across the water to see you. Write to me care of the Regiment. You have the address.

God Bless and Keep You,

Your Loving Brother

Jo.

The second letter was slightly longer, and on thinner cheaper paper.

20th of December 1899

Near Mafeking

Dear Paddy,

What a time it has been! Now we are here I can tell you we sailed along with the Royal Inniskilling Fusiliers, the Border Regiment, and the 1st Dublin Fusiliers on The Bavarian. We landed at the Cape on the 28th and thence to Durban. Together we are known as the Fifth Irish Brigade. Is that not grand? And I can tell you that we were landed straight in the thick of it. Only last week at a place called Colenso we had the blackest day in the history of the Regiment. We were made to do parade drill before we set off to ford a river and take the village. The guide took us to the wrong place and put us in full view of the Boer guns. As we tried to cross they opened up on us. Twenty four of my comrades were killed, one hundred and three were wounded along with two officers. Another twenty three are missing, and must be dead or captured. It was a truly sorry day. For my part I got to the bank and laid down covering fire. Then I went in and pulled a few of the men out to safety. They are saying I was a hero but it was no more than any man would have done. I do not tell you any of this to make you worry. But I have to tell someone. I certainly cannot tell Charlotte. So who better than my favourite brother? And don't you be worrying about me. Didn't I always live a charmed life?

God Bless and Keep You,
Your Loving Brother
Jo

PS. I have enclosed a photograph took shortly after we arrived. It's my platoon, though sad to say Gerry, whose stood to my left, we buried on Friday, and Sergeant O'Malley is still in the hospital tent. In case you don't recognise me with my short hair (the curls aren't suited to the heat, and the lice, and they look daft sticking out from under my helmet) I am the handsome looking one on the back row with the straight back and the fine moustache!

Niamh picked up the photo. There he was staring back at her. Just twenty one years of age, in the first flush of manhood, everyday an adventure, fearing nothing. She wondered how much of a rude awakening the battle had proved, and if the youthful bravado evident in his letter masked the first intimations of his own mortality. She placed the photograph back on the table, and picked up the next letter. She thought she detected a change in the handwriting, as though his hand was shaking.

25th of February 1900
Langerwachte Spruit
Dear Paddy,

Happy New Year. Let's hope this new Century is better than the last!! I am writing this by the light of a candle in our tent. I hope you can read it. We have to keep the lights down because the Boers are close by. They've taken to crawling through the brush as close as possible and firing their long barrelled rifles. Praise God this day a truce has been declared to allow for the recovery of the dead and wounded, and there has been no gunfire. We've had another bloody engagement. The day before yesterday the Brigade advance on the Langerwachte, a steep hill heavily fortified. We were met with terrible fire and fierce resistance and had to clear their defences with our bayonets. We lost many gallant men, and I two of my closest friends. The Inniskillings, the Dublins, and the Imperial Light Infantry had the worst of it. Over three hundred men they reckon. The hell of it was listening to the wounded lying out there in the open, crying out with pain and thirst, picked off by snipers if they tried to move. The hill is still not taken, and the road to Ladysmith still closed. Tomorrow will be another day, but for now I thank God that the truce has put an end to the suffering on the hillside. I've heard tell that they are calling it Hart's Hill for our General, I think it would be better named Inniskilling Hill, in memory of the fallen.

I have some other news Paddy. It is the reason I am writing to you. I had a letter from Charlotte shortly before we mustered to engage the enemy. It seems we are to have a child. This news has left me happy, and miserable, by turns. Were we already married I should be delighted, though still mindful of my great responsibility in the matter. Fearful also that this war might leave our child fatherless. But since we are not married I am more concerned for Charlotte. She has not told her parents, and I fear that her father may turn her out. I would not see her and our child in the Poorhouse. If you could send a little money to enable her to see herself through this difficult time until we are able to marry, then I should be in your debt for ever. You know dear brother that I shall repay you however long it takes. If you could send it to me at the Duke of York's Barracks in London with a covering letter, our Captain assures me that although we are not based there he can see to it that it will be held for Charlotte to collect.

God Bless you Paddy,
Ever Your Loving Brother,
Joseph.

PS. Please do not tell Mammy and Daddy. Charlotte is a Protestant, though it's of no consequence to me. She could be a Hebrew for all I care. But you know what that will do to them! I need to break it gentle. Who knows, she may turn for me, and no harm done.

Niamh read it again, trying to contain her excitement. Here was mention of another Caton, albeit conceived out of wedlock. She had found no such mention of a child in any of the searches through which she had unearthed Tom's branch of the family. Perhaps Charlotte had never gone full term? Perhaps the child had died in infancy, or before its birth could be registered? Perhaps it had been adopted, a rarity in those days? More probably, it had been raised with its mother's maiden name. There were too many unknowns. She picked up the next letter. It was brief, and to the point.

Fifth Irish Brigade.
1st Battalion, The Connaught Rangers
"Quis Separabit"
Brigade Headquarters
Spion Kop
28th February 1900

Dear Mr Caton,
It is my painful duty to inform you that your brother, Private Joseph John Caton, was killed, yesterday forenoon, during an attack on enemy forces at Pieter's Hill. It was characteristic of Joseph that he died whilst single-handedly attacking, and silencing, a trench from which the scathing fire of a Maxim gun had scythed down many of his comrades. I hope that it will be a small

comfort for you to learn that this was the second occasion on which he had behaved in such a heroic manner. I have learned today that he will be mentioned in Lord Buller's next dispatch to the War Office, and recommended for a posthumous award.

Private Caton asked specifically that if this letter should needs be written, it should be directed to you. I must tell you that in due course a formal notification of your brother's death will be sent from the War Office to your parents in Ireland. You may feel that it would be kinder to inform them first yourself, but that is a matter for you.

It only remains for me, on behalf of the entire Battalion, to express our sympathy at your loss, and deep regret that we were unable to bring Joseph safe home.

I am Sir,
    Your Obedient Servant,

    Captain Thomas James Egerton

The final letter was the shortest of them all.

Office of the Regimental Adjutant
Duke of York's Headquarters
King's Road
Chelsea
June 17th 1900.

Dear Sir,
I am returning to you, with this letter, the money order which you sent on behalf of your brother Private

Joseph John Caton, of the 1st Battalion the Connaught
   Rangers, to await collection by one Charlotte Roberts.
I regret to say, that despite attempts to elicit the
whereabouts of Miss Roberts, the money order, and your
letter, have remained uncollected. I have taken this action
based on advice from the Adjutant at the Headquarters
of the Connaught Rangers in Renmore, County Galway,
to whom any questions you may have with respect to this
matter should be addressed.
   I am Sir,
   Your Obedient Servant,

   Albert Edward Makepiece. (Lieutenant)

It was only when Niamh came to fold the letter to
place it back in the envelope that she discovered that
something had been written on the back. Just six lines,
in a hand that she recognised as belonging to Patrick
Caton.

Not a day goes by, but that I offer up prayers for
Charlotte Roberts, and her child, and for the repose of the
soul of my poor, brave, and foolish brother Joseph. I swear
that I have done everything, short of sailing to England,
to carry out the promise that I made to him. Were it not
for the fact that our little Joseph is not yet two weeks old,
and Mary still weakened by her confinement, I should
have done so. In the Fall, when they are both strong,
perhaps I shall go then.

Niamh wondered if Patrick had actually managed
to make it to London. If so, had he found Margaret,

with or without a child? It was, she knew, idle speculation. She packed everything up, and placed it back in the box, just as she had found it. Then she picked up the phone, and dialled.

Max Madera was busy out Hookset way. Something about a body in the reservoir. Was it important enough to interrupt him? No it wasn't, but she asked them to leave a message to say she'd called, and would he ring back when it was convenient. She checked the time. Four in the afternoon. Ten in the evening in Manchester, England. Tom would understand. She dialled again. He picked up on the second ring.

'Tom, it's me, Niamh,' she told him.

'Good timing Niamh, I was just about to ring you. I only just got in.'

'Are you sure it's OK?' she asked. 'You must be bushed.'

He laughed. 'It's Friday night. The course finished at midday. Kate's out with the girls, and I've just had a couple of hours with The Alternatives.'

'Alternatives?' It sounded like a pop group.

'It's a Reading Group. Male only. Once a month. More of an excuse to have a few drinks, and chew the cud, than a literary occasion. Though I'm lucky to make it at all these days.'

'Chew the cud?' Her mind was working overtime. 'What does that entail?'

He laughed again. 'Ruminating, like the cows do. Look, let's talk about you. Are you alright?'

'I'm fine, but I've found something, and I need your help.'

'Hang on,' he said, 'Let me get a pen and paper.'

'Let me get this straight,' Tom said. 'Joseph, who we assumed had died childless, may in fact have had a son by his fiancée Charlotte Roberts. If that's so, that son would now be...'

'One hundred and eight!'

'Right, but if that son had children, say when he was about thirty, that would make them around seventy or so.'

'And if *they* had children,' Niamh said excitedly. '...they would be anywhere between thirty and fifty right now. And if their children had children...'

'But hang on,' Tom cautioned her. 'Didn't you say you'd done a search through the births, deaths and censuses and, apart from my family, you drew a blank?'

'That's right but don't you see, I was looking for Catons. What if Charlotte didn't identify Joseph as the father? He'd have been registered as Roberts.'

'And so would his sons, and so on.'

'Exactly!'

'What if she named someone else as the father?' he speculated. 'After all, a woman on her own, with a child to raise...'

'I didn't think you were a sexist Tom,' she said pointedly. 'Plenty of women manage to do that perfectly well.'

'Granted they do nowadays, not in 1900 they didn't. You said yourself Joseph was worried she'd end up in the workhouse. I don't know what they were like in New Hampshire, but I can assure you that over here she and her child would have been parted sooner rather than later.'

'Shoot! I never thought of that. How would we follow that up?'

'Easy. Start with the mother's name, and take it from there.'

'There's just one problem with that.'

'Which is?'

'That if Joseph's name never appeared on the birth certificate, how would any of the subsequent offspring know they were related to Joseph Caton?'

'And, therefore, that they were related to John James Clark, the very rich, very sick, billionaire?'

'Exactly.'

'So we have to assume that either his name did appear on the birth certificate, or that Charlotte told her children the truth, and they passed that on.'

'But without the letters in my possession, how on earth would they be able to prove it?'

'With the letters that he sent to her?'

'Why didn't I think of that? I know, because you're the detective.'

'No. Because you're too close to it. It's all about perspective.'

'And you're not? If we are right, and there's a maniac out there determined to get his hands on JJ's fortune, you're just as much in the firing line as I am. Or had you forgotten?'

'No, I hadn't. This is why I'm going down to London in the morning.'

'Where to?'

'To the London Metropolitan Archives.'

'On a Saturday? Kate's not going to be too happy about that.'

'Too right she isn't,' Tom said. '...but I'm back at work on Monday morning, and as you so rightly pointed out, there's a maniac out there who is unlikely to be keeping holy the Sabbath Day!'

Max rang back ten minutes later. He sounded flustered.

'Niamh, are you alright?'

'I'm fine Max. I didn't want to disturb you, but you did say that as soon as anything came up...'

'Damn right I did. What is it?'

She told him.

'In which case I'm going to add the name Roberts to the trawl we're doing through the lists from the Immigration and the Airlines. If you get anything more from Tom let me know immediately. Are you sure you're OK?'

'I'm good to go. All the better for hearing your voice.'

'Well I'd love to be able to say I can come over tonight,' he told her. '...but I've got a floater here who doesn't look like he intended going for a swim.'

'Someone pushed him in?'

'Let's just say "assisted entry". He had a bag of rocks tied to his feet. '

'Give me a ring when you can?' she said, as she fought to push the image from her mind.

'You bet. And you take care.'

Niamh replaced the phone. She stood there for moment thinking. She felt energised by the discovery that she had just made, but impotent to do anything about it. Both Tom and Max had more than enough to keep them busy, whereas she had no idea what to do next. She had no intention of hanging around the house waiting for something to happen. There was only one way to release all this pent up frustration. She went across to the computer, and booted it up.

22

It was gone midnight when Kate arrived home. Tom was still up watching a late night thriller. She dropped her bag on the sofa, sat on his lap, threw her arms around his neck, and gave him a sloppy kiss.

'Sauvignon Blanc, or Pinot Grigio,' he ventured.

'That's not a very nice way to welcome me home,' she said pretending to be peeved. 'You'll be telling me what I had to eat next.'

'That's easy. Something with garlic, probably pasta.'

'Close.' She laughed, and kissed him again.

'Definitely pasta,' he said. 'Carbonara. Heavy on the cream. Not enough bacon.'

This time she punched him on the arm.

'Hey, that hurt,' he complained. 'I've still got a bruise from the last time.

'Well you deserved it.' She slipped from his lap, and snuggled in beside him. 'Aren't you going to ask me if I had a good time?'

'Given half a chance,' he said. 'Well, did you...have a good time?'

'Brilliant! Lots of catching up and lots of gossip. Bernie's got a new job at the Infirmary - Theatre Sister - really responsible. Nicky's got a new man at last. And unbelievably, this one isn't married.'

'As far as she knows.'

'You do have a point' she said. 'It wouldn't be the first time a man had spun her a yarn.'

'What about Mel, how's she getting on?' he asked.

She regarded him suspiciously. 'Mel claims to be unattached, and loving it. Why do you ask?'

'No particular reason...I just wondered.'

'I think you've got the hots, for Mel,' she said. 'I think you have ever since I introduced her to you.'

'Well you can hardly blame me,' he said, preparing for the onslaught. As she began to rain playful blows in his direction he grabbed her wrists, pinioned her against the back of the sofa, and pressed his lips to hers. He felt her relax beneath him, and released her wrists. She lay back, with her hands behind her head, as he began to unbutton her blouse.

'That was mean,' Kate said as she came out of the bathroom, turned back the sheet, and slipped into bed. '...and underhand. I think I'm beginning to see another side of you now that we're living together.'

'What was mean?' Tom asked, plumping up his pillows, affecting ignorance.

'You know very well,' she said. 'Making love, and then informing me that you're going to London tomorrow. Saturday of all days. Did you think that if you told me first you wouldn't get your evil way?'

'It never occurred to me.'

'Like hell it didn't! You knew very well what would happen.'

'Well there you go then,' he said. 'Better to go to bed with something nice to remember.'

'And then take the edge off it?' she protested.

'At least there was something to take the edge off.'

'Why is it so bloody difficult to have an argument with a man?' she fumed.

'Because we don't let emotion get in the way of reason?'

'You wait till one o'clock on Saturday morning to tell me that you're swanning off down to London in six hours time. How did you think I'd react?'

He shuffled down the bed and sank his head into the pillows. 'Just like this. Not that I blame you. I'm really sorry, but I didn't know myself until a couple of hours ago. He reached out for her shoulder. 'I'll be back in time for dinner I promise, and then we've got the whole of Sunday to ourselves.'

'Big deal,' she said, turning away from him, and switching out the light.

They lay there, back to back, for several minutes, the tension like a wall between them. Then he felt her turn over. Her left arm curled around his chest and her lips brushed the nape of his neck. 'Just you take care Tom Caton,' she said. 'And come back safe. Or I'll kill you.'

Caton was on the doorstep of the London Metropolitan Archives when it opened at dead on nine forty five. It helped that it was only just over a mile from Euston Station. Even more important when it came to the return journey. He'd promised, on pain of death, that he would be back by seven thirty. That meant catching the fourteen forty seven, or at a pinch the fifteen seventeen which, if it was on time, would mean arriving at the apartment just ten minutes late. That gave him less than five hours to track down

Charlotte Roberts and her issue…if any. Despite the fact that he had been here before, and knew his way around the system, he doubted it would be long enough.

He was first at the Information Point. The archivist was positive and upbeat, until he was told Caton's deadline.

'Ah, that might be a problem,' he said. 'The Family Records Office has recently closed, and moved over to the National Archives at Kew. If you want to search the General Records Office Indexes for births, deaths and marriages you'll have to go over there. If the woman you're looking for did end up in the workhouse though, you've come to the right place,' he shrugged. 'But it would help if you knew which one. Otherwise you're going to have to plough through them one at a time.'

'How many are there?' Caton asked.

He had to think about that. 'When it comes to London you'll find them organised by county. North of the Thames, we've got thirty two in Middlesex. Then there are nine south of the river in Surrey. And there are three in Kent.'

Caton did the maths. Forty four sets of records. It sounded like a needle in a haystack. 'Does it help if I can narrow it down to one or two years?' he wondered.

The archivist smiled. 'It will certainly help me. And you'll have fewer request cards to fill out for a start. But you'll still have to get lucky…and that's if she was even in the system at all. Come on, let's get you started.'

By twelve thirty Caton had got through twenty three sets of Admission and Discharge Books, each of them listing those admitted to the workhouse, those who had been discharged, and those who had died each day. The roll call of workhouses was like a game of Monopoly, the list of pauper names like a dirge. His eyes were beginning to ache. He had had nothing to eat, and only two cups of coffee, and copious beakers of water to keep him going. It was beginning to feel like a fool's errand. Wearily he started on number twenty four, St Pancras.

Five minutes into his search he almost missed it, and had to go back. On the 17th of April 1900, Charlotte Roberts, Spinster, had been admitted to St Pancras Workhouse. Her age was given as twenty one, and her occupation as domestic servant. Her birthplace was Clerkenwell. There was no mention of a child. Caton had to check his notes. Of course there was no child. Unless she had miscarried she would be not less than five months pregnant; enough to show, enough for her parents to turn her out onto the streets. Hurriedly, he copied down the details, and returned the records to the archivist.

'If she was pregnant would there be a record of the birth?' Caton asked.

'Of course, in the Register of Births. And you're in luck, because if my memory serves me right there was a maternity ward at St Pancras. In fact after 1904 none of the children born there were stigmatised by having the workhouse shown as their place of birth. I'll get you the register.'

Five minutes later Caton was staring at an entry for one Charles Joseph Roberts, born on August 6th 1900, to Charlotte Roberts. In the space for the father's name to be recorded, there was a single letter.

'Father unknown or undisclosed,' the archivist told him. Since you're pushed for time, I had a look in the Workhouse Register of Baptisms for you but there's nothing there.'

Caton looked at his watch. 'I've got just under two hours left,' he said. 'Where should I look next?'

'That's easy. Let's start with the Discharges. I say easy, but you've seen for yourself what the turnover was like, over a thousand a year. You'd better hope she and her son weren't there too long or, worse still, died inside.'

With an hour to go Caton came across another entry. In October 1907 Charlotte Roberts was discharged in order to go into service. There was a note against it which he was unable decipher, and another date that looked like the fourth of September 1907. He asked for the Archivist's assistance.

'It looks like DNRftb,' he said. 'I've only seen it a couple of times before. I assume it means Did Not Return.'

'What about the child, Charles Joseph?' Caton said.

'I'm assuming that's what the ftb stands for: Did Not Return for the boy.' He pointed to the remaining letters. LIS. 'Leavesden Industrial Schools,' he explained. 'It was set up in the countryside north of London, in Hertfordshire. Originally for children who were abandoned and destitute, or at risk of being sucked into a life of crime. The Asylum for Imbeciles was built right next door. God knows what poor unfortunates ended up in there. The Industrial School is where the boy would have been sent. Not such a bad regime as you might imagine. He'd have got a decent basic education, plenty of physical activity... they had two swimming baths for example...better regular medical checks than he would have done outside, and some skills training to help him get a job when they discharged him.'

'And there would be a record of that?' Caton asked anxiously glancing at his watch.

'Oh yes. I know you're pushed. I'll bring you their Admissions and Discharges book. Don't worry,' he said lowering his voice, glancing furtively around. 'I'll fill out the request form to save you time. Just don't tell any of the others.'

Caton returned the records at twenty five minutes past three. That left just twenty two minutes to get to the station, and onto the train.

'Did get what you wanted?' the archivist asked.

Caton nodded. 'Charles was there until his fourteenth birthday. Then he was discharged into apprenticeship with a master bricklayer.'

'That was what...1913?'

'1914.'

The archivist shook his head. 'Two years later, if he hadn't already volunteered, he'd have been conscripted to fight in the trenches. I suggest your next stop is the General Register Index of Deaths,' he said grimly

'The trouble is I've run out of time, and it'll be next weekend before I could possibly come down to Kew,' Caton said. 'But thanks for all your help. I couldn't have got this far without you.' He made for the door.

'Hang on a sec,' the archivist called after him. 'Manchester wasn't it?'

Tom half turned, desperate to get away. 'Yes, Manchester.'

A grin spread over the archivist's face. 'Then you haven't got a problem. No need to come back down here. There's a full set of Civil Registration Indexes at the Manchester Records Office Marshall Street. Monday to Friday.'

Tom would have given him a hug, but there wasn't time. He exited the building like a bat out hell, hot foot towards the Euston Road.

He found it halfway down Deansgate. It was the fourth estate agent in quick succession. Unlike the others this one appeared to deal exclusively with lettings rather than sales. More importantly, it had a number to let in New Islington. He opened the door, and went inside.

'Short term let?' the salesman straightened one of the cuffs on his shirt, and sniffed as though encountering a bad smell. 'How short exactly?'

'A month...two at the most.'

'Not possible I'm afraid. Six months is the best I can do...unless you're lucky, and we have an "in-betweeny". Even then it would have to be at least three months.'

'An in-betweeny?'

'A gap between two longer lets. It can happen. Did you have a particular area in mind?'

'New Islington. As near to the Wharf as possible.'

The salesman sashayed across to his desk, and sat down at the computer. 'Well there's nothing on the

Wharf,' he said, scrolling through the pages. 'But we do have something that's just come up.' He shifted a gear into enthuse mode. 'Urban Splash, Chips development. Very nice apartment. Two beds, beautifully appointed. Surrounded by water on three sides would you believe? On the site of the former Ancoats Hospital. Very convenient for the city centre. One mile to Canal Street, Less to Piccadilly Station, and only...'

The man cut him off in full flight. 'Can you show me exactly where it is?'

The salesman got up and crossed to the wall on which a large scale map of the city was displayed. Here you are,' he said stabbing dramatically at a point on the map. 'Perfecto.'

Close, he decided, but not close enough. 'Have you anything near here?' he asked, scribing a semi-circle with his finger.

The salesman sniffed again, and walked back to his computer. It took several minutes of tutting, and dramatic sighs.

'Ah. We do have this. Bit big for you I'm afraid, unless you'll be holding parties?' He looked up expectantly. The client's face might as well have been a mask. 'No, I don't suppose you will,' said the salesman, swivelling the flat screen so the client could view the gallery of photos. 'Three bedrooms, two bathrooms - one ensuite. Balcony with wooden decking and glass balustrade. Former resident of the Cardroom Estate due to move in four months time. He's got to see out his existing lease on the property he's been in for the past three years. Three months would suit nicely.' He got up, and led the way back to the map. 'Here you are. What do you think?'

The man studied it closely. No line of sight on Caton's apartment, he decided, but a good view of the main entrance. 'I'll take it,' he said.

The salesman's eyebrows shot up. 'Don't you want to know the price?'

The client was already reaching for his wallet.

'Well, just so there's no misunderstanding,' the salesman continued. 'It's nine hundred and fifty pounds per calendar month. The first month to be paid up front. Plus, we'll require a standard deposit of five hundred pounds returnable at the end of the lease, less that which might be required to cover breakages, damages, or cleaning.' His fixed smile broadened as he attempted a little humour. 'Of course that won't be a problem in your case. What with you not throwing any parties.'

It takes all sorts, the salesman reflected as he watched the client cross over Deansgate, and walk off towards Quay Street. James Charles Roberts, according to the name on the contract, and his credit card. He had looked like such a nice young man when he entered the salesroom. Just goes to show how appearances can deceive.

'How did you get on?' Kate asked as Tom parked his briefcase, and slipped off his jacket.

'Not bad at all,' he told her. 'Although I'll have to follow up on it tomorrow. God knows when I'm going to find the time.'

'Well you can tell me all about it over dinner,' she said. 'Soup to start. You freshen up while I pour the wine.'

On the way back from the bedroom Tom noticed the heading on the web page up on the computer screen. "Kissing Cousins." He smiled to himself, and took his place at the table, just as she brought their meals across.

'It it was good enough for Queen Elizabeth, and Prince Philip,' he said. 'Then it must be OK for me.'

She stopped with the plates in mid air. Her fingers began to burn. She almost dropped the plates in her haste to put them down. 'Damn!' She raced over to the sink, and ran her fingers under the cold tap. 'What on earth are you talking about?'

'Kissing Cousins,' he said. 'I take it that's not a co-incidence? You were wondering about Niamh and me?'

A tell tale flush of pink began to spread from her neck towards her chest. 'That's not fair,' she said, turning off the tap, and sucking her fingers as she came back to the table. 'You've been spying on me.'

'Hardly,' he said, laughing. 'You left it up there for all to see. But, since you're clearly interested, did you know that there is no more consanguinity between third, let alone fourth, cousins than any other random couple? So there wouldn't be anything to stop us getting married, having children, the works.'

He ducked as her bread roll came flying through the air.

23

They slept late on Sunday morning, not stirring until 10 am.

'It looks like a beautiful day out there,' Tom said as he padded into the bedroom with a tray of tea and bacon rolls. 'I think we should get out, and make the most of it. There won't be many more this side of winter.'

'Be careful with those,' Kate said anxiously. 'I don't want tea stains on the sheets, and crumbs all over the floor.'

'They're my sheets as well,' he reminded her, placing the tray on the floor. He handed her a mug. 'So, are you up for it...a walk in the fresh air?'

She blew across the surface, and took a sip. 'It depends.'

He sat down carefully on his side of the bed. 'On what?'

'On where we walk, and how far it is.'

'I thought Daisy Nook. It's what, ten minutes drive? And as for how far, that's up to you. I thought we might start out from Crime Lake, and go up to Hartshead Pike and back. About five miles.'

'She bit into her roll, and wiped a smear of ketchup from the side of her mouth.' Is that your five miles, meaning it's more like seven?'

'If you're going to insult me, you can make your own breakfast next time.' He stood up, and took his mug and bacon roll in the direction of the lounge.

'Don't you think you're over-reacting?' she asked.

'I was only teasing,' he said as he disappeared from sight, 'I've just got an email I need to send.'

'Oh, Tom...' she called after him. 'It's Sunday!'

Tom knew that in all probability Niamh would still be asleep, but he didn't want to have to wait until they got back from their walk and be accused of spoiling their evening. In any case, it would only take two minutes to explain what he'd discovered, and what he intended to do next.

When he'd finished he asked her to copy the email to detectives Madera, and Foley so they could include the name Roberts in their analyses of the immigration and passenger lists. Then he reminded her to take care, and pressed send.

He sat there for a moment wondering if this was going to be the breakthrough they had been looking for. If so, was somebody called Roberts sitting out there right now watching him, and Kate? Or was that person several thousand miles away zeroing in on Niamh? He hadn't felt this powerless since the time two years ago, when his involvement of Kate in the Bojangles case had put her in jeopardy. He hoped to God it wasn't going to happen again. He went into the bedroom, made sure that Kate was still busy in the bathroom, removed the holster containing his expandable baton from his drawer, slipped it onto his belt, and made sure it was hidden beneath his sweat shirt. Just a sensible precaution he told himself.

They'd almost made it easy for him. Except when they had walked around the lake. He wondered if Caton had done that just so that he could check if they were being followed. It was unlikely. After all why should he? Perhaps it was just a touch of occupational paranoia, a policeman watching his back. Once the two of them had moved in among the trees and bushes, they had presented what would have been an ideal opportunity but for the other people strolling around the country park.

Now that they'd left the well trod paths, and headed up towards the hills, they were alone. With his bob hat pulled down, and dark glasses on, had anybody chanced upon him, he would have been just another walker. Medium height, medium build, in a dark green anorak, and combat jeans. But he had not come prepared. Not for that. This had always been another recon. Establishing routines...patterns of behaviour. It hadn't occurred to him that Caton would present such an opportunity in broad daylight. In any case, he had never intended to include the woman. What he'd done so far, what he'd set out to do, it wasn't indiscriminate. Keep it in the family. That had always been his intention. He smiled to himself. "Keep it in the family." He liked that. On the other hand, if he were to take out the two of them, that would break the pattern. Make it harder for anyone to join the dots.

He adjusted the pocket field glasses, and focused on the woman. She bent to pick something up... a wild flower...a stone? She showed it to Caton, and then threw her head back, laughing, her auburn hair, rich red in the autumn sunlight. Collateral damage, that's what they called it. Collateral damage. Pity, he reflected. Such an attractive woman. Wouldn't mind a bit of that myself. His breath began to mist the lenses. Not today though. Not prepared. Have to stay focused...disciplined. Not today. Not here.

'Welcome back Boss.'

It was DS Carter who spotted Caton first as he walked into the Major Incident Room. The others looked up from their computers, and joined in with a chorus of greeting. Joanne Stuart, standing beside the water dispenser, raised her cup. Ged, the Office Manager, beamed a big smile. The warmth of their reception confirmed that he'd made the right decision, not to go to the Promotion Board, nor to take the invitation to join the Serious and Organised Crime Agency. He couldn't put it off indefinitely without having the door closed in his face for good, but right now this was where he belonged. He looked around the room. Two weeks away and nothing had changed. The team were busy beavering away at their desks, poring over files, bent over their computer keyboards. Someone tapped him on his shoulder. He turned to find DS Gordon Holmes grinning at him, like a great silverback gorilla that has just become the dominant male.

'Great to see you back Boss,' Gordon, told him. 'About time too! And have I got something to tell you!'

They were hardly inside Caton's office when Gordon started.

'Marvin Brown shooting,' he said. 'Turns out it wasn't the drive by that sparked it off after all.'

Caton was intrigued. 'Go on,' he said.

'Danny Wilkes took his woman to a meet with Brown. Showing off, strutting his stuff. I say woman, all of seventeen. Legs up to her arm pits, skirt shorter than a pelmet, belly button ring, tight tee shirt, no bra. You know the type. Seems Marvin took a fancy to her, and she sussed out straight away who was the bigger man of the two. Danny with a mountain bike, Marvin with a Merc...not rocket science is it? Danny finds out,' He made a gun with two fingers, and the thumb of his right hand. 'Boom Boom! Good night Marvin Brown.'

Caton nodded. 'It had to have been something personal, close up like that, splayed across the children's roundabout. He was sending a message: nobody makes a fool of Danny Wilkes and walks away. How did DI Tyldesley put it all together?'

'Holmes grinned. 'Little bit of help from yours truly. Though, to be fair, it was mainly down to her.'

Caton sensed a bit of the old sexism creeping back in. 'What do you mean Gordon?'

The DI smiled smugly. 'I suggested she ask the Drugs Team for a full log of any observations they'd done involving Marvin. They not only had a record, they had photos of Danny's bird coming and going to Marvin's flat. Tyldesley pulled the girl in, and put the squeeze on her. She was clearly terrified, and upset. Didn't give too much away, but as soon as Diane let her go she went straight round to Danny Wilkes's, shouting and screaming. So much so, the neighbours dialled 999. Uniform turns up and Danny does a runner. So does his mate. Uniform has no idea why, but they give chase. Corner the two of them hiding in a vacant Industrial Unit. They're about to let them go because they've nothing on them. Just then DI Tyldesley arrives because she was banking on something like this happening. She gets Tactical Aid to do a search of the area around Danny's house. Guess what?'

'They find the gun?'

'Nope, but they found a pair of bloodstained trainers and a load of half burnt clothes at the bottom of a bin round the back of the Unit. Like they say...if the clothes fit.

'And they did?'

'Trainer's were Danny's, clothes belonged to both of them. His so called mate was quick to confess. Of course Danny planned it, did the shooting, made him help move the body. He had no idea any of it was going to happen.'

'Naturally.'

'Which should be worth a minimum of seven years, and upwards of twelve for him.'

'And life for Danny.'

Gordon grinned. 'Not bad for a fortnight's work. While you've been playing dolls houses with Kate, and make believe with SOCA.'

Caton chose to ignore it. Not least because it was basically true. This was about as rewarding as police work got. Taking scum like Danny Wilkes off the streets, and giving the law-abiding public a few years respite. 'Close the door Gordon, and sit down,' he said. 'I've got something I need to pass by you.'

'Bloody Hell!' said Gordon Holmes. 'That's not a lot to go on is it? It may not even be just one person.

For all you know there may be a rat's nest of them out there. Or another branch of the family that neither you nor your cousin…'

'Niamh.'

'…Niamh, has found out about.'

'That's why I need to make this official,' Caton said. 'I felt I had to run it by you before I spoke to DS Gates. See if you thought it was something she'd take seriously.'

'If there are two other police forces working three murders, possibly four, I can't see any reason why we shouldn't get involved.'

'Because no crime has been committed over here,' Caton reminded him. 'Let alone within our jurisdiction?'

'So what are you suggesting? That we sit around and wait till someone takes a pop at you? Don't forget that whoever it is has done a bloody good job so far. Hundred percent record, and leaving everyone chasing shadows.'

'Thanks Gordon,' Caton said ruefully. 'That's just the reassurance I was looking for.'

Detective Superintendent Helen Gates heard him out in silence. When he'd finished, she eased her chair back, and folded her arms.

'If it wasn't you telling me this Tom,' she said. 'I'd have to say it was too fanciful for words.'

'You don't think that there are people who would consider five point one billion dollars worth killing for?'

'I'm not denying that' she said. 'I don't believe in coincidence on this scale any more than you do. But

276

let's face it…four or five deaths, several thousand miles apart. Someone would have to be going to considerable lengths to pull this off. And how does he or she know anymore than you do about how many family members there are still out there, standing between him – assuming it's a him – and all that money?'

'Don't you think I've been asking myself that?' he said.

'And?'

'And he's either several steps ahead of us, or he's just happy to be reducing the competition, and increasing his share.'

'Eliminating is a more appropriate word I think.' She unfolded her arms, and placed her hands palm down on the desk. 'So Tom, I take it you want me to authorise your team to engage in a little catch up with your elusive relative?'

'Not the whole team Helen. Nor full time. Just permission to use someone else to help me follow this latest lead at the Records Office here in Manchester.'

'And?' she said, perceptive as ever.

'And, if we come up with one or more names, to use Duggie Wallace to search through the databases - HOLMES2, CATCHEM, the Driver and Vehicle Licensing Authority, National Insurance, TV Licences - whatever it takes to track them down.'

She pursed her lips. 'You know as well as I do that Chief Superintendent Hadfield is unlikely to go along with that unless you come up with something more substantial within our jurisdiction.'

Caton knew she was right. Hadfield's nickname in the Force was Jobsworth. Earned way back when he was still an Inspector, and his favourite response to anything carrying the slightest risk was "More than my job's worth."

'What if,' Caton said. 'We were to get an official request from a fellow European Force, to assist them with an enquiry relating to a multiple murder investigation?'

'Say from somewhere in the Republic of Ireland?' she said with a widening smile. 'Routed via Europol?'

'I was thinking Interpol,' Caton said. 'Europol's remit is really to do with serious organised crime isn't it?'

'Fair comment,' she acknowledged. 'But then we don't know this isn't serious organised crime do we? Seems pretty serious to me, and certainly organised.' She steepled her fingers. 'Get them to send it for my attention. I can probably keep it from Martin for forty eight hours or so.'

'In which case, I'd better get cracking.' Caton said. 'And thank you Helen. You've no idea how much this means to me.'

'Oh I've a pretty good idea.' She stood up to see him out. 'And don't think for a moment that I'm being purely altruistic here. There's no way you're going to be able to concentrate on anything else until this is resolved. What good is that to me?'

Hope it hasn't messed you about too much Jo?' Caton said as he and DS Stuart waited for the records to be retrieved. 'Pulling you off that job?'

'Not at all Boss,' she replied. 'Been at it since last Thursday. Making my head spin. Just what I needed, to get out of the office for a bit.'

'I don't suppose this is going to be all that different.'

'Well, you know what they say. A change is as good as a rest.'

That was one of the things Caton liked about Detective Sergeant Joanne Stuart. She was ever an optimist. A perfect counterpoint to Gordon, and his irrepressible cynicism. Though to be fair, he had been improving lately.

'You clear about what you're looking for?' he asked.

She held up her notebook. 'I think so. I'm going to take the Marriages, you're covering the Births. Hopefully each will connect with the other. With any luck, we might both be able to divide the Deaths up between us somewhere mid afternoon.'

There it was again, he reflected. Eternal optimism.

As it happened, she was right. Charles hadn't died in the Great War. After he'd come out of his apprenticeship he'd become a builder, and in May 1922 married a Margaret Barton at the Watford Register Office. This discovery by DS Stuart enabled Caton to skip a few years, and saved him at least a half an hour's work. He swiftly came across the births of Philip in 1922, still in Watford, and then of a daughter Caroline, in November 1936. Nothing then until April 1956 when Philip – now thirty four years of age – married an Ann Fitzmaurice, eight years his junior, at Church Road Baptist's, Acton, in North London. DS Stuart worked through another eleven years of records before she came across the birth of what proved to be their only child, Peter Charles Roberts. Ann was recorded as the mother, but there was a notation that Caton hadn't seen before. The archivist had a pretty good idea what it was, but went to check it anyway.

'I was right,' he said. 'Deceased. The mother died in childbirth. Shortly before the child was born. Hence the annotation.'

"...was from his mother's womb, untimely ripp'd." Caton observed.

'Macbeth?' The archivist said confidently.

Caton shook his head. 'The other one. The one who ended up killing him...Macduff.'

He went to tell Joanne Stuart. 'I've asked for a copy of the birth certificate,' he said. I'll keep going through the Births in case Philip remarried, or Peter had any children. I suggest you start on the deaths.'

By twenty past four in the afternoon they had exhausted all the possibilities. Philip had died in 2002 aged eighty. He had not remarried. His son Peter married an Emma Charlesworth in 1992, when he was twenty five.

'Westminster Cathedral,' Joanne Stuart observed. 'That's a turn up. From Baptist Chapel to Roman Catholic Cathedral in one generation. Either he saw the light, or his wife was a Catholic, and he converted for her sake.'

'In 1992 he probably didn't have to,' Caton reflected. 'Just so long as he agreed to bring up the children in the Faith.'

'Not that there have been any children,' she observed.

'That's it then,' Caton said. 'All we've got still alive are Mr and Mrs Roberts. Last known address in South Kensington, South West London. We'd better get back to the station, and find out where they are right now.'

'Surprising what we can discover in just one hour when we put our minds to it, isn't it Boss?'

Caton stared at the single sheet of paper Gordon Holmes had brought him. Discounting parking fines – which in London were a given - neither Emma nor Peter Roberts had ever fallen foul of the law. They had, however, divorced just three months into the new Millennium, after eight years together. But the biggest revelation of all had come when Duggie Wallace checked out the National Insurance details. In December 2006 Peter Charles Roberts had changed his name by deed poll to Peter Cayton.

'Tricky little sod,' Gordon continued. 'Changing his name like that. But you'd think he'd at least have spelt it right.'

'It depends on how he found out who his Great Grandfather really was, and from whom,' Caton said. 'It's equally possible he did it to give more credence to his claim on John James's billions, whilst making it that little bit harder for anyone to track him down.'

'In which case, it hasn't worked has it Boss? That's his current address right there. Duggie checked with the Greater London Council. Pays his council tax monthly by direct debit. Doesn't mean he's resident though. He could have leased it…included the council tax in the rent.'

'Let's find out,' Caton said reaching for his phone. 'I've got a pal in the Met who can check it out. In the meantime, you get on to his bank, and credit card companies. Let's see if his spending pattern places him in New Hampshire, or Ireland, in the relevant time period.'

'I'll need a warrant,' Gordon reminded him. 'And

you said yourself we don't have grounds for that, not yet.'

Caton smiled. 'Maybe we don't, but I know someone who does.'

'Detective Inspector Sean Foley, how can I help you?' He sounded frazzled.

'I was hoping I might be able to help you Sean. It's me, Tom Caton.'

Foley's tone lightened. 'Tom...they didn't tell me it was you. Thanks for the tip off about Roberts by the way. Though a first name wouldn't have gone amiss.'

'I've got an update on that. The name is Peter Roberts, but ...wait for it...he changed his name by deed poll to Peter Cayton, with a Y, two years ago.'

'The tricky little beggar!'

'That's what my DI said. Or words to that effect.'

'So now we're looking for both Peter Roberts and Peter Cayton?'

'That's right. Can you let Detective Madera know for me?'

'No problem. We're in contact daily over these wretched passenger lists. It's a nightmare I can tell you.'

'Cayton's address is in London,' Caton told him. 'Someone's checking his whereabouts as we speak. But I've got a problem.'

'Which is?'

'I need a warrant to access his bank and credit card details. He's done nothing on my patch that would convince a magistrate to give me one. Whereas...'

'I'm conducting a multiple murder investigation,' the Irish detective said.

'Exactly.'

'Consider it done Tom. I'll email you everything we turn up.'

'Likewise.'

'It's great doing business with you.'

'My thoughts entirely.'

Caton spent the next hour and a half catching up on the mountain of paperwork that had accumulated while he was off, plus over three dozen emails whose senders had chosen to ignore his Out of Office message. It was gone six when Ged put the call through.

'It's DI Brooks, Metropolitan Police, Sir,' she said. 'He sounds like a nice man.'

Caton chuckled. 'That's not the consensus of opinion in Pentonville prison.' He pressed the receive button. 'Jack...thanks for this. How did you get on?'

'Curate's egg Tom, some good, some bad. '

'Give me the good news, I need cheering up.'

'He still lives there. Has done for the past two years.'

Changed his name and his address at the same time Caton reflected. 'And the bad?'

'He's not at home, and according to the neighbours he hasn't been seen for the past three months.'

'Not at all?'

'Not unless he's crept in after dark, and out again before dawn.'

'Did he stop the milk...the newspapers?'

'Blimey, don't tell me they still deliver the milk up North? This is London Tom. Anything left on the doorstep gets nicked. And no one down here has time to read the morning papers.'

'Anything else?'

'Short of breaking in, there's not a lot else I can tell you. When he is home, he's a bit of a loner by all accounts.'

'Where does he work?'

'Where did he work, you mean. Somewhere on Canary Wharf, according to Mr Nosey Parker in the ground floor flat.'

'What about his post?'

'Letterbox is sealed up. Some circulars left on the floor outside. I reckon the postman takes everything back to the sorting office.' There were noises in the background. 'Look, I'm sorry Tom, but I've got to go.'

'Thanks Jack,' Caton said. 'I really owe you on this one.'

Jack Brooks gave a throaty laugh. 'You said that last time. It's about time I came up there and collected.'

'Any time.' Caton told him.

'I'll hold you to that,' he said, and put down the phone.

Caton went through to the Incident Room, and found them all still at it. 'You lot. Home, now!' he told them. 'I'd rather you came in bright eyed and bushy tailed first thing in the morning.' He looked across at his DI. 'Gordon, a word.'

Holmes came over. 'Yes Boss?'

'First thing tomorrow, I want a copy of Peter Cayton's photograph. Either from his passport, or his driving licence – whichever is the most recent.'

'Likely to be the same Boss,' Gordon reminded him. 'The one on the driving licence is digitally mastered straight from the passport.'

'Right,' Caton said. 'And secondly, I want him put on the Missing Persons list. I want someone to check on his local sorting office. See how he arranges to pick up his mail. And finally, I want all of the local hotels and guest houses up here checked out, just in case. Tell them if he's not staying with them at present, we'd like to know if he has ever stayed with them before, and to be informed immediately if he does happen to check in.'

'Bit of a long shot Boss. Be lucky if any of them remember to tell all of their reception staff.'

Caton knew that he was right. 'Even so. It's worth a try. And don't forget the Apart Hotels.'

Three months away from home. That's where I'd set up base, Caton decided. A self-contained apartment. Come and go as I please, least likely to be checked. That's if he is here. If he's in New Hampshire, I only hope for Niamh's sake that Madera is taking this as seriously as I am. But then, he told himself ruefully, why should he? It's not his neck on the line.

24

Niamh was still digesting the information in Tom's latest email when another one appeared in her inbox. The sender's address caused the hairs on the back of her neck to stand up: mcaton6@wannaby.co.uk. Without a moment's hesitation, she opened it up.

Hi Niamh.

My name is Michael Caton. I've just seen your web site. I think it's brilliant!!! Especially your family tree. I think it's part of my family tree too. Saved me loads of time. And how about this? I've only just started researching mine but my Great, Great, Great, Grandfather was called Joseph, and his wife was called Mary McCarthy. Just like yours. That can't be a coincidence can it? I live in London, England. I have a fear of flying so I don't think I will ever get to visit the US of A but if you're ever over here it would be great to meet up. It would be great to hear from you.

All the best,

Mickey (that's what my mates call me) Caton

Niamh found it difficult to believe. Between the two of them, she and Tom had traced all of Joseph's offspring. The only way this Michael could possibly be telling the truth would be if they had missed something. She checked the time. It was far too late to be calling Tom, and in any case he would want to know more, as did she. Instead, she decided to respond. To see if she could tease out something further for them to work on. Then she would email Tom, and ring Max. Keep them both in the loop. Her fingers flew across the keys.

Hi Mickey.

What a surprise it was to hear from you! I'm glad you liked my website. And that it's proved helpful. That's why I did it, so that we Catons all over the World could build up the definitive family tree! So, I'm intrigued. If Joseph was your Great, Great, Great Grandfather, which of his sons was your Great Grandfather? Was it Frederick, Colum, or Joseph John? I know it wasn't Patrick, not unless there are skeletons in my own family that my dad kept from me!!! Maybe you could include the names that you've dug up in your next email?

Looking forward to hearing from you soon.

Niamh

Only when she'd pressed send did she wonder if she'd made a big mistake opening up his first message. From what little she knew about computer viruses she doubted it. After all there had been no attachments, and she hadn't actually downloaded anything. But she couldn't be sure. She vaguely remembered the IT guru at City Hall warning them not to open any email whose addressee they didn't recognise. In practice it had proved to be one of those rules that was impossible to adhere to. No member of the public would have ever got a response. Even so, the seeds of doubt had been sown. Perhaps Michael

Caton was even now crawling through her computer, copying her address book, reading her emails. Oh my God, she thought, he'll know everything that Tom's told me. And what Max, Tom, and the Irish police are doing. At that moment she received another message alert. It was from him. She hesitated for a moment, and then decided that if he was in already it wouldn't make any difference whatever she did. She clicked on OPEN.

Hi Niamh. I can't believe how quickly you got back to me! Is'nt the internet amazing?! I cant send you a copy of the family tree Ive done so far because Im having a problem with my software. But my Great Grandfather was called Joseph John if that helps?

You dont say if your likely to be coming over here anytime. It would be great if we could meet. I could show you around London. Look forward to hearing from you.

Mickey.

She read it through twice. Warning bells rang loud and clear. According to the letters in Miriam's loft, and Tom's research, Joseph John had died childless, except for the boy born to Charlotte Roberts and raised with her surname. None of his descendants bore the name Michael. In which case this Mickey could only be Peter Roberts aka Cayton, crawling out from the woodwork at last. She had to tell the others. But for now, she decided, I mustn't risk losing him, or give anything away. Thank heavens, she reflected, that Tom stopped me adding anything to the website as soon as we found out about John James Clark, and his billions. She decided to send a holding response.

That way, she reasoned, he would be less likely to suspect that she was on to him. This time she proceeded slowly, and read it back several times before pressing send.

> *Mickey,*
>
> *What a nice surprise! You'll know from my website that I haven't been able to trace any record of a marriage for Joseph John, or any children. So this is really good news. Unfortunately I've agreed to go out this evening, so I've got to stop now, but I will email you tomorrow.*
>
> *Niamh*

Next she composed an email to Tom in which she described what had happened, and told him that she was getting straight on to Max Madera, and did he want her to forward the emails from Michael Caton. As soon as the message was sent she rang Max. For once, he was in the office.

'Forward them to me,' he told her. 'I'll get our IT guys to have a look at them. With any luck we should be able to pin down his email account, and the servers he's routed through. I can't believe he's tipped his hand like this. It could be what we've been waiting for. But whatever you do Niamh don't drop your guard. Just because he claims to be in London it doesn't mean that he is. I'll come over first thing in the morning. Until then, just sit tight.'

Detective Lieutenant Supervisor Max Madera pitched up on her doorstep just in time for breakfast. He seemed a little awkward, hovering on the porch, his smile lost somewhere between shy and embarrassed. I should have kissed him that first time, when I had the chance, she chided herself as she closed the door, and followed him down the hallway.

'I'm sorry Niamh,' he said. 'This is one clever customer. Our guys say the mail box appears untraceable. They mentioned something about public key cryptography. It might as well have been Chinese as far as I'm concerned. We've asked the FBI Computer Crimes Task Force to see what they can do, but it'll take time.'

She tried not to let her disappointment show. 'So what do I do in the meantime?'

'Humour him,' he said. 'Like with a blackmailer.'

'I don't have much experience with blackmailers,' she said.

He grinned. 'Enough with the graveside humour. Just keep him talking…metaphorically that is. Copy everything to me. Just don't agree to anything without checking with me.'

'Such as?'

His forehead crinkled, the eyebrows seemed to meet. Nice eyebrows she decided. Thick but immaculately groomed. Groomed? Did he really groom them himself? She hoped not. Probably his barber.

'Such as agreeing to meet him,' he told her.

Most likely Houle's Barbers on Stark Street, just a couple of blocks from Police Headquarters she thought.

'Niamh. Are you OK?' There was genuine concern in his voice. Enough to jerk her out of it.

'I'm sorry,' she said. 'I was miles away. It's happened a few times lately.'

'I think you'd better sit down,' he said.

'No I'm fine. I just need a cup of coffee. I'm sure you could do with one. I'm having some granola with yogurt and berries. I can fix you waffles if you like.'

He grinned. Like a big bear she thought. Strong and cuddly both at the same time. 'Waffles would be great,' he said, sitting down at the kitchen table. 'Have you seen a doctor about these episodes?' he asked as she hunted for the maple syrup.

'They're hardly episodes,' she said. 'My mind just wanders that's all.'

'Even so,' he persisted. 'That bang you got on your head in Ireland. No telling what it might have done. Not to mention the trauma of seeing your cousins burn to death.'

Her immediate reaction was one of anger. He was patronising her. That wasn't what she had expected. Not from him. 'I'm fine!' she snapped, slamming the jar down on the marble kitchen top. Her arms began to shake uncontrollably.

'Whoa...' he said, getting down from the stool.

She felt his hands on her shoulders

'It's OK Niamh.' His arms encircled her, holding her tight until he felt her body relax, and the shaking stop.

She realised that she didn't want him to let go.

'I think you should sit down, and let me do that.' He took the jar from her hand, turned her gently, and made her sit down on one of the stools.

'I'm fine, really I am,' she told him. 'They gave me the works when I got home. Scan, X Rays, reflexes, you name it.'

'Where do you keep the waffles?'

She pointed. 'In the cupboard. Behind the pancakes.'

'What about the trauma?' he asked. 'Have you seen a counsellor yet?'

'I don't feel I need to.'

He gave her the look her mother had used when she was really disappointed.

'First off I didn't actually see my cousins die,' she said.

The look intensified.

'OK so they were in there. But I didn't know for sure. Not until afterwards. And I hardly knew them.'

He cocked one eyebrow. Disappointment morphed into incredulity.

'I was unconscious.' Even she realised just how stupid it sounded. 'Alright, alright, I'll make an appointment later today.'

The other eyebrow joined its companion. Those damned eyebrows.

'OK, OK, this morning. As soon as you've gone.'

He smiled, and began to fix breakfast.

'It's probably just stress,' he said, wiping the syrup from around his lips with a napkin. 'Hardly surprising, given what you've been through lately.'

'So what do you recommend for stress relief Officer?' She could hardly believe that she'd said it. That she was turning this into an opportunity to flirt. But what the hell. She was running out of time, and if he needed a push...'

His eyes seemed to bore into hers. She could tell that he was weighing things up. Right and wrong, checks and balances, did she really mean it? She smiled reassuringly. At least she hoped it was reassuring, not just plain crazy. She concentrated hard, trying to send him a message. It's OK, you can kiss me, her eyes were saying, I won't bite. For God sake just do it, her mind was screaming. In slow motion he put the napkin down, leaned across the table, cradled her face in his hands, and kissed her. Gently at first, then long and hard.

'How's that?' he said, sitting back down.

'That might do it,' she said. 'But you'd better try it again...just so I can be sure.'

As he started to lean across the table again she began to laugh.

'What the heck!' he said, looking pained and confused.

She stifled the giggles with one hand, pointed with the other. 'You've got yoghurt all over your tie,' she spluttered.

He looked down, cursed, and began to mop it with his napkin, smearing it across the silken surface.

'That's no good,' she said getting up. 'You're just going to make it worse. Come over to the sink.' She wiped his tie with warm water, then started to dab it dry with a kitchen towel.

Hold still,' she said.

He had no intention of holding still. He took hold of her shoulders, and kissed her until the last vestiges of maple syrup, and very berry yoghurt, had blended into something closer to nectar.

Niamh had a pretty good idea what the next step would have been, had the phone not started ringing. She tucked a loose curl behind her ear, and picked up.

'Niamh. It's me...Tom. I got your email. How are you?'

'Tom. I'm fine.' She looked across at Max. He rolled his eyes skyward. She shrugged. 'You didn't have to call, you could have emailed me back.'

'It's OK,' he said. 'I'm at work. I thought it better to speak to you direct on this one. It must be Peter Cayton. There's no other possibility.'

'That's what I thought.'

'Can you forward his emails to me straight away? I'll have our IT people have a look at them.'

'Max has already done that. He says they're untraceable.'

'Max Madera? Detective Madera?'

'That's right. He's with me right now. He's sent them to the FBI to see if they can do anything with them. Do you want a word with him?'

Max held out his hand for the phone.

'No, it's alright,' Tom told her. 'I'd better have sight of them first. If you could forward them right now, then I'll ring you both back.'

'OK,' she said. 'I'll do that. Bye Tom.' She put down the phone.

'What...he didn't want to talk with me?' Max said. She wondered if there was trace of annoyance in his voice. Professional jealousy perhaps?

'Not till he's seen the emails. He says he'll ring straight back. When he does I'll put him on the speakerphone.'

'OK,' he said. 'Better get them sent. Then we can start over.'

'There's no doubt about it,' Tom said. 'There's no chance there is another Caton out there anywhere, unless Joseph John had another illegitimate child before he met Margaret Roberts.'

'That is a possibility though,' Max observed.

'Possible, but unlikely.' Tom said. 'First off, there is no record of a birth with him as the father. Secondly, look how he felt about becoming a father. If he'd known about a child by a prior relationship he would almost certainly have married the mother.'

'Catholic guilt.' Niamh observed.

'Well we both know something about that,' Tom said.

'We all know something about that.' Max added. Niamh looked at him in surprise. Not that she should have been, Mediterranean surname and all.

'And there's something else about these emails of his. It's obvious he's lying.' Tom said.

'I agree,' said Max.

'How do you know?' she asked.

'It's all in the syntax,' Tom replied. 'The way he words everything. Constructs his sentences. For example, he's trying too hard to leave out the possessive apostrophes, as though he's not that well educated, but he forgets every now and then.'

'And some of the sentences are too sophisticated for the rest of them. They stand out like a sore thumb,' added Max.

'Exactly.' Tom agreed. 'He just can't help himself. His normal grammatical style just keeps popping out. So if he's lying about that, we can assume that he's lying about some of the content too.'

'Including where he says he's emailing from?' asked Niamh.

'Possibly. What did your IT people have to say about that Max?'

'Like Niamh said. The source is untraceable. He's bouncing between servers all over the world, and the source is expertly encrypted. But they do reckon it's somewhere in Europe. Possibly the UK.'

'Could be London then?'

'Could just as easily be Russia, or an Eastern European country. Lot of illegal traffic heading out of there these days.'

'Hang on a second,' Tom said. 'I've got a message.'

They heard a muffled exchange. When Tom did come back on he sounded pleased with himself. 'That was Detective Inspector Foley,' he said. 'It turns out that a Peter Roberts flew into Dublin airport a fortnight before you did Niamh, and flew out again a week after you left. Outward bound from Luton airport, inward bound to Manchester.'

'Manchester!' Niamh exclaimed.

'That's Manchester England, not Manchester New England.' Tom told her.

'Where's he been since then?' Max wondered out loud.

'I've got my team checking that right now,' Tom said. 'Sean Foley suggested you might like to check it out too…as well as hurrying them up on whether he was around when Niamh's aunt was run over. Incidentally, Sean says it looks like he was using his dead father Philip Roberts' credit card instead of his own.'

'I'm on to it.' Max replied, blowing Niamh a kiss, and heading for the hallway.

'Hang on Tom,' she said. Max is just leaving.' She put the phone down and caught him on the porch. 'When will I see you again?' she said.

'It's difficult,' he replied. 'Don't forget I've got your house under surveillance. If anyone put two and two together…well…you know what I mean.'

'But you could come over to discuss progress. Give them an hour off, while you're here?'

He shook his head. 'It doesn't work like that. If we suspect that someone might be planning to make a move on you we have to know if they're casing the place. I can hardly do that from the inside. It's not just about deterrence, it's about catching him.'

'You could come over for a half an hour or so though?' she persisted.

'That's not a problem. I'll give you a ring. And look, when this is all over, I'll be free to do what the hell I like.'

She liked the sound of that.

'All the indications are that he's in London,' Tom told her, picking up where they'd left off. 'Why else would he want you to meet him there?'

'If I'm ever over there, that's what he said. Not like straight away.'

'Yes, but look at the next one he sent. "It would be great if we could meet up." That sounds like he's hiking up the pressure.'

'So, what are you suggesting?' she asked.

'Why don't you tell him you're coming over? Agree to meet with him. Only when he does turn up, he'll find it's me, not you.'

'That won't work Tom. If I'm not there why would he show himself? If we're even half right about what's going on he's bound to be suspicious. And if he was the one that killed Aunt Miriam, well he's bound to know exactly what I look like.'

'I'll use one of my team,' he said. 'Put her in a wig. She can sit with her back to the window, whatever. We can work out the details when we know where he suggests you meet.'

'He's far too bright to fall for that. You said so yourself. He hasn't put a foot wrong so far. Why would he start now? There's only one way. I've got to be there.'

'No way. I'm not going to risk that.'

'It's not you doing the risking.'

'It is if I'm setting it up.'

'OK,' she said. 'Then I'll set it up myself.'

25

Tom did his best to dissuade her. When it was clear that Niamh would go ahead without him he agreed to work with her, on condition that she arranged to meet this Michael Roberts in Manchester, England.

'Are you going to break it to Lieutenant Madera, or would you like me to?' he asked.

Niamh had a pretty good idea how Max would react. Especially now. 'No, please don't do that,' she said. 'Leave it to me. I want to choose when to tell him. I have no idea how he'll react. Professional jealousy, and all that.'

There was something about the speed and force of her response that told Tom there was more to it than that. 'Well just make sure you do,' he said. 'He'll have to be told because he's working the investigation at your end.'

'Don't worry,' she said. 'I will.'

The truth was, she knew perfectly well that Max would forbid her to go. And he probably had the means to stop her, or at the very least make it really difficult. She hated having to deceive him but could see no other way. She would leave it until the last minute, when it would be too late for him to do anything about it. She hoped it wouldn't jeopardise what had only just begun between them. Surely, she reasoned, he would understand.

The first thing she did was to check that her visa was still valid, and that since both Ireland and England were member states of the European Union she would be able to make it to Manchester. Then she checked her mail. Sure enough, there was one from the mysterious Mickey.

Hi Niamh. You said you were going to email me today. Just thought I'd let you know I was around all day. Hope to hear from you soon.
Mickey.

Clever, she thought, insistent without appearing to apply any pressure. Insidious, like water torture. Drip, drip, drip, till you gave in. She composed a reply. The one she had agreed with Tom.

Hi Mickey.
Good News. I can come over right away. I've got some leave owing, and I'd already agreed to meet up with another relative. A fourth cousin. Tom Caton. You must have spotted him on my website - on the family tree. Tom is the great, great grandson of Frederick, your great, great grandfather's brother. The only thing is he lives in Manchester. How far is that from London?

How pathetic I must sound, she thought. Can't even pick up an atlas, or open Google Earth. But then that was the idea, to lull him into a false sense of security. On the other hand, if he had checked out

Tom – and why wouldn't he – he would know he was a detective. Surely that would put him on his guard? Tom had convinced her it was a risk worth taking. Not to mention him at all would have raised suspicion. Would she really come all this way and not look her other cousin up? And how else would they persuade him to come up to Manchester? The reply took longer than she had expected. She was on her second mug of coffee, dangerously close to chewing her nails, when the mail alert popped up.

Niamh. FANTASTIC NEWS! I cant wait to see you. When are you coming over? Perhaps we could ALL meet up. That would be GREAT. Can you both come down to London? It's only two and half hours on the train by the way.
Mickey.

This was the tricky bit. Tom had been adamant. It had to be Manchester, or forget it. Niamh had already rehearsed her reply.

Hi Mickey.
Yes it's great isn't it? I'm really excited because I've never been to England before. I've already spoken to Tom and he says I can stay with him and his partner, and he'd love to come along too. Unfortunately he can't get away from work…he's a policeman would you believe? And I've only got five days off in total, and with the flights, and jet lag, it doesn't leave me long in England. Can you possibly make it to Manchester? It would be a real pity to come all that way, and not meet you.

This time his reply was swift, and to the point.

No problem Niamh.   Of course I'll go up to Manchester. Just let me know when and where. I only know Old Trafford (that's Manchester United's Football Stadium …home of David Beckham…you must have heard of him? Oh, and there's the Trafford Centre – that's a shopping mall. That would be a good place to meet. You get to shop, and I could come on the motorway in the car and go back the same day. No need to go into the city centre at all. Let me know what you think. And make sure I've got your cell phone number in case I get lost.'
Mickey

Niamh forwarded it to Tom. He rang back fifteen minutes later.

'He's clever,' he said. 'The Trafford Centre is huge. A typical shopping mall, on the American scale. There are multiple entrances and exits. Five or more car parks. Masses of people around throughout the day. He wants to make sure he can check us out without us seeing him.'

'Do you want me to suggest somewhere else?'

'No. That would definitely put him on his guard. In any case, it cuts both ways. The place is crawling with CCTV, and my team will be able to blend in just as easily as he will…if not more so. The only thing that bothers me is how he knows about it. I suppose he could have come up here to one of the gigs at the MEN. Or he could even be a United supporter I suppose.'

'What about my phone number, should I give it to him?'

'Yes, but ask him for his as well, just in case we get stuck in a traffic jam, break down, go to the wrong place, that sort of thing. My guess is he won't give it to you. He'll find some kind of excuse not to. He'll know that if we are onto him I'll be able to use it to trace him. He'll probably use a pay phone when he needs to contact you. Or a pay as you go, and then ditch the SIM card.'

'What do I do if he does say no?'

'Act the innocent. Say you understand perfectly. That you'll just have to make sure we get there early.'

Mickey's final email was characteristically upbeat, manipulative, and elusive. Just as Tom had predicted.

Hi Niamh

Glad you're both happy with the Trafford Centre. Much the best for me! Let me know where. The only place I remember is the Food Hall. We could meet by the big screen. If you send me a photo I'll be able to recognise you. Me, I'll be the handsome one with the black hair looking lost!!! Thanks for your number. I won't use it till I'm setting off on Wednesday. Sorry I can't give you mine yet. Im changing it. Network I've got at the moment is a waste of space! Cant wait to meet you both.

Your Cousin
Mickey.

Knowing that it was happening at last, Niamh had mixed feelings. On the one hand she couldn't wait to get it over with, on the other she was genuinely scared. She felt like the character must have done in a trashy romantic novel she had read as a teenager. "Propelled by a need to know, excited, and fearful turn and turnabout, Miranda hurtled towards her fate." With a growing sense of apprehension she went upstairs to pack.

Max was incandescent. Niamh held the phone a foot from her ear.

'There's no need to shout, Max,' she said, trying hard to keep her own voice down, conscious that people on the seats either side were staring. Even the man in uniform at the gate had stopped talking to the cabin crew, and was staring at her.

'There's every need,' Max bellowed. 'I've got egg all over my face here. How the hell did you give my man the slip?'

'Is that all you're concerned about?' she asked, worried that it might be.

'Of course it's not! You ring from the airport to inform me that you're about to board a plane for England, to meet a guy we both know wants to kill you. How the hell am I supposed to feel?'

'I'm sorry Max. But if I'd told you before, you'd have tried to stop me.'

'Damn right I would! And I'm still going to. If you think I'm going to let someone I care about commit suicide, you've got another think coming. You stay right there, I'm coming over.'

'I'm sorry Max,' she said. 'I'll be alright. I'll ring you when I've landed.' She ended the call before he had a chance to say any more, and just as the call came over the tannoy.

"Passengers travelling on British Airways flight 212, to Manchester England, via Heathrow, please make your way immediately to Gate 22, where we are about to board."

Niamh put her phone back in her bag, stood up, and joined the queue. "Someone I care for," she told herself. That's what he said. I only hope he cares enough to forgive me.

'You can't be serious Tom? Please tell me you're not.'

He had never seen Kate this angry before. 'I'm sorry,' he said. 'But I am. I can't see any other way round it.'

'You could wait for your manhunt to find him instead of staking yourself out like a sacrificial lamb.'

'It's hardly a manhunt. We don't have the resources for that. Besides, all the time we're looking, he's the one who's doing the hunting. Better to have him come to us, on our terms, on our territory.'

'Listen to yourself,' she told him. 'You sound like Rambo on a mission. "Heroes never die, they just reload." Rambo is make believe. You do know that don't you?'

'Sarcasm doesn't suit you,' he said. 'We do this kind of thing all the time. He won't get anywhere near us. Do you really think I'd let Niamh do this unless I was one hundred percent confident?'

'It's not her I'm worried about.' She stood up putting the sofa between them. 'And that's another thing. Telling her she could stay here. What were you thinking about?'

He held out his arms. 'Come on Kate. What else was I supposed to do? Book her into a hotel and make it easier for him?'

'I don't know. But not this. For God's sake Tom, our first home together. We've been here less than a week.'

'Surely you're not jealous? Of a woman neither of us has even met?'

For a moment he thought she was going to throw her laptop at him. Instead, she swore, and stormed into the bedroom.

The final leg from Heathrow up to Manchester was a revelation for Niamh. They were below what little cloud cover there was, and a patchwork of countryside - the fields and woods, the rivers, lakes and reservoirs - was laid out beneath her. Now she understood why back home was called New England. Except that here the towns seemed to run one into the other linked by the ubiquitous superhighways, snaking like arteries across the landscape. She had no idea that England was this crowded. Not that she hadn't done her research. She knew that the Manchester to which she was flying was almost the size of Boston, and over four times the size of her own city. With 452,000 people in the city proper, and four and a half million in the metropolitan area, it was the second largest urban zone in the UK, and the fourteenth most populated in Europe. And somewhere among all of those people, was a man who needed her dead.

Her case was packed. She stood by the door, checking in her handbag that she had everything she needed. Her anger had subsided. All that was left was cold, hard, reason.

'You don't have to do this Kate,' he told her. 'Please stay.'

'I think I do,' she said. 'And not for the reasons you think. If I was really jealous do you think I'd leave the two of you alone together?'

'I'm sorry,' he said. 'I shouldn't have said that.'

'No you shouldn't. Up until then I thought you knew that I trust you implicitly.'

'It was just the heat of the moment.'

'That's usually when we say what we really feel, rather than what other people want to hear.'

'Not this time it wasn't. It was stupid, but I was just goading you.'

She extended the handle on her case. 'Well it worked. But like I said, that's not why I'm going. I know I said that if you were determined to get yourself killed I didn't want to be there to see it. Well I'm sorry I said that.' She smiled thinly. 'Heat of the moment. The truth is I know you're good at what you do. I've been there remember? Seen it at first hand. So I know you'll be alright. But I'm just going to be in the way. A distraction. The last thing you need is having to worrying about me too.'

He wondered how he could ever have doubted her.

'You're right about that. And the last thing in the world I want to do is put you in harm's way again.'

'I'll have a great time,' she said. 'Staying with Gem for a few days will be like being students again. We can shop till we drop.'

He could tell it was false bravado. He took her in

his arms and gave her a big hug, ignoring the angle of her case biting into his thigh. 'Thank you,' he said. 'I know this is hard; it is for me too. But it'll soon be over. I promise.'

She reached up, and gave him the briefest of kisses. 'Just make sure it is.' She looked at her watch. 'Niamh will be landing shortly. You'd better go; me too.'

Their kiss was fuelled by serious apprehension.

Tom was late at Arrivals. As it turned out, he was still in plenty of time. Immigration took longer than either of them had bargained for. When Niamh came through the gate he was not the only person waiting. Despite the fact that they had never exchanged photographs of themselves, they recognised each other immediately. Their first embrace had been so natural. Like old friends. More like brother and sister he decided. The sister he had never known. Now her case was unpacked in the spare bedroom, and she was in the bathroom freshening up. The phone rang. It was Max Madera. He sounded even more anxious than the last time.

'Tom,' he said. Has Niamh arrived? She promised she was going to call me as soon as she landed.'

'She's right here with me,' Tom told him. 'Having a shower.' There was a momentary silence on the other end of the phone

'You've got the phone in the shower?' Max said. The humour was forced. Tom picked up on it straight away.

'It's all right Max,' he said. 'She's in the shower, I'm in the lounge.'

'Sure you are. Don't suppose Kate would approve of mixed showers. 'He laughed to show how he was cool with it.

'Kate's not here. We thought it safer that she was out of the firing line.'

The laughter tailed off. 'The two of you are alone in the apartment? For God sake Tom what are you thinking of. At least get yourself some back up in there.'

'I've got the entrances covered,' he said. 'And we'll have back up from the second we leave the apartment block. You don't need to worry Max, nothing is going to happen to Niamh, or to me.'

'I hope to hell you're right, because checking on Niamh wasn't the only reason I called you. There was something on the news today that you need to know about. Something that ups the ante on this.'

There was no mistaking the edge to his voice.

'I'm listening.'

'It was on the TV early evening news...just before I called you. John James Clark passed away an hour ago, in his sleep.'

Tom's brain was working overtime.

'Tom, did you hear what I just said?'

'Yes Max...JJC is dead.'

'You know what that means?'

'Peter Cayton, or Roberts, or whatever he's calling himself right now is going to want to get this over with sooner rather than later.'

'Sooner than that,' Max reminded him. 'Have you forgotten that stuff Niamh's lawyer... Bill Fitzgerald dug up?'

'The 120 hour rule!'

'Exactly. And by my reckoning, taking the time difference between the two of us into account, there are just one hundred an thirteen hours remaining!'

'Are there usually that many policemen with dogs and guns at Manchester Airport,' Niamh asked as she walked into the lounge. 'Or was it just for my benefit?'

Tom replaced the phone, and looked up. She was drying her hair with a towel. Her skin was pink, and glowing, against the stark white of Kate's bathrobe – a size too small – hugging her figure in a way he would under normal circumstances have thought incredibly sexy.

'I think you'd better sit down,' he said.

26

Exhausted from the journey, and desperate to catch up on six lost hours, Niamh had taken a sleeping pill, and slept like a log. Tom was making a mug of coffee to take into her when the phone rang. It was Kate.

'Tom,' she began. 'I thought I'd ring to see if Niamh arrived safely...and if you're OK.'

'She got in more or less on time,' he told her. 'Had a little supper, took a pill, and went straight to bed. She's still fast asleep, if the snoring is anything to go by. I'm just making a coffee to see if I can wake her up.'

'What are your plans for today...or shouldn't I ask?'

He hesitated for a moment, wondering how much to tell her. As a Home Office profiler intimately connected with his work, it would be pointless trying to pull the wool over her eyes.

'The meeting's on for later this morning,' he said. 'I made all the arrangements at our end yesterday. I couldn't risk taking Niamh into Longsight with me in case he's already up here, and watching us.'

'You will let me know as soon as it's over won't you? There's no way I'm going to able to concentrate on my work till I know you're safe.'

'Of course I will. Kate. Everything will be fine.'

'Make sure it is,' she said. 'I don't know what I'd do if I lost you.'

Now she was beginning to shake his confidence. 'Nobody's losing anybody,' he said. 'Look, I've got to go. Speak to you later I promise.'

'I love you.'

'I love you too.'

He listened for the sound of her breath, and willed her to terminate the call. When it was clear she wasn't going to he whispered 'I love you Kate.' And ended it himself.

Penned between the Motorway, a towering indoor ski slope complete with alpine village, and the first Industrial Park in the world, the Trafford Centre is in every sense a temple to mammon. Tom locked the car. They walked together between the fountains towards the entrance. A pair of white marble lions on granite blocks stood either side of soaring sandstone pillars supporting a portico guarded by mythical beasts. Four angels with golden garlands, and trumpets, proclaimed the new Millennium before a massive dome of emerald glass.

'I had no idea,' Niamh said.

'What about?'

'How big it would be. That you had malls like this.'

'Twenty screen cinema, sixty restaurants and bars, hundreds of stores. Two miles of retail heaven or hell, depending on your point of view. There's even a police station. With any luck, you'll get to see it when we charge him. Come on, I'll show you the Food Hall.'

'This is amazing,' she said. 'Like something that belongs in Vegas.'

The Hall had been designed to simulate the top
two decks of a cross-Atlantic liner. Where the bows
would have been a massive screen presented music
videos for the hundreds of diners at tables set out
around the central ornamental swimming pool. Puffy
white clouds scudded across the blue curved ceiling.

'I think that's the general idea,' he told her.
'Shopping as a leisure pursuit. Shame about the
credit crunch.'

She stared at the crowds of people swarming like
ants up the stairs, and escalators. 'It doesn't seem to
have stopped people from coming.'

'No different to gambling. Just another form of
addiction,' he said.

Around the sides she counted more than a dozen
restaurants and food outlets: American, Chinese,
Indian, Spanish, Mexican, French, and Italian among
them. Tom followed her gaze.

'There are another twenty upstairs. One for every
one of the cinema screens on the poop deck.'

'You were right,' she said. 'He's chosen well. I don't
think I could spot him among all these folk. Not until
he was right on top of us.'

'And hopefully he can't spot my people either,'
Tom reminded her. 'But I thought we agreed not to
talk about it.'

'In case he can …you know…' she whispered the
words. '…lip read.'

'And if he can,' Tom pointed out. 'Whispering isn't
going to help. It'll just be more obvious. Come on,
we're early. Let's take a walk. As though I'm showing
you around.'

She grinned at him. 'You are.'

Tom smiled back. 'There you go then. We don't even have to pretend.'

'So far, so good.'

Gordon Holmes took the cap off his Starbuck's coffee, gave the liquid a blow, and replaced it. 'How's your smoothie, blue eyes?'

Joanne Stuart grimaced 'Smoother than you, that's for sure. And just in case you haven't noticed my eyes are brown.'

'Hazel I think you'll find,' he replied triumphantly.

They were leaning over the railings beside the Indigo's Juice Company stall. To all appearances they were colleagues. Lovers at a push. Given the age difference, more likely adulterers. Jo hoped none her of friends had decided to pop in over their lunch break to do a spot of shopping.

'If he's here we'll get him.' Gordon said, his lips pressed hard against the cardboard cup to mask them.

There were a dozen officers from the Tactical Aid Team scattered around this floor and on the one below that held the Great Hall. DS Carter and DI Sarah Weston were with the in-house security team studying the banks of monitors covering every inch of the malls, and other open spaces. On the desks in front of them were blow ups of Peter Roberts' passport photograph. The similarity to Tom had been remarked on by everyone. Age, colouring, hairline, and bone structure. He wasn't quite a doppelganger, but near enough. 'Fourth cousins... just goes to show the power of genes.' Ged, the office manager, had remarked sagely when she had seen it.

'Do you think the stab vest Niamh is wearing was a mistake?' Jo asked.

Gordon watched through the side of his eyes as Tom and Niamh strolled beneath them, past the Namco Station techno bowling centre, and out of sight in the direction of Pizza Hut. 'No, just looks like she's got a fleece under her anorak,' he said.

'This one's got more than a fleece under his sweat shirt,' said Jo, digging him in the ribs, and nodding towards the nearest metal stairway. A man of indeterminate age, weighing all of twenty stone, was hauling himself breathlessly upwards, one painful step at a time. He wore a plain, white, long sleeved sweatshirt tucked into a pair of outsized track suit bottoms. They could see the sweat trickling from beneath his blue baseball cap, glistening momentarily on the short ginger hairs on his neck, before adding to the dark damp stain creeping across his back and chest. An impatient queue had already built up behind him.

'Makes you wonder why he didn't take the escalator.' Gordon said, secretly pleased that this vision of corpulence put his own spreading waistline into some kind of perspective.

'Perhaps he needs the exercise,' said Jo, setting them both off laughing. They turned away as he reached the top of the steps, and headed painfully in their direction.

'A fiver says he doesn't stop at the smoothie bar,' Gordon proposed.

'You can forget that,' muttered Jo. 'But I bet you a fiver he does stop at Muffin Break.'

They heard him wheeze past them. When they looked over their shoulders, his back was towards them. He had come to a halt just ten yards away, in front of the Muffin Break stand. They watched as he attempted to extricate his wallet from the mound of flesh pressing against his rear trouser pocket.

'That makes us quits,' said Gordon.

'They're back,' said Jo nudging him, 'Centre right, going into Costa Coffee. Must have done a complete circuit.'

Gordon looked at his watch. 'Fifteen minutes to go,' he said, draining his coffee.'

'It's no good Niamh. He's not coming,' Tom told her. 'We've been standing here for almost an hour. He hasn't rung you. And he didn't send you his phone number like he promised.'

'You were right then,' she said. 'He must have been using it to check us out. Does him not turning up mean that he's decided we were setting him up?'

'God knows. It's just as likely he got cold feet, and never set off.'

'He doesn't seem like the kind of person who would get cold feet. First Miriam, then Oonah, and Matty and Billy.'

'You're right,' he said. 'He doesn't. But there's no point in hanging around here any longer. Let's go and have some lunch. I don't know about you, but I'm famished.'

She smiled, and linked her arm though his. 'So am I. I could eat a horse.'

Tom looked around the Food Hall. 'I don't think they do horse. At least, not that they're telling.'

They were in Cathay Dim Sum when Niamh's

phone rang. Half of the watchers had been stood down. DS Stuart and DI Holmes were across the way in Tampopo, watching the entrance over bowls of chicken and seafood ramen.

'It's from him,' she said. 'A text.'

'What does it say?'

Niamh read it through then passed him her cell phone.

'See for yourself.'

Niamh So Sory!!!! U wont bleve it. Broke dwn on M42. Culdnt get a signal. AA toing me home. Culd try train 2morrow if yaw still there. Mickey.

'He's right. I don't believe it,' Tom said. 'The man from the AA would have lent him his phone. Or they could have stopped at a service area, and used a public phone.'

'So what do you think?' Niamh asked.

Tom had a casual glance around the restaurant, as though hoping to catch a waiter's eye. When he was sure they were not being watched – other than by the two guys from the TAG team in the corner nearest the door – he turned to face her. 'He hasn't cried off. He wanted to make sure that you'd really come over here, and to get us both together. He knows this place is too public to make a move, but a great place to hide among the crowds. So whether he spotted our people or not, I think he's just biding his time. He's just hoping to find the right place...the right moment.'

'If he's learnt that John James is dead, then he'll know he hasn't got a lot of time to bide,' she reminded him.

Tom shook his head. 'He might not. It hasn't made

the news here yet. By the time it does, it may be too late for him to act on it. To be honest, I hope he does know. The less time he has to plan, the more chance he's going to slip up.'

Niamh found that less than reassuring. Until now, despite the stab vest, she had been sure that everything was under control. 'Chance,' she said, nervously. 'Is that what it's going to come down to? Maybe you'd better tell me what the odds are, then I'll know how hard to pray.'

He waited until he got into the bathroom before he removed the wadding from the inside of each cheek. There were great patches of damp across the front and back of his sweat shirt, and the arm pits were sodden. The cloth clung like a limpet as he struggled to extricate himself. The fat suit proved easier to divest. He pushed it to one side with his feet, took off his tee shirt and pants, wrung them out over the sink, and left them there while he climbed into the shower cubicle.

The shock of the pinprick jets of ice cold water was rapidly offset by the speed with which his body temperature returned to normal. He turned the temperature up a little, and began to lather himself with body wash. All in all, he decided, it had been satisfactory. As far as he could tell the disguise had worked a treat. If it had been a trap, and he had found nothing to suggest that it was, then he would surely have been picked up. And he wasn't. Nor was he followed back to the apartments. He was as sure of that as anyone could be.

For that last half hour he had bought himself one

of Nando's famous platters to share. A whole peri peri chicken, with a large portion of chips, and a large coleslaw, on the side; it would have been ambitious even without the wadding to contend with. He had taken it to one of the tables at the edge of the Hall, well back, facing away from the screen. The last thing he wanted was to be seen watching them. Instead, from beneath the rim of his baseball cap, he had casually scanned the areas from which others might be watching. The fact that he spotted none meant nothing. The management made much of the CCTV coverage on their web site, and in their promotional material. As much, he suspected, to deter gangs of shoplifters and pickpockets, as to keep the crowds flowing smoothly. The nearest he got to looking directly at Niamh and Tom was out of the corner of his eye as he glanced up at Leona *Bleeding Love* all over the big screen.

He switched off the shower, and stepped down onto the bathroom floor. The fat suit lay crumpled in the corner like a flayed pig. Brilliant value, he told himself as he towelled dry. Just fifty pounds on the internet, plus four pounds postage. He took his underwear out of the sink, and dropped it in the black bin bag. No point in washing it. Plenty more where they came from. And in future, well, it would not be just the pants that were disposable. A brand new life…brand new everything. He took the bottle of dye from the bathroom cabinet, and read the instructions. Before he unscrewed the top he set it down, leaned over the hand bowl, and wiped the condensation from the mirror. Then he separated the lids of one eye with the finger and thumb of his left hand, and used the finger and thumb of his right hand to locate and remove the coloured contact lens. He smiled at himself in the mirror. One eye brown, one eye green. Now wouldn't that confuse them? He discarded the lens in the bowl, and started on the other eye.

DS Gates was adamant.

'I'm Gold Commander,' she said. 'You two stay in that apartment. Let him come to you. We've tried it the other way, and it didn't work.'

'We don't know that,' Tom replied. 'Only that if he was there, then we didn't spot him'

'But that was the whole point! To catch him. That's the only way we can be sure to keep you both safe. So there's no discussion on this one. Have you got that?'

He pictured her standing in the control room, surrounded by other officers, her message for their benefit as much as his own. She was right of course. Not that it made it any easier to eat humble pie. He took a deep breath. 'Yes Ma'am.'

'Good. Keep your radio on. And don't take any unnecessary risks.'

'Yes Ma'am and no Ma'am.'

This time her she lowered her voice so that he could hardly hear her. Even so her words were charged with menace. 'This is not the time to be taking the piss Detective Inspector,' she said.

'No Ma'am,' he said. 'By the way,' he added, knowing that she was willing him to say it. 'It's Detective Chief Inspector.'

'Not for long,' she hissed. 'Not if you're going to keep this up.'

'I wish there were a few more cars parked out

320

there,' Joanne Stuart said. 'I reckon we stand out like a blind cobbler's thumb.'

Gordon Holmes shook his head. 'No, we're fine here, between this van, and that people carrier. Providing you don't decide to take a walk, the only people who are going to know we're here are ones in the apartments straight ahead of us.'

'Or if they come right past us to, or from, the entrance.'

'Well if he does, we'll just jump out and nab him. And if he's already in one of those apartments, there's not a lot we could do about it anyway.

'Not much chance of that is there? We've already checked out the occupants.'

'Unless last night he picked up a bird that lives in one of them, went back to her place, and convinced her to let him stay on. That's what I'd do.'

'I bet you would, you randy beggar.'

'It's Detective Inspector to you,' Gordon reminded her.

He sat by the window. The lights in the apartment were off. He hardly noticed that his backside ached. His eyes had been focused on the entrance for almost three hours. Plenty of comings and goings, but neither of them had stirred. Behind him the doors of the fitted wardrobe were open. Inside on the hangers, hung an anorak, two jackets, two pairs of chinos, and three pairs of jeans, one black, two blue. On the shelves, pullovers and sweat shirts were neatly stacked. A brown hooded sweat shirt from Fat Face lay on the bed. Beside it was a pair of brown Ecco shoes, and two pairs of trainers, one brown, one black. It had taken over a fortnight of careful observation to put it all together. Bluetacked to the inside of the wardrobe – beside the mirror, was a head and shoulders photo of Tom Caton. The one he had used to style his hair. On the lap top, the video of Tom and Kate at Daisy Nook that he had used to perfect his gait. He was as ready as he could be. Now all he needed was a little luck.

27

'Do you think we should get someone to clear those hoodies off the children's play area?' Joanne Stuart wondered. 'They're getting on my nerves. Can't be doing much for the residents either. Who'd want to shell out a two hundred thousand for a posh apartment, and then have this little lot hanging around your front door?'

'Two hundred thousand? And the rest.' Gordon Holmes unscrewed the top of the flask. 'I blame the supermarket. Someone's selling them booze. They're like cockroaches, back and forth, back and forth.' He poured himself a coffee. 'D'you want one Jo?'

She shook her head. 'No thanks. What d'you reckon then? Shall I ask control to send a couple of Community Support Officers to move them on?'

'I don't think DS Gates would thank us for bothering her over them. If he is watching, having a couple of CSO's turn up might just scare him off. Best to let them be.' He lifted the cup to his lips.

Jo suddenly sat up. 'Hang on,' she said. There goes the Boss.' Her elbow caught Gordon's arm. Hot coffee sloshed over the rim of the cup scalding his lip, and spilling into his lap.

'Christ!' He yelped. He put the cup down in the floor well, searched frantically for his handkerchief, and began to mop his trousers.

Sorry Boss,' she said, her eyes firmly fixed on Tom Caton's retreating back.

When Holmes looked up the DCI had disappeared. 'Are you sure it was him?'

'No question. He came out of the entrance, and turned left.'

'What the hell's he's doing?'

'Popping down to the shops I suppose. Maybe they ran out of something. It's not as though he's really leaving the apartments is it? Not with the supermarket built into the ground floor.'

'We better let control know though,' Gordon said, mopping furiously. 'Just in case.'

She reached into the glove compartment, took out a bottle of water, unscrewed the top, and handed it to him. 'Here, you'd better try this,' she said.

He grabbed it, poured some into his mouth, and some onto his trousers.

'Hang on,' she said, 'He's back. Blimey, that was quick. I wonder what he's got in the bag.'

Niamh heard the buzzer, and went to the video phone. Tom was standing in the corridor, his back towards her - looking towards the lifts. 'Tom?'

You're not going to believe this,' he said, half turning, then looking back again.' 'I forgot my wallet.'

She pressed the door release, and walked down the hallway to meet him. The door opened, and he entered. Her hand flew to her mouth. The constriction in her throat choked off the scream.

'Hello Niamh,' he said, pushing the door closed behind him.

'Here come DI Weston, and DS Carter,' Joanne Stuart said, pointing towards the playground. 'Good idea of Superintendent Gates...having us pair up like this.'

'Star crossed lovers, I think not.' Holmes muttered.

'Oh I don't know, he could always be her toy boy.'

Gordon chuckled. 'Don't let them hear you saying that. I don't reckon either of them would thank you.'

Nick Carter, several inches shorter than DI Weston had his arm around her waist. Her head was on his shoulder as they ambled along. Suddenly they stopped and half turned towards the apartment block behind them. Kate Weston raised her arm towards her chest.

Gordon Holmes' radio burst into life.

'Juliet, to Paris. I thought you said Hamlet had already returned. Over.'

Holmes and Carter stared at each. Gordon grabbed his radio. 'He did, five minutes ago. Over.'

'So how come he's here right now?'

Stuart and Holmes craned their heads forward in time to see their boss reach the entrance, and go inside.

'That's impossible,' Gordon exclaimed. 'It can't be him.'

'Well it looked like him,' said Jo, equally incredulous. 'But it can't be can it? And if it is...well that means...'

'Bloody hell!' Gordon shouted, bursting into action. 'We've got to warn him. 'Try to ring him. Use his phone. And for Christ sake tell Control.'

He was out of the car and running, shouting to Kate and Nick to join him. Together they burst into the reception area. It was empty. One of the lifts was climbing, already at the fifteenth floor. Gordon ran to the second lift, and pressed the button. It was on the fourteenth floor, beginning its descent.

'We're too late.' Nick Carter pointed to the number on the screen above the other lift. It had stopped on the nineteenth floor.

DI Weston slammed her hand against the lift door. 'Shit! What the hell are we going to do now?' Their radios crackled simultaneously.

'Juliet…Paris…this is Gold. Report your situation please. Report your situation…'

'I got Chinese,' Tom called out, as he closed the door behind him 'I hope that's alright?'

As he walked down the empty hallway, his phone began to ring. In the doorway to the lounge he shifted the carrier bag to his left hand, and took the mobile from his pocket.

'I'll take that thank you.'

Tom looked up. His hands frozen by his sides. Niamh was standing at the angle where the kitchen area began. Beside her stood a man more or less his own age, height, weight, and colouring. He wore identical clothes to his own, black jeans, his favourite Fat Face hoodie, and black trainers. It was like looking in the mirror. Except that his alter ego was holding a gun to the base of Niamh's head. Tom cancelled the call, and held out his phone, inviting him to come and get it.

'I don't think so,' the man said smiling grimly. 'Switch it off, place it on the floor, and kick it over here.'

'It is off.' Tom told him. He did as he had been instructed. It clattered against the side of the dividing wall, and spun off towards the patio windows. 'Are you alright Niamh?' he asked. It was a stupid question. The only one he could think of. She nodded and tried to smile.

'Yes. I'm alright,' she said. The tremble in her voice belied her words.

'And if you want it to stay that way, just do as you're told,' the man said. 'Nothing more, nothing less. Exactly what I tell you.'

'May I put this down?' Tom held up the carrier bag.

'On the floor. Then step away from it.'

'It's going to make a mess of the floor,' Tom said, drawing on his training as a negotiator, trying to sound as relaxed and matter of fact as possible.

'I don't think that's going to matter do you?' the man said. 'Just do what I say…remember? It's not difficult, but it's really important. Ask Niamh.' He dug the barrel of the gun harder into her neck, causing her to gasp.

Resisting the temptation to let fly, Tom gritted his teeth, and lowered the bag to the floor, his mind racing.

'Very good,' the man said. 'Now walk slowly over to balcony windows, and open them.'

Tom remained where he was. 'You don't have to do this Peter, 'he said calmly. 'There will be more than enough money to go round. You do know that don't you?'

The pressure eased on Niamh's neck as Peter Cayton registered what Tom was saying. He was unable to mask his surprise. 'So you know who I am?'

Tom nodded. 'Peter Cayton, formerly Peter

Roberts. We've been expecting you Peter.'

'And you know about Clark?'

'About his billions? Yes.'

Peter Cayton's eyes narrowed. 'And that he's dead?'

'That too.'

The gun was hard against Niamh's neck once more. 'So you know why I'm here?'

'We know about Miriam, and Oonah, Matty and Billy,' Tom said. 'None of that was necessary and neither is this. Put the gun down Peter, and let Niamh go.'

'Why should I?'

'Because the wharf is surrounded. That phone call you wouldn't let me take? That will have been Superintendent Gates, trying to alert me to the fact that you are here. Any minute now the phone will ring in this apartment. It will be the Force negotiator for you. I told you we were expecting you.'

Tom could see indecision written all over his face. Then it cleared.

'So why didn't they stop me before I entered the Apartment block?' he said, triumphantly.

Tom had been wondering the same thing himself. 'Presumably because your disguise was just too good,' he said. 'I have to congratulate you on that.'

Peter Cayton stood there for a moment struggling to discount the flattery, and weigh the cold hard logic against his instinct that he could still pull it off. Instinct won. He looped his left arm around Niamh's neck, and shifted the gun so that it pointed at her right temple. 'I gave you an instruction,' he said. 'Do it. Go to the balcony windows, open them, step outside, and move to the furthest corner.'

Tom stayed where he was.

'Do it now,' Cayton said. 'Or I'll shoot her, and then you.'

Tom walked across to the windows, slid them back, and stepped onto the balcony. Peter Cayton pulled Niamh across to the balcony, placed his left hand in the small of her back, and shoved her hard into Tom's open arms. Then he pulled the curtain across, stepped outside, and slid the windows closed behind him. Inside the apartment the phone began to ring.

28

Tom held Niamh tight. He had no idea whether she was shivering because she was in shock, or if it was the cool wind whistling through her short sleeved blouse. Peter Cayton stood in shadow in the corner of the balcony, the metal table between them, the gun held steadily in both hands. Tom had already calculated the risk of moving Niamh to the side, and launching himself at their captor. Ten per cent or less, he'd decided, and likely to cause him to shoot whether he intended to or not. In the distance he could hear the hum of the city centre traffic, and the occasional wail of a siren that whooped for a while, then faded away as it passed out of range.

High overhead planes were circling as they waited to come into land at the airport just ten miles to the south. There was the faint chatter of a helicopter heading away in the direction of North Manchester Hospital. It was cold and lonely up here. He knew that there would be only limited line of sight to this balcony from any of the surrounding buildings. Not until the ones on the other side of the canal had been completed. In any case, Roberts – as he preferred to call him in his mind – had been clever. He made a poor target standing there in the dark. Tom cursed himself for his stupidity, for his pride, above all for underestimating this man. It took all of his concentration to drag himself away from the slide into self-recrimination, and to draw on his training. To his surprise, Niamh beat him to it.

'Why are you doing this Peter?' she asked.

'I'd have thought that was obvious,' he said out of the darkness.

'No, not just this…all of it. Why kill all of those people. Your own flesh and blood?'

At first, when he didn't reply, Tom feared they had lost him. When he finally spoke his voice had a different edge to it. Not so much harder, as bitter.

'Flesh and blood?' he said. 'I'll tell you about flesh and blood. How would you like to have been brought up by a father who could barely bring himself to speak to you, let alone play with you? Who drank himself senseless most weekends? Who had no one else to take his anger out on? As I got older, I told myself it was grief at the loss of his wife, my mother. That way I could handle it. It was only when he finally found the courage to hang himself that I discovered the truth. That his own father had been plagued all his life by the belief that he had been deserted by his father and by his mother.' He went silent.

'We know that your great grandfather died a hero…at Mafeking.' Niamh said.

'I bet you don't know that the woman he got pregnant, my great grandmother, went into service with a respected Member of Parliament?' he said.

'No we didn't,' she replied.

'Or that he expected "extra services." That he raped and abused her? That when she tried to complain she was told that if she continued with her wicked accusations her son would be thrown out of the orphanage?'

'No we didn't.'

'Well, that's exactly what happened. When the MP lost his constituency he took her back with him to the North East, where she disappeared.'

It was Niamh's turn to go silent.

'You can use your own imagination as to what might have happened. I certainly have, and I've no doubt my grandfather and father did before me.'

'How did you find all this out?' Tom asked, picking up the thread, keeping the conversation going.

'I didn't. My grandfather did. When he got out of the workhouse he was given a cardboard box his mother had left behind. In it were letters from his father to her. Love letters. Promising to marry her...promising that he would look after the baby. He tried to track her down, but it was too late. He wrote it all down in a letter to his own son, and put it in the box for him to read when he died. He thought he was doing him a favour.'

His laugh was hollow, and deeply sad.

'Some favour.'

'Were you ever in the forces?' Tom asked.

'What, you think it's in the blood? Following in my great grandfather's footsteps?'

'No, I just wondered. The way you've planned all this...it's like a military operation.'

'You're good...very good.'

He paused as though deciding whether to reply.

'I did seven years in the Army. So just in case you were wondering, I do know how to use this.' He waved the gun in the half shadow. 'I joined up straight from school...just missed out on the Falklands War. It was the only way I could get away from home...from him.'

'What did you do after that?'

'Drifted from job to job...driving mostly, some security work. I was a trader for while in the City. Had a Porsche, nice house down by the River, everything. When the markets crashed I was one of the casualties. More ways than one. The wife left. She said because of my mood swings. I never believed that. She couldn't live without the money.'

'What did you do then?' Niamh asked.

'Sold the Porsche, and the house. Got a flat. That left me enough to live on comfortably for a while. Then my father died. I hadn't seen him in over twenty years. Among his papers was my Grandfather's letter. So I began to research the family tree, and came across your web site Niamh.' They saw him shift his position, transfer his weight against his left shoulder, and lean on the wall. 'So you see,' he said. 'You only have yourself to blame.'

'If you've done your homework as well as it seems you have,' Tom said. 'Then you'll know that the concept of intestacy is a lot less important than most people realise. Under civil law a will is far less important. That means that the doctrine of legitime – or forced share - gives a deceased person's relatives automatic title, to a large part of the estate, if not all of it, regardless of the deceased person's attempt to reverse that through a legacy.' He wondered if Peter Cayton understood what he was talking about. He wasn't that sure himself.

'So what?'

'It means that even if there is a will, and even if you go to prison. You can still inherit a share of John James Clark's estate.'

'I don't intend to go to prison.'

'So far you've been careful. There's no real evidence to connect you with any of the deaths. If you kill us, all that changes. By the time you get out, if ever, you'll be too old to enjoy any of it.'

There was silence while he thought about it.

'They'd charge me with threatening the two of you though?'

'True, and with using a gun to do it. That means a mandatory seven years. With good behaviour you could be out within four. Maybe less.'

'What if you're lying?'

'I'm not. Pick up the phone inside. They'll tell you the same.'

'I meant about there being no evidence. What if I had done it? If I had slipped up, and you weren't telling me about it? What would I get then?'

Unlike those desperate final minutes with Bojangles Tom could tell that this man was actually envisaging an alternative outcome. He knew that everything hung on this conversation. He had to be careful to tell enough of the truth, however unpalatable, or risk blowing it completely.

'In Ireland?' he said. 'For three premeditated murders? You would undoubtedly be given life. But that would be reviewed after seven years, with a view to release on parole. The typical person serving life in Ireland spends no more than twelve years in prison.' He hesitated, and then ploughed on. 'Of course, if the American's seek your extradition for the murder of

Miriam...' he felt Niamh's body tense beneath his hands...'

'They'll never be able to pin that on me.' Cayton said.

'You were in America at the time.'

'Researching my family tree. Whatever they think they've got, it'll be circumstantial. They won't be able to convict on that.'

'You're probably right. They might not even be able to extradite you.'

'So what would be my chances of parole?'

'It depends.'

'On what?'

'On how much remorse you showed.'

He shifted his weight again. 'I can do remorse.'

'And if you were to use your inheritance to support charitable organisations, that would go down well with the Parole Board.'

'All of it?'

'Not necessarily. Just enough to convince them you were serious....And if you agreed to undergo treatment...'

His voice was suddenly hostile again. 'Treatment, what do you mean, treatment?'

'Well I'm assuming that the balance of your mind must have been disturbed for you to commit those murders. To threaten us here, right now. That in itself would the basis for a plea of mitigation.'

'And a lighter sentence?'

'And if you co-operated, an earlier release date.'

In the silence they sensed a smile spreading across his face.

'But if you continue with this,' Tom pressed on.

'You won't have a hope in hell of any of that happening. My colleagues are probably out there in the corridor right now, trying to decide whether to break in, and take you down, or try to talk you into giving yourself up. Either way, what it comes down to is this; you have no way out...except in custody, or in a body bag.'

It was obvious that he was close to surrendering, but something was stopping him. Tom knew the questions that would be flashing through his mind. *What if this is all a con? What if there is nobody out there? What if there is and I've slipped up somewhere? Left enough evidence for them to put me away for good?* By laying down the gun he would be throwing away both his freedom, and the full inheritance. He moved out from the shadows, looked across at Tom, and their eyes met.

'You can't kid a kidder,' he said.

Tom felt Niamh begin to tremble in his arms.

'I don't believe you can do this Peter.' he said. 'Not like this. Up close. Looking into our eyes.'

'I think you'll find I can.' He shifted his weight evenly onto his feet and held the gun out in front of him. 'Niamh, get that chair, and move over to the railings,' he said. 'Then I want you to climb up on it.'

'It won't work Peter.' Tom said, 'If you shoot us here my people will hear you. You'll never get out of this apartment.'

'Who said anything about shooting? You're going to jump. A suicide pact. Neat isn't it?'

'And if we refuse?'

'Then I'll have to shoot you.'

'So it comes down to the same thing,' Tom said.

'They'll still hear you.'

'Hopefully not.' He extended his arm so that the gun protruded into the pool of moonlight. A silencer had been screwed onto the end of the barrel. 'So I'll tell you just one more time. Niamh, get that chair, move over to the railings. Then I want you to get up on it. At least this way you'll have a fighting chance.'

'Stay where you are Niamh,' Tom told her. 'And, if you're going to do it Peter...' he raised his voice, shouting the words. 'Do it now!'

'Are you serious?' Peter Cayton said .

'Do it now!' Tom repeated. Her fingers dug into his arm. 'Or put the gun down, while you still can,' Tom eased her hand away from his arm, and drew her behind him.

The noise that had been a distant chatter became a thunderous throbbing roar. Resplendent, in midnight blue and gold, India 9 swooped up and over the tip of the glass and steel shard that was the highest point of the building above them, and hovered miraculously, just four blades widths from the balcony. The airwaves thudded across the narrow space, assaulted their eardrums, and slammed them back against the wall. In the open doorway of the helicopter knelt a man in the black protective clothing, and peaked cap, of a firearms officer. The snub nose of his short-barrelled 9mm semi-automatic pointed straight at Peter Cayton's head as he cowered in the centre of the searchlight beam. The front mounted loudspeaker, designed to be heard above the noise of the helicopter boomed out.

'Armed Police. Drop Your Weapon. Do it now!

Without removing his hands from over his ears he opened his fingers, and let the weapon fall to the tiled floor of the balcony.

'Kick it away from you. Do it now.'

He sent it spinning. It ricoched off a leg of the patio table, and came to rest beside the aluminium planter at Tom's side.

'Get on your knees. Do it now.'

He bent one leg, and then the other, until he knelt there, his hands clamped to the sides of his head.

'Lie down, and put your arms out to your sides. Do it now!'

He used his elbows to support his torso as he lowered himself to the metal floor.

'Put your arms out to your side. And cross your legs. Do it now!'

He took his arms away from his ears, and slid them out sideways. He lay his head on one side, his eyes sought out his cousins huddled together in the opposite corner of balcony. He smiled a sickly smile and mouthed some words. Tom could have sworn that he was thanking them.

The patio door slid open, and the balcony filled with figures in black. Carter, Stuart, Holmes and Weston, crowded the lounge behind them.

'You guys sure know how to put on a good show,' said Detective Supervisor Lieutenant Max Madera as he pushed his way between them.

29

'Somewhat premature,' said Tom, as they waited for Henry Mayhew, the solicitor, to return.

'What was?' Niamh asked.

'His thanking me, if that's what he was doing.'

'Why's that?'

'Because I wasn't strictly truthful with him.'

'In relation to what?'

'To all of it. Not that I told any lies. It's just that I didn't tell him everything.'

'Omission then…rather than commission?'

'If you like.'

'How exactly?'

'Well, the part about a life sentence was true, as was the possibility of review after seven years. What I said about the average being twelve years was also true, but there are plenty doing thirty years, and more, without reprieve. There isn't a hope in hell that he will get parole…ever. Not for three premeditated murders, and a further two planned. Especially if it meant he would come out to enjoy his ill gotten gains.'

'What about the bit about the balance of his mind being disturbed?'

'That would mean he would spend the rest of his life in a psychiatric wing. In any case, my radio was on send the whole time. When they play the tape to the jury, it will back up everything we say. They'll know he was planning to con the court.'

'What about his share of the inheritance?'

'That was another omission. What your man Fitzgerald told Rob Thornton is that the State of New Hampshire takes the line that a share of an inheritance can be decreased on account of some very specific misconduct by the heir. In particular, one directly related to defrauding others of their rightful share. Especially, I would have thought, when it includes murdering them. In any case, the latest legislation over here means that the Serious and Organised Crime Agency can automatically recover any assets resulting from criminal activity.'

'So basically...what you're saying... he's screwed?'

'Tighter than the bolts on the Verrazano-Narrows Bridge.'

She stared at him in surprise. 'What do you know about the Verrazano Bridge?'

'That it links Staten Island, and Brooklyn, across The Narrows. That each of the towers has a million bolts, and three million rivets.'

She shook her head in disbelief. 'How would you know that?'

He grinned. 'I ran the New York City Marathon three years ago. That's where it started, on the bridge. There was a history of the bridge in the hand out literature in our goody bags.'

Mayhew entered the room and found them laughing like naughty children.

'I have the copies of the will for you,' he said, affecting a serious demeanour more appropriate to the occasion. 'I suggest that you read them at your leisure. They make interesting reading. In essence, the estate of your cousin John James Clark, after death tax rates staged at thirty seven percent and fifty five percent respectively, and sundry debts, came to two billion, seven hundred and fifty three million, and one hundred and seventy seven dollars. He left a sum of two hundred thousand dollars each to his long term nurse, and his factotum. He bequeathed twenty million dollars to the town of Listowel, in Count Kerry, in the Republic of Ireland, on the condition that it be used to set up The Caton Foundation for the Advancement of Gifted and Talented children in Kerry, with special provision for children from those families least well placed to meet their children's needs.

The residue of his estate – two billion, seven hundred and thirty two million, seven hundred and seventy seven dollars – he had already made arrangements for. It seems that shortly before he lapsed into a coma he signed the papers setting up a Trust with three primary aims: Firstly, to provide clinics across the United States to assist the recovery of people with gambling addiction, secondly to carry out research into gambling addiction, and thirdly, to develop a rigorous programme to educate children and young adults about the inherent dangers of gambling.'

'The Caton Foundation...not the Clark Foundation? Niamh noted.

'That's correct, the Caton Foundation.'

She turned to Tom. 'So he wanted to remember his roots, the humble beginnings from which his fortune had grown.'

'And to redress some of the damage that he did building up that fortune,' said Tom.

It left a hollow feeling in the pit of her stomach.

'So everything Peter did – killing Miriam and Oona, Matty and Billy - was completely pointless?' she said.

'It always was,' Mayhew said, holding up the file. 'If this will had not existed – as Peter Roberts erroneously assumed – each of the six cousins would have received approximately three hundred and twenty million pounds sterling. More than enough not to have to go around murdering all of his relatives. However, it is only a statement of his wishes. Under New Hampshire law you can still contest it. There is every chance that you could be awarded a sum of some kind – particularly in view of what you've both been through.'

They looked at each other, and shook their heads in unison.

'I've still got Miriam's house,' Niamh said. 'And this was never why I started to trace my roots.'

'And I've learned more about my family than I might otherwise have known.' Said Caton. 'And best of all, I've found a cousin I never knew I had'.

She gave him a dig. 'I'll think you'll find that I found you.'

They thanked Mayhew, took their copies of the will, and walked out of the office to the reception area, where Kate was waiting for them.

'Do I get a hug?' she asked.

Niamh opened her arms wide. 'Am I forgiven then?' she said.

'Whatever for?'

'For putting Tom's life at risk.'

Kate laughed. 'As he's proved several times before, he's perfectly capable of doing that all on his own. Even if you hadn't made contact, it's likely that Peter would have tracked you both down, and tried to eliminate you. So I ought to thank you for putting Tom in the picture, before he was in your cousin's sights.'

'What are you going to do now Niamh?' Tom asked.

'I'm selling up my apartment. That'll give me enough to live on while I have a go at doing what I always wanted to do.'

'Which is?'

'Write. I think I'll start by telling our story, if that's OK with you? Digging up the past, tracing your roots, reclusive billionaires, murder and mayhem. It's got best seller written all over it. And I know just the person back home to help me with it.'

'Max?'

'Exactly.'

'Go for it,' Tom told her. 'Just remember to send me a signed first edition.'

'Count on it,' she replied. 'How about you two, have you any plans?'

'Well,' he said. 'Now there are just you and I left, I thought that Kate and I had better get on with rebuilding the Caton dynasty.'

Niamh hugged Kate a second time. 'At least with you...' she said, '...there's a chance of breeding out our wayward genes!'

The Author

Formerly Principal Inspector of Schools for the City of Manchester, Head of the Manchester School Improvement Service, and Lead Network Facilitator for the National College of School Leadership, Bill has numerous publications to his name in the field of education. For four years he was also a programme consultant and panellist on the popular live Granada Television programme *Which Way*, presented by the iconic, and much missed, Tony Wilson. He has written six crime thriller novels to date – all of them based in and around the City of Manchester.

His first novel *The Cleansing* was short listed for the Long Barn Books Debut Novel Award.

A Trace of Blood, in manuscript, reached the semi-final of the Amazon Breakthrough Novel Award.

If you've enjoyed
A Trace Of Blood
Try the other novels in the series:
The Cleansing
The Head Case
The Tiger's Cave
A Fatal Intervention
Bluebell Hollow
Available through Booksellers and Amazon as paperbacks and Kindle EBooks

www.billrogers.co.uk www.catonbooks.com
THE CLEANSING
ISBN: 978 1 906645 61 8
Grosvenor House Publishing

The novel that first introduced DCI Tom Caton.
Christmas approaches. A killer dressed as a clown haunts
the streets of Manchester. For him the City's miraculous
regeneration had unacceptable
consequences. This is the reckoning. DCI Tom Caton
enlists the help of forensic profiler Kate Webb,
placing her in mortal danger. The trail leads from the site
of the old mass cholera graves, through Moss
Side, the Gay Village, the penthouse opulence of
canalside apartment blocks, and the bustling
Christmas Market, to the Victorian Gothic grandeur of the
Town Hall. Time is running out: For Tom, for Kate...and
for the City.

Short listed for the
Long Barn Books Debut Novel Award

THE HEAD CASE
ISBN: 978 1 9564220 0 2

Roger Standing CBE, Head of Harmony High
Academy, and the Prime Minister's Special Adviser for
Education, is dead. DCI Tom Caton is not short of
suspects. But if this is a simple mugging, then why is MI5
ransacking Standing's apartment, and disrupting the
investigation? And why are the widow and her son taking
the news so calmly?

SOMETHING IS ROTTEN IN THE CORRIDORS

OF POWER.
THE TIGER'S CAVE
ISBN: 978 0 9564220 1 9

A lorry full of Chinese illegal immigrants arrives in Hull. Twenty four hours later their bodies are discovered close to the M62 motorway; but a young man and a girl are missing, and still at risk.
Supported by the Serious and Organised Crime Agency, Caton must travel to China to pick up the trail. But he knows the solution is closer to home – in Manchester's Chinatown - and time is running out.

A FATAL INTERVENTION
ISBN: 978-0-9564220-3-3

A SUCCESSFUL BARRISTER
A WRONGFUL ACCUSATION
A MYSTERIOUS DISAPPEARANCE

It's the last thing Rob Thornton expects. When he finds his life turned upside down he sets out on the trail of Anjelita Covas, his accuser. Haunted by her tragic history and sudden disappearance Rob turns detective in London's underworld. A series of rhyming messages arrive, each signalling a murder. Rob must find Anjelita and face a dark truth.

DEEP BENEATH THE CITY OF MANCHESTER LIES
A HEART OF DARKNESS

BLUEBELL HOLLOW
ISBN: 978 0 9564220-2-6

DCI Tom Caton's world is rocked when he learns that he has a son by a former lover. Then the first of the bodies is discovered at the Cutacre Open Cast Mine. The victims appear to have addiction in common. Suspects include a Premiership footballer, a barrister, and just about everyone at the Oasis Rehab Clinic in leafy Cheshire. As Caton digs deeper his world begins to fall apart.

Staffordshire
Legends

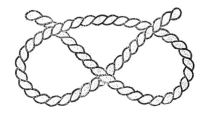

Alan Gibson

Dedicated to Robert (Bob) Harrison,
late of Crowtrees Farm, Whiston

Acknowledgments
The Staffordshire Advertiser and A. J. Standley - his work on transcribing
assize records and newspaper articles have proved invaluable.

A forged or 'flash' note.

CHURNET VALLEY BOOKS
6 Stanley Street, Leek, Staffordshire. ST13 5HG 01538 399033
thebookshopleek.co.uk
© Alan Gibson and Churnet Valley Books 2002
ISBN 1 897949 86 3

Foreword

Hanging Stone, Swythamley

Loxley Hall

Doveridge Hall

ONE
Robin Hood Revisited

The story of Robin Hood read to us at school was probably the Sir Walter Scott version of a story that had already been in existence for 700 years then. The story we are so familiar with revolves around Robin's adventures in Sherwood Forest, his prowess as an archer and his numerous battles with the Sheriff of Nottingham. He was the most loyal supporter of King Richard the Lionheart and the sworn enemy of King John.

This is all very well until you look a little more carefully into the historical and geographical background of Nottingham's favourite son. Simply look around and note the various place names that relate to Robin Hood locally. His name crops up in the most unusual settings like Uttoxeter, Loxley and Doveridge. An old book on the history of Uttoxeter refers to the hamlet of Loxley about two miles to the west of the town. But the inference by some that Loxley is the place of Robin's birth does not stand up well to scrutiny even if the suggestion is sufficient enough to create much interest.

Even more interesting is the fact that the Kynnersleys of Loxley Hall had in their possession 'Robin Hood's Horn'. The Horn apparently originally belonged to the Ferriers family of Chartley. The horn bears the initials R. H. plus three horseshoes which obviously relate to the De Ferriers who came over with William the Conqueror and were employed as farriers.

A more likely explanation for the horn's existence may lie a few miles away at Abbots Bromley where the annual horn dance celebrates the story of Robin Hood. In this case the horns are the antlers of deer but Robin's hunting horn would be well placed in such a setting.

The Doveridge connection is even more obscure although the substance of the claim is more evident. A reference to Doveridge occurs in rhyme form and is probably taken from *The Vision of Piers Plowman* written by William Langland in 1377.

This battle was fought near Tutbury town when the bagpipes baited the bull.
I am King of the fiddlers and swear tis the truth, and call him, that doubts it a gull.
For I saw them fighting and fiddled a while, and Clorinda sang Hey, derry down.
The bumpkins are beaten, put up thy sword Bob, and now lets dance into town.
Before we came in we heard a strange shouting, and all that were in looked madly,
and some were a black bull, some dancing a morrice, and some singing Arther a Bradley.

Chartley Hall (Plott's *Natural History of Staffordshire* 1686)

A mystery play in the Middle Ages much as would be seen at the Tutbury Feast.

And then we saw Thomas our justice's clerk, and Mary, to whom he was kind,
and Tom rode before her and called Mary madam, and kissed her full sweetly behind.
And so may your worship - But we went to dinner with Thomas and Mary and Nan.
They all drank a health to Clorinda and told her Bold Robin was a fine man.
When dinner was ended, Sir Roger, the parson of Dubbridge, was sent for in haste.
He brought his mass book and bid them take hands, and he joined them in marriage full fast.
And then as Bold Robin and his sweet bride, went hand in hand to the sweet bower,
The birds sung with pleasure in merry Sherwood, and it was a most joyful hour.

The rhyme refers to the priest from Doveridge and to Robin's bride Clorinda. The reference is largely ignored by historians and remains something of an enigma. The most obvious conclusion may lie in the nature of the traditional revelry of the Tutbury Feast. Could our modern Carnival Queen be a descendant of Clorinda? Was Clorinda a pretty girl chosen to be Queen of the Tutbury Feast and was Robin chosen to be King for the day?

References to Robin Hood are not just part of local legend - such references are spread far and wide across the Country. Such names as Robin Hood Buttes, Robin Hoods Cave and Robin Hoods Well are to be found in various parts of the Country and offer no more proof of his whereabouts than the fact that Robin must have been remarkably well travelled to have visited even a small percentage of the places that bear his name.

Our search for the true home of Robin Hood has to take a more practical route. A look through archives, court records and the publications that record the scholarship of those who have made an in-depth study of the outlaw. Even then there is conflict of opinion. The one over-riding fact is that the exploits of Robin Hood took place not in Sherwood Forest but in Barndale Forest. To complicate matters further two Barndales appear, one to the north of Nottingham and one to the south.

The greater claim favours the forest of Barnsdale that covered an area in South Yorkshire between Doncaster and Ferrybridge, about fifty miles away from Nottingham. An early publication *The Guest of Robin Hood* set many of Robin's adventures in Yorkshire with reference to Watling Street, Sayles and Wentbridge. The Great North Road that ran through Barnsdale was referred to as Watling Street, although strictly speaking Watling Street was the road between London and North Wales. More precisely Sayles, or Salis, and Wentbridge are definite landmarks as is Kirklees which enters the story at the time of Robin's death. From the Gest, the following verse enforces the case as

Robin speaks to Little John;

> And walk up to Sayles
> And so to Watling Street
> And wait after some unknown guest
> Perchance you may them meet

Salis is now the name given to a plantation in the village of Wentbridge.

In other ballads Wentbridge is quoted as the scene where Robin encounters the potter in the story *Robin Hood and the Potter*. The name Sherwood does not emerge until the 15th century when ballads begin to mention Merry Sherwood. Local landmarks such as Robin Hood's Cave at Rainworth do not appear until 1700.

Two other factors also emerge that support Barnsdale. First there is the compelling suggestion that one Robert Hood of Wakefield married Matilda de Toothill. Matilda was the daughter of Hugh de Toothill, a widower who married a widow, Joan de Stayton. Elizabeth, the daughter of Joan, and Matilda became half sisters and so Elizabeth becomes Robert's sister-in-law when Matilda marries Robert. This relationship becomes more intriguing when Elizabeth eventually becomes the Prioress of Kirklees Monastery and later betrays Robin at the behest of her lover, Sir Roger of Doncaster.

The story now turns to the Lancaster revolt. Thomas, Earl of Lancaster, petitioned the King (Edward II) to enact reforms to aid his tenants who were suffering starvation after a series of crop failures. When the King reneged on his promise of support, Lancaster mounted a rebellion in March 1322. In the event the rebellion was crushed and Lancaster's army routed. Many of his followers, not daring to return to their native villages, fled to the forests and became outlaws. It is thought, but without proof positive, that Robert Hood was one of the Lancastrian men that took refuge in the forest.

He was later joined by Matilda. The names Robin and Marion, whether nicknames or otherwise, became common in legend and Robert and Matilda disappeared from the local scene.

If the above were the case then the traditional theme where Robin meets Richard the Lionheart is not possible, simply because of relevant dates. Edward II, the great law-maker ruled from 1307 to 1327, the courageous Richard I died in 1199 over a hundred years before.

The second salient point surrounds the use of the longbow and Robin's expertise as an archer. The longbow was simply not used during the reign of

King Richard and King John. It was not until 1282 that the longbow gained popularity and came into common use.

It is also worth noting that the archives' office in Nottingham has no record of Robin Hood or any documents indicating the involvement of the sheriff with outlaws during the reign of King Richard and King John. In reality, and if we are to follow the research, it seems likely that the period of Robin Hood's tenure would be from 1282 until 1350 and that the reigning monarchs were Edward II and III.

These dates coincide with the visit to Nottingham of Edward II in 1323. The sheriff at that time was Sir Henry de Faucumberg who had been granted lands previously owned by Lancastrians who were now outlaws. The fact that Henry was a follower of the King and was also in possession of unwarranted estates would almost certainly have caused anger and reaction. It is also a fact that Henry had at one time resided in the Wakefield area.

As well as being Sheriff of Nottingham he was also Sheriff of Yorkshire and would have known the Barnsdale area well. Such was his power that he also held positions of authority in Derbyshire, Staffordshire and Shropshire and part of his remit was to obtain for the King any Lancastrian land available and to rid the countryside of villains and outlaws who stood in his way. An obvious contender for the position of Robin's enemy for ballad writers and playwrites.

The story of Robin Hood's association with the Yorkshire forest of Barnsdale is almost complete except for his demise at the Priory of Kirklees to where we will return. However, before taking the easy option of accepting Wakefield, Doncaster and Barnsdale as the scenes of Robin's exploits we must, in fairness, consider the research of those who suggest otherwise.

The Barnsdale that lies to the south of Nottingham covers an area of Rutland now known as Rutland Water and lies between Oakham and Stamford. Not only is the area littered with place names relating to Robin Hood but the Great North Road also skirts the area. In the 12th century the forest of Barnsdale became a Royal hunting ground and one of the notables who served the King was the Earl of Huntingdon. This, of course, fits very well with Robin's allegiance to King Richard around the period 1194. To confuse matters more the Earl of Huntingdon appears to be David, the brother of King William, who was known as the Lion of Scotland, and held estates in Rutland. Certainly Scotland has its own version of Robin Hood and local writers engaged their imaginations in the pursuit of legends.

Whatever the truth it appears that legend and fact, dates and people are well and truly mixed. Whether for religious or political reasons is impossible to say. The playwrites of the 15th and 16th centuries seemed more concerned with a story that suited their audience than one that suited a researched history.

The scene of Robin's death is at least on common ground. Most historians seem to agree on Kirklees Priory. The Prioress, probably Robin's sister in law Elisabeth, had a long running affair with her lover Sir Roger of Doncaster. The goings on at Kirklees must have been common knowledge at one time because the records show that the Bishop had expressed great concern over the rumours surrounding the sexual activities of the nuns. As Sir Roger was also a priest he had the perfect disguise to conduct his affair with the Prioress.

Sir Roger and Robin were bitter enemies and it is thought that Sir Roger persuaded the Prioress, against her better judgment, to invite Robin to Kirklees. The confrontation was to lead to a viscious sword fight in which Sir Roger was killed. Robin Hood received serious injuries and within hours was also dead. The story of Robin's death tells of how, on his death bed, he called for Little John and asked him to place his grave on the spot where his final arrow landed. As his life ebbed he drew on his bow and fired the final arrow to its destination. The Prioress, according to historical records, disappears from the scene within a few months. Did she take her own life as an act of remorse at the death of her lover, Sir Roger? Was there also a feeling of guilt over her treacherous betrayal of Robin Hood?

And what decision do I reach about Robin Hood? Without the reputation of the historian to worry about it matters little whether I am right or wrong. My vote goes to Yorkshire. But it just could have been Needwood after all!

References

Robin Hood: The Man Behind the Myth. Phillips & Keatman. Michael Omara Books.
Robin Hood: Study of the English Outlaw. Stephen Knight. Blackwell.
Robin Hood. Sir Walter Scott.
The True History of Robin Hood. J. W. Walker.
Robin Hood. Spirit of the Forest. S. Wilson.

Robin Hood meets Maid Marian.

Lud Church today, and inset, an illustration from Miller's *Olde Leeke* 1891

Two
Lud Church. An arena of violence

What are we to make of Lud church, this fissure of rock that appears out of nowhere, bearing an aura of innocence and beauty? It is an area where the landscape between Leek and Macclesfield transforms itself within a few miles. In no time at all the rugged moorland is replaced by the streams and forests of the Dane Valley.

The scenery is splendid by any standard and given half a chance many ramblers disappear into its wilderness. The area has changed little since the days of the Ancient Briton and neolithic and bronze age relics bear testimony to the tribal wanderings of yesteryear. The area abounds with myth and legend, fiction soon becomes fact, and tales of ritual sacrifice mingle with stories of battle and bloodshed.

How much is fact and how much is fiction is impossible to say, but three distinct areas present themselves for our examination:

1) The Tale of Sir William de Lacy
2) The Viking Connection
3) The Arthurian Poem, *Gawain and the Green Knight*

Each are worthy in their own right, although the tale of Sir William de Lacy is the story that has been handed down through the centuries, whilst the other two have been largely ignored. As is so often the case, numerous writers and historians have used their own words to relate the same events, often with very little research into the records. The origin of the story relates to one Sir William de Lacy who visited the district during the reign of Henry VIII.

One: The Tale of Sir William de Lacy

In the summer of 1546 Sir William visited an old friend, Trafford of Swythamley and, after enjoying his hospitality, he made his departure and set off on his steed towards Buckstone. Sir William speaks eloquently of the beauty of the wild countryside and the splendid trees within the forest. Seeking to escape the heat, he rides along the banks of the River Dane and into the coolness of the forest.

A well beaten path leads him into an area of unsurpassed beauty and at length he reigns in his horse to survey the scene. As he does so he is startled by a loud noise. Turning around he sees a large wolf in desperate combat with a goat. The wolf, being the natural aggressor, sinks its teeth into the neck of the goat. The goat, unable to free itself, drags the wolf deeper into the forest. Sir William, fascinated by the encounter, follows through the dense undergrowth until he finds himself at the mouth of a gloomy looking, narrow glen. In places the glen was so narrow that its damp walls rose high above until almost all light was excluded. Sir William was overcome by a feeling of solemn awe, and as he stood and gazed at the scene he perceived that the goat had emerged victorious. The wolf lay on the ground, gored to death by the goat who, now suddenly aware of the intruder, scampered off into the forest. As William returned to his horse he saw a neatly dressed old man seated at the base of a large oak tree engrossed in the words of a worn bible.

"This is a very odd looking cavern," said William.

"True, my friend," replied the old man, *"but the almighty, whose power can exalt the humble, and lay low the high, has been pleased to make this cavern, insignificant as it appears, the instrument of many righteous works".*

With that the old man recited the legend that has lived for so long in the minds of the local people. The following extract appears verbatim in various books about Lud Church including those of Brocklehurst, Rathbone and Miss Dakeyne. The words, if we are to believe the story of Sir William de Lacy, belong to the old man he encountered on that hot summers day of 1546.

The immediate followers of Wicklif - the dawning star of the Reformation, as he is called - were denominated Wicklifites, or Lollards. The latter word is by the best authorities, supposed to be derived from the German word lollen, signifying to sing aloud, in an allusion probably to the extreme fondness of this sect for vocal music. Walter de Lud-auk was one of the most zealous supporters of the Wicklifite doctrines; so that the ecclesiastical authorities sought every opportunity to criminate him. This cave was once much larger than at present, but one of those strong convulsions of nature, which undoubtedly formed the ravine at first, by a second stroke caused it to collapse into its present narrow condition; and perhaps, (said the old man) another stroke may close it for ever.

However, Walter de Lud-auk was in the habit of repairing to this cavern during the summer months, with several of his friends, where their devotional exercises might be conducted with safety. Sometimes they made this place their abode, while they spread themselves over the country, extending their doctrines among the peasantry. Many were the searches made for them; but at that time the forest was so large and dense, and the cavern so well concealed, that all search was bootless. On these occasions the Lollards kept close, while food was conveyed to them by Henrich Montair, the head forester, who was devoted to their interests.

It was a fine summer afternoon, when the Lollards assembled to perform divine service in the natural cavern of Lud Church. Upon an elevated mound, in the upper part of the church, stood the good old minister. Walter de Lud-auk was about seventy years of age: his hair was bleached like the hoary top of Snowdon, yet his form was erect; and what was still more strange, his broad massive brow was unclouded with a single wrinkle. Neither his voice nor his intellect had suffered from the iron and relentless hand of time: the former was strong and melodious, and was equally fitted for vocal praise or pious exhortation; the latter could, with the same ease, grapple with the keen and subtle arguments of the Romish champions.

Walter de Lud-auk was a man eminently fitted for the post and faith which he had chosen; his strong mind and indomitable will were well calculated to brave the wrath of the Catholic Church; while his gentleness, exemplary pity, and the weight of learning and age, could not fail to make a favourable impression. The assembly, fourteen in number, was ranged in a circle, having their pastor at their head. On his right hand stood a beautiful girl, Alice de Lud-auk, his granddaughter, whose parents, dying when she was an infant, left her to the care of her grandfather, whom she generally accompanied in his journeys. She was about eighteen years of age, rather taller than the generality of women. Her form was light and sylph-like, with a head exquisitely shaped; her brow broad and fair like her grandfathers; indeed her fine features and graceful form made up a picture of loveliness which the stern old walls of Lud Church rarely viewed. Among the rare qualities with which she was endowed was a matchless voice; indeed all her family were blessed with this enviable gift but she, like a diamond surrounded by less precious stones, surpassed them all.

Separated from the rest of the congregation, and almost at the entrance of the cavern, stood, or rather leaned against a wall, the Herculean form of the head forester. Henrich Montair was of gigantic stature and strength; his features were cast in that striking style, called Roman - large, dark, full eyes, keen as the falcons; the aquiline nose, and curved and haughty mouth. The expression of his features was rendered still more striking by his bronzed complexion and curling black beard. He was clad in a coarse dress of Lincoln green; his legs were protected by strong buskins of deer-skin. In his belt was a heavy broadsword, a huntsman's horn, and a long dagger. At his feet lay a crossbow and a sheaf of arrows.

After a short but earnest prayer from the pastor, the opening hymn began. How beautiful and solemn did that hymn sound, as every note and every voice rose in strict accordance and harmony with each other! The lofty and sweet tenor, with the deep and musical bass, mingled their dulcet notes together in fervent praise to the Most High. At a certain part of the hymn, the other singers stopped, and the wild, birdlike strains of Alice de Lud-auk warbled with an almost unearthly sound - so remarkable was the compass of her voice - through the vaulted chamber. And when her voice was at the highest pitch, and when all eyes and thoughts were engaged in devotional contemplation, a quick trampling of feet, and a ringing of arms was heard. Before any movement could be made, a tall and powerful man, clad in steel, rushed in at the entrance, followed by others.

The voices of the singers were hushed - the man stopped short, and, waving his sword, cried, *"Yield, in the name of the blessed Church, and his most Gracious Majesty King Henry."* The Lollards seized their weapons, and prepared to stand on the defensive, but were commanded to desist by their pastor. All obeyed, except the forester, who darted forward, and seizing the officer in his iron grasp, dashed him with such force among his followers, that they were irresistibly borne back to the entrance of the cave; then drawing his sword, he called to the Lollards to escape through the other outlet, while he defended the pass. One of the men levelled his arquebus, and fired, as the forester pressed forward; the bullet whistled past his ear, but a loud shriek burst from behind.

The forester turned hastily round, almost afraid to trust his eyes; his foreboding was but too true; he saw the beautiful Alice supported in the arms of her grandfather, - the fatal bullet was lodged in her bosom. Uttering a terrible cry, the forester sprang forward, and flung himself, with the desperation of a wild beast, upon his foes. His great stature and strength, and the narrowness of the pass, were formidable obstacles to the assailants. Two had fallen, cleft to the teeth by the mighty arm of the forester, whilst all shrank from encountering those terrible, death-dealing strokes.

There was a pause. The men held back; and the giant forester leaned on his bloody sword, his dark eyes flashing fire from beneath his shaggy and lowering brows. A low sound now issued from the violated temple, like the plaintive sighing of the wind; it grew stronger and stronger; till at last the lofty and solemn death-chant of the persecuted Lollards could plainly be heard, swelling in rich, yet mournful strains, as it rolled forth from the cavern and floated on the breeze, then declining in cadences of touching tenderness and melancholy pathos, it ceased - and the songs of the Lollards never more issued from Lud Church.

So solemn and wild was the place, so awful the event which had called forth the beautiful, yet unlooked-for hymn, that even the rough natures of the soldiers were touched, while the strong chest of the forester heaved with emotion. A few moments after the last sounds of the chant had passed away on the wind, Walter de Lud-auk, bearing the fair corpse of his granddaughter, and followed by the Lollards in solemn procession (carrying with them pickaxes and spades), issued from the church. At a few yards from the entrance, the Lollards began to dig the last resting place of Alice de Lud-auk. The soldiers were grouped around in silence, for there is nothing which makes so great an impression on the mind, as a glimpse at that state through which the perishable matter of all earthly things must pass. The grave was dug, the corpse lowered, and soon the earth covered the lamented remains of her who, one short, fleeting hour before, lived in the possession of youth and beauty. Thus do the temporal things of this world pass away, like morning dew before the midday sun.

The good old pastor, upon whose countenance grief was strongly depicted, but who, with the Christian fortitude of all good men, bowed in submission to the will of his God, kneeled down and signing to his companions in adversity to do the same, offered up a short, but fervent prayer. Then rising with a dignity which no misfortune could overcome, he, with his friends (including the forester), peaceably submitted to the soldiers. Little more of this melancholy legend remains to be told.

On the way to London, the forester conceived his plan of escape for the whole party, but they refused to profit by it; De Lud-auk, however, aware of Montair's danger for his imprudent resistance to the officers of justice, ordered him, on pain of his strict displeasure, to convey several papers of importance to France. After considerable resistance, Montair obeyed, made his escape, and embarked for France, where he resided until the invasion of the English, whom he joined. Of De Lud-auks companions, some were imprisoned for a short time, and the rest pardoned; the fate of De Lud-auk himself was never known, but it is supposed that he died in prison.

Wycliffe, who produced the first English bible and his followers

After the old man had concluded, he rose from his seat, and laying his hand impressively on my shoulder, said, *"My son, if thou art of the Protestant religion, and art called upon, by the despotic rulers of this land, to abjure thy faith, remember the Lollards of Lud Church, and stand firm."* I thanked him for his advice, and desired him to show me the grave of the unfortunate Alice. *"Thou hast sat in the shadow of the tree which grows over it,"* he replied. I turned to the oak and broke off a leaf from its broad branches, which I deposited in my bosom, as a momento. Then, thanking the venerable old man again, I mounted my horse and rode away, my mind filled with sorrowful reflections.

The story narrated by the old man to Sir William de Lacy bears the hallmark of truth. Whether Lollards were named after the Germanic impulse to sing loudly or the English definition to drone it is apparent that both descriptions sit easily in the pulpit of church reform. Lollards was the name given to followers of John Wycliffe (1329-1384), the famous religious reformer and translator of the bible. Athough many of his beliefs and ideals would be considered very reasonable in later years he quickly became an outcast in 14th century England.

It must be remembered that at this time England, like the rest of Europe, suffered badly from the devastation of the plague. The huge number of deaths left the population much depleted. Serfs, so long at the beck and call of their lords, were now in great demand. Labour was so scarce that wages threatened to spiral out of control. The ruling classes found themselves temporarily under pressure as the serfs formed themselves into groups in an effort to improve their lot. As Parliament endeavoured to retain the status-quo the last thing they wanted was an ecclesiastical revolt. Wycliffe, it seems, was simply in the wrong place at the wrong time. The lower classes flocked to his cause as Lollards. The response of Parliament and the established clergy was predictable. Wycliffe and his small retinue of priests, lay readers and peasant followers were branded heretics. Punishment for those caught in the act of heretic worship was severe in the extreme. Burning alive became the order of the day.

Little wonder that the Lollards held their services in secret. The venue, in a very isolated area of the Dane Valley must have seemed safe, but obviously not safe enough. As for Lud Church, there can be no better explanation for its name. What else could it be but the Church of Walter de Lud-auk.

Two: The Viking Connection

Volume II of Miller's Olde Leeke published in 1900 contains a chapter dedicated to the story of William Shirley's uncle, of Sheen in the Staffordshire Moorlands. The story is about the exploits of King Ludd who sailed across the North Sea with the intention of gaining the riches that lay in wait in a country at that time in a state of turmoil and lacking a good defence.

Around the year 800 AD Ludd reached the east coast of England and made his way into the mouth of the River Humber. Leaving the Humber he turned left into the River Trent and headed up river, probably aided by the tide, until he reached a small settlement where he and his followers disembarked. The settlement, now called Luddington, lies a few miles away from Scunthorpe and is still little more than a hamlet.

Ludd then followed the course of the river toward Nottingham leaving in his wake a trail of plunder and destruction. Whatever the size or importance of Nottingham at the time it failed to repell the marauding Vikings. Ludd burnt down the castle and caused great devastation in the neighbourhood. He also now took on the name of 'Captain' Ludd.

From Nottingham they travelled west and fought their way through the Derwent and Dove valleys. The waters of the River Dove obviously agreed with them for after refreshing themselves they named the place of Ludswell.

They now travelled on towards areas more familiar to our story. Their forays took them through Glutton and Thirklow before they made camp at Dane Bower in the Dane Valley. Now the Dane Valley had long been a place of religious ritual where local tribes made sacrificial offerings on a stone that lay above a large fissure of rocks and caverns. Ludd met with strong resistance from these local clans as he neared the rocks but after a fierce struggle the Vikings emerged victorious and in the aftermath of battle he offered human sacrifices to the Gods Thor and Woden on the alter stones above the woodland chapel. The victorious Vikings declared the arena to be Ludd's Church.

By now the story of Ludd's exploits and savagery preceded him, and when they approached Gawsworth the locals were ready and waiting. The Monks of Gawsworth with a mixed army of supporteres confronted Ludd at a point where he needed to ford a river. The battle that followed was fierce and brutal, and finally Ludd's men were routed, their heavy losses exacerbated by the numerous drownings as they were forced back into the river. Ludd and his depleted band

Vikings

Sir Gawain.

were forced to change course and leave Gawsworth to the monks and some time later the Hug Bridge was built across the river in celebration of the victory.

Ludd, still intent on joining fellow invaders, pressed on towards Shrewsbury. With the county in the grips of the invaders Shrewsbury offered little resistance to his men. The cathedral was burnt down and all the monks killed. At this point the story comes to an end with all trace of Ludd lost - except we are told that Ludd's final resting place was to the south of Shrewsbury. Here a burial chamber or low was built to house the Viking warrior's remains. Henceforth the place was known as Ludlow.

This wonderful story of blood and gore is all very convenient except that it fails to coincide with historical fact. There seems to be no record of Ludd's travels in recorded history and even the names of places fail to stand up to scrutiny. Assuming that Ludd did indeed come down the Trent the hamlet of Luddington is said to derive its name from the Luda which is an old English reference and not Norse.

He could conceivably have landed at other places on the east coast. Boston with its long established history as a port springs to mind. Nearby the town of Louth stands on the River Lud with its obvious connotations. But again we reach a negative conclusion. The Anglo Saxon derivation indicates Louth and Lud as Loud, with neither names relating to the Viking Ludd.

The same explanation is reached again when Ludlow is considered, where we learn of the settlement that stands by the waters of the loud river.

We are now left only with the destruction of Nottingham and Shrewsbury and once again we draw a negative conclusion. Obviously Nottingham could be reached by following the Trent and no one denies the possibility of Vikings in the area. The castle, however, is of Norman origin and was not in existence. It was common enough practise to build wooden stockades before then which would have been easy enough to burn down but no records are available to support this idea.

In Shrewsbury the story flounders again. A relatively modern cathedral stands in Shrewsbury but no structure is recorded in pre-conquest days. Even the old Abbey stood on virgin ground and was not built until 1080. All of which leaves the story of Lud Church as mysterious as ever and probably commits the story of William Shirley's uncle to the realms of fantasy.

Three: Sir Gawain and the Green Knight

The third of our possible origins of Lud Church concerns the Arthurian legend *Sir Gawain and the Green Knight*. But we must first ask ourselves whether King Arthur himself actually existed. Over the years the answer to this question has been as varied as the many myths and countless stories that surround Arthur.

Yes, certainly there was a warrior king we now refer to as Arthur. Both Gildas and Nennius, our most reliable historians of the period recognised Arthur as a noble warrior and place him firmly at the battle of Badon. The date of that battle is subject to much debate although it appears to precede the year 500 AD. Bede, the English monk and historian, adds credence to the events of the 4th and 5th centuries with his Chronicle of English history.

More recently the works of Geoffrey Ashe and the detailed research of Phillips and Keatman not only confirm Arthur's existence but pinpoint with logical precision both the site of the battle of Badon and the origins of Arthur's birth. A hill outside the city of Bath is thought to be the site of Badon and Arthur himself is placed with some authority as Owain Ddantgwyn, son of the King of Gwynedd. The Kings of Gwynedd were known as the head dragons and the name Uther Pendragon appears in chronological lists appertaining to Arthur. Owain was destined to become King of Gwynedd and Powys, and was called the Bear, which has long been considered the origin of the name Arthur.

No one now doubts his existence. What is in doubt is most of legends surrounding the Knights of the Round Table and the sagas that have been handed down over the centuries. The names of Lancelot, Guinevere, Gawain and most of the characters who play such an important part in the story of King Arthur and the Knights of the Round Table simply do not appear in real history. They are fictitious, the creations of the long succession of story tellers who not only passed on the story but added their own bit of romance. Some stories, laboriously written by clerics, gave an air of authority but were fantasy.

By the 12th century production of the legend was in full spate. Geoffrey of Monmouth produced his *Historia Regum Britanniae* (History of the Kings of Britain) in 1135. Other writers selected the Arthurian theme, notably a Jersey poet by the name of Wace who introduced the Round Table. Christian de Troyes then introduced Sir Lancelot and Camelot, and in the 1190s Robert de Boron introduced the story of the Holy Grail.

Gawain, the subject of our story makes an appearance in the *Historia* but then disappears until 1400. Sir Gawain and the Green Knight was composed by an anonymous writer thought to be from the North West Midlands and may well have been based on a fictional French hero called Walwanus - the exploits of Walwanus being very similar to those of Gawain. By the time William Caxton produced his printing press the story of Arthur was just waiting to be a best seller, and its further impetus came from Sir Thomas Mallory who gathered together the works of Geoffrey of Monmouth, the stories of Arthur known as the Vulgate cycle and virtually all the other fictitious information available.

Mallory's book *Le Morte DArthur* (The Death of Arthur) was garnished and polished into the story we now know so well, and the printing presses and mass production gave Mallory an unassailable place in Arthurian history despite the fact that much of his work was copied and bore little semblance to fact.

As for Gawain, his story has also been told many times and the yet scenes of his exploits remain as elusive as ever. The author is thought to be an anonymous cleric who displays a sound knowledge of the North West Midlands. His knowledge of courtly procedures, of hunting and feasting, and his ability to produce an exceptionally fine narrative poem featuring Sir Gawain, singles him out as a gifted writer. The poem, written about 1390, has created much speculation over the years with scholars placing him firmly within the speech patterns and writing mode of the English Midlands. Some consider that he may have been a clerk in holy orders with John of Gaunt as his patron. Conveniently this would place him at Tutbury, near Burton-On-Trent. Tutbury was also the seat of an active monastery from whence the monks travelled far and wide in their pursuance of Christian converts.

Whether they would have ventured towards Leek and thence to Ludchurch is a matter of conjecture as is the thought that the anonymous writer may have been a cleric at Dieulacres or Gawsworth. The answers are far from clear as the story unfolds:

> At Camelot the festive season was in full swing. Christmas was upon them and a new year but a few days away. In the great hall, Arthur, his knights and Guinevere with the other wives were in good voice. Singing and laughter preceded the rich feast which was being laid on the sagging trestles. The great assembly, amidst much banter, took its place at the bulging tables. Arthur, true to his dignity, waited patiently for all to be served before sitting to join the others.
>
> As the meats were about to be consumed they were disturbed by a commotion and a clatter of hooves. The doors burst open and into the great hall rode a spectacle

Steps at the top end of Lud Church before it opens onto the moorland plain.

that amazed the assembly. Standing before them was a huge knight. A man of mighty proportions, muscular, tall but well balanced, lithe and strong. The intruder was dressed from head to foot in green, with threads of gold here and there. Even his face was green as were his limbs. His horse was coloured green as also its saddle and harness. *"All of green were they made, both garments and man."*

> *A green horse great and thick,*
> *a stallion quick to quell.*
> *in broidered bridle quick*
> *he matched his master well.*

The Green Knight addressed the assembly in measured tones. In the silence he explained that he had come to issue a challenge to the knights of Camelot. A challenge they scarcely dare accept but could not refuse if their reputation was to remain intact. The Green Knight addressed Arthur.

"I challenge you to take my battle axe and strike me with one blow. In return I demand the right to return the blow one year hence on the first day of the new year."

The foolhardiness of the challenge caused much consternation as Arthur reluctantly accepted the challenge that would result in the certain death of the unknown knight. Gawain with his love for both Arthur and Guinevere intervened so forcibly that Arthur reluctantly agreed to stand down and allow Gawain to take up the challenge instead.

The Green Knight, now on the ground, prepared himself for Gawain's blow. Placing his left foot forward he pushed his hair to one side and lowered his head leaving his naked neck and ready for the blow.

> *Gawain gripped on his axe, gathered and raised it,*
> *from aloft let it swiftly land where twas naked*
> *so that the sharp blade shivered the bones,*
> *and sank clean through the clear fat and clove it asunder.*
> *The fair head to the floor fell from the shoulders,*
> *and folk fended it with their feet as forth it went rolling*
> *and blood burst from the body bright on the greenness.*

What followed astounded the assembled knights even more. The Green Knight never faltered or fell but strode forth and grasped the head and held it aloft. He mounted his horse, settled himself in the saddle and turned towards Gawain. The head spoke and instructed Gawain to meet him as agreed for the return blow. Gawain must prepare himself and come to the green chapel or be called a craven. With that the Green Knight spurred his horse and, with his head still in his hand, hastened out through the hall door. As calm returned Arthur and Gawain, marvelling at the encounter, returned to the table as the feasting continued.

The new year arrived quickly enough and with the challenge of the Green Knight never far from his mind Gawain anticipated the coming seasons with much concern. As weeks turned to months spring was replaced by summer and in no time at all it seemed to Gawain that the autumn was upon them. Now Gawain began to compose himself. Whatever the challenge he was a man of honour. He would accept his fate as befits a true knight of Camelot. As the festive season once again descended Gawain mounted his trusty steed Gringolet, and set off in search of the green chapel. Trusting only in God he rode through the realm of Logres (England) enquiring always of the whereabouts of the green chapel. He travelled into North Wales, by Anglesey and Holy Head and then towards the wilderness of Wirral.

Unable to find the green chapel he journeyed on into the moors and forests of the Midlands. With the winter weather now blowing bitterly he reached his lowest ebb among the cold streams and naked rocks of an unfamiliar land. He sought once more   .....*the guidance so far denied.*

The knight did at that tide
his plaint to Mary plead,
her riders road to guide
and to some lodging lead.

The following morning he was in much better spirits and rode on through the oaks and hazels of a large forest until suddenly he noticed, through the trees, the outline of a fine moated castle. Spurring Gringolet on they hastened towards the castle. The drawbridge was immediately lowered and Gawain entered the castle and received a most cordial welcome. The knight of the castle, a sturdy and jovial man, not only gave food and shelter to Gawain but offered to accommodate him over the festive season. After Gawain had bathed and rested, the knight and his good lady sat with him in long conversation. Gawain explained the purpose of his mission and the knight readily agreed to help him to reach the green chapel. In the meantime during the few days that remained until the first day of the new year, Gawain was invited to remain at the castle.

Each morning his host would go out and hunt wild boar and deer and each evening he would share his spoils with Gawain. Much impressed by the civility and manner of his host Gawain agreed to the arrangement. On the morning of the first hunt Gawain was awakened by the noise of someone entering his bed chamber. To his surprise the lady of the castle approached his bed and sat beside him. The intentions of this lady, even more beautiful than Guinevere, were plain to see. Gawain, with the respect of his host in mind, managed to resist temptation until, with a sigh, the lady kissed him and retired from the room.

The second morning it happened again. The lady was even more determined and Gawain found himself struggling to resist the feminine charms of his seductress. After much gentle conversation she once again kissed him and departed. On the third morning Gawains mind was in a turmoil. He had to resist the ambitions of this lovely lady even though his human frailties were all too apparent. With splendid restraint he managed to resist the seduction but succumbed to the kiss which he returned passionately. This time, as the lady was about to make her exit, she took off part of her dress and revealed a green lace girdle which she removed and gave to Gawain as a token of her love.

Not that Gawain's masculinity was in dispute. He simply had life-threatening matters on his mind. The new years day was upon him and he enquired once again where he could find the green chapel. This time he was successful and was told that the place he sought was no more than two miles away. Seeking more precise directions he set forth as instructed and rode down the yonder rock side until he reached the bottom of a baleful valley. Here, a little to the left, he was told to look oer the green and see the self same chapel.

> Then he put spurs to Gringolet, and espying the track,
> thrust in along a bank by a thickets border,
> rode down the rough brae right to the valley;
> and then he gazed all about: a grim place he thought it,
> and saw no sign of shelter on any side at all,
> only high hillsides sheer upon either hand,
> and notched knuckled crags with gnarled boulders;
> the very skies by the peaks were scraped, it appeared.
> Then he halted and held in his horse for the time,
> and changed oft his front the Chapel to find.
> Such on no side he saw, as seemed to him strange,
> save a mound as it might be near the marge of a green,
> a worn barrow on a brae by the brink of a water,
> beside falls in a flood that was flowing down;
> the burn bubbled therein, as if boiling it were.
> He urged on his horse then, and came up to the mound,
> there lightly alit, and lashed to a tree
> his reins, with a rough branch rightly secured them.
> Then he went to the barrow and about it he walked.
> debating in his mind what might the thing be.
> It had a hole at the end and at either side,
> and with grass in green patches was grown all over,
> and was all hollow within: nought but an old cavern,
> or a cleft in an old crag; he could not it name aright.
> Can this be the Chapel Green,
> O Lord? said the gentle knight.
> Here the Devil might say, I ween,
> His matins about midnight!

As Gawain alighted and looked around he was distracted by the sound of an axe being whetted on a grindstone. Then as silence returned the Green Knight appeared and bid Gawain to take his stance and prepare for the blow. Grasping his courage Gawain pushed his hair to one side and offered his neck to the Green Knight's axe. Twice the axe was raised and twice it was lowered. A third time the axe was raised and this time it was brought down on the edge of Gawains neck causing little more than a graze. A relieved Gawain watched as his blood dripped red onto the snow. It was but a minor wound from which Gawain could easily recover. As he pondered the actions the Green Knight spoke. *"I am your host, my name is Sir Bercilak. My intent was to test the resolve and integrity of Arthur's knights. You have acted in a most noble fashion and your life has been spared."*

Gawain, recovering from his ordeal, was obviously much relieved. Sir Bercilak continued: *"The graze to your neck is to remind you of your one moment of weakness. My wife was acting on my instructions. Twice you resisted her but on the third occasion you responded with passion and you accepted her girdle."*

With that Gawain was released from his obligation to the Green Knight. He returned to Camelot a much chastened and embarrassed man and confessed his weakness to a forgiving court.

The analysis of our final story lies not so much in the exploits of Sir Gawain and the Green Knight which we know to be fictitious, but in the location of the green chapel. Experts have placed the location in Derbyshire or Staffordshire and the clerics, assuming he knew the area well, could have come from Tutbury or even Dieulacres or Gawsworth. There is nothing in the translated text that relates specifically to his base.

As for the description it can, with imagination, be almost anywhere. Perhaps this was the writer's intention. In reality Ludchurch fits well enough. Its knuckled crags and gnarled boulders, the water, the concealed entrance with its hollows and cavern all sound familiar. Even the descriptions of the surrounding countryside speak of heath and moor and rocky outcrop. The Staffordshire Moorland sweeping around the Roches as it falls toward the Churnet Valley springs easily to mind.

To the people of Leek and Macclesfield it may well sound convincing. It remains unproven but local claims are as valid as any and better than most. Whatever the truth Ludchurch remains an enigma. So much written, so much assumed. But even without proof one can be forgiven for thinking - *there's no smoke without fire.*

THREE
The Babington Plot

Many plans were made to free Mary, Queen of Scots, from captivity and to place her on the English throne. The Elizabethan period at times seemed to thrive on lies and innuendo and supported a spy network that perhaps makes today's subterfuge pale into insignificance. The background to Mary's so called act of treason has all the hallmarks of lies and deceit.

Mary, a true catholic, had experienced a lifetime of tragedy by her mid-twenties. She married at the age of sixteen to become Queen of France and by eighteen was made a widow when the young French King died of illness brought about by a septic ear. Within a year she returned to Scotland where she resumed her role as the Scottish Queen, a position she had held from childhood.

She was not short of suitors despite her recent bereavement, and it was only a matter of time before Mary's wishes became clear. Her marriage to Henry, Lord Darnley, came as no surprise to those who had witnessed the carnal desire that was apparent between them.

But such a marriage was almost doomed to fail. Darnley succumbed to the sexual urges of youth and quickly established himself as a womaniser. Mary rejected him, although her own conduct was also subject to many rumours, as she dallied with other admirers, and instead of the divorce that had been discussed at length coming to pass, evil deeds were set afoot and Darnley was murdered. His home was first blown up in an attempt to kill him. He escaped this only to meet his death by strangulation as he fled from the scene.

Whether or not Mary was fully aware of the plans for Darnley's death is difficult to ascertain. Suffice it to say that Darnley died before his twenty-first birthday. Mary continued to bewitch both the Scottish and English nobility and swiftly selected a third husband. This time it was the devious Bothwell, who had been involved in the murder of Darnley, who was Mary's consort.

This marriage was to prove no more secure, for now the politics and ambitions of those who coveted the Scottish throne turned to open revolt. A series of battles and skirmishes in which Bothwell and Mary stood shoulder to shoulder eventually took their toll and, in a last ditch attempt to free himself of Mary's overwhelming problems, Bothwell deserted her. She was never to see him again.

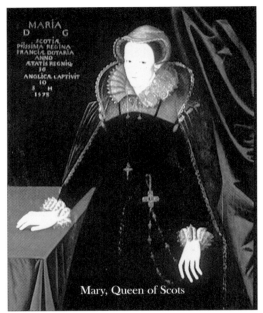

Mary, Queen of Scots

The ruins of Tutbury Castle.

Now, under ever increasing pressure, Mary decided to leave Scotland, and with a small retinue of loyal servants she landed in Northumberland in 1568. Her decision to flee proved disastrous. Her troubles in Scotland, her French upbringing and catholic tastes, plus her tenuous claim to the throne of Elizabeth I, made her an unpopular migrant to supporters of the Church of England and the English throne.

Lord Cecil, close to Queen Elizabeth, was ever aware of such dangers, and he initiated an enquiry into the death of Darnley. A Westminster Conference reached the decision that Mary was a danger to Elizabeth and should, henceforth, be kept under close surveillance. To achieve this end meant the virtual imprisonment of Mary and her staff.

Initially the surveillance allowed a degree of freedom and respect for her Royal life. Hunting trips and visits to Buxton were not uncommon as Mary awaited Elizabeth's pleasure. She was to wait a long time as Elizabeth procrastinated and did nothing. As shrewd as Mary was she had met her match in Elizabeth. A Mary that was free to engage catholic sympathies, both nationally and abroad would always be a threat to her throne. Far better that Mary should be kept under constant surveillance and control.

What to do with the Scottish Queen taxed the thoughts of nobles and politicians alike. After a short spell in Bolton castle she was sent to Tutbury, in 1568, where she came under the control of Talbot, Earl of Shrewsbury. Soon plots were being hatched for her release, so she was moved to Wingfield Manor in Derbyshire and then later back again to Tutbury. By 1572 she found herself transferred to Sheffield where she remained for several years despite further brief interludes at Tutbury and Wingfield.

In 1585 she returned yet again to the draughty and insanitary conditions of Tutbury. This time her jailer was Sir Amyas Paulet who despised her and set about enforcing the harsh regime he considered appropriate. As well as being an ardent supporter of Elizabeth, Paulet was close to Elizabeth's allies, Sir Francis Walsingham and Lord Burghley - and between them they were to prove instrumental in Mary's final downfall.

In 1585, Robert Giffard, a catholic exiled to France and in the pay of the French Embassy, returned to England. He was detained when he landed in Sussex and found to be carrying a letter of introduction to Mary. As Gifford's parents lived near to Tutbury he was an obvious choice for such a communication. Walsingham, having been advised of Giffard's arrest took a personal interest in his examination. A series of threats and 'persuasion' placed Giffard in an unenviable position and by the end of Walsingham's interrogation he agreed to change his allegiance and, in effect, become a spy for Walsingham whilst deceiving his French paymasters.

Giffard contacted the French embassy and gave them details of a foolproof way of passing letters to Mary. A brewer from Burton who delivered barrels of beer to Tutbury was now to deliver beer to Chartley Hall where Mary was in temporary residence whilst her Tutbury quarters were being improved. The 'honest' brewer now became part of the plans but when he decided the extra journey merited a price increase in his beer from sevenpence to tenpence a gallon, it did not go down very well with Walsingham - but he had little option but to accept. The brewer was vital to his plans.

A specially adapted barrel, into which a secret water-tight compartment was fitted, was to be used by the brewer and Gifford. Into the compartment went secret letters to Mary - and then Mary's replies. The French embassy immediately tested the system and in due course received a reply from Mary. Walsingham allowed the communications to continue and while the confidence of the correspondents grew their letters were being intercepted, deciphered and then allowed to continue to their destinations. Using an interpreter called Philippes, Walsingham was privy to all the dealings of the French and, over a period of time, built up a case against Mary that smacked of treason.

At this point, and totally fortuitously for Walsingham, Sir Anthony Babington entered the frame. Babington, a prominent member of an old catholic family, was a Derbyshire Squire and at one time a page in the Shrewsbury household where Mary had been held prisoner. Wealthy and well-educated, Babington was not without influence and he, with a group of fervent supporters now planned the release of Mary.

Using contacts in France, Babington was put in touch with Gifford who immediately invited him to correspond with Mary via the Burton brewer system. Babington's letters to Mary now gave precise details of the plot surrounding her intended escape. They were far too open and explicit for his own good! Babington's movements were closely monitored and it proved simple enough for Walsingham to discover the names of his fellow conspirators.

In the meantime, and much to the delight of Walsingham, Mary replied to Babington. This was Walsingham's greatest piece of good fortune. Not only did Mary embrace Babington's proposals she also made it plain that Elizabeth's

STAFFORDSHIRE LEGENDS

The death warrant for Mary, signed by Elizabeth.
Below: Queen Elisabeth with her ministers and a painting of the Babington conspirators.

assassination should be carried out prior to her own release. To Walsingham this was the perfect response and clear treason.

Babington and his supporters were arrested and tried without ceremony. All were found guilty and, in keeping with the law of the day, were hung, drawn and quartered.

As for Mary, she was apprehended whilst out riding a few miles away from Chartley and taken to Tixall for questioning. The case against her was overwhelming. She was held at Tixall, and later at Chartley, while Walsingham gathered support for his actions. A Bond of Association had previously been signed by politicians and nobles which stated that any threat to Elizabeth's person should be treated as an act of treason. Walsingham needed to ensure that the Bond would hold before presenting Elizabeth with a fâit acomplit.

The question of treason was discussed at length in both the Commons and the Lords. Ponderous speeches proclaimed allegiance to Elizabeth and condemnation of Mary. Not a single voice was heard in her favour. There were delays and adjournments but slowly the parliamentary proceedings took their course until finally the obvious conclusion was reached and a warrant of execution granted.

As Paulet accompanied Mary to Fotheringhay from where her execution was planned to take place, Walsingham had the task of persuading Elizabeth that the execution should go ahead. Elizabeth's past resistance may well have been a mixture of politics and a desire to be thought compassionate to someone of royal blood. She now refused to add her signature to the deed and only relented at the last moment. Her reluctance to agree took them all by surprise, but she eventually succumbed to pressure and added her consent on the 1st of February 1587.

Walsingham and Burghley went straight to Paulet at Fotheringhay where they set proceedings in motion for Mary's execution on the 8th of February, Mary spent the previous evening completing her will and handing over purses to her servants. The following morning at 9.30 she was led to the wooden stage, and with great dignity she laid her head on the block and awaited her death. The first blow missed her neck and cut into her head - a second blow was required to sever her neck.

The executioner held the head aloft and cried *'God save the Queen'!* There was movement from Mary's crimson petticoats and her pet Skye terrier appeared. It had remained with her to the end.

F O U R
The Plague

The Plague, the Black Death, the Pestilence; call it what you will, the disease struck fear into the heart of every citizen in the land. Rich or poor, wise man or fool, if you caught the plague there was little chance of survival. It was a disease that, at its height, devastated the population of villages, towns and nations. With the benefit of time we now know that the plague was an infectious bacterial fever transmitted by the rat flea.

The disease manifests itself in three forms. Bubonic, which is characterised by the swelling of lymph nodes or buboes; pneumonic which affects the lungs; and septicaemic in which the bloodstream is flooded with the bacillus Yersinia Pestis. In the latter the bloodstream is invaded so quickly and so vigorously that death occurs before either bubonic or pneumonic plague has time to appear. In urban areas the disease spread rapidly leaving huge numbers of deaths in its wake. Rural areas escaped more lightly.

Despite the fact that much of Staffordshire, especially the north, was sparsely populated and so escaped the worst of the disease, the devastation was still felt. In the 14th century the Black Death wiped out up to 25,000,000 people in Europe with some countries losing up to two thirds of their population. England probably saw its population halved. It left a much reduced workforce and chaos as labour became a valued commodity and tithes remained unpaid.

In Britain it is thought that the disease was brought by rats that had entered the ports via merchant ships. The disease is primarily restricted to rodents but the death rate among rats may reach such proportions that their population decreases, and the fleas turn their attention to man. The milder infection is bubonic, with recovery still unlikely but death not quite as violent as with pneumonic or septicaemic. With pneumonic plague the lungs fill with fluid and death occurs within a few days. With septicaemic plague brain damage occurs within 24 to 36 hours and it is always fatal.

In general the plague had an incubation period of three to six days and began with shivering and vomiting, headache, giddiness, intolerance to light, pain in the back and the limbs, sleeplessness and delirium. Temperatures would reach 104F before falling rapidly. An early characteristic was the appearance of buboes - glands - in the groin or armpit, which had the appearance of a red, swollen ring - the "ring a ring of roses". In a vain attempt to cure the disease herbalists prepared a mix of flowers and herbs to sweeten the air and ward off the infection that they considered to be transmitted through the air. But the nosegay, "a pocket full of posies", did nothing to prevent the spread. The flu-like symptoms preceded death, "Atishoo, Atishoo, we all fall down."

Waves of the plague were rampant in Britain for over three hundred years, first appearing as the Black Death in May of 1348. It was only after the plague of 1664/65 which devastated London with up to 7,000 deaths a week, and over 100,000 in the course of a year, that the disease began to disappear in Britain. The great fire of London in 1666 may well have helped to wipe out the disease in the City. The fire broke out near to London Bridge in a narrow street of wooden houses. All in all some 13,000 dwellings including St. Paul's and 89 churches were destroyed. But also destroyed were the rats and the fleas. After this the black rat, the main carrier of the disease, was replaced by the brown or sewer rat in our towns. There was also a marked decrease in import for a few years with its obvious advantages.

Many of the records of the time were ill kept at best or neglected totally at worst. But we do have the journal of Daniel Defoe who was born in London in 1660 and subsequently recorded the memories of an uncle who witnessed the events first hand. Despite the fact that Defoe's account relates solely to London the remedies and descriptions are very much at home in the rest of the country.

The physicians, the quack doctors, the herbalists and the witches, all concocted remedies to cure the plague. They were no more successful than the illustrious philosophers of ancient times. Thucydides, Procopius and Boccaccion all tried to cure the disease which was considered to be air borne.

One eminent member of London society, William Kemp, described the bubo or botch as *"a swelling about the bigness of a nutmeg, walnut or hen's egg and cometh in the neck or behind the ears if the brain be effected, or under the armpits from the heart or in the groin from the liver."* The recommended cure would come as no surprise to followers of witchcraft: *"For the cure where of pull off the feathers from the rump of a cock hen or pigeon and rub the tayl with salt and hold its bill. Then set the tayl hard to the swelling and it will die."*

On occasions efforts were made to sweeten the air by the lighting of huge fires or the discharge of gunfire. Vinegar became widely used as a way of combating airborne infections and it was said that *"vinegar is a noble thing in tyme of pestilence."* Thomas Phaser widely recommended it as a prophylactic and a fumigant as early as the 15th. century and in 1665 the College of Physicians commended its vapours to be inhaled in any room to correct infectious air, especially with the addition of wormwood, masterwood, bay leaves, rosemary, rue, sage, scordium (water germandium), valerian or Ssetwell root, zeodoary and camphire.

A vinegar seller

In North Staffordshire where the population perhaps might be sparse enough to avoid the plague, tradition speaks otherwise. The stone crosses around Cheddleton, Leek and Werrington may well have been used as way markers and boundary points but are also thought to have been used as remote trading posts during periods of pestilence. The plague stone at Birchall near Leek and the Butter Cross on the outskirts of Cheddleton have long been considered places where local people traded their wares after coins had been washed in vinegar. Leek is said to have suffered seriously from the plague in 1646 and 1647.

Cheadle Cross

Records at the William Salt Library in Stafford and the histories of Stoke-on-Trent and Staffordshire may cast doubt on the extent of the plague in the moorland area but there is sufficient evidence to suggest that the disease was far from uncommon. Some of the larger towns in the area, with populations in excess of 1000, lived in constant fear of an epidemic. Uttoxeter, Lichfield, Walsall, Wolverhampton, Stafford and Eccleshall considered themselves especially vulnerable as their diversity of trade attracted many visitors.

Lichfield suffered badly in 1564 and again in 1593 when 1100 deaths were recorded in a single year. Wolverhampton and the Black Country also lived in dread of the plague which from time to time left its mark. The people of Walsall were so concerned that in 1665 and 1667 the constable of the borough was instructed to appoint four housekeepers to keep all strangers from the town unless they had certificates showing that they did not come from an infected place. Ale houses were told to refuse all guests save under the same conditions. Any inhabitant who was considered the slightest risk could be placed in quarantine for a period of four weeks, his house shut up and his wares enclosed.

At the same time the plague visited Stafford (1646) and left the people so poor that they called for *"some speedie course to be taken for their relief unless the meaner sort of people break out for want of sustenance"*. Excessive deaths are recorded in 1604 in the villages of Colwich, Oulton and Stone and in 1557 the village of Leigh recorded 37 burials. In 1563/64 London had a serious epidemic and outbreaks occurred in Derby, Leicester and South Staffordshire.

The plague also visited the potteries which at the time really only consisted of small moorland villages producing crude earthenware vessels from the local marl. Ward records that the plague visited the parish of Burslem in 1647 and that many of its inhabitants died of the malady. It is said that a female domestic employed by the Biddulph family at Rushton Grange imported the disease on her arrival from Italy. The lady, employed to educate the children, had 'liberated the disease' (fleas) whilst unpacking her clothes.

The woman and several of the children were early victims as were members of the related Bagnall family. The disease spread to the lower parts of Burslem around the Hole-House and Hot Lane areas and caused such terror that people were afraid to go near the infected. The dead, instead of being interred in the church, were buried in pits dug near the Grange where the family Priest administered Holy Communion. The location of the burial ground became known locally as Singing Kate's Hole after the warblings of the Italian lady.

Such was the severity of the plague that local magistrates issued an order for taxing several neighbouring parishes in aid of the Parish of Burslem. The weekly sums raised were:

	£	s	d
Burslem	1	00	00
Wolstanton	1	05	00
Stoke on Trent	1	05	00
Norton in the Mores		10	00
Newcastle	1	00	00
Keele		13	04
Trentham	1	03	04
Cheddleton		10	00
Audley	1	03	04
Madeley		13	04
Leeke	1	00	00
Barleston		13	04
Swinnerton	1	03	04
	12	00	00

BAGNALL CROSS

The villages that were to form the conurbation of Stoke-on-Trent in later years were certainly rural in the 16th and 17th centuries. Even more rustic were the moorland hamlets around Leek and Ashbourne. The worst excesses of the plague took its toll in July 1538 when fourteen deaths occurred at Ellastone and twenty eight at Alstonefield during a period described as the 'great sweat', although it is difficult to differentiate from influenza. Death from influenza was not uncommon, but the number of deaths seems excessive. The Alstonefield records have disappeared but the village was still aware of the plague over a century later when the death of Ann Walton was recorded: *1-7-1646 Ann daughter of Thomas Walton. Died of plague.*

Alstonefield recorded 37 deaths in 1664 which again seems excessive for a small isolated village although no mention of plague occurs on that occasion.

Bearing in mind the admiration that is justifiably given to the villagers of Eyam in Derbyshire, who deliberately isolated themselves from outsiders in an effort to contain the plague, it is strange that the catastrophe's of Leigh and Alstonefield remain unmentioned.   Perhaps people wanted to keep it quiet.

References
History of Stoke Upon Trent Ward Hanley Library
Victoria History of the Counties of England Vol I/Vol II Uttoxeter Library
A Journal of the Plague Year Daniel Defoe Keele University Library
Death and Disease in Staffordshire 1540-1670 David Palliser, William Salt Library, Stafford

The present Staffordshire Moorlands area
as seen in Plott's Map of 1686 in his *Natural
History of Staffordshire*

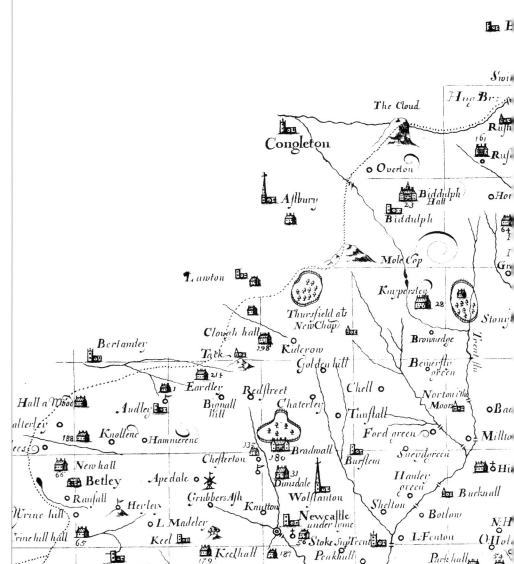

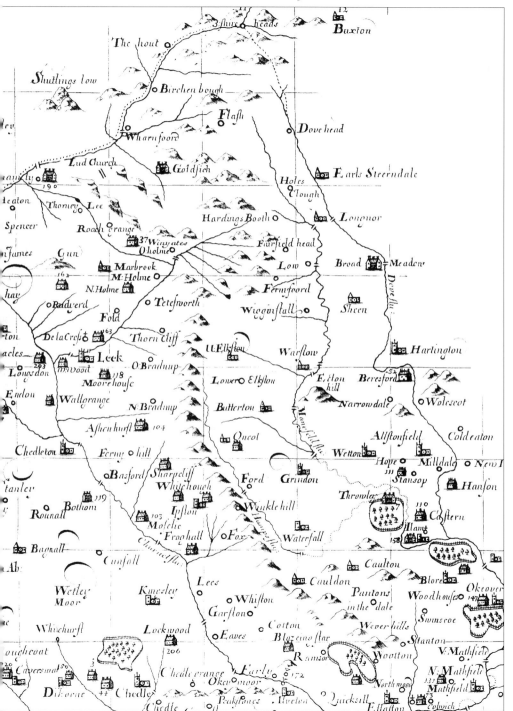

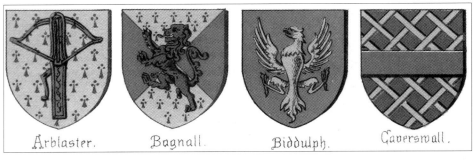

Arblaster.   Bagnall.   Biddulph.   Caverswall.

Ford.   Hammersley   Kynnersley.   Rudyerd.

More old North Staffordshire families.

When old John Botham died a few weeks short of his 100th birthday in the 1920s, his obituary in a Liverpool news-papert reminded us that he was the cousin of the famous Mary Howitt (née Botham).

42

FIVE
The Bothams of North Staffordshire

One of the mysteries that intrigues the student of local history hereabouts surrounds the original occupants of Botham Hall in Cheddleton. From the research of Mr J.D. Johnstone who lived in the area, we know that Botham Hall stood to the south of Cheddleton on the site now occupied by Ashcombe Park. Ancient maps confirm its position and long forgotten road names support the claim. Basford Bridge Lane which runs along the northern edge of Ashcombe Park was long known as Bottom Lane by the people of Cheddleton.

Anomalies exist and facts are difficult to come by if only because the source of origin is often omitted from the limited information that is at our disposal. The work of Mr Johnstone was considered sound enough by local historians and from him we discover that Botham Hall was an Elizabethan stone house with mullioned windows and many gables.

The earliest reference to the Bothams appears to be Hugh de Botham who is mentioned in 1215. From that point on, the Bothams disappear from Cheddleton records and reappear several hundred years later and a few miles away at Apesford. Whether or not the Bothams of Cheddleton and the Bothams of Apesford are one and the same is open to debate but the proximity would lead to this conclusion.

It appears that the Bothams were replaced at Botham Hall by the Hammersleys. The reference to Hugh de Botham is not substantiated by an original source but Botham and Botham Hall certainly begin to appear in documents from 1333 when Robert de Hammersley of Botham is listed on the Subsidy Rolls. The Hammersleys obviously acquired the Hall before that date. A William Hammersley of Botham is recorded in 1344 as a surety in Cheddleton and is said to have founded a family and held land there for two hundred years. By 1348 he was an attorney at Cheddleton and Newcastle and in 1354 became attorney for Ralph, Earl of Stafford. He also became a Member of Parliament for Stafford and a little later for Newcastle under Lyme.

William's descendants include Robert Hammersley who lived at Botham Hall in 1562. Robert also owned land in Kingsley and Cheadle. A later descendant, Thomas Hammersley, mortgaged Botham Hall to Anthony Rudyeard of Dieulacres in 1640. Thomas's heir, William Hammersley, then sold the title to Rudyeard in 1641. William also sold Cheddleton Grange before purchasing property at Basford and Southlow near Cellarhead in 1693.

It is significant at this point to note that William's son, Thomas, was visited by George Fox, who founded the Society of Friends, in 1654 and 1657. The Society was to find a permanent place in the lives of the Hammersleys and the Bothams.

The Hammersleys were replaced at Botham Hall by Anthony Rudyeard who later sold the estate to William Joliffe who died in 1699. Joliffe's descendants remained at Botham Hall until 1765 when their estates were leased to Ralph Leake. Although Leake had a very modest option on the estate he declined to purchase and it was eventually sold to Simon Debank. From Debank it passed to his daughter Jane Debank around 1773.

When Jane married William Sneyd in 1796 the estate passed to him and there it remained, with the Sneyd family, until 1926. The Sneyds demolished Botham Hall between 1806 and 1810 and replaced it with Ashcombe Park. The Sneyds were followed in 1926 by Miss Wardle, the daughter of Mr Arthur Wardle (of Sir Thomas and Arthur Wardle, Dyers, Macclesfield Road, Leek). Miss Wardle and her sister lived at Ashcombe until 1960. A Mr Durose purchased the estate and lived there briefly before selling it to Mr and Mrs John Haigh in 1961. The Haighs still occupy Ashcombe Park at the time of writing.

The fact that the house demolished by William Sneyd is described as Elizabethan leads to the conclusion that the house occupied by Hugh de Botham in 1275 may well have been replaced itself in the 16th century. From what little we know, the name of Botham faded from Cheddleton memories from 1810.

What happened to the Bothams themselves, especially between the 13th and 17th centuries remains a mystery and it is only through the pen of Mary Howitt (nee Botham), and the endeavours of the Botham descendants that a little light can be cast. We come to the assumption that the Bothams remained in the North Staffordshire area where they prospered as moorland farmers.

Mary Howitt, formerly Mary Botham, of Uttoxeter, was one of the foremost writers of her day and from Mary's autobiography we learn that her ancestors originated from Appsford in the Staffordshire Moorlands. The name has long been Apesford rather than Appsford and its situation on the road between Bradnop and Basford would have made the walk to the Quaker meetings at Basford easy enough.

The Bothams, like the Hammersleys of Botham Hall, had long been members of the Society of Friends and, as likely as not they would have been laid to rest in the Quaker burial ground at Basford. The burial ground had been granted to Quaker trustees by Thomas Hammersley in a deed dated 15. 9. 1667 *"for the sole use of a burying place for the bodies of all such who in their lifetime may desire to be laid within"*. Although through the following years it served their purpose well, with 139 burials being recorded, the burial ground ceased to be used in 1842. Controversy marked its final years. By 1841 there were no serving trustees and the Quakers failed to renew the trust agreement. As a consequence the owner, John Sneyd, wrote to the Clerk of the Staffordshire Monthly Meeting, William France, claiming his historic right to the property. The Staffordshire Friends reluctantly gave up their claims to the property quoting *"this burial ground is lost through inattention to the renewal of trust and owing to its being conveyed in sale illegally to John Sneyd.'*

The Basford burial ground is our most positive link with the Bothams of Apesford, with five members of the family being laid to rest there. The Quaker records are as follows:

1713	Mary, daughter of Mary of Apesford	Buried at Basford
1714/15	Mary, widow of Apesford	Buried at Basford
1754	Jane, daughter of John & Barbara of Apesford, age 28	Buried at Basford
1761	Barbara, wife of John of Apesford	Buried at Basford
1767	Ann, wife of Michael and daughter of Edward King	Buried at Leek
1769	John, son of James & Mary, age 87 -	Buried at Basford
1771	Rebecca, wife of John, age 55 -	Buried at Uttoxeter
1776	Michael, grocer of Leek, age 48 -	Buried at Leek
1807	John, of Uttoxeter, age 83 -	Buried at Uttoxeter
1821	James, of Uttoxeter, age 89 -	Buried at Uttoxeter
1823	Samuel, of Uttoxeter, age 66 -	Buried at Uttoxeter

The earliest birth recorded by the Society of Friends is that of Mary Botham in 1718, Mary being one of six children born to John and Barbara Botham, whilst the earliest marriage is that of Sarah, who was the daughter of James and Mary. Sarah married David Hall of Cheadle Grange, Morrage, at John Mellor's house at Whitehough in 1695. Assuming Sarah married sometime between the age of sixteen and twenty our earliest reference would be James in about 1655.

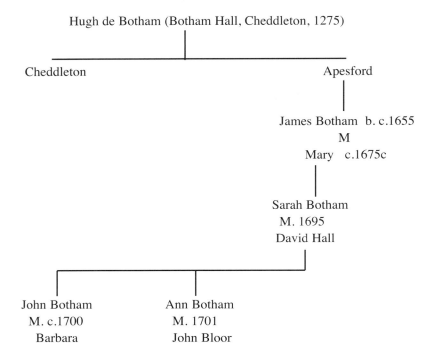

Hugh de Botham (Botham Hall, Cheddleton, 1275)

Cheddleton

Apesford

James Botham b. c.1655
M
Mary c.1675c

Sarah Botham
M. 1695
David Hall

John Botham
M. c.1700
Barbara

Ann Botham
M. 1701
John Bloor

The parish registers of St Edwards Church, Leek, record the baptism of Mary, John and Elizabeth Botham on August 12th, 1635 and John and Elizabeth Botham on December 16th, 1637, but there is no positive link between them and James of c. 1655

The Bothams may well have been moorland farmers but that did not prevent them from travelling far and wide in their pursuit of business or religion. Botham descendants are found in Liverpool, Chester and North Wales, as well as locally in the Moorlands, and in Uttoxeter.

It was in Uttoxeter that the young Mary Botham spent her childhood before finding fame and fortune. Mary was destined to become one of the foremost and most avidly read writers of the 19th century, as was her husband, William Howitt. Such was Mary's worldwide fame, she was consistently voted by the people of America to be that country's most popular author. It is surprising that such writing is now all but forgotten by the country of her birth. Uttoxeter itself displays little pride in the woman and her books are out of print, her autobiography a collectors' item. Mary's sole supporter appears to be Joy

Dunicliff of Uttoxeter whose recent biography makes a valiant and worthy effort to give Mary the fame she deserves.

It is from Mary's own pen that we learn a little of her ancestors. Mary's father, Samuel, is described as being from a long line of farmers who lived at Appsford in the Staffordshire Moorlands. Mary describes the nearby town of Leek:

"The town of Leek, in itself a primitive place, might be called the capital of this wild district. It was the resort of rude farmers on the occasion of fairs and markets. Strange brutal crimes occurred from time to time, the report of which came like a creeping horror to the lower country. Sordid, penurious habits prevailed; the hoarding of money was considered a great virtue."

By Mary's time the Bothams were well established as Quakers and, as such were regular attenders of the First Day Mornings at the Leek Meeting House. The Bothams were not without spirit and were prepared to suffer for their faith. Another Mary Botham was placed in the stocks and then put into jail in Bedfordshire for spreading her beliefs in that area.

A later Botham, John, was known as the quiet friend. John was living at Apesford in 1745 when rumours were rife that the Scottish rebels were coming. The thought of invasion filled the moorlanders with terror and John hurried his wife and children to safety before burying his money and his valuables. Their fears were unfounded. The Highlanders demanded food and nothing more. They sliced John Botham's big round cheeses and toasted them on the end of their claymores in front of the kitchen fire. The youngest son of the house, James, related the story of the Highlanders to successive generations of Bothams until his death, at the age of 89, in 1821.

It was James brother John, the eldest son, who decided to seek his fortune elsewhere and, in 1750 at the age of 26, he settled in the market town of Uttoxeter. John plied his trade as a herbalist and his moorland remedies brought him a modest living. He sought out and joined the local Society of Friends which consisted mostly of two families, the Shipleys and the Summerlands.

William Shipley's sister, Rebecca Summerland, was a well endowed widow in her mid thirties. Rebecca was an attractive catch for anyone, and had turned down a number of suitors before John came on the scene. John wooed and won Rebecca, six years his senior, and they were married in 1755. Rebecca handed over her malting business to John, an act that found little favour with her sons by her previous marriage.

John Botham and Rebecca had two sons, James who was born in 1756 and Samuel who was born in 1758.

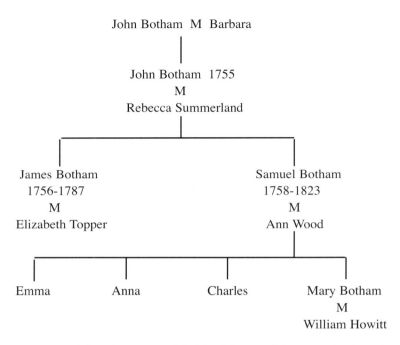

The resourceful Rebecca provided both boys with a sound education at the best Friends' school of the time, which was run by Joseph Crosfield at Hartshill in Warwickshire. After leaving school both were placed in apprenticeships, James with a merchant in Lancaster and Samuel with William Fairbank of Sheffield. Fairbank was a land surveyor of some repute.

Rebecca died in 1771 and with her death the good housekeeping and prudence which had served James and Samuel so well, disappeared. Around 1784 Samuel returned to Uttoxeter to take up his profession of land surveyor and upon doing so discovered an appalling state of affairs. His father had mortgaged much of his wife's property and what little income remained was needed to pay the interest.

Undaunted Samuel sold some of the less valuable property to pay off the main debt and took up residence himself in a humble tenement they owned in Carter Street. It was from this impoverished abode that Samuel set out to establish himself in his chosen profession. After a slow and inconspicuous start his fortunes changed for the better. Samuel was employed to enclose the Heath, an area of common land to the north of Uttoxeter. His surveying of the Heath was extremely accurate and quickly led to other commissions.

He and his brother James, who settled in Liverpool, worked diligently for several years to remove the remaining mortgages and to re-establish the families estate. James died in 1787 when he suffered a fever only six weeks after his marriage to Elizabeth Topper. The young Elizabeth and her posthumous daughter, Rebecca, returned to her parents in Chelmsford.

Samuel continued to revive the family fortune and his reputation for accuracy gained him commissions to survey large estates in Staffordshire, Shropshire and South Wales. He also tried his hand in other ventures, notably iron founding but fell foul of sharp practice and dishonesty. Samuel Botham met and fell in love with Ann Wood while in Neath, South Wales. Ann was a descendant of a remarkable family, her grandfather, William Wood, being a patentee of Irish coinage and an assayer of note.

Samuel and Ann married on the 6th December 1796, in the Friends Meeting House in Swansea. The marriage was blessed with four children, Emma, Anna, Charles and Mary. Mary was born at Colesford while her parents were working in the Forest of Dean, and came to Uttoxeter at an early age, when they returned to his home town. This time Samuel decided to remain in Uttoxeter and pursue his career in the area he knew best, surveying.

Mary Botham, with her privileged background in a prosperous market town, had a comfortable existence which allowed free reign to her imagination. In 1821 she married William Howitt, a druggist working in Hanley in Stoke-on-Trent, from a Yorkshire family. The marriage took place in Uttoxeter and as William and Mary Howitt they were to gain worldwide fame as authors and poets. They were prolific writers and an important part of the literary scene at the time, helping and working with many famous names like Charles Dickens, Mary Gaskell and Hans Anderson.

They later travelled greatly and William and two of his sons became important names in the exploration of Australia and New Zealand. William and Mary finally settled in Italy. Mary lived to an old age in Rome, receiving a pension from Queen Victoria in recognition of her achievements, and eventually converting to Catholicism before she died there.

References

Miscellaneous notes of Mr J. Johnstone.

J. Sleigh. History of Ancient Parish of Leek.

Joy Dunicliff. Mary Howitt, Victorian Authoress. Churnet Valley Books 1999

Basford Graveyard. Warwicks, Staffs & Leicester Trust Property Book.

Extracts from Digest Registers. The Botham Family.

Bothams Births, Marriages and Deaths.

Miscellaneous notes of Mrs Audry Baker, Ruthin, Clwyd.

Special thanks are extended to Sylvia Carlyle, Library of the Religious Society of Friends in Britain.

Other references attributed to Mr Johnstone indicate that the Hammersleys originated from Ombersley in Worcestershire. An extensive search of the Worcester County Archives and the Local Studies Library failed to reveal the name of Hammersley or anything similar. Likewise, enquiries in Ombersley were unsuccessful.

Two illustrations taken from the biography of Mary Howitt and her family, *The Traveller on the Hill-top*, by Joy Dunicliff. (Left, by Mary's sister, Emma, right by Mary Noon.

Top: One of Mary
Howitt's many books.

Middle: Mary Botham's
childhood home in
Balance Street, Uttoxeter.

Below: The Friends'
Meeting House in
Uttoxeter today.

Poems by Mary Howitt

The Spider and the Fly

"Will you walk into my parlour" said the Spider to the Fly.
"Tis the prettiest little parlour that ever you did spy.
The way into my parlour is up a winding stair
And I have many curious things to show when you are there".
"Oh, no, no," said the little Fly "to ask me is in vain"
"For who goes up your winding stair can ne'er come down again".

"I am sure you must be weary, dear, with soaring up so high,
Will you rest upon my little bed" said the Spider to the Fly.
"There are pretty curtains drawn around, the sheets are fine and thin,
And if you like to rest a while, I'll snugly tuck you in!"
"Oh no, no," said the little Fly, "for I've often heard it said,
They never, never wake again, who sleep upon your bed!"

Said the cunning Spider to the Fly: "Dear friend, what can I do
To prove the warm affection I've always felt for you?
I have, within my pantry, good store of all that's nice;
I'm sure you are very welcome - will you please to take a slice?
"Oh, no, no," said the little Fly, "kind sir, that cannot be,
I've heard what's in you pantry, and I do not wish to see!"

"Sweet creature," said the Spider, "you're witty and you're wise;
How handsome are your gauzy wings, how brilliant are your eyes!
I have a little looking-glass upon my parlour shelf,
If you'll step in one moment, dear, you shall behold yourself."
"I thank you, gentle sir," she said, "for what you're pleased to say,
And bidding you good-morning now, I'll call another day."

The Spider turned him round about, and went into his den,
For he well knew the silly Fly would soon come back again;
So he wove a subtle web, in a little corner sly,
And wet his table ready, to dine upon the Fly.
Then he came out to his door again, and merrily did sing,
"Come hither, hither, pretty Fly, with the pearl and silver wing;

Your robes are green and purple, there's a crest upon your head:
Your eyes are like the diamond bright, but mine are dull as lead!"
Alas, alas! how very soon this silly little Fly,
Hearing his wily, flattering words, came slowly flitting by:
With buzzing wings she hung aloft, then near and nearer drew, -
Thinking only of her brilliant eyes, and green and purple hue,

Thinking only of her crested head - poor foolish thing! At last
Up jumped the cunning Spider, and fiercely held her fast;
He dragged her up his winding stair, into his dismal den,
Within his little parlour - but she ne'er came out again!
And now, dear little children, who may this story read,
To idle, silly, flattering words, I pray you, ne'er give heed:
Unto an evil counsellor close heart, and ear, and eye,
And take a lesson from this tale, of the Spider and the Fly.

The Fairies of the Caldon Low: A Midsummer Legend

"And where have you been, my Mary,
And where have you been from me?"
"I've been to the top of the Caldon Low,
The midsummer-night to see!"

"And what did you see, my Mary,
All up on the Caldon Low?"
"I saw the glad sunshine come down,
And I heard the merry winds blow."

"And what did you hear, my Mary,
All up on the Caldon Hill?"
"I heard the drops of water made,
And I heard the corn-ears fill."

"Oh! tell me all, my Mary,
All, all that ever you know,
For you must have seen the fairies,
Last night on the Caldon Low."

"Then take me on your knee, mother,
And listen, mother of mine,
A hundred fairies danced last night,
And the harpers they were nine.

"And their harp-strings rung so merrily
To their dancing feet so small;
But oh! the words of their talking
Were merrier far than all."

"And what were the words, my Mary,
That then you heard them say?"
"I'll tell you all, my mother;
But let me have my way.

"Some of them played with the water,
And rolled it down the hill;
And this, they said, shall speedily turn
The poor old miller's mill.

"For there has been no water
Ever since the first of May;
And a busy man the miller will be
At dawning of the day.

"Oh! the miller, how he will laugh
When he sees the mill-dam rise!
The jolly old miller, how he will laugh,
Till the tears fill both his eyes!"

"And some they seized the little winds
That sounded over the hill;
And each put a horn into his mouth,
And blew both loud and shrill:

" And there, they said, the merry winds go,
Away from every horn;

And they shall clear the mildew dank
From the blind old widow's corn.

" Oh! the poor blind widow,
Though she has been blind so long,
She'll be blithe enough when the mildews gone,
And the corn stands tall and strong.

"And some they brought the brown lint-seed
And flung it down from the Low;
And this, they said, by the sunrise,
In the weaver's croft shall grow.

"Oh! the poor lame weaver,
How he will laugh outright,
When he sees his dwindling flax-field
All full of flowers by night!

"And then outspoke a brownie,
With a long beard on his chin;
I have spun up all the tow, said he,
And I want some more to spin.

"I've spun a piece of hempen cloth,
And I want to spin another;
A little sheet for Mary's bed,
And an apron for her mother.

"With that I could not help but laugh,
And I laughed out load and free;
And then on top of the Caldon Low
There was no one left but me.

"And all on top of the Caldon Low
The mists were cold and grey,
And nothing I saw but the mossy stones
That round about me lay.

"But coming down from the hill-top,
I heard afar below,
How busy the jolly miller was,
And how the wheel did go.

"And I peeped into the widow's field,
And, sure enough, were seen
The yellow ears of the mildewed corn,
All standing stout and green.

"And down by the weaver's croft I stole,
To see if the flax were sprung;
But I met the weaver at his gate,
With the good news on his tongue.

"Now this is all I heard, mother,
And all that I did see;
So, prythee, make my bed, mother,
For I'm tired as I can be."

The Roches.

S I X
John Naden of Leek

In the early years of the 18th century, before the introduction of the turnpikes, the oldest road in the area linked Leek with Macclesfield and Buxton. So old is this ancient way that first references to its existence can be found in 1230.

The road twists and turns its way through some of the loneliest and most picturesque of moorland scenery. It begins in the town and soon wends its way across the River Churnet, passing Abbey Green and Fould and on towards Meerbrook. At this point the road splits into three. Ahead lies the Roches, Gradbach and Flash. To the right it heads back towards an ancient road that leads to Buxton and to the left it follows a scenic and wooded route towards Danebridge, Wincle and Macclesfield.

The subjects of our story would have been as familiar with the Macclesfield road as they would with the landmarks of Gun-Hill and Gun-Common. John Naden was the son of an established Leek family who lived on the edge of the town at Hores Clough. Modern maps do not record Hores Clough but gradual changes in pronunciation have probably resulted in the name of Horsecroft, more familiar to the citizens of Leek. This land around Haregate with its proximity to the River Churnet and Abbey Green would have been a pleasant area for the Naden family to live and prosper.

The family, solid and dependable but as poor as most moorland families, made the best of their lot. Despite their hardship, they bestowed upon John an education in excess of the expectations of such a poor family. John attained a decent standard, competent in reading and writing, and the promise of youth and ability foretold a comfortable and happy life.

Whether John's character was flawed is difficult to ascertain, but it seems he lacked the strength of character to make anything of himself. In the end he found employment as the servant to Robert Brough, a grazier who resided at White Lea in the parish of Prestbury, in the County of Chester, a few miles to the north of Macclesfield. Brough was married to a woman much younger than himself and the arrival of young Naden highlighted the difference between the young man and a plodding, but good hearted, husband.

Mrs Brough, with the artfulness and experience of a married woman whose desires were unsatisfied by her husband, quickly ensnared the willing servant. In a very short time she and Naden embarked upon an illicit and passionate affair.

Early in the relationship she gave Naden a ring, expressed her love for him and intimated that they could be very happy together should anything happen to her husband. Mrs Brough made her intentions very plain and encouraged John to murder her husband and become master of the house.

The affair was to last for more than four years until Naden, somewhat reluctantly, went along with a lover whose impatience grew daily. The fact that Naden, at one time, saved his master from drowning only served to increase the pressure from Mrs Brough.

The suspicion that her husband had recognised the passion she felt for Naden now spurred her on to greater efforts. Naden succumbed and first tried to kill Brough as he returned from Congleton market. His clumsy attempts involved trapping Brough between his horse and a stone gate post and, although the attempt failed, it frightened Brough enough for him to relate matters to his drinking friends a few days later.

Those in the pub obviously decided that the drink was talking and ignored him. The conversation was forgotten and Naden continued in the employ of Robert Brough; but now in fear of losing his job. The botched attempt led to even more pressure on Naden and a couple of weeks later, in the middle of June 1731, he decided to try once again to murder his master.

When Robert Brough decided to go to Leek Fair, Naden made his plans accordingly. While Brough enjoyed the attractions of the Fair, John Naden spent the day in the Town's ale houses providing himself with Dutch courage. He left Leek sometime before Brough with the intention of waylaying him at a lonely spot near Danebridge.

He chose a spot on the edge of Gun Moor, and on a narrow section of the road he placed an obstruction which would cause his master to stop and remove it before proceeding. (Sleigh's *History of Leek* indicates a large stone). Lying in hiding Naden awaited the arrival of Brough. As anticipated, he stopped, and as he bent down to remove the obstacle Naden attacked from behind. Stunned, Brough fell to the ground. As he lay there Naden, taking Brough's own knife, slashed him on his wrist and then in a frenzy cut a great gash across his mouth which almost severed his head from his body.

Having finally fulfilled his mistress's wishes he hurried away from the scene, stopping only briefly at a house en route where he asked for a drink of water. At White Lea he acquainted Mrs Brough with the facts. As soon as the family had gone to bed she left the house and went to the spot where her husband lay dead, and went through his pockets. She also found the blood stained knife and threw it over the hedge. By 3.00 pm she was back at White Lea where she plotted with John Naden and came up with a false alibi which lay the blame on a William Wardle. Naden was to say that he actually saw Wardle do the deed. Shortly after, the body was discovered they were questioned and Wardle was subsequently arrested and held in jail.

At this point the hand of justice intervened. A woman came forward claiming that Naden had called at her house and asked for a drink of water. She noticed that his hands were covered in dried blood. At the same time Wardle's friends submitted positive evidence of his good character and innocence. Naden was arrested and committed by a local magistrate, Thomas Hollingshead of Ashenhurst.

Naden appeared before the Coroner, Thomas Palmer, and was examined on the question of murder. He denied the deed but with the evidence so plainly against him he was committed to Stafford jail on the 25th June in readiness to stand trial at the following assizes.

The trial began on Thursday 19th August 1731, at Stafford, and Naden once again pleaded not guilty. However, as more and more witnesses appeared and gave credible statements on behalf of Wardle, Naden finally succumbed to his guilt and confessed. He begged Wardle's forgiveness and affirmed the man's innocence in open court.

Naden was found guilty of murder. The Judge pronounced sentence that on Tuesday 31st of August he should be brought to his master's door, where he committed the act, and there be hanged till he was dead, and afterwards conveyed to Gun-Common, near Danebridge, and there hanged in chains .

Naden's written confession told of his infatuation with Brough's wife and of her persuasive endearments. But it was simply Naden's word against hers and the authorities were powerless to act. Naden ended his confession:

In the meantime, I beg forgiveness from all I have injured, and do declare and solemnly affirm this my confession to be exactly true, as I am a dying man and expect in a few days to appear before the tribunal of the great God of Heaven; as witness my hand this 27th. day of August 1731.

On the night before he was hanged, Naden was returned under guard to Leek. In a house on the corner of Stockwell Street and the Market Place, possibly the Cock Inn, the last rites were administered to him by the Reverend Mr Corn. He was said to be easy with himself saying, *"God's mercy was very great, or there would be no pardon for him, and though he had been a vile wretch he hoped for pardon through the merits of Jesus Christ."*

Meantime the inns of Leek were doing a roaring trade. Both locals and visitors had gathered for the hanging, with scenes of drunken revelry evident throughout the town. Many of them gathered the next day to accompany Naden and to witness the hanging.

Mr Corn and another clergyman attended Naden on his journey from Leek to the place of execution. Bizarrely, by today's standards, groups of singers from Leek, Bosley and Wincle sang psalms with him at Gun-Gate, and at the place of execution they all sang the 51st Psalm (one of David's when the prophet Nathan came to him after he had been into Bethsheba).

Naden climbed the ladder at 12.00 o'clock on a very hot day. He raised his hands, shook his head and desired Wardle to forgive him as he went to meet his maker. The manner of his death was grisly to say the least. From Miller's *Olde Leeke* the following extract remains as vivid today:

In another moment the rope, which had been fastened to the tree, was adjusted on his neck, and the ladder was removed, leaving the body suspended in the air. As this was done a thrill of horror ran through the crowd, some of the women shrieked and fainted, and the most hardened and calous-hearted men quaked at the terrible sight as they beheld the wretched man dangling from the tree. When the ladder was removed the body gave several violent spasmodic jerks, a gurgling noise was heard in the throat, the legs and arms worked convulsively for some minutes, the chest heaved heavily, the face became black as suffocation became more intense, the eyes almost burst from their sockets, and blood began to ooze from the mouth, nostrils, and ears of the unfortunate man. Then all was over. He died a hard and violent death. After the body had hung from the tree three-quarters of an hour it was cut down. The cavalcade was then reformed, and the corpse was borne to a place called Danebridge, or Gun Common, and there hanged in chains to a gallows erected for the purpose, and it is said that the body hung there until one limb fell from another.

S E V E N
William Palmer - Serial Killer

Doctor William Palmer, of Rugeley in Staffordshire, became one of the most notorious people in the Country when the news of his arrest for murder, and later the details of his trial, became public knowledge.

His notoriety came as no surprise to the people of Rugeley, nor to those of Kings Bromley, who knew of his background. Today we would perhaps speak in terms of bad genes; in the middle of the 19th century they simply spoke of bad blood. Palmer's background certainly left much to be desired. His maternal grandfather appears to have been an out and out rogue. After a liaison with a Madam who ran a brothel in Derby, he is said to have disappeared with a considerable sum of money which he used to good effect when he settled, some time later, in Kings Bromley.

His daughter was obviously worthy of pursuit, if only for financial reasons, and she managed to attract two main suitors. One was a sawyer by the name of Joseph Palmer and the other was the steward of the Marquis of Anglesey, who had large estates in the area. The daughter had no doubt inherited her father's morals for she opted to marry Joseph Palmer whilst continuing her liaison with the steward. Joseph Palmer, in turn, decided to use the liaison to his own advantage and, whilst his wife dallied with her lover, Palmer set about fiddling the haul of timber that came from the Marquis's estate. He is also said to have been engaged in a similar fiddle which involved timber from the Bagot estate.

The net result of Palmer's enterprise was a great deal of money which he used to purchase a substantial house in Station Road, Rugeley. It was here that William Palmer was born in September 1824, and he was christened in nearby St. Augustines Church on October 21st.

William's schooldays were anything but successful. His father placed him at Rugeley Grammar School, a school of good repute, under the control of headmaster the Reverend Thomas Bonney. Whilst other scholars, most notably Thomas Bonney, the head's son, advanced, Palmer quickly gained a reputation for dishonesty. He had about him a sly charm which he used to good effect persuading fellow pupils to write his thesis and complete his exercises. He was all too willing to use threats, or money stolen from his family, to achieve his

ILLUSTRATED AND UNABRIDGED EDITION

OF

The  Times

REPORT

OF THE

TRIAL OF WILLIAM PALMER,

FOR POISONING JOHN PARSONS COOK,

AT RUGELEY.

THE TALBOT ARMS, RUGELEY, THE SCENE OF COOK'S DEATH.

FROM THE SHORT-HAND NOTES TAKEN IN THE CENTRAL CRIMINAL COURT
FROM DAY TO DAY.

objectives. One fellow pupil by the name of Timmis remembered Palmer well and described him as *"a thoroughly bad boy who did not mind how he cheated"*.

What little discipline existed in William Palmer's life ended in 1837 with the sudden death of his father. Joseph left a sum of over £70,000, in a unsigned will, but sufficient for his wife and family to arrange distribution of his assets. The seven children were five brothers and two sisters, and it seems that each of the boys inherited a sum of £7,000 with the remainder going to the widow on the proviso that she did not remarry. In 1837 the sum of £7,000 represented a considerable fortune but it was to prove totally inadequate for the free spending womaniser, gambler and horse racing fanatic that the young Palmer was to become.

Despite their dubious background the rest of the children managed to live their lives without resorting to murder and crime. Joseph, the eldest, became a wealthy merchant who traded in Liverpool, George became a local solicitor, Walter made nothing of his life and was an alcoholic, and Thomas became a Church of England clergyman. Of the daughters, the elder was very much like her brother Walter and drank herself to death whilst the younger daughter proved to be a charming and accomplished lady, well respected by all. A mixed bag indeed.

The restrictions of the will had little effect on Joseph's widow and, although she determined never to marry again, she entertained a number of male friends. The most amorous was a Mr Duffy, a man twenty years her junior who lodged at the Shoulder of Mutton pub in Rugeley. Duffy, a fair haired and handsome man, eventually tired of her affection and disappeared, leaving his case behind containing many love letters from Mrs Palmer. Duffy's place was quickly filled by a Rugeley solicitor, Jerry Smith.

In the meantime William completed his education at Rugeley Grammar School and began his working life by being apprenticed to the firm of Evans and Evans, wholesale druggists in Liverpool. With little discipline outside his place of work, William played the field and was known to have seduced at least one young girl.

He was a great gambler and he began to pay for his exploits by stealing from his employers. It became his practice to intercept the mail and remove any money enclosed - it was common practice at that time to settle debts by forwarding cash by post and Palmer was not slow to take advantage of this.

His dishonesty soon became apparent but, although traps were set, Palmer found a way around them for a while, before he was actually caught opening one of the firm's letters and they were able to dismiss him. Ever supportive of her son and anxious to avoid a scandal Mrs Palmer agreed to replace the stolen money, and to avoid family disgrace, William's own brother was allowed to complete the apprenticeship.

For William the die was now cast. At the age of eighteen he embarked on a second apprenticeship, this time for five years with Dr Edward Tylecote of Great Haywood, a village but a short distance from Rugeley. His penchant for sex and gambling continued unabated, as did his dishonesty. His mother continued to pay off his debts including a record of £5 to a local farmer.

Visiting local patients gave William the ideal opportunity to call on his lady friends and his reputation steadily worsened. On one occasion he took one of his favourites, Jane Widnall, to Walsall and remained with her until his brothers discovered his whereabouts, settled his debts and returned him to Great Haywood. He still managed to see Jane by various ruses. The most notorious was to attend church with Jane's parents and then arrange to be called out to see a patient. While her parents were in church William made love to Jane.

As was to be expected in such a small and tight knit community, their meetings were soon discovered. To appease Jane's parents William agreed to marry her although such a promise meant absolutely nothing to him.

He was no longer welcome in Great Haywood and left the employ of Dr Tylecote to take up a position at Stafford Infirmary. It was here that Palmer discovered the poisons that were eventually to be his downfall. Palmer's interest in the Dispensary reached such proportions that he, and other pupils, were forbidden to enter the room. It seems, however, that the damage was done. The use of poisons, along with his cravings for sex and gambling, had found a place in Palmer's devious mind.

The first of Palmer's probable victims came to grief during his time at the Infirmary. It is said that he got into a minor dispute in a public house with a local man called Abley. Abley was challenged to a drinking bout and was thought to have had poison placed in his drink. Whether that was the case or not, Abley staggered outside and was violently sick in the adjacent stables. He died shortly afterwards. An inquest followed and a verdict of *Death from Natural Causes* was returned. The foreman of the Jury was unhappy with the verdict and was convinced that Palmer had poisoned Abley. This was to be the first of many occasions when death and Palmer were in close proximity.

(Although over a century later a relative of Abley, researching his family tree, was to draw a totally different conclusion over his ancestor's death.)

Even if we conclude that Palmer may not have killed Abley, the fact remains that his wayward life continued unabated. In 1846 Palmer went to London to complete his training to be a doctor under the guidance of Dr Stegale. Far from becoming a serious student Palmer embarked upon a life of parties, prostitutes and heavy gambling. His reputation in the capital became as bad as it was in Rugeley. One of the hospital officials refused point blank to allow Palmer to lodge with him on the basis that to do so would place his daughters in moral danger.

As for his studies, Palmer showed little aptitude for learning. He finally promised Dr Stegale the sum of 50 guineas if he would cram him to pass his examinations. By some miracle Palmer did pass but then reneged on his promise to Dr Stegale. Dr Stegale was forced to enter into litigation. The case was found in his favour and Palmer had to pay. Even though the trial was in London, an account published in a newspaper fell into the hands of Dr Bamford of Staffordshire. Palmer's exploits in London came as no surprise to the people of Rugeley.

On his return to Rugeley, armed with his newly acquired Diploma of the Royal College of Surgeons, Palmer set up in practice and settled into a house in Market Street. Shortly afterwards Ann Brookes entered his life.

Ann was the illegitimate child of a Colonel Brookes, who, on retirement from the Indian Army, settled in Stafford. Brookes was part of a family much prone to suicide. Although Brookes never married he had a mistress, Ann Thornton, his former housemaid. Ann Thornton took to drink, became an alcoholic and caused him so much distress that he shot himself. It is said that all Brookes' four brothers also committed suicide.

During his liaison with Thornton a daughter was conceived. Ann Brookes was born in 1827. The Colonel left a will in which his mistress and daughter inherited considerable wealth. However, legal complications caused delay in the settlement and Ann became a ward in chancery and was placed under the guardianship of a Charles Dawson of Stafford.

Dawson also had a country house in Abbots Bromley and it was here that she fell for the charm of Dr William Palmer. Whether or not Palmer was aware of Ann's financial status, the courtship, and eventual marriage, was certainly to his advantage. Despite the objections of Charles Dawson, who was aware of

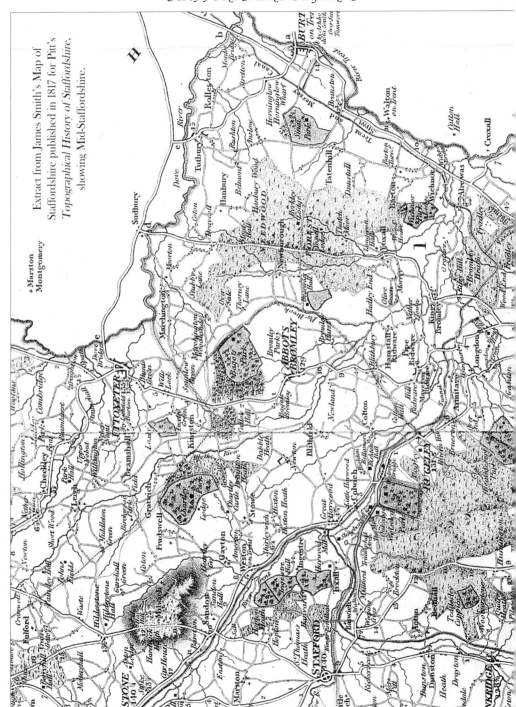

Extract from James Smith's Map of Staffordshire published in 1817 for Pitt's Topographical History of Staffordshire, showing Mid-Staffordshire.

Palmer's reputation, the wedding went ahead and they were married at Abbots Bromley on the 7th October 1847.

A year later, on the 11th October 1848, their first child was born. Christened William he was destined to survive the four later children who all died in infancy. Whether Palmer resented the expense of children or simply the encumbrance is unclear. At this time he still had some money and the ability to earn a living, although his practice was already failing, as he spent more and more time pursuing his interest in horse racing. The death of his four other children, according to the family nurse Ann Bradshaw, was due to Palmer's unthinkable method of poisoning. Bradshaw claimed that Palmer would nurse the children and allow them to suck his finger which had been coated with poison and dusted with sugar. Ann Bradshaw was not slow to make her feelings known in the nearby public house, but her remarks were obviously insufficient to be taken seriously, or to bring about retribution.

Palmer continued on his wayward path. An affair with a Rugeley woman, Jane, resulted in an illegitimate child which also died. Meantime heavy losses on horse racing began to take their toll. Palmer's reputation plumbed new depths as debts remained unpaid and money lenders began to apply pressure.

In an effort to placate his creditors, Palmer approached his mother-in-law, Ann Thornton, who initially refused to lend him money but relented after much pressure and the fear that her daughter's life would be made a scandal and a misery. The sum of £20 he obtained did little to ease Palmer's problems and, hoping to obtain more, he invited her to stay awhile with him and his wife. She accepted the offer with some reluctance and with a prophecy of doom that proved to be remarkably accurate. She died soon after arriving at the Palmer residence. As it turned out, her death was to no avail, as Palmer gained no benefit at all from Ann's will.

By now even the slow-witted were beginning to wonder what sort of man they had in their midst. On the face of it the jovial and charming doctor was all 'hail fellow, well met', whilst in his wake lay a trail of suspicious deaths. Some recalled previous deaths, including that of Joseph Bentley, an uncle of Palmer's who lived near Uttoxeter. Staying with Palmer, the two engaged in a bout of heavy drinking, and the following morning Bentley was so ill that he failed to recover and died three days later.

The death of a Mr Bladon from Ashby-de-la-Zouch seemed equally suspicious. Bladon had visited Palmer in May 1850 to collect a debt. During the meeting Bladon became ill. Palmer, in an effort perhaps to spread any blame, sent for Dr Bamford and asked him to prescribe medication. Somehow Bladon's wife got to hear about his illness and arrived to see him. But Palmer persuaded her not to send for other relatives as the journey to Ashby and back would take too long.

Bladon died and was buried with undue haste. His widow showed surprise at the small amount of money he had with him when she knew he had set out with a considerable sum. Not only had Palmer avoided payment of the debt, Bladon's money had disappeared also. Bladon's brother was highly suspicious but was prevented from taking action by Mrs Bladon who refused to embarrass Mrs Palmer by accusations when there was no evidence of a crime being committed.

Even within the family Palmer was now viewed with suspicion. When a visiting aunt complained of feeling unwell Palmer gave her medication in the form of some pills. The aunt decided not to take the pills. The following morning a belligerent Palmer urged her to take the medication but she declined and some time later disposed of the pills by throwing them out of the window into the yard. It is said that the poultry in the yard ate the pills and promptly died. It certainly seemed that Palmer's medication left something to be desired.

Whatever money Palmer managed to obtain it was still insufficient to meet his debts, and he again sought salvation in the demise of his creditors. One such was a Mr Bly of Beccles. Bly had met Palmer at a race meeting and during the course of the meeting had won the sum of £800 from him. Later Bly, complaining of feeling unwell, was treated by Dr Palmer. Needless to say he died soon after, but not before telling his wife that Palmer owed him £800. When Mrs Bly approached Palmer for the £800 he claimed that Bly must have been deluded and that it was really Bly who owed the money to Palmer.

Around this time Palmer began attempts to obtain large sums of money by insurance fraud. He had discovered that Colonel Brookes, in his will, had left his daughter - Palmer's wife Ann - only a life's interest in his estate, after which the property would pass to the next heir. Palmer sought to insure his wife's life and, although several companies declined, he eventually obtained life cover of £13,000. Ann Palmer's days were now numbered. After visiting Liverpool, in September 1854 to attend a concert, Ann caught a chill. Feeling unwell she returned next day to Rugeley and took to her bed. Naturally Palmer attended her and although she managed to consume some tea and toast she vomited shortly afterwards.

Also in attendance during Ann Palmer's illness was Dr Bamford of Rugeley and Dr Knight of Stafford. Dr Bamford prescribed pills and medicine and called again two days later to find that only one pill had been taken. Within days Mrs Palmer had died and Dr Bamford, now into his ninth decade, certified English cholera as the cause of death. Cholera was common at the time and the cause was not questioned by Dr Knight, or indeed by a third man Benjamin Thirlby, an associate of Palmer. The insurance company reluctantly paid Palmer the sum of £13,000.

His wife was laid to rest in the family vault in Rugeley churchyard where Palmer was seen to be greatly distressed and weeping profusely. His distress did not last too long as he was consoled that night by his housemaid Eliza Tharme. Nine months later, in June 1855, Eliza gave birth to Palmer's illegitimate son. The son was to survive just six months before dying on the 13th December 1855!

By now Palmer had cleared some of his debts but had disposed of the £13,000. To sustain his lifestyle further he began to forge his mother's signature on bills which he attempted to discount in London. Although his mother became aware of this deception she found it impossible to be too severe on William who had long been her favourite.

Now in an effort to obtain greater sums and to satisfy his main money lender, Mr Pratt of London, Palmer attempted another insurance swindle. William Palmer's brother, Walter, was an alcoholic who lived in Stafford. He lived off his inheritance and the private income of his wife which amounted to £450 per annum. William promised Walter a large sum of money in return for having his life insured. Six companies were approached for sums of around £82,000 and although caution had been advised a policy was finally obtained, albeit for a smaller amount. Walter was not a good candidate - his life was plagued with illness through his excessive drinking.

At the first opportunity William began administering to the medical needs of his brother. What he treated him with is open to conjecture but he was seen purchasing prussic acid in Stafford and making up a mixture in the Junction Hotel. Walter's death came following a day at the races. He was taken ill for a while and then took a turn for the worse. He died while his wife was visiting her relatives in Liverpool and, during her absence Palmer saw that Walter was quickly buried in the family vault at Rugeley. Palmer arranged to meet Walter's

RUGELEY, FROM THE SOUTH, LOOKING TOWARDS THE RAILWAY.

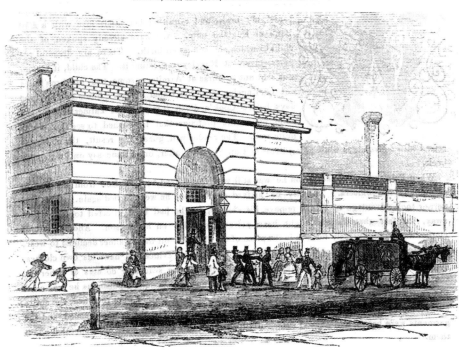

Stafford Gaol

[19 to 21] **November** — 19 MONDAY [323–42] — 11th Month **1855**

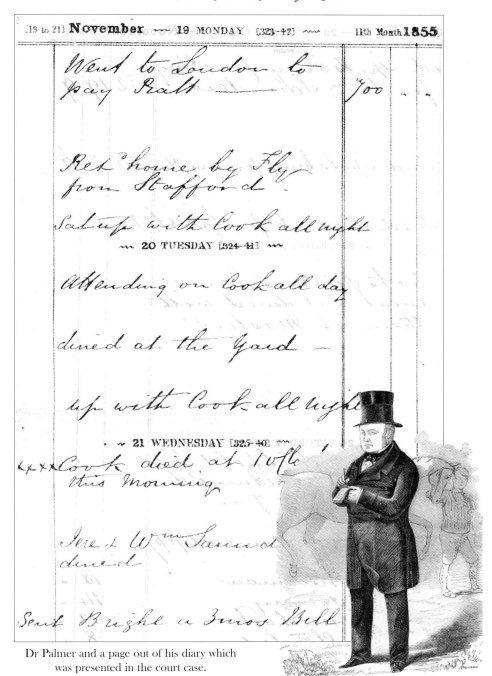

Went to London to
pay Pratt _____ 700 . . --

Ret'd home by Fly
from Stafford.

Sat up with Cook all night

— 20 TUESDAY [324–41] —

Attending on Cook all day

dined at the yard —

up with Cook all night

. ~ 21 WEDNESDAY [325–40] —

xxxxCook died at 10½
this morning

Jere & W'm Saunders
dined

Sent B—right a 3 mos Bell

Dr Palmer and a page out of his diary which
was presented in the court case.

wife and escort her from Liverpool where he broke the news to her of her husband's death and internment. He attempted to persuade her that it would be wise if she gave up her interest in the insurance policy.

As it happened the insurance company became most suspicious and refused to pay the claim. Legal action was threatened and Palmer reluctantly dropped his claim. The insurance company contacted two local men, a George Bate and a Tom Myatt, and both referred to occasions when Palmer had tried to persuade them to undertake life insurance. Myatt also claimed that Palmer tried to poison him by lacing his drink. Needless to say insurance proved difficult for Palmer to come by from that moment on.

Now even more desperate, and under pressure from his money lender, he found himself in more trouble. A Stafford girl, Jane Bergen, the daughter of a policeman, began to blackmail Palmer. It appears that Palmer and Jane had an affair and, when Jane became pregnant, she was forced to have an operation and abort the child. Using the contents of a number of explicit love letters Palmer had sent her, she set about extracting money from him on the threat that she would reveal all to her father if he did not cooperate.

With pressure from the money lender and from Jane Bergen, Palmer embarked upon his final desperate attempt to obtain money. John Parsons Cook, from Lutterworth, was an ex-solicitor who used his private income to support his hobby of horse racing. Cook was on friendly terms with Palmer and they attended race meetings together. Cook also owned race horses and one by the name of Polestar won the Shrewsbury Handicap and the sum of £1,700.

Cook and Palmer celebrated that night in the Raven Hotel and returned to the racecourse again the next day. The following night Palmer plied Cook with excessive amounts of drink and was seen paying particular attention to a tumbler of liquid. Cook became very sick. Although he suspected Palmer of foul play, their friendship continued and they returned to Rugeley where Cook took a room at the Talbot Arms Hotel, opposite Palmer's house. Later Cook dined at Palmer's house and by the following morning was feeling violently sick again. Palmer caringly prepared some soup for the invalid and sent it across to the Talbot Arms.

Cook was immediately sick again. Palmer now began to attend Cook continuously and also persuaded Dr Bamford to also prescribe pills for him. More broth was sent to Cook. This time a chambermaid, thinking it smelled nice, decided to sample it. She vomited immediately.

Palmer now sent for a friend of Cook, a Mr Jones, to come to visit the patient. Whether Palmer obtained Cook's money is difficult to ascertain, although he made a quick trip to London while Jones was in attendance at Rugeley. On his return to Rugeley, Palmer was observed purchasing three grains of strychnine. He later obtained a further six grains, plus some prussic acid. Palmer, with the assistance of Dr Bamford, made a number of tablets which were later administered to Cook along with a dark coloured liquid. Jones, sleeping in the same room as Cook, awoke around midnight to find Cook in great pain. Palmer was sent for and gave Cook two more pills.

The effect of the pills on Cook had catastrophic results. He began to shriek and scream in pain, tossing about and going into convulsions. His muscles contracted, his body became arched and rigid and in this appalling state, he died. Palmer quickly laid out the body - presumably taking the opportunity to search for any incriminating evidence.

Cook's stepfather, Mr Stephens, hearing of his death, came immediately to Rugeley and, after questioning Palmer as to the circumstances, became most suspicious - his doubts compounded by the absence of certain documents that Cook had been in possession of, and now nowhere to be found.

Palmer asked Dr Bamford to sign the death certificate - the cause of death to be recorded as apoplexy. A post mortem reported that Cook's *"intestine was healthy and showed no indication of syphilis"* although Cook was thought to have been a sufferer. Palmer however was no doubt anxious about any further tests and he attempted to tip over the containers of intestines and stomach which were ready to send for analysis. Then when they were sent away Palmer tried to bribe a cab driver by offering him £10 to break the jars. The driver refused.

Palmer now tried to bribe the Rugeley postmaster, Mr Cheshire, and in this he succeeded. By intercepting a letter from London, Palmer discovered that no trace of poison had been found. A relieved Palmer was heard to exclaim *'I am as innocent as a baby'*. Palmer then tried to bribe the coroner to return a verdict of death by natural causes. The coroner would have none of it and, perhaps swayed by Palmer's reputation, and the recent purchase of strychnine, recorded a verdict of willful murder.

Palmer now became ill and took to his bed, but upon recovery he was arrested for the murder of John Parsons Cook. Shortly after the arrest, the bodies of Ann Palmer and Walter Palmer were exhumed and post mortems carried out. Walter's body was in a grotesque condition with swollen limbs and

PALMER'S STABLES FOR BROOD MARES AT RUGELEY.

cheeks, the smell from his body making the examiner quite sick. Ann Palmer's body was in better condition. The inquest proved inconclusive on Walter but Ann was found to have been killed by antimony poisoning.

The trial of Dr William Palmer took place in London and he was eventually found guilty and sentenced to death by hanging. He was transferred to Stafford gaol for execution. Such was Palmer's fame by now, the streets of Stafford in the vicinity of the gaol were crowded with spectators to witness the event at 8.00am on the morning of June 14th 1856. Between 30,000 and 40,000 people surrounded the scaffold to witness his demise.

Palmer, despite the entreaties of family, friends and officials refused to acknowledge his guilt and stood quietly while the hangman, George Smith, prepared him for his final moment. Smith placed the rope around his neck and shook hands with him. Palmer said, *God bless you*, and went to his death.

The transcript of the trial makes interesting reading and has, over the years, become famous in the annals of legal history. Initially his trial was to have been held in Stafford but it was thought that local bias would have made a fair verdict impossible. Instead a hastily passed act of parliament enabled the trial to be held in London, between the 14th and 22nd May 1856.

Controversy has surrounded the trial ever since. Despite the concerns of local bias the case became a source of gossip, speculation and general news throughout the land. It is extremely doubtful that any member of the jury would have been unaware of the circumstances surrounding the case. Opinions would almost certainly have been formed before the trial even began.

Ward, Coroner.   Dr. Rees.   Thirlby. Smith, Solicitor. Sup. Hatton,   Dr. Taylor.
INTERIOR OF THE TOWN HALL, RUGELEY, DURING THE INQUEST ON THE BODY OF JOHN PARSONS COOK.

The trial itself is distinguished by the attitude of the Attourney-General, Lord Campbell, who was thought by some to be determined to hang Palmer, and by the excessive amount of circumstantial evidence upon which a verdict was reached. It should be remembered that Palmer was on trial for the murder of Cook only and not for any of his other probable victims. It should also be remembered that strychnine was given as the cause of death and in 1856 the ability to diagnose the presence of strychnine was limited. It should also be noted that strychnine was at the time used by doctors in small doses in tonics - and continued to be so used to the middle of the 20th century.

The similarity between strychnine and tetanus upon the body confused both prosecution and defence. Add to this the conflicting opinion of eminent doctors and the picture that emerges is one of doubt. Very little attention seems to have been given to the evidence of Dr Nunnerly of Leeds who shortly before the Palmer trial was involved in the trial of a Dr Dove, also of Leeds, who had been accused of murdering his wife by strychnine. In that case it was ascertained that traces of the poison were found in the body. For some reason Dr Nunnerly was called for the defence and not the prosecution. A description of Dr Dove's wife showed symptoms very similar to those of Cook.

During his summing up the Attourney-General advised the jury that strychnine kills by causing tetanic fixing of the respiratory muscles, which matched Cook's symptoms. We also learn that Cook visited a Dr Savage frequently and was concerned about his health long before he became involved with Palmer. Dr Savage initially prescribed a mild dose of mercury which was later replaced by a tonic when Cook failed to improve. The tonic seems to have improved Cook's health although the swelling around his throat and the follicles under his tongue remained and were noted during the post

DRS. TAYLOR AND REES PERFORMING THEIR ANALYSIS.

mortem. He also had ulcers on his lips and seems to have been in poor health despite claims to the contrary. Later opinion pointed to secondary syphilis.

Two other comments are worthy of note. Mr Edward Duke Moore, a surgeon, said that he prescribed a small amount of strychnine to a patient who subsequently became stiff in every limb, his head drawn back, his spine arched and he screamed in pain - the effects of strychnine poisoning. William Herepath, Professor of Chemistry at Bristol Medical School, stated that he had detected strychnine in the stomach of a patient who died from strychnine, three days after the death. He had also detected it in animals two months after death. He believed that even small amounts of strychnine could be traced.

So why was no trace of strychnine found in Cook's body even though all the symptoms pointed to strychnine poisoning? The answer seems to lie in the limitations of the people carrying out the examinations and in the botched transfer of organs from Rugeley.

Mr Serjeant Shee, the main defence council, made great play of the lack of concrete evidence although he did Palmer's cause no good at all by constantly pointing out the fact that this innocent man was being persecuted by a biased prosecution. Too many people had read about Palmer's exploits to consider him anything but a rogue. Despite the eloquence of Mr Serjeant Shee's defence, the Attourney-General remained unconvinced, and so did the jury.

After a long and detailed summing up the jury retired. They took little over an hour to reach a guilty verdict that few would argue with, regardless of its basis on circumstantial evidence.

E I G H T

Flash. Fact or Fiction

The village of Flash sits high in the Staffordshire Moorlands, and at a height of 1500 feet above sea level claims, with some justification, to be the highest in England. Its remoteness and geography are easy enough to substantiate; if they were its only claim to fame the village would be allowed to rest in peace. However, its greater fame relates to its reputation as a centre for counterfeit notes and coins. The search for the truth about this continues unabated, although there is very little evidence to substantiate the famous stories that surround this otherwise ordinary moorland village.

The place Flash existed long before the tales of forged notes and coins began to circulate. Flash means a swamp or wet land, and Quarnford, of which Flash is a part, was originally Quernford - or 'millford'. But the word flash later came to have connotations with such words as 'spiv' or 'top-show', and ostentatious displays of wealth - the words flash and flashy are still used.

The first reference to Flash as a centre of disrepute appears to be that of a Dr Aiken in a book published in 1795. Dr Aiken's text, plus several others that follow, have a similarity that leads to the conclusion that the later publications may well have been simply based upon Dr Aiken's original publication. From Dr Aiken's *Description of the Country from 30 to 40 miles round Manchester* (1875):

In the wild country between Buxton, Leek and Macclesfield, called the Flash, from a chapel of that name, lived a set of pedestrian chapmen, who hawked about these buttons, together with ribands and ferreting made at Leek, and handkerchiefs, with small wares from Manchester. These pedlars were known on the roads which they travelled by the appellation of Flashmen, and frequented farmhouses and fairs, using a sort of slang or canting dialect. At first they paid ready money for their goods, till they acquired credit, which they were sure to extend till no more was to be had; when they dropped their connections without paying, and formed new ones. They long went on thus, enclosing the common where they dwelt for a trifling payment and building cottages till they began to have farms, which they improved from the gains of their credit without troubling themselves about payment, since no bailiff for a long time attempted to serve a writ there. At length, a resolute officer, a native of the district, ventured to arrest several of them; whence their credit being blown up they changed the wandering life of pedlars for the settled care of their farms. But as these were held by no leases, they were left at the mercy of the lords of the soil, the Harpur family, who made them pay for their impositions on others.

Three Shires Head and some 'flash' notes.

Another set of pedestrians from the country where buttons were formerly made, was called the Broken Cross Gang from a place of that name between Macclesfield and Congleton. These associated with the Flashmen at fairs, playing with thimbles and buttons like jugglers with cups and balls, and enticing people to lose their money by gambling. They at length took to the kindred trades of robbing and picking pockets till at length the gang was broken up by the hands of justice. We cannot but remark, that Autolycus in Shakespeare seems to have been a model of this worthy brotherhood.

And from Samuel Smiles *Life of James Brindley* in *Lives of the Engineers*. (1861)

In order to favour the button trade, an act of Parliament passed about 80 years ago, inflicting a penalty upon the wearing of moulds covered with the same stuff with the garment; and this, after having fallen into neglect, was again attempted to be enforced with rigour in 1778 and hired informers were engaged in London and the country to put it into execution - an odious and very uncommercial mode of enforcing a manufacture. The result of which was rather to promote the use of metal and horn buttons. The trade is still however considerable.

And from *Notes on the Northern Borders of Staffordshire* by the Rev. William Beresford in *The Reliquary Vol. V 1864-5.*

In the third year of the reign of George I ... the first English canal engineer was born in a remote hamlet in the High Peak of Derbyshire in the midst of a rough country, then inhabited by quite as rough people. The nearest town of any importance was Macclesfield where a considerable number of people were employed about the middle of last century in making wrought buttons in silk, mohair and twist such being then the staple trade of the place. These articles were sold throughout the country by pedestrian hawkers, most of whom lived in the wild country called "the Flash" from a hamlet of that name situated between Buxton, Leek and Macclesfield. They squatted on the waste lands and commons in the district, and were notorious for their wild half barbarous manners and brutal pastimes. Travelling about from fair to fair, and using a cant or slang dialect, they became generally known as "Flashmen" and the name still survives. Their numbers so grew and their encroachments on the land became so great, that it was at length found necessary to root them out, but for some time no bailiff was found sufficiently bold to attempt to serve a Writ in the district. At length an officer was found who undertook to arrest several of them, and other landowners, taking courage followed the example, when those who refused to become tenants left to squat elsewhere; and the others consented to settle down to the cultivation of their farms. Another set of travelling rogues belonging to the same neighbourhood was called the "Broken Cross Gang" from a place called Broken Cross, situated to the southeast of Macclesfield. These fellows consorted a good deal with the Flashmen, frequenting markets and travelling from fair to fair practicing the pea and thimble trick, and enticing honest country folk into the temptation of gambling. They *proceeded to more open thieving and pocket picking until at length the magistrates of the district took active measures to loot them out of Broken Cross and the gang became broken up. Such was the district and such the population in the neighbourhood of which our hero was born. James Brindley first saw the light in a humble cottage standing about midway between the hamlet of Great Rocks and that of Tunstead in the liberty of Thornsett some 3 miles to the northeast of Buxton. The house in which he was born in the year 1716 has long fallen to ruins.*

"It is now (1864-5) it seems more than 200 years since the coal trade and the button manufacture were introduced into this wild country. Intimately connected with the latter, as pedestrian hawkers, were the noted " Flashmen", living in the last century, and already mentioned. They squatted on the moors about Flash, and made it their business to carry buttons over the country for sale. Travelling from town to town and speaking a sort of cant, or slang dialect, they soon obtained their peculiar name, and became notorious for their rude, half savage manners, and brutal pastimes. Increasing in numbers, they became a nuisance to the vicinity and it was then resolved to eject them; but no bailiff could, for a while be found sufficiently bold for the purpose. When, however, an officer was procured who undertook to arrest several of them, other landlords followed the example of the prime mover; they who refused to become tenants left the district and formed the " Broken Cross Gang " whilst the more peaceably disposed consented to settle down in the cultivation of farms, and some of their descendants remain on the spot to the present day".

And from *Round About* by William Bullock, Macclesfield. (c. 1877)

"The trade of the town (Macclesfield) consists chiefly of the manufacture of ladies and gentlemens silk handkerchiefs. About 250 years ago Macclesfield was celebrated throughout England for its manufacture of curiously wrought silk buttons, mohair and silk twists.

These goods were hawked through the country by a set of pedestrian " chapmen" who lived in the wild country between Leek, Buxton and Macclesfield, called "The Flash".

These men, who had now earned the name of 'Flashmen', assisted by another set called 'Broken Cross Gang', having acquired all the goods they could by fair or foul means thereby nearly ruining the town, had to be broken up by the strong arm of the law. After this the trade revived, and in 1720 an Act of Parliament was passed to protect the trade, and forbidding any person to wear buttons made of the same material as the garment".

In later years the article by Dr Aiken was roundly condemned as being without proof or authenticity, but, although there may be some justification in this, it must be assumed that even hearsay or rumour has a source of origin. Where the truth lies remains a mystery.

Perhaps the best known book is *Flash* by Judge Reugg which was published in 1928. Reugg for his part lays no claim to historical fact and simply wrote a novel about the life and times of Longnor and Flash during the early days of the 19th century (1830) using forgery as his main theme. He was shrewd enough to use his local knowledge and legal acumen together with common names to give more credence to his story. But the integrity of Judge Reugg remains firmly intact as can be seen from a letter that he sent to a Mr Duncalf who had posed the obvious question.

Highfields Hall
Uttoxeter
Staffs.
15th August 1940

Dear Sir,
I am glad you liked my book Flash. I made many enquiries when writing it but could find no evidence of false notes being made there.
All I could discover you will find in the note on page 227 of the book.

Yours sincerely

A. H. Reugg.

The story could end very neatly here; except that assize records point to a very different story. There can be no doubt whatsoever that counterfeiting was rife in the moorland areas. Despite the fact that forgery was a hanging offence until 1831 the temptation to improve one's lot and escape the appalling poverty of the time was greater than the threat of hanging or deportation. Let us distance ourselves from supposition and consider the facts.

The Bank of England (Bank of England Museum; Derrick Byatt, Spinks, London, 1994) acknowledge that the forged notes were a common problem. In addition to straight forward forgery, attempts were made to produce notes that were genuine products but fraudulent by design. For example a note would be made to look similar to a £20 note except that the promise was for 20 pence, the forger, if caught, hoping to be charged with the lesser offence of fraud. Other notes carried headings like 'Bank of Engraving' or 'Bank of Elegance'. Such notes were claimed to be forms of advertising but served their illegal purpose very well when used as 'flash' notes. The forger or the flashman could look the part by having a wad of counterfeit notes with a few genuine ones on top.

One local magistrate (Miller's *Olde Leeke*) who served the area from 1810

More 'flash' notes and above, the beautiful, but at times bleak, Staffordshire Highlands.

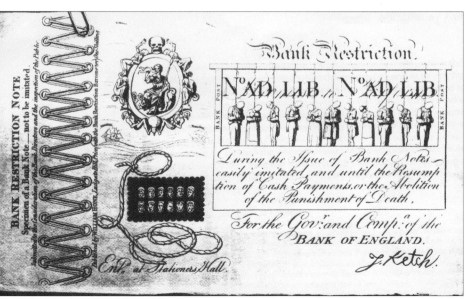

felt quite certain that the forged notes were manufactured at Flash as can be seen from the following extract:

> *What is the origin of the word "Flash" as applied to base coins? - I never heard of the term "Flash" being applied to coin, though I have known the locality where the term was used from 1810.*
>
> *But I know it perfectly well as applied to forged notes. I became a magistrate more than 52 years ago, and between 1810 and that time what I am about to mention occurred:*
>
> *At, or in the neighbourhood of Flash, the manufacture of forged notes was carried on: and they were sent to Birmingham by the higglers, I think, from the "Bottom House" a public house on the turnpike road between Ashbourne and Leek, and they received the name of "Flash" from the place where they were made. A family of the name of Wardle, unless my memory deceives me, was concerned in the forgery, and I think some of them were executed at Stafford, and another, a woman, being imprisoned for forgery, was let out of prison by one of the officers of the prison, who gave himself up on a threat by the magistrates in quarter sessions that, unless the person who let the woman escape was produced, all the officers should be dismissed. This, I believe, I heard from the magistrate who suggested the threat to be used. The record of circuit, or books of the prison, if the latter exist so far back, would probably throw light on the matter.*

One would assume that a magistrate would have justification for such comments and at least some part of his claims match the legal records of trials that took place at Stafford. From the assize records we know that counterfeit coins were produced in the moorlands area and that from time to time the criminals were apprehended, tried, and either hanged or deported to Australia.

One such event concerned the Meg Lane forgers. It appears that a coining machine was discovered at a farm near Meg Lane at Sutton near Macclesfield. The road from Macclesfield to Leek, now known as Leek Old Road passed through Sutton en-route to Leek and the moorland villages of Quarnford and Flash. The trial of the Meg Lane forgers took place at Chester in 1784 and included a John Oakes and a John Orme who both lived in Sutton. A guilty verdict resulted in the ringleaders being hanged and several others deported.

Further evidence of forgery was discovered many years later during a road widening scheme in Leek. During the removal of a roadside building, possibly an old mill, a coin mould was found hidden within the wall. The impression indicated that the mould was used during the reign of George III. The fact that coins were produced in the area comes as no surprise. Macclesfield and Leek were traditionally involved in the silk and button making trades and the skills required to make buttons could easily be adapted to the art of making blank disks and coins. Add to this the engraver's art required for fancy buttons and you have all the skills necessary to produce good quality coins.

Movement of coins was simple enough. A slight adaptation plus a covering of cloth and a coin would pass for a button to all but the most discerning observer. At one time the government was so concerned that it passed an act prohibiting the covering of buttons with cloth or silk to match clothing. Such an act, however well intended, had little hope of halting the trade in counterfeit coins and only the intervention of private detectives and a local constabulary, that had yet to be formalised, stood in the way of the forger.

If the use of forged coins was rife, the use of forged bank notes was even more so. One particular case involved George Fearns who kept the Bottom Public House (now the Green Man), a few miles away from Leek on the Ashbourne road. Fearns was trapped by a Mr Nadin, Assistant Chief Constable of Manchester, who had been assigned to the task by the Bank of England, in an effort to eliminate an illegal trade that could seriously undermine the financial stability of the country. (By coincidence Nadin, whose family came from the Buxton area, was from the same family as the John Naden hanged for murder in 1731 **see Ch 5** - Reference: Leek Library; Rev. Dennis Lloyd Nadin. *Roots and Branches*, Vol. 1, No. 2, 1989)

Nadin, using the name of William River and assisted by a constable, Mr Marshall Knowles, using the name Mr Marshall, disguised themselves as hawking pedlars and called at the Bottom Public House. They had with them all the goods of their trade including considerable quantities of cambrics, muslins, prints etc. which they carried in a one horse chair (cart).

They asked for accommodation for the night and were attended to by Fearns himself. Wishing to avoid suspicion they made few observations that night, except to comment that it was difficult for a man to live honestly in such bad times.

The following morning Fearns joined them for breakfast. Nadin ordered milk and rum, and, finding fault with it, asked Fearns where he had bought it. Fearns replied *"off a man in Manchester"*. Nadin decided to put Fearns to the test. He told Fearns he dealt in that article (rum) and that he could supply some very cheap. Fearns responded by asking Nadin ('River') if he was a smuggler and how much would it cost. The price of six shillings and sixpence per gallon was attractive enough for Fearns to order immediately. He questioned Nadin about how he transported the rum and was told a cask of twenty gallons of rum was placed into a barrel of American flour. The excise men would have no reason to doubt the authenticity of barrels of flour. Fearns thought it a very good plan and was willing to go along with the scheme.

Nadin and Knowles, having established Fearns willingness to trade in illicit goods, now enticed him further. After showing him their swag, which they said was already spoken for, Nadin put down a forged Halifax guinea note. Fearns declared he was unable to change it. Nadin said he wanted it to be examined, not changed. Fearns duly examined the note and, after some deliberation, stated that the note was a forgery and a poor one at that.

The subject further turned to screeves (forged bank notes) and Fearns began to show a more friendly and amicable attitude. Fearns observed that the screeve business had been very good two or three years ago but since then a man by the name of Jackson had played the devil with it. Nadin asked who Jackson was and was told he was out of the Country at present buying heifers.

Nadin now showed Fearns some forged Bank of England notes and Fearns declared that they were also badly executed. Nadin said that he found such notes were very easily disposed of - the quality was satisfactory and he could no doubt dispose of many more. He said he had got them from a man called Ben Baker but was at a loss as how to get more as Baker had run away. Fearns asked Nadin how much he would give for a £1 screeve and was told eight shillings and sixpence, and fourteen shillings for a two pound screeve.

Fearns advised them not to trade them in Leek or Congleton as the area was under scrutiny. He had almost been caught when someone had snitched on him. He asked Nadin if he ever used five or ten pound screeves, to which Nadin replied that he had never even seen any but if he had some he would probably go to Ireland and use them to buy some salt beef and pork, as any amount of forgeries could be passed there. Knowles, who had left the room, returned to say that a caller from Manchester had arrived. Nadin told Fearns not to let anyone into the room in case they were all caught out. Before Fearns left the room he passed Nadin a five pound screeve and left it with him.

After a considerable time had passed Nadin grew concerned about Fearns' absence and began to think he would not see any more notes. Under the guise of going for more swag, Knowles was ordered to fetch the constables from Leek so that Fearns could be apprehended under the Act of Parliament for having notes in his possessions. Fearns returned after an hour, before Knowles and the constables from Leek, and in his hand he had two notes which he passed to Nadin. Nadin offered him three guineas for them. Fearns, not too happy about the offer said *"aye man, but one is a ten pound screeve"*. Nadin then agreed with him to pay three guineas for the ten pound note and one and a half guineas for the five pound note.

Nadin was shown other notes that were not for sale as they were to be disposed of in Yorkshire soon by Fearns, where they would realise their full value. Nadin was advised how to soil the new notes before trading them. Fearns told him not to squeeze or rumple them as the imitation water mark was done with a stiff substance that would break into holes. He added *"These are a good sort - my brother Tom and I played the devil with them in Wales last Chester Fair. We went to the Fair and from whence to Wales where we smashed (traded) about five hundred pounds worth"*. Nadin asked how he used the forged notes and was told that cattle and horses were purchased and resold later in Nottinghamshire - Fearns had a license to deal in horses.

Fearns asked Nadin if he knew Long Tom. *"Do you mean Tom Marley?"* Nadin replied. Fearns said he did not know the surname, however, the man he had the money off *"comes here once a month. He will be here again next week and you may have any quantity"*.

At that moment the constables from Leek arrived and Fearns was promptly arrested. Nadin and Knowles had achieved their objective with greater success than they could have dreamed of. Fearns was taken into custody and the next morning was committed to the County Gaol at Stafford by the Rev. Mr Powis, where he was to stand trial.

The trial of Fearns took place at Stafford in July 1801. Nadin himself underwent a severe cross examination by Mr Sergeant Williams. His evidence was both precise and accurate and fully confirmed by Marshall Knowles. Mr Glover, an inspector from the Bank of England, confirmed that the bills purchased by Nadin from Fearns, and also those found upon him, were forged.

An objection was raised by Fearns' counsel on the grounds that the number on the notes were not under the figure of Britannia. Mr. Glover agreed that this was the case. Either way His Lordship considered the objection frivolous. Counsel then objected that the indictment was too loosely worded in using the words bank note instead of promissory note. Again His Lordship disagreed saying *"The words of the Act (15 Geo 11 Cap 2) were bank note and it was quite sufficient that the terms of the Act were followed."*

Fearns himself claimed to know nothing of the notes and that he had a witness to prove it. The witness was one James Bloor who claimed to be a bread maker who lived near to the Bottom Inn. On the day in question he said he had business to conduct at the Inn where he had arranged to meet one John Chadwick of Waterfall regarding the sale of some flour. During his time at the Bottom Inn he claimed to have witnessed the events of that day, he recognised both Nadin and Knowles and stated that no such conversation with Fearns had taken place.

In the event Bloor proved to be a very poor witness and his evidence was clearly a tissue of lies. His description of Nadin and Knowles, and of their attire, was inaccurate. He had not been observed by the Leek constables and, to make matters worse, he claimed to have had no contact with the Fearns family prior to the trial. Knowles at this point made it known that Bloor had been seen many times with the accused's family at the Trumpet, an inn in Stafford where the Fearns' father and brother were staying as well as Bloor! Mr Thomas Kent, who kept the Trumpet Inn, proved that Fearns' father, brother and servant were there and that Bloor had supped with them on Thursday night and that they had slept together on both Wednesday and Thursday nights. This was corroborated by Margaret Brown, Mr Kent's servant.

Bloor had sworn to His Lordship that he did not know Fearn's father, brother or servant. Not only was Bloor's evidence dismissed, but he was taken into custody, the solicitors of the Bank undertaking to prosecute him for perjury.

As for Fearns, the jury found him guilty without hesitation. In passing sentence His Lordship told Fearns, *"His was a crime that prevented any application of mercy. The paper credit was now the security of the affluence, the riches and the power of the country, and if forgeries were so frequent and so well imitated the originals that the most wary might be deceived. They must be stopped or there would be an end to commerce and an end to us as a country"*.

He went on to add that there was another bar to mercy for the prisoner, another high aggravation of his crime - *he hath brought forward a man who, in the most gross, most impudent and shameful manner, came into Court to commit willful perjury who swore that he had not seen the father, brother or servant of the prisoner since he came to this place, when by the most respectable witnesses it was clearly proved he had been with them, ate and drank with them and even slept with one of them!*

Addressing Fearns directly His Lordship told him that the Law must take its course and accordingly Fearns was sentenced to death.

As an aside to the conviction of George Fearns, his brother, Thomas Fearns, was committed to Stafford Gaol either in late March or early April in 1802 charged with uttering counterfeit notes. With a co-defendant he appeared at the summer assizes in Stafford but did not receive a sentence. He was then transferred, in late August or early September, to be tried at Ruthin Assizes, Denbighshire, with a co-defendant, Green. Fearns was subsequently acquitted and Green was convicted.

As a further aside, a record of Nadin's employment by the Bank of England may be seen from the following expenses payment, indicating that he had been used by the Bank for several years and not just in the Fearns case:

> Paid Joseph Nadin the expenses incurred in several prosecutions prior to March 1797 including also a reward of £20 for his services as directed by the Lords Commissioners of the Treasury as per voucher No. 103 and therein parts authorised £67 1 6d.

If the trial of George Fearns lends credence to the words of our magistrate then the story of Sarah Wardle adds to it even more. (A.J. Standley and Staffordshire Advertiser, 21/8/1802)

Sarah Wardle was born at Ipstones in 1783 and was married to a cabinet maker. When she was committed for trial on the 4th July 1817, she was 34 years of age and had three children. Sarah had been charged with uttering counterfeit shillings at Leek in Staffordshire. She appeared at the summer sessions held in July and was sentenced to twelve months imprisonment.

Sarah was later charged with having in her possession at Leek a forged one pound note knowing that the note had been forged. She was tried for that offence later in July and for her pains received a sentence of fourteen years transportation. The sentence entailed Sarah being kept in custody at Stafford Gaol until such time that a berth was available in one of the boats used by the Government to transport female prisoners to either New South Wales, Australia, or Van Dieman's Land (Tasmania).

Sarah was no fool and had no intention of being transported if she could avoid it. Using her feminine charms she managed to form a relationship with a turnkey by the name of Bould. While awaiting transportation, Sarah was found work in the female hospital housed within the prison, in a room in the upper part of the gaol. Access to the hospital was gained via the hallway of the prison

Governor's house. Bould was in the habit of visiting Sarah and on one occasion had allowed Sarah's daughter to bring provisions in and to stay the night.

Such acts were strictly forbidden but it seems that Thomas Bould either enjoyed sexual favours from Sarah or financial reward. Inevitably Sarah plotted her escape - with the help of Bould, or otherwise, remains open to doubt.

Embroiled in Sarah's escape was a prisoner called George Walker who was serving twelve months hard labour for stealing a pig. George, realising the futility of being obstructive had become a model prisoner and was given a degree of trust. He secured for himself the position of cook and also that of watchman. In the latter capacity George walked the grounds of the prison during the late evening ensuring that all was well.

On to George fell the blame for Sarah's escape and after questioning he admitted to his involvement. He also claimed that he acted on the behest of Bould. According to George, Bould had been locking up the Debtors on the evening of the 4th of January and later approached him by the 'necessary' (lavatory) that was near the gate lodge. Bould told him that he wanted to see Mrs Wardle who at the time was looking after another prisoner, Hannah Nicholls. Both were locked in the female ward. George was instructed to take the keys, walk quietly through the Governor's house, release Mrs Wardle and bring her to Bould. George removed his shoes and went softly through the house to the ward where he found Sarah waiting for him. George then locked the door, descended the stairs and waited a few minutes for Sarah to get clear. He heard a dog bark at the time he reckoned Sarah would have reached the lodge and thought it would be the dog belonging to Kendedine, a turnkey who worked near the lodge.

George never saw Sarah again but was certain she had not gone over the wall but through the lodge gate. He still believed this to be the case even though a ladder was found leaning against the wall the following day. The gaol walls were twenty feet high and would have challenged a determined man let alone a matronly woman.

Not surprisingly, Bould had his own version of events prepared and ready. He claimed to have locked up Wardle and Nicholls just before nine o'clock. He then went to the gate lodge and placed the keys in the basket kept for that purpose. George Walker entered some time later to have 'a warm'. Apparently this was his custom and a frequent occurrence. Bould alleged that Walker could have taken the keys during one of his visits, released Mrs Wardle and then returned the keys. The keys were definitely in their accustomed position in time to be handed over to the Governor for the night.

The hue and cry that followed the next morning can be imagined. As well as a reward of £10 being offered for Mrs Wardle's return, a full investigation was undertaken. Bould being on duty that night was of course questioned and under pressure admitted to allowing Sarah's daughter into the prison and to allowing her to stay all night. Although there was a supposition as to Bould's intimacy with Sarah Wardle, the Governor found no reason to believe this. His behaviour had, however, left much to be desired and he was dismissed.

George on his own admission was very much involved and as a consequence took most of the blame. George Walker stood trial in April 1818 and was duly found guilty of feloniously assisting Sarah Wardle to escape from gaol. As was the custom of the day George's sentence had to match the sentence that Sarah was serving. He therefore received fourteen years transportation. George Walker left Stafford prison on the 24th May 1818 and was placed on board one of the old ships that was used to accommodate the large number of prisoners who left our shores in such an inglorious way. From Sheerness he sailed towards an uncertain future and out of our story.

As for Sarah, and despite the Bank of England increasing the reward to £60 for her capture, she now disappeared without trace. Until, that is, fate took a hand. When Sarah left Stafford she had headed south and eventually arrived in a small town outside Gloucester. Here, in the guise of a lady's maid, Sarah stayed the night at the local inn. She left the next morning only to return a few days later on the pretext that her mistress in Cheltenham had gone on a visit and that her services were not required for a few days.

After a few days Sarah left again on the pretext of meeting her mistress. Yet again she returned and this time advised everyone that her mistress was on a visit to Ireland and would be away for some months. During this time the mistress would send remittances for Sarah's sustenance. Sarah now established herself as a lodger and was soon to point out to her elderly hosts the inadequacies and dishonesty of their own servant. As a result the servant was dismissed and, although such duties were considered beneath the dignity of a lady's maid, Sarah took her place and soon became indispensable to the couple.

The frailty of the elderly lady was such that she passed away shortly afterwards and the elderly widower became dependent both physically and emotionally on Sarah. Sarah's feminine wiles served her well and before long the locals began to assume a wedding would take place. But here fate played its hand. A woman from Staffordshire was visiting the area and, much to her surprise, noticed Sarah standing outside the inn. She approached Sarah who, naturally enough, denied her identity, but whether it was the thought of the reward, or a sense of justice, the lady promptly denounced Sarah to a local magistrate. The magistrate did his duty, apprehended Sarah and placed her on bail pending formal identification by justices from Stafford.

Sarah, true to form, decided to leave while the going was good. Her elderly husband now became certain of her guilt by her flight, and suffered the added financial strain by the loss of his bail bond. He found it all too hard to bear and put an end to his existence. The bank notes that Sarah had claimed to have received from her mistress turned out to be forgeries which she distributed through trade at the inn.

Sarah's latest narrow escape heralded the end of her luck. Within a month, in April 1822, she was finally apprehended under the name of Ann Layshaw and was once again charged with uttering counterfeit notes. She appeared before the magistrate at a Lambeth Police Court in London and was shortly afterwards committed to Chelmsford Prison. Here Sarah was identified by Stafford prison officer, Richard Coombs, who travelled to London with the Stafford Governor, Thomas Brutton, with evidence of her conviction at Stafford.

There was also the latest charges to be faced, this time at the Essex Summer Assizes. A conviction resulted and Sarah, under the name of Ann Layshaw, was sentenced to death. The sentence was later commuted to transportation for life and in June 1823 Sarah, along with other female convicts boarded the *Mary III* and left for Hobart, Van Dieman's Land.

In Hobart Sarah, still known as Ann Layshaw, was assigned as a servant or worked in the female factory. In November 1825 Ann married Charles Jefton. By 1853 she disappears from official records - but she would by now have been 70 years old.

In conclusionI think the claims of forgery, in the village of Flash itself, remain unproven - just about!

Extract from James Smith's Map of Staffordshire published in 1817 for Pitt's Topographical History of Staffordshire, showing North Staffordshire.

Wetely Rocks in the late 1800s.

N I N E
The Powys Family - Mysterious Death

Even the most prestigious family lines disappear. The desire to perpetuate the family name and wealth came to nothing when a marriage failed to produce a son. Even nowadays wealthy families and those in power will endeavour to see their children marry 'well', but there was no pretence to do otherwise in the 18th and 19th centuries and although the Powys family were wealthy in their own right they would have been well pleased when Martha Powys married Edward Arblaster of Rownall. Arblaster was the last of an ancient line and, as Lord of the Manor of Cheddleton, he was an excellent catch.

When Edward died in 1783 without issue his estates passed to Martha and upon Martha's death, in 1791, to her brother, the Rev. Edward Powys, Rector of Stapleton in Shropshire, who came into possession of the Arblaster rights and privileges. He settled at Westwood Hall in Wetley Rocks and was Vicar of Cheddleton from 1791 to 1815.

He was also a Justice of the Peace for Staffordshire and played an important role in local affairs. He was a major in the Volunteers or Pikemen, a body of soldiers raised in 1805 to keep the peace and quell disorders at a time of civil unrest.

He was certainly resolute in his duties as witnessed by the 400 Blanketeers who arrived in Leek in 1817 intent on marching from their Manchester homes to London in an attempt to draw attention to their working conditions and abject poverty. So called because of their simple garb of blanket cloaks, the Blanketeers caused little trouble as they marched through Leek and on towards Ashbourne. But any sympathy from the people of Leek was not shared by the Rev. Powys. At the head of a troop of Yeomanry and in his position as High Constable, Powys caught up with the marchers at the Hanging Gate Bridge where they were promptly dispersed. About thirty returned to Leek and were then escorted to Macclesfield by a body of special constables sworn in by the Rev. Powys.

For convenience we must refer to him as Edward I as he was succeeded on his death by his eldest son, Edward II, who also became Vicar of Cheddleton. There was a second son, John and a third son, Thomas (*Cheddleton*. Ed. R. Milner; indicates also other children who died). John appears to have inherited

Westwood and later sold the estate to his brother Thomas for £13,100 in 1829.

Edward II remained as Vicar of Cheddleton from 1815 until 1851, during which time his life as a bachelor was in direct contrast to the demands of the church. To put it mildly he was considered by many to be unworthy of his office. Not that this mattered to Edward who continued to enjoy his lady friends throughout his life.

The younger brother, Thomas, was cast in the mould of his father. He became a Captain in the Coldstream Guards, a Colonel in the Staffordshire Militia and a Justice of the Peace. It was Thomas who, as Justice of the Peace, read the Riot Act in Burslem Market Place when the Chartist Pottery Riots were at their height in 1842. A grateful government thanked him for his action and an even more grateful gentry presented him with a dinner service bearing the ancestral crest of the Powys family and the Staffordshire Knot.

If the Captain was upholding the family traditions the Reverend Edward most certainly was not. In a small community, indiscretions were quickly spotted and made a source of gossip and innuendo. The philandering of the Rev. Powys had long been common knowledge but on this occasion he managed to incur the wrath of both his lover's, and his own family. A family by the name of Critchley had recently moved into a moorland cottage and the Reverend in his role of clergyman had duly paid them a visit. He was delighted to discover their very attractive daughter. From that point on she became the object of Edward's desire and on the pretext of visiting the mother he tried to win the daughter's affections.

In no time at all the tongues began to wag. The son of the house, sensing the trouble ahead, warned his sister to end the association. His words fell on deaf ears and his sister continued to meet the parson whenever possible. One Sunday the parson arrived as usual and, after hitching his horse to the gate post, went with the daughter into the cottage. The brother, with the help of two accomplices, unhitched the horse and took it to a nearby pit shaft. Without ceremony the unfortunate animal was driven towards the shaft and fell to its death, although during the scramble the reins became entangled with Critchley's boot and only the sudden drop snapped the reins saving Critchley from the same fate as the horse.

The loss of his horse embroiled the parson in a tissue of lies. He had no ready money to purchase another horse and had to explain its disappearance. The following morning Captain Powys received a note from his brother describing the narrow squeak he had had when his horse had fallen from under him while out riding. He asked for the loan of one of the Captain's horses until such time as his annual tithe payment would enable him to buy a replacement. The Captain, being wise enough to doubt the story, questioned the bearer of the note. The young lad promptly told him all he knew, including the whereabouts of the Critchley's cottage.

Despite the entreaties of the boy, the Captain instructed that the stables should be locked until he had investigated further. Arriving at the moor the Captain drew his horse to a halt next to an old woman picking bilberries and asked her if she knew the way to the Critchley's cottage. Pointing a finger toward a nearby hill, she replied in her dialect, *"The'er bin sum new foke wot an taken a cott o'er yon bonk. Theer's a muther an' darter an the darter's a flashy sort o' wench. They sen a man o' quality kapes her. Mehap them's o you arter."*

The Captain arrived at the cottage and demanded to know the fate of the Parson's horse. The daughter gave some evasive replies, but was persuaded to be more open when the Captain, changing his tactics, tried a more friendly approach. Gradually she confessed, not only to the events surrounding the parson's horse, but to her brother's involvement and the liaison.

The Captain agreed not to punish Joe Critchley on consideration that he was taken to the scene of the accident. Now satisfied with the explanation the furious Captain went immediately to South Low, near Cellarhead, where the parson lived. Conveniently the parson was out and, despite several attempts during the week, the Captain was unable to confront his brother. It was easy enough for the parson to be absent for his clerical duties which included the livings of Bucknall, Bagnall and Cheddleton. Nevertheless Captain Powys persisted and finally caught up with Edward on Sunday at the evening service.

The Captain told Wood, the sexton, to tell his brother that he wanted to see him on business immediately after the service. Several of the congregation resolved to remain behind to see what would happen. When Wood eventually emerged he spoke quietly to the Captain who immediately went into the vestry where he found his brother with another woman. Now totally enraged he bundled the parson out on to the path and set about him with the hunting crop. As he vented his anger he shouted, *"You think more of your cursed concubines than the cloth you wear."*

The comment was undoubtedly true as can be borne out by the poor attendance. On one particular occasion the only people in the church were the sexton and the parson. Unabashed, the Parson proclaimed *"Dearly beloved brother, let's put on our hats and go home."* It is likely that more people attended his thrashing than his service.

As for the Captain, he died in 1851 in the most strange circumstances. During the summer of that year, with the hay-making well under way, the Captain stationed himself in the shade of a small oak tree. From this vantage point he watched as the men raked the hay into piles, and the horse and dray made its way slowly across the field. The afternoon turned to evening and still the Captain sat beneath the tree. One of the workmen, wondering if anything was amiss, went across and as he approached he could see something was indeed dreadfully wrong. The Captain was delirious and muttering to himself, *"And then another,"* and *"Yet another,"* and *"The grass"*. With some effort the men managed to get him back to the hall. The doctor was sent for but, despite his best endeavours, he was unable to prevent the Captain's health from deteriorating. He lingered on for a few days deliriously muttering the same phrases he had uttered beneath the tree.

After the Captain had been declared dead the undertaker was sent for to measure the body for the coffin. When putting the body into the coffin he noticed that it had not stiffened and it remained in this state even to the time of the funeral, the undertaker becoming more and more concerned. After the funeral he was heard to complain that he did not think the Captain was dead. *"All the folks I have buried were stiffuns but the Captain's joints were all a limber."* Equally unusual was the spot where the Captain had sat under the oak tree. The grass where his boots had rested had withered and, shortly afterwards, disappeared altogether, leaving bare patches.

The mystery would no doubt have faded from memory or been put down to imagination except for a repeat performance. A few years later the tenant of the farm was taken ill in the same field and died within a few days. His body never stiffened like the Captain's. When the area of the field where he had sat was examined it was also noted that the grass had withered away leaving four bare patches where the heels and soles of his boots had rested. In *Cheddleton: A Village History*, Ed. R. Milner, there is a reference to a third death in similar circumstances.

What are we to make of such a story? A hundred years later the similarity of the two deaths, and the phenomenon of the scorched grass still leaves room for conjecture. A heart attack plus the heat of the sun may be the answer. Perhaps a brain haemorrhage or infection, perhaps meningitis.

The question of rigor mortis must be considered. In normal weather conditions, when death occurs, the natural heat of the body dissipates over a period of a few hours. In hot conditions, or in tropical climates, the loss of body heat may take much longer but it would be unlikely to have been many days. Rigor mortis itself is only temporary and as the body begins to deteriorate - and decompose - it once again becomes flexible. Normally in the brief period between death and burial a condition of rigor mortis prevails but, in this case deterioration could have been rapid. The fact that the undertaker witnessed no stiffening of the Captain's body leads to another possibility. Was the Captain in a deep coma? Even with today's sophisticated methods it is not unknown for medical practitioners to mistake deep coma for death. Certainly exhumed coffins have been known to have scratches and inbedded finger nails in the underside of the coffin lid! As it appears that the death of the Captain was not questioned by his family and that the comments of the undertaker were not taken seriously we can only assume that the Captain was well and truly dead when he was buried. Or can we?

The other part of the mystery is even more difficult to explain. Withered grass! Bare patches! It is worth remembering that the Captain lived in superstitious times when education was limited. Custom and folk-lore were rife in an area where 'witches' still existed and herbal cures were held in great respect. Local legend tells of the Witch of Rownall and another witch who kept the good people of Burslem in check. But why, in his delirium, was he heard to utter *"the grass"*? Clearly something was troubling him as he sat beneath the oak tree. 1851 was far too early for the burial of toxic waste. The Captain may simply have shuffled his feet for some time and, in doing so, worn away the grass. The hot weather would have added to the scorching and breaking up of the grass.

Then again could the marshy ground have been the cause. Marshes by nature create rotting vegetation which, in turn, gives off an odourless, colourless and usually invisible gas. Under certain conditions this gas takes on the appearance of light airy strands of mist, known by country dwellers as Will-o-the-Wisp. Marsh gas is a simple hydro-carbon - methane (CH_4) - and it is toxic. Again the suggestion is probably no less feasible than any other.

The derelict farm buildings of Whiston Eaves Hall.

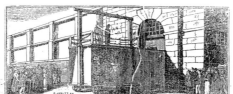

EXECUTION OF WILLIAM COLLIER

At Stafford, on Tuesday, August 7, 1866, for the Murder of Thomas Smith, jun., of Whiston Eaves, near Cheadle.

Staffordshire Summer Assizes.

Before Mr. JUSTICE SHEE.

The Murder at Whiston Eaves.

WILLIAM COLLIER, farmer, was indicted for the wilful murder of Thomas Smith, the younger, on the 4th July, 1866, at Whiston Eaves parish of Kingsley.

The following are the leading facts of the case, as proved by the witnesses called:—

Mr. Smith was the eldest son of Mr. Thomas Smith, a gentleman well known in Cheadle and the neighbourhood. He is lord of the manor of Whiston, and is also a farmer in a considerable scale. Deceased was his eldest son, and about 24 years of age. He was an active, frank, agreeable young man, and popular with a l classes in the neighbourhood, and was familiarly known among the villagers as the young Squire. He recently joined the Oakamoor Cricket Club, with the humbler members of which he was a great favourite, and gave other evidences of a desire to live on pleasant terms with his neighbours. The man Collier, was a man of indifferent repute in the parish. It was not alleged that he occasionally poached in the covers surrounding his farm and his house, which is very near to some of Smith's plantations, was used as a rendezvous by poachers. At the same time he was not regarded as a thoroughly vicious or abandoned man; nor is there anything in his countenance to indicate gross depravity. He is a fair, light-haired man, with blue eyes, and his countenance is of a type common enough in the "moorlands of Staffordshire. A certain measure of determination of purpose is indicated by the lines of his mouth and lower jaw, but the whole of his countenance is a common p ace one—t at of a small farmer without educ tion or natural intelligence, but at the same time not suggesting a murderous disposition. He is 35 years old and has a wife and seven young children. The circumstances attending the murder may be thus briefly summarised—For some time Collier entertained considerable bitterness of feeling against Mr. Smith, his unfortunate son', and those who were employed to watch the preserves, for fourteen months ago a friend of his asked him how he was getting on with his neigh

c urse ran down the middle of the plant tion, the bott-m of the plantation, where deceased was found there was a large quantity of briars. t ne goes. The first thing he saw on on entering the plantation was the body of the deceas d l ng in t o hollow, near the watercourse, quite dead. He was lying on his face with one arm under his head. His h nds and face were col l. There were two c ts, ne on each side his brow, and the back of his head had been knocked about and was matted with blood. It was about half-past nine o'clock when he found the bo y. He is also found the trigger of a gun and a ram r n. The ramrod was about six yards from the body, whilst he was searching on the plantation he saw the prisoner two fie ds off hoeing turni s Prisoner was apprehended at three o'clock on Friday morning. After that time he a d witness s were together at Moor croft's house. He said "Now, Jim, how should-t thee have felt if thou hadst been in Mr. Smith's place?" He replied, "I suppose I should have felt the same as Mr. Smith if I had received the same blows." witness also said, "This wil never daunt me; I shall be as brave as ever for it s" Prisoner then said, "I don't know; it's the best way to be cautious." Prisoner next said, "Hidst see no any where?' and witness said, "Hidst thee see me any where?" Prisoner ma d no reply.

...it yourself to prayer and by repentance to the poor Judge who is above you, you may, notwithstanding the horror of a public execution, find a happier lot as respects tho long eternity which awaits you ed, then if your life had been extend d to the utmost span of man's life It s now my painful duty to pronounce upon you the awful sentence of the law, which is that you be taken from home to the prison from whence you come, that you be taken from thence to a place of execution, that you be there hung by your neck until you be dead, and that your body be buried within the precincts of the prison in which you shall have been last confined. And ma the Lord God, of His infinite mercy, have mercy on your soul.

Confession of the Murderer.

In a letter written on Collier's behalf to the mother of his victim, he confesses that he left his home at 3 a.m. on July 5th, t king with him a double-barrel ed gun, both barr s loaded; and that before he met the young man he killed two rabbits with one barrel. He loaded again but did not ram down the wad. He met young Smith a out 50 yards from where the body was found, with whom he exchanged a word or two; and on the young man t urning round he fired at him, hitting him on the back of the head. As soon as he was hit he r mb'e l a nd exclaimed "Don't hur more

Governor in the customary form to deliver up the body of the culprit for public execution.

The culprit was taken into the corridor of the new prison, where the officers of justice and the Rev. M O'Sullivan with the last executioner of the law, Smith, the hangsman awaited his arrival. After a deliberate arrangement of all the sad details of the execution, the procession started for the place of execution.

The procession having arrived at the lodge, the culprit was taken into the Governor's office and underwent the process of pinioning, in the presence of the officials.

A few minutes were occupied in this painful duty, and and at eight o'clock the culprit was ushered upon the scaffold under the charge of several officials and accompanied by his Spiritual guide.

His appearance on the scaffold excited considerable sensation amongst the crowd assembled, who now watched the scene with intense interest. The culprit appeared calm and yielded unresistingly to the hands of the executioner. who at once placed him in a position on the drop, the halter hanging over him, suspended from the beam.

Revolting Mishap at the Execution.

The Executioner having speedily adjusted the rope he shook hands with the prisoner, and descended and drew the bolt, when, to the horror of the multitude, the rope loosened from the beam, and the wretched culprit fell prone and helpless to the bottom of the scaffold. Great consternation appeared amongst the officials on the drop, who instantly descended to the rescue of the culprit, and amidst the execrations of the spectators

The article in the Staffordshire Advertiser covering the murder, the court case and the hanging.

TEN
The Moneystone Tragedy

The rustic routine in the more remote villages of North Staffordshire was seldom disturbed, but it was shattered when William Collier, a farmer from Moneystone, was found guilty of murder and became the last man to be publicly hanged outside Stafford gaol.

Moneystone now lies on a country lane between the villages of Whiston and Oakamoor in the Churnet Valley. In more recent years the road has become the access to the quarries of British Industrial Sand (now Hepworths), but in 1866 the lane was little more than a cart track which, en-route to Oakamoor, led to Whiston Eaves, and Park and Crowtrees farms. Branching off to the north was the original Blakeley Lane which has long since disappeared beneath the earth movers of BIS. A couple of hundred yards further on toward Oakamoor, and now classed as the new Blakeley Lane was the narrow, grassy track that led to the hamlet of Moneystone. Here a few stone cottages and farmhouses straddle the road and overlook an open cast quarry long used to produce the fine silica sand much sought after by the glaze-makers of Stoke-on-Trent.

The track to Moneystone petered out near to Rock Cottage where a convenient footpath directed the traveller to the old Blakeley Lane. Almost immediately the lane passed Oldfields farm on the left before continuing towards Blakeley farm where it joined with the Garston road.

Oldfield farm was the home of William Collier and although not large, its thirty six acres supported his family, with seven cows and a few chickens. It must have been a meagre existence, and to supplement his income Collier resorted to the activities of countrymen from time immemorial. He poached the game of the local gentry.

The Smiths of Whiston Eaves Hall, along with the Bolton family from Oakamoor (Moorside Hall, Farley Lane), were by far the most prosperous landowners in this part of the Churnet Valley. Collier had been at odds with the Smiths for a while and recent altercations over a water course had done nothing to heal the rift. The Smiths were not used to insubordination and they found Collier an unacceptable hindrance. The difference between the two could not have been greater. One a small time farmer with a disregard for authority and a penchant for poaching, the other wealthy, yeoman farmeing 'gentry'.

The Smiths' land covered most of Whiston and Moneystone and included many of the tenanted farms. Whether Collier's farm was owned by the Smiths is unknown. If so they would surely have evicted him. The laws of 1866 were very much in favour of the landowner and at a time when villains could be transported to the colonies or even hung for what would now be considered a minor offence, the Smiths would have had little difficulty in getting rid of William Collier from a tenancy.

As it was, the Smiths decided to concentrate on catching Collier in the act of poaching. The job fell to Thomas Smith, the twenty three year old eldest son, and heir to the family fortunes. Tom's plans to confront Collier at the scene of his crime involved the assistance of Bamford, one of the farm hands. On the night of July 5th 1866, Bamford and Smith retired to their beds with the intention of rising early to watch the game covers in nearby plantations.

Bamford rose at 4.00 am and went to rouse Thomas only to discover an empty bed. From the lack of warmth in the sheets Bamford reached the conclusion that Thomas had left his bed at least an hour earlier. Bamford now left the house and, with no specific instructions to help him, wandered aimlessly around the estate. Tom, it appeared, had risen shortly after 3 am and, with the aid of a full moon, had headed towards the covers in the Barn plantation.

Collier must have risen about the same time and with his new gun cocked over his arm, he too headed towards the plantation. The two men must have reached Barn plantation at about the same time and a surprised Collier found himself confronted by Smith. A row followed and Collier, in an uncontrollable rage, went for Smith. As Smith turned to run, Collier raised his gun and fired.

Recollections later referred to two shots in quick succession and Collier himself spoke of shooting at a rabbit. Regardless of the detail, the fact remains that the blast from Collier's gun caught the fleeing Smith on the back of the head, tearing away his hat and leaving him seriously wounded. Still in a fury Collier then set about his victim, striking him about the head with the gun until Smith lay prostrate on the ground.

It should be realised that the consequences of being caught poaching at that time were dire. Collier's future was very much at stake from the moment of the confrontation. Whether he thought in rational terms or whether he acted in panic the result was the same. He had murdered Thomas Smith in a brutal manner. His only hope lay in the fact that no one had witnessed the event.

Collier quickly left the scene and hurried away to his own adjacent land.

He reached the edge of one of his fields and walked alongside the boundary wall before reaching a land drain where he knelt and deposited the gun an arm's length into the opening - hopefully out of sight and mind. He then returned home and awaited the morning.

The Smiths, totally unaware of the night's event, rose as usual and only realised that something was amiss when Tom failed to appear for breakfast. Bamford could throw no light on Tom's absence but related the plans that he and Tom had prepared to apprehend Collier in the act of poaching. Fearing an injury, or worse, Tom's father became more and more concerned and shortly after breakfast ordered his men to go into the plantations in search of Tom.

The search party came across Tom's battered body where it lay near to the game covers in the Barn plantation. Using the door from the nearby field barn they carried the body back to his family at Whiston Eaves Hall.

As always in a close knit community, news travelled fast, and by noon the residents of Moneystone and Whiston were aware of the death. As tongues began to wag, residents spoke of shots being fired in the night. Opinion flowed freely and in some quarters the name of Collier was bandied about. His disputes with the Smiths were common knowledge as was his poaching.

During the morning, in a show of normality, Collier worked in his fields. He observed Tom Smith's body being carried away and awaited the aftermath he surely knew was sure to follow. Within a short space of time a police officer from Leek was handling the case and asking pertinent questions of local people. Almost immediately suspicion fell on William, but he vehemently denied any involvement.

The police officer would have none of it and Collier was forced to attend an inquest at Whiston Eaves Hall. He still denied his involvement but the police were far from satisfied and placed him under arrest whilst they undertook an intensive investigation. They had a suspicious death, they had a suspect, and now they set about obtaining sufficient evidence to justify Collier's detention.

Retribution was swift in the 19th century but the speed of Collier's investigation and trial beggars belief. Within days he was formally charged and bid his wife an emotional farewell at Oakamoor before being removed to Stafford goal. His trial was fixed for July 28th 1866. During the intervening days between his arrest and the trial the police sought to establish their case. Collier had not confessed to the crime, and the evidence upon which the prosecution based their case was suspect to say the least. But, this was 1866, before the art of forensic science, and before the rights of the common man became fundamental.

The case put before the court was clumsy and unprofessional. In a modern court it would have been torn to shreds if only because it was totally circumstantial. No one had witnessed the murder. The prosecution called Eliza Taylor of Moneystone who stated that on the night of the 5th she heard two shots being fired at about 3.00 am. It should be remembered that poaching was common in the area and it was not unusual to hear shots.

The gun had been discovered in the culvert. Henry Goldstraw, who gave his address as Udall Town, stated that he heard two shots fired in succession at about 3.30 am from the direction of Black plantation. Goldstraw was followed by Eliza Moorcroft who claimed that she saw Collier walking by the stone wall close to where she lived on the Garston road and heading towards the edge of his fields. Quite what Eliza was doing at 3.30 am was not considered. Neither was the question of her eyesight or the distance involved. It was obviously a moonlit night because she related matters to her husband who told the court how, the following day, he conducted a search of Collier's field and found the stock and barrel of the gun pushed arms length into a drainage culvert.

Eliza and Thomas Moorcroft, either by genuine observation, or by deduction, played a vital role in the prosecution's case. Part of Eliza's statement seems strange. The road that passes Collier's farm is called Blakeley Lane by the locals and Garston road is not reached until it joins another road beyond Blakeley farm. Eliza referred to the road as Garston road, a mistake easy enough for a stranger to make but not for a local. It is tempting to reach the conclusion that the Moorcrofts were 'helped' by the police to issue their statements. Certainly with the gun lock, and stock and barrel, containing pieces of hair and traces of blood, the police would have felt justified in their case.

Rupert Mellor, a gunsmith from Hollington was examined and said he sold the gun to Collier a few months earlier. At first Collier denied all knowledge of the gun and suggested that it could be the property of a Mr Bowler, a man who had lodged with him for a while but left just prior to the death of Tom Smith. He also suggested that a band of travelling gypsies may have been involved although this was quickly dismissed.

Ownership of the gun became a vital issue and the defence resorted to what can only be described as a blistering attack on the integrity and ability of Rupert Mellor. Mellor was lambasted for his lack of precise records in the sale of firearms. It was suggested that he was more a general dealer and merchant than an expert in guns. But whatever he was, and however suspect his records were, he was able to pinpoint his own purchase of Collier's gun. Not only did Mellor recall the purchase he could also advise on markings on the gun that related to the previous owner.

Mellor's sale of the gun to Collier was the subject of much discussion. At least four other people verified that the markings on the murder weapon were identical to the markings on the gun purchased by Collier. The case for the defence was in tatters and only an instruction from the judge could save Collier.

The judge had been far from happy with the case from the outset and even as he summed up he stressed to the jury that the evidence surrounding the death of Tom Smith was far from satisfactory. He instructed the jury to consider the evidence very carefully before reaching a verdict.

Within an hour of retiring the jury returned. The foreman stated that they were dissatisfied with statements involving Collier's lodger Mr Bowler. Why had he left Moneystone? Where had he been at the time of the death? Bowler's explanation seemed honest and to the point - a few days earlier he had been caught poaching and was due to face the consequences of law. Hoping to avoid arrest he had fled the scene and would have remained out of sight had not the actions of Collier curtailed such hopes. He also confirmed categorically that the murder weapon belonged to Collier. He stated that two other guns in the Collier household were in such a poor state of repair that Collier only had one useable piece - the murder weapon.

Satisfied with Bowler's explanation the jury retired once more. After a very short deliberation they returned to the court. The foreman of the jury gave their decision without hesitation. Guilty! He added that Collier's previous good conduct be considered and a degree of leniency extended by the judge. But having received the verdict the judge addressed Collier. Not only could he expect no mercy he would now face the ultimate penalty and should be prepared to meet his maker. With arms folded Collier quietly accepted the sentence and calmly left the court.

The date of the execution was set for Tuesday 7th August at 8 pm, in front of Stafford gaol. As he awaited death Collier confessed to the crime. The details were almost identical to the conclusions reached by the police. He described how he had left home with both barrels of his gun loaded. With one barrel he shot at two rabbits and then encountered Thomas Smith. He fired and hit Smith in the head and when his victim turned to run away he struck him repeatedly with the gun until the barrel broke. Full of remorse Collier now wrote to Smith's family expressing his regrets and acknowledging his guilt.

Come the day of execution, the usual collection of onlookers began to arrive. From as early as 5.00 am people sought a vantage point and throughout the day they were joined by country folk who had made the long journey to Stafford and swelled the crowd to over 2000. Even women and children were assembled behind the barricades.

Shortly before 8.00 pm, Collier and his executioner, a cowkeeper from Dudley also called Smith, walked calmly onto the scaffold. For a few minutes Collier prayed audibly, before, with his arms pinioned, he took his place on the trap door. The executioner placed the noose around Collier's neck and moved the lever which operated the trap. With a click the trapdoor swung open - and Collier dropped heavily to the floor taking the rope with him. Badly bruised but alright, Collier stood shaking against one of the scaffold supports. A stunned hangman went down the steps to Collier and then led him back to the scaffold.

The crowd, equally stunned by the mishap, now found their voice. Hoots of derision, cries of 'shame' and demands for 'liberty' were heard amid the roar of disapproval as the officials went through the procedure once more. This time there was no mistake and Collier's life came to a merciful end.

The horrific scene outside the gaol proved to be beneficial in one area at least. It had been too much even for the hardened prison officials. The Collier execution was to be the last public hanging in Stafford.

With justice done, the Smiths were left to come to terms with their loss. The brother of Thomas, John Eli, became heir to the estate. He married and had two children, Thomas and Mary, but when he died, sometime after the First World War, the family were faced with unsustainable death duties, and the Whiston Eaves estate was broken up. Much of it was sold but Tom and Mary continued to live at the Hall in reduced circumstances. Neither ever married. In 1947 Tom caught a severe chill walking to Whiston during one of the worst winters on record and died. Mary lived on for several years.

Much of the Whiston Eaves Hall estate, including Barn plantation became the property of British Industrial Sands. The Hall fell into dereliction, but not before the fine staircase and interior fitments were sold.

ELEVEN
Of Fighting Men

The multi-million pound business that surrounds boxing today has its roots in more humble times. In the 18th and 19th centuries bare knuckle fighters entertained the crowds with fights that ended only when one man was left lying amid the blood and gore of battle. A lack of consistency in rules and weights and a spectacle, often over sixty or seventy rounds before the loser was either unconscious or too weak to continue, made exciting 'sport'..

The rounds did not consist of a standard three minutes but varied to suit the fight. A round was considered over only when one of the contestants was knocked to the ground, and the next round followed as soon as the fighter was able to continue. With the crowd baying for blood, and a suitable purse at stake, the protagonists would fight to the bitter end.

Traditionally fighters came from travelling gypsies, fairground workers and the working classes. For the down-trodden masses of industrial Britain boxing was seen as a salvation. A chance to earn in a single night more money than they could in a month of employment. Virtually every village, town and city had its champion, a local hero prepared to take on all comers.

Stoke-on-Trent was no exception and each of the five towns produced its own favourites. Among the very best of the locals were the fighting Catons of Golden Hill. This rural village was just a short walk from the town of Burslem, long considered the queen of the potteries, but in reality, with its mass of kilns, engulfed by a pall of smoke and grime that clung to everything and everybody. It produced fine earthenware that brought wealth to the potters and a meagre living for their employees.

If the conditions were tough, the men and women of the Potteries were tougher. The same can be said of almost any of the industrial towns and cities of the Midlands and certainly of West Bromwich with its cottage industries of chains and nails. Just as Burslem produced Harry Caton, West Bromwich produced Emmanuel Tinsley who was known to his vociferous supporters as 'Nailer Boy'. Tinsley was born to a family of nail-makers who also kept the Jolly Nailer public house in Taylors Lane.

By the age of seven Tinsley was working with his father and by the age of sixteen he was old enough to stand up for his father who was being intimidated

BOXING!

STAGED BY H. W. BROMIGE, B.B.B.C.

Victoria Hall

HANLEY,

Tuesday, July 17th,
1934.

AT 7-45 P.M.

DOORS OPEN AT 6-30 P.M.

SENSATIONAL FIFTEEN ROUNDS CONTEST

JOHNNY QUILL

(London). This boy k.o. Pat Haley, in London, in his last fight. Quill is out with a £500 Challenge for a fight with Mason.　V.

PAT HALEY

(Hanley). Leading contender for the Title by reason of his recent win over the Champion at Mile End Arena, London.

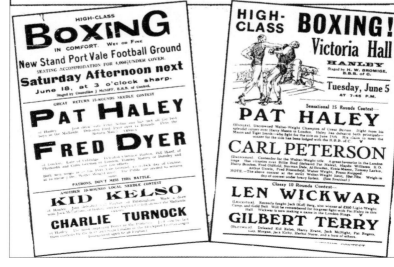

by a local bully. In the skirmish that followed, and despite a considerable difference in weight, Tinsley taught the bully a lesson he would never forget.

His natural skills were apparent to all and he was soon encouraged to become involved in the local fight scene. Weighing little more than ten stone, he took on and defeated anyone and everyone regardless of weight or size.

The Catons of Burslem were a family of prize fighters, the father and his nine sons. Ned was the champion of the potteries and Harry and William were both good enough to take over his mantle. It was Harry Caton who instigated the fight with Tinsley. Both fighters had been at Hednesford and Caton had insulted Tinsley so a fight became inevitable.

The fight was arranged for the 6th April 1840 at Woore in Shropshire and thousands turned up to witness what was billed as the fight of the century. Caton, aged twenty four, stood five feet eight inches and weighed eleven stone seven pounds. He had the advantage of both height and weight over twenty year old Tinsley at five feet six inches and ten stone and three pounds.

Nailer Boy was not to be intimidated, his speed and intelligence was more than a match for the Potteries' champion. Caton, with his rugged, brutal attacks, often overwhelmed opponents but Nailer Boy was ready for him. As Caton prepared to rush forward Tinsley skipped towards him and delivered a hard blow to Caton's eyebrow and just as quickly retreated, leaving blood trickling down Caton's face. The Potteries' man came again. Nailer Boy side-stepped and hit him on the ear. Caton stumbled into one of the ring posts, and fell to the ground. The round was over and Nailer Boy was looking confident.

Harry's corner ordered him to change his tactics and to Caton's credit he did just that. For over twenty rounds the fight swung first one way and then the other, but Tinsley was still relatively unmarked. By the twenty seventh, Caton decided to engage Nailer Boy in closer combat. As the two tangled in the centre of the ring they fell to the floor and a badly shaken Tinsley was carried back to his corner.

The twenty eighth round began. Caton appeared to rush at his opponent but suddenly stopped in his tracks and before Nailer Boy realised what was happening two hard blows in the ribs had knocked him to the floor. The Potteries crowd were delirious as they sensed victory. Nailer Boy thought otherwise. Round after round he dodged Caton's blows. At one stage Caton was floored by several blows to the stomach and as the fight wore on Nailer Boy inflicted more and more damage to his eyes. Caton, was going down frequently.

Bare-fist fighting, 1870.

and the fight in the end dragged on for seventy-two pitiful rounds with him virtually blinded and fighting by instinct. But now Nailer Boy made one of his rare mistakes and tangled with Caton in the centre of the ring. Both fell heavily to the floor and as they were being separated Caton held up a lacerated finger claiming that Nailer Boy had bitten him.

Rightly or wrongly, and despite the vehement protests from Tinsley's corner, the referee ruled it to be a foul and stopped the fight. In the mayhem that followed Tinsley's mouth was examined by the umpires who stated that Caton's wound had not been caused by a bite, but despite being called back to the ring Caton's team stuck to the referee's decision and claimed the fight.

In truth Nailer Boy was a worthy winner and returned to West Bromwich as popular as ever. Both fighters continued to dominate their local scene but luck deserted the Nailer Boy. He remained undefeated by another man for two years before losing a battle to typhus. He died at his home on the 28th of December 1841, still not twenty two years of age.

The barbaric savagery of such fights continued for many years despite the introduction of more rigid rules and controls that made bare knuckle fighting illegal. In the Staffordshire Moorlands, Three Shires Head was the venue for an illegal fight between the Burslem Bruiser and Preston Pat. With a prize of

Fighting often ran in families as this Staffordshire family of boxers typifies.

£2000 at stake the fighters were prepared to defy the threats of the magistrates in Leek. When a magistrate arrived to stop the fight the organisers resorted to a well used ploy and promptly moved the fight out of Staffordshire into Cheshire - and the magistrate, his duty done, stayed on to watch the fight!

Gradually the organisers of fair play won the day and fights became professional and controlled. North Staffordshire in general, and Stoke-on-Trent in particular, stood on the brink of a golden era. Between 1900 and 1938 the area produced a glut of fighting men who can only be described as outstanding.

Tommy Harrison was the only Potteries' boxer to be an international champion. Harrison won the European bantam championship in October 1921 when he defeated the Frenchman Charles Ledoux over twenty rounds at the Palais-de-Danse in Hanley. Strange as it may seem, Harrison became the European champion before he gained the British championship in 1922, defeating Jim Higgins of Scotland. Ledoux took his revenge later when he beat Harrison on two occasions, but Harrison had earned his place in Stoke-on-Trent's hall of fame.

FOUR LOCAL HEROES

Jack Matthews - featherweight

The first of our four was a typical Potteries' man. Prepared to work hard at his profession of hairdresser and devote his spare time to physical fitness and training, Jack was determined to be the very best. With his slick black hair and waxed moustache he looked a formidable opponent. Born in 1883 Matthews was a familiar figure in the Hanley, Burslem and Etruria areas where he pounded the city streets and parks in his quest for physical perfection.

It is said that Jack Matthews was a late starter but in typical 'Matthews' fashion he continued to box until the age of forty two by which time he had lost just nine out of three hundred and fifty bouts!

He was making his presence felt by 1912 when he was a last minute replacement against George Mackness of Kettering at London's National Sporting Club. He could hardly have been at his best having just had twelve teeth removed but Matthews was never short of courage.

The fight that followed was hard fought indeed and one that neither fighter deserved to lose. Jack, the underdog, stood toe to toe against the favourite, Mackness. Eleven times Matthews was hammered to the floor and on six occasions Mackness suffered the same fate. It was purely fitness and courage that kept Matthews in the fight. It also gained him an unexpected victory when Jack called upon all his reserves and produced a right hook that sent Mackness to the canvas and out for the count. This was a featherweight with a real punch - the champion of the potteries could no longer be considered just a local fighter.

In 1913 he fought another local man, Billy Gerkin of Newcastle, at the Olympia Skating Rink, Hanley. With a purse of £110 and side stakes of £110 Matthews was a valued commodity. With a family to keep and a business to run Jack worked hard for his money. Despite his age he continued to defeat all comers and would undoubtedly have gone on to contest the national featherweight championship had the First World War not intervened.

Jack remained a force to be reckoned with even after the War and, despite his age, at least two people had good reason to respect him. Tancy Lee had defeated the great Jimmy Wilde to hold the Lonsdale Belt, but he met his match at the Staffordshire Sporting Club in Stoke in September 1921 when Matthews beat him over fifteen rounds, another fight that remained long in peoples' memories.

In 1920 Jack, now in his late thirties was matched against the up and coming Tommy Harrison, eleven years his junior, and later to be European champion. Billed as the championship of the Midlands, the young pretender against the old master, it was a match not to be missed.

Jack Matthews

Few expected Matthews to stand up to a boxer of Harrison's potential and not many of the 6,000 people who crammed into the old Port Vale ground in Hanley would have put their money on him. The master was in decline. The opening rounds only served to prove the point. Harrison, younger and quicker, was outclassing Jack as the fight reached the half way point.

Once again Jack dug into his reserves of stamina and courage. He was not prepared to accept a humiliating defeat. The second half of the fight saw him revitalised. In a bruising encounter he was landing the quicker and harder punches and by the fourteenth round it was Harrison who fell to the ground. The count was brief before Harrison was up again and slogging it out.

The battle royal continued until the final bell at the end of the twentieth round, when the referee, without hesitation, raised the arm of both fighters. What better result than a draw for an old favourite who had seen it all before and a young favourite who had Europe knocking at his door.

Benny Jones - bantamweight

Benny was born on the 13th September 1913 at Etruria Road in Hanley just a few yards away from his later hero and role model Jack Matthews. With the exception of his uncle, Jack Jones, Benny's family had no experience of boxing and could not have dreamed of the fame that awaited their new arrival.

As Benny grew he became more and more interested in boxing. Every spare minute was spent reading about his heroes or listening to anecdotes in the local gymnasium. For the most part Benny was self taught and learned the hard way how to pace himself, how to avoid being hit and how to take the fight to his opponent, and by the time he left school at the age of fourteen he had already decided to be a professional boxer. For a few years he fought as an amateur and a sparring partner to local professionals until he felt ready to take on the world.

Benny Jones

Ironically he was not ready enough. On 22nd December 1931 he was matched against a far heavier opponent in what would now be described as a mis-match. The result was inevitable and the inexperienced Benny suffered his first defeat. But it would deter him and within a week he was back in the ring and fighting three times a day to win a local bantamweight competition.

For a while he won every contest he entered and for 18 months his confidence and reputation grew in tandem. He then was brought down to earth again with a bump on 7th November 1933 when he lost on points to the experienced Jack Lilly of Congleton - Jack beat Benny again at a later date which is indicative not only of Lilly's ability, but the depth of talent at the time.

Many will say that Benny's boxing skills were his prime asset but it takes more than ring craft to turn a good boxer into a great boxer. Benny had the raw courage, the determination and the intelligence to go with it, and this combination carried Benny towards the peak of a career that ended prematurely with the outbreak of war in 1939.

Between December 1931 and July 1939 Benny Jones fought no fewer than ninety times. He lost on twenty three occasions in fights that would raise a few eyebrows today. On occasions Benny fought when he was ill, injured or outside his weight limits. It is an indisputable fact that when Jones was matched correctly he was one of the finest boxers in the country. His fights with the great Phil Milligan became the source of legends, and his battles with Jackie Brown, the ex-world flyweight champion caught the imagination of the nation.

If Brown thought he was in for an easy ride with Benny Jones he was in for the shock of his life. The first bout between Jones and Brown took place at the Victoria Hall in Hanley on 7th September 1937 and produced a controversial decision that still rankles the boxing fraternity of Stoke-on-Trent. For twelve rounds Benny traded punches with the ex-champion and looked to be well on top by the twelfth and final round. To the disgust of the crowd the referee thought otherwise and raised Brown's arm in victory. Years later Jackie was to admit that Benny was the real winner. They fought again two more times. The second match resulted in a much disputed draw and on the third occasion a leg injury put paid to Benny's hopes in a fight that was going his way.

Benny now received a letter from the British Boxing Board advising him that he had been selected to fight in a series of eliminators for the British bantamweight championship. Other contenders were his first opponent Pierce Ellis and his old adversary Phil Milligan who was to fight Jim Hayes.

Ellis was an excellent fighter but then so was Benny - he had already beaten Milligan and was confident that he could bring the British championship to Stoke-on-Trent. Unfortunately a much longer battle was looming and as Britain declared war on Germany, all boxing was suspended, and Benny's career came to an end.

Some of the boxers who fought with Benny Jones became household names themselves in North Staffordshire. Tut Whalley a local southpaw and Tiny Bostock from Leek are our other two heroes but even they had to work hard to beat one of the also rans - Darkie Baker of Newcastle under Lyme who was among the most courageous of boxers. Darkie was the most gentle and good natured man imaginable and it is hard to picture him in the ring trading punches. But trade punches he did. He fought Benny Jones on no fewer than seven occasions, winning once, drawing once and losing five times. As the arguments rage about the brutality of boxing the debate takes many twists. Many of the old fighters fought hundreds of bouts and retained their faculties well into old age. On the other hand, although Darkie remained competent, he did display all the hallmarks of a boxer who had continued too long.

With a flattened nose, cauliflower ears and speech that was slurred, he would have made an ideal target for the opponents of boxing. They would no doubt ignore the fact that he was a happy man. At times he displayed a ready wit although it was not always intended. He could also take a joke at his own expense, as friends who remember him when he worked at Meaford Power Station will tell. The one instance that is printable occurred when the decorators were painting the Engineers' shop. Darkie observed their skills with a growing admiration and when they got around to putting the finishing touches to the toilet block it knew no bounds. The top half of the walls had been painted light blue and the bottom half a deep grey. Now, where the two colours met, the painter was carefully painting a narrow black line. It all looked very artistic - so much so that Darkie exclaimed to us all, *"That painter would make a good typewriter"*. He was not allowed to forget that slip for a long time!

Tut Whalley

Sometimes a person becomes so popular that a nickname outlives their real name. It was like that with Tut Whalley. He was born in 1913 and no doubt his parents were happy enough with the name of Tommy when they christened him.

Tut was a small boy but he more than made up for his size when he took on the school bullies. Perhaps it was the harsh lessons in the school playground that turned Tut into a polished fighter. Whatever the reason, he followed the path of many before him and took up boxing when he left school.

In a career that lasted until the outbreak of the Second World War, he beat virtually every champion in the world outside the United States of America. At this crucial point in his career he was about to take on the American champion 'Small' Montana when he was called up to join the nation's fight against Germany. It was a sad end to an epic journey during which his boyish good looks and fighting skills had earned him a well deserved reputation.

He became the Potteries' school boys' champion at the age of eleven and continued to dominate the sport at junior level until he left school at fourteen. He immediately set about joining the 'big boys' and enrolled with the 'Black Boy' gymnasium in Cobridge. From there he progressed to his first professional fight at the age of seventeen.

As was so often the case with flyweights, Tut had to fight heavier opponents on a regular basis. That first fight, against Billy Sale of Nantwich in 1931, resulted in a winner's fee of 12s. 6d and a third round knockout. The public had witnessed a natural southpaw with a lethal left hand. With more sympathetic management Whalley would surely have been a world champion. With the inexperience of youth he signed up with promoter and manager Jack McNiff and in doing so became matched against numerous champions and ex-champions. The McNiff strategy was to arrange for two minute rounds instead of the usual three minutes. Because of this no matter how many fights Whalley won or how convincingly he won them the results were always unofficial.

The whole sorry saga came to a head when McNiff arranged a bout between Tut Whalley and Jackie Smith. Amazingly McNiff forgot to advise the press or the public and after a sparsely attended evening at the Queen's Hall McNiff found himself unable to honour his financial commitments. Whalley felt he had no option but to end their relationship. His contract was examined by the British Boxing Board who ordered McNiff to pay his debts, including Tut's fee, or forfeit his licence.

Whalley's next manager was the more professional Jack Fitzgerald and under his guidance he went from strength to strength. Fitzgerald arranged a fight against the world champion Kenny Lynch in Dundee. The purse of £1,000 was an astronomical sum in 1934 and Tut had every intention of winning it. In a bruising battle Tut put Lynch down five times, finally connecting on the chin for what would surely have been the final knock down. Instead of raising Tut's

Tut Whalley

arm, the referee, who was also Lynch's uncle, disqualified him for a low blow. The crowd were in uproar, with even the partisan Scottish fans shouting their disapproval. Despite the furore the verdict stood and Whalley had lost.

Fitzgerald continued to match Whalley against the best including Jackie Patterson of Newcastle. Patterson drew with Whalley before going on to become champion by beating Peter Kane - who had previously beaten Lynch. Tut Whalley was obviously in good company and it must now have seemed a far cry from his early days when he once had to fight eight times in twelve days. On one occasion in Birmingham, he knocked out his opponent in two rounds. On his way home he stopped to watch a tournament in Smethwick. The officials discovered they were a boxer short and persuaded Tut to stand in. He won with a fifth round knock-out.

Fitzgerald handled his boxers with great care but he was also an astute business man. The talk around the potteries had always been about who was the better man among the local fighters. In truth it was too close to call. One of Tut's closest friends was the Leek boxer Tiny Bostock. Bostock, like Whalley, was a gifted athlete and they often trained and sparred together. Such was their friendship and respect that the last thing they wanted was to enter into professional rivalry. But Fitzgerald could see the attraction of sucha match as could the boxing fraternity.

Whalley and Bostock were matched in an eliminator for the Northern area championship in 1938, and on a rain soaked night they entered the ring before a massed crowd at the Port Vale ground in Hanley. On the night it was Whalley's greater experience that gave him a narrow points' victory.

This fight with Bostock may have been the one that remained in the minds of the local fans but Whalley had many other great victories to be proud of. During a career spanning 378 fights he won 192 by knockouts and became the number two flyweight in the world rankings. He was in some ways an enigma, for whilst he managed to get the better of both Benny Jones and Tiny Bostock he lost to Phil Milligan.

For the most part Tut Whalley's defeats occurred at the beginning and end of his career. With the amazing number of fights pre-war boxers packed into their lives some defeats were inevitable. But make no mistake about it, Tut Whalley was a great fighter - and a Potteries man to boot. In his prime Tut was even capable of beating heavier opponents as can be borne out by his three victories over Jim Brady, the European bantamweight champion.

It was Tut's left hand that accounted for most of his opponents but he did not need it to dispose of Irish man Al Sharpe when they met in Hanley. From the opening bell Sharpe danced around Whalley without a blow being struck. As Tut advanced towards him Sharpe backed away and in a few farcical seconds toppled over the ropes, fell out of the ring, struck his head on the floor and was counted out. The Potteries sense of humour must have come to the fore on that night - no doubt, Tut smiled all the way home.

Tiny Bostock

The most diminutive of our boxing heroes was Tiny Bostock. The tiny baby who was born in a small cottage in Leek in 1917 was christened Ernest after his father who was then away at the Front. He was destined never to return and, like so many others, he lost his life in the Great War. But Ernest had a conventional and happy upbringing, and it was a contented small boy who attended Compton school.

His greatest asset, even at the tender age of six, was a sweet treble voice that placed him in the probationers' choir stall at All Saints Church. In no time at all he was a regular member of the choir and making a name for himself. He was good enough to be included in a party that was invited to sing at Lichfield Cathedral and from time to time he was also allowed to be absent from lessons to learn principal parts in musicals. Such favours did little for his popularity in the school playground. He was so small that he avoided the usual rough and tumble of playground fights. It would have done nothing for his confidence to be classed as a sissy but that is precisely what happened.

In later years the experiences of his schooldays were to alter the course of his life. He remained a devout Christian but his mind was far from settled during his early youth. For a while he sang at Leek Town Hall on Sunday evenings and also teamed up with a friend to sing duets in the local cinema. He became a member of the Leek Operatic Society and so good was his voice that a career as a singer seemed a foregone conclusion.

He started work at fourteen at Whites Silk Mill, one of Leek's major employers. Before the age of sixteen he found a better job at Joshua Wardles' at Leekbrook. He also decided that he needed to toughen up, so he visited Carr's Gymnasium, Leek's finest. Among all the activities in the gymnasium boxing was by far the most popular and was under the control of Ted Crumbie.

Crumbie was an excellent instructor and even the diminutive Bostock was

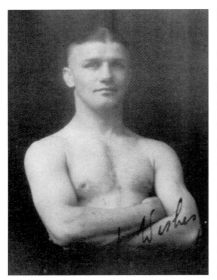

Ernest 'Tiny' Bostock

inspired to have a go against all comers. With a muscular and lithe body Crumbie cut an impressive figure and was very popular with the youngsters. Under his guidance Ernest began to build up his stamina and technique and, despite his light weight, his confidence grew considerably. Even so he must have looked a comical figure with his thin arms and oversized padded gloves.

One of Ernest's heroes was Jack Sharkey, a heavyweight in the boxing elite of the Midlands. When Sharkey decided to open a gymnasium in Leek Ernest was one of the first to join. One night as Ernest was working furiously on the punch bag, Sharkey's manager, Jack Fitzgerald walked in. He chuckled at the sight of the tiny boxer. *'Who's your new heavyweight?'* he said. *'Oh him'* said Sharkey. *'He's a wonderful little boxer but I do not know what to do with him.'* *'What weight do you think he is?'* Fitzgerald guessed at seven stone but was way out. *'He is six stone eight pounds'*, said Sharkey. Fitzgerald smiled, *'In that case he must be a paperweight!'*

Even so Fitzgerald was impressed enough to take an interest in him. Ernest was christened 'Tiny' and Sharkey and Fitzgerald set about building the Leek boy into a seven stone flyweight.

Tiny's earlier fights as an amateur had begun as he approached his fifteenth birthday with side bets of £5, but it was a fitter and wiser boxer who entered into his first professional fight at the age of seventeen. Weighing a little over six stone he won the bout and a purse of ten shillings. Three years later, under the guidance of Fitzgerald, he was a contender for the British title only again to have his career cut short by the second world war.

During those three eventful years Bostock astounded the boxing world. He also proved to be a fighter with a difference, for after his fights he would return to the ring and sing to the fans! A particular favourite *Waltzing in a Dream* went down particularly well after a knockout victory.

The church with whom he was so popular did not know what to make of

Tiny. On one occasion he was banned from singing in a charity concert at a service in Golden Hill. Elsewhere his christian commitment was accepted with enthusiasm and he performed as a soloist at All Saints Church in Leek with the full support of his friend the reverend W. G. Kenworth. Tiny had no difficulty in combining his beliefs with his boxing.

He continued to win his fights on a regular basis. During his brief career he took on the very best. He beat the Scottish champion Jimmy Campbell and shortly afterwards the American champion Small Montana. He also defeated the IBO European champion Ernest Weiss, the Austrian flyweight. On the few occasions when he lost he was usually successful in reversing the decision when they met again. Among the exceptions was Peter Kane who went on to become world champion.

The most pertinent fact in Bostock's career was his age. When the War cut short his progress he was still several years away from his peak. Given these extra years Tiny would surely have improved and become almost unbeatable. Like the other fighters in our story the War probably

Tiny as a chorister

prevented him from being a world champion. He fought on for a short while after the War before retiring to concentrate on his textile business. In a short but active career he had 200 fights and lost just ten. He was truly a gifted boxer who deserves to stand side by side with North Staffordshire's greats.

After the Second World War a period of austerity was followed by a prolonged period of social change and an ever improving standard of living. Even the labouring classes felt the benefit of a national health service and full employment. The popularity of boxing, so long the sport of the underdog, began to decline. The gymnasiums, the boys' clubs and the boxing competitions were gradually replaced with less physical sports. Stoke on Trent still produced the occasional boxer good enough to be worthy of its past reputation, but the glory days were at an end.

Strangely enough. and against all the odds, the sport was resurrected for a few years in the unlikely town of Uttoxeter and the man behind it was an ex-Romany by the name of Bartley Gorman. Gorman had the ideal pedigree for a boxing promoter except that his experience was gained outside Queensbury rules. Bartley was the Gypsy bare knuckle champion and as such his exploits in the ring were more relevent to the 18th and 19th centuries than to the 1960s.

No doubt Bartley's performances were frowned upon by the powers that be, but the locals around Uttoxeter had no such reservations. Gorman was popular both inside and outside the ring and when he joined forces with Harold Groombridge in 1970 to become a promoter there was no shortage of boxers at his gymnasium behind the Wheatsheaf pub in Bridge Street. The partnership was immediately in conflict with the British Boxing Board and Bartley resolved the problem with a typical piece of independence. By approaching the International Boxing Federation they gained approval to stage fights under New York State rules. Thus BGHG Boxing Promotions were able to stage boxing legally, albeit unofficially as far as the British Boxing Board was concerned.

The USA Pirate Boxing Rules were observed in a four round exhibition match between Sam Gorman and Don Halden. Don was probably the best boxer in the area and Gorman was among the hardest. The local boxers had a huge following and the locals got what they wanted, a local fight between local fighters. The unlikely venue was the Old Chapel in Rocester.

They were in sharp contrast as they entered the ring. Halden with his blonde hair and white robe and Gorman wearing an old hessian sack draped over his jet black hair and his shoulders. Exhibition match it might have been but neither man gave an inch as they fought toe to toe before the roaring crowd. It was held on a no decision basis but it was enough to prove to the people of Rocester and Uttoxeter that BGHG promotions were worthy of support.

In point of fact the BGHG promotions were always well organised with first class referees and doctors in attendance. Bartley's popularity and reputation no doubt attracted the local pugilists such as his brother Sam, John Peaty, John Wheeldon and Chris Morfitt. The better known Don Halden of Rugeley and Tommy Beardmore of Cheadle were also proud to fight for the Uttoxeter promoters. For a few years the Elite Cinema and the Town Hall attracted capacity crowds to Uttoxeter, and national and international fighters.

On one occasion Sam Gorman was matched against a much fancied

American, Olanze Johnson. Instead of the anticipated twenty round battle, Sam made short work of the American by flattening him in the first round. BGHG were in demand and promotions were regularly held in Hanley's Victoria Hall.

Perhaps the most memorable was the fight between John Peaty, one of Gorman's fighters, and Zue Shaw, who was managed by the Bodell stable in Swadlincote. (Jack Bodell had been British heavyweight champion and produced many well-trained boxers). On this particular night it was the hard hitting Uttoxeter heavyweight who came off best although he was several stone lighter than Shaw. At six feet two inches and sixteen stone Peaty was a giant of a man but he was dwarfed by Shaw who weighed twenty three stone and stood seven feet six inches tall! Shaw lasted just four rounds - he may well have underestimated Peaty who was an excellent boxer with a terrific punch.

In 1972 Gorman launched a bid to establish a more creditable organisation under the name of the Anglo American Boxing Federation. At the group's first meeting at Wilfred House in Uttoxeter the name was changed to the International Boxing Federation. Whether or not the IBF actually originated in Uttoxeter is not clear, but is now an international force that once boasted the great George Foreman as the World Heavyweight champion.

Bartley Gorman

The story of the decline of boxing in Uttoxeter is also clouded in mystery. Around 1975 Bartley Gorman was subjected to a violent assault outside the ring. Gorman spent two months in hospital and eighteen months on crutches. By the time Bartley had made a full recovery his club was in decline. It closed in 1977. The old pub was demolished twenty years later.

References

Stoke-On-Trent library, Hanley
Staffordshire Sentinel
Uttoxeter Advertiser
The Bugle

Biography of Benny Jones, G. Deakin
The Black Countryman magazine, William Salt
Library, Stafford

Hanbury now: The crater where Upper Castle Farm once stood, the church, the school and the Cock Inn

TWELVE
The Fauld Explosion 1944

In 1937, as a precaution against the growth of Nazi Germany, the Government purchased from the Duchy of Lancaster part of a gypsum mine near Fauld in Staffordshire. The mine was to be used as a bomb storage dump. The entrance to the mine was housed within the RAF camp at Fauld, and about a mile away from the more substantial village of Hanbury.

Early in the War an adjacent mine belonging to Peter Ford was also purchased. The workings of the two mines were separated below ground by around 120 yards of rock and earth and, perched high above was Upper Castle Hayes Farm, the home of tenant farmer Maurice Goodwin and his wife Mary.

Were the Goodwins fully aware of the danger that lay beneath them? That the storage dump existed was an open secret. What was not so well known was the huge amount of bombs stored within the chambers and passages of the former mine. In all some 14,975 tons of bombs, including giant American 4,000 pound blockbusters, were being held on a fateful day in 1944. The Goodwins, and no doubt other locals, would have been extremely worried had they been aware of the disastrous history of similar dumps in other parts of the country. To put it in short, explosions were not uncommon.

The discipline within the RAF camp certainly gave an aura of control. In 1944 the bomb store was manned by No. 21 Maintenance unit. Also present were employees of the Air Ministry and the Ministry of Aircraft Production, the Air Ministry Works Department and the Air Maintenance Inspection Department, (AID) - being specifically responsible for the inspection of bombs and any maintenance required, they were crucial to the safety of the site.

About 1,033 people were employed at RAF Fauld, half of them civilians, plus a contingent of Italian co-operators seconded to the camp.

The morning of Monday 27th November 1944 was typical of late autumn, a sharp frost later challenged by bright sunshine, as Doveridge men climbed onto the lorry for the mine. Present that day were Bill Coker, Bill Robinson, Bill Dainton, Bill Hudson, James Haire, Jack Hudson, Jack Freeman, Mr Wall and Mr Langley. Leaving from home at the same time was Frank Beckett who was to witness events from Sudbury Camp where he worked as a joiner.

At about 11.00 am Maurice and May Goodwin locked the doors of Upper

Castle Hayes Farm to go to market, setting in their car off down the narrow lanes that bordered the mine workings. At eleven minutes past eleven a single short explosion was heard. This was followed immediately by a very long explosion that reverberated for 30 seconds. The sound was heard over 100 miles away and shock waves were recorded as far away as Casablanca.

The explosion was the largest involving conventional weapons the world had ever known. The effects were devastating. A crater 900 feet across and 80 feet deep was ripped out of the Staffordshire farmland. Upper Castle Hayes farm simply disappeared. Surrounding farms, Hanbury Fields and Hare Holes farm were severely damaged. In nearby Hanbury, buildings were shattered. Fire and shock waves caused further damage. The Cock Inn and the village hall were virtually flattened. By some miracle no one in Hanbury was killed and the village school, with its full intake of pupils, remained intact.

The full force of the blast removed a large part of the hillside above the Peter Ford works. This also destroyed the water reservoir that supplied the mine and six million gallons of water mixed with soil and debris formed a wall of mud and slurry twenty feet high that engulfed the works and a row of cottages.

Thousands of tons of rock and debris which had been blasted 300 feet into the air, fell to earth. A huge shadow blocked out the daylight as three million cubic yards of soil, stone and boulders descended. Houses that escaped the initial blast were now smashed by the debris up to eleven miles away. In the immediate vicinity of the crater the debris lay 20 to 30 feet deep 70 yards from the edge. Trees stuck out of the ground, roots uppermost and, in the nightmare scene, dead and injured animals littered the ground. Around 200 cattle and 100 sheep were killed and many of the surviving cattle died during the night.

The human casualties took longer to assess as the gruesome task of recovery got underway. Rescue workers raced to the scene. Mine rescue, fire brigades, ambulance teams and personnel from the American camp at Foston came to help. Seventy people died and twenty were injured. In the bomb store itself 5 servicemen and 15 civilians together with 6 Italians were killed. Those in the immediate area were atomised. Some died from carbon monoxide poisoning and others from the mud slide, including Maurice and Mary Goodwin in their car. Nine farm workers died, including one man whose legless trunk was found buried head first. By some miracle none of the Doveridge contingent was killed, although one farm worker from the village died whilst driving a horse and cart on one of the farms near Fauld.

The old Fauld alabaster works and the massive crater made by the explosion

The inevitable inquiry followed and was conducted by the Royal Air Force at Fauld between December 5th and 12th 1944. Despite rumours of sabotage and enemy action, the conclusion reached was far more realistic. It had been the practice, against all instructions to the contrary, to use a brass chisel when extracting the exploder charges from dangerous bombs. A brass chisel struck against steel could easily create a spark, and it was this simple but foolhardy practice that was thought to have caused the explosion. If standing orders were adhered to a bronze chisel would have been used.

If heads were expected to roll it was not to be. The RAF Acting Chief Equipment Officer and the AID Chief Inspection Officer, *'although not absolved from responsibility'* for the lax procedures, were simply reprimanded and transferred. The Commanding Officer of 21 Maintenance Unit had been on leave on the day of the explosion and escaped without censure.

Whatever the shortcomings, the reaction and contribution of the numerous organisations afterwards illustrates the British response to a crisis. Help arrived very quickly indeed. So much so that the area was swamped as assistance poured in from all directions. The police from Tutbury and Burton were quick to pass on details to the various authorities. Soldiers from the US military base at Foston rushed to the area, the civil defence, the woman's volunteer service and the auxiliary fire service. Water supplies were quickly reconnected.

Rescue parties searched the village of Hanbury and local fields. The Cock Inn, demolished except for the saloon bar, managed to provide refreshment.

Over the next few days the reality of the situation sank in. The task of discovering and removing bodies, the clearance work and rebuilding would take months rather than days. Teams of miners from Midland collieries volunteered to help. Convicts from Stafford goal joined with individuals from the local area to help with the relief work. Major Dobson co-ordinated the work on behalf of the civil defence and it was he who recognised the health risk imposed by the dead cattle. Within a week 118 carcasses were disposed of. He also reported that *'eighty four houses in the Tutbury Rural have been damaged'. Four other houses were damaged beyond repair and two others were very badly damaged'.*

Major Dobson battled on against overwhelming odds but the task was simply too great. On the 5th December, civil contractors Messrs Robert Douglas of Birmingham became involved. With the help of 170 troops working three shifts and with local coal miners using breathing apparatus the task of re-entering the mine continued. Fauld was unique in terms of emergency action.

At times chaos reigned but, with the exception of bureaucratic disputes over the priority of procedures, work continued unabated. Local heroes emerged as common sense prevailed and officialdom was put in its place.

Ministers and Members of Parliament visited the scene. Promises were made of compensation to the families. As always it was more political hyperbole than honesty. National newspapers carried front page stories. Families did eventually receive compensation, but nothing like that hoped for. The hazardous nature of the work in the bomb store resulted in an average wage of around £6 a week. As compensation widows received 32 shillings plus 11 shillings for each child with a proviso that no one would receive less than £2 10 shillings. Compensation for property damage was also unsatisfactory. An initial response, shortly after the explosion helped, but full compensation took months to reach the victims. The detail was typically ambiguous:

'The awards will be of amounts those concerned might reasonably expect to receive in a successful action for damages under the Fatal Accident Law, the Reform Act, or at common law. Claimants have been invited to seek legal representation either through their solicitors or trade union machinery. Any reasonable legal costs will be paid'.

Little comfort to the people of Hanbury and Fauld. Almost as soon as work began, rumours and incrimination started. The Governnent, anxious to keep control, insisted on any inquiry remaining confidential, and the 30 year rule prevailed. It was not until the late 1970s that full details began to emerge.

The Government's penchant to withhold information from the general public was still in evidence in 1962. Earl Harrowby sought information from Lord Carrington, who replied, *'the cause of the explosion at Fauld was never established. It was not the practice to publish the reports of RAF boards of enquiry and, notwithstanding the lapse of time, it would not, in my opinion, be in the public interest to make an exception in this case'.* In some ways Carrington's statement says it all. A report from the RAF about the RAF.

The local people knew the truth well enough. Negligence, poor supervision and a blasé attitude contributed to an unprecedented disaster. When facts did emerge we discover that the explosion was caused by about 4,000 tons of explosives held in one area of the mine. It was also established that rumours about sabotage and Italian prisoners of war were totally untrue.

Despite the secrecy and the buck-passing, the local people come out of it as shining examples of stoicism, determination and honesty. Inquiries are one thing, but someone had to find and identify the dead. The local people took on the task. Mr John Auden, coroner for East Staffordshire was assisted by P.C. Mackey and Mary Elizabeth Cooper. Auden was moved to write about Mackey and Cooper. Of Mackey he wrote, *'For 72 days, without rest, he carried out the removal, cleaning and identification of bodies in every state of mutilation and decomposition. In addition to this he has kept me informed and done most of the clerical work of which there was a considerable amount daily. At no time has he shown signs of nerves and his cheerfulness has helped everyone through an exceedingly difficult period'*. Of Mary Cooper he wrote, *'This woman, of her own free will, has cleaned and scrubbed a very gruesome temporary mortuary every day for 72 days. The work has been indescribable. She has helped with the undressing and also with the washing of clothes removed from the bodies. One of the first victims she had to deal with was her very own husband. In most cases that would have been sufficient for a middle aged woman to undertake without volunteering to continue the work with all the remainder. She survived the wrecking of a farm at which she was looking after an old lady, and it is probably due to her actions that the old lady's life was saved!'*

For Auden there was no-one to sing his praises. Records retained by his son W. H. Auden of Anslow, the inquest details when eventually released, and an article by Trevor Jones (pub. Keele University) redress the balance. Auden found himself in the middle of political interference from all angles. The Civil Defence and the police were anxious to bring matters to a conclusion and a return to normal. The RAF wanted to continue with the distribution of bombs. On the other hand the coroner had legal obligations to consider which included an inquest into the deaths and a satisfactory appraisal of any bodies that would be impossible to recover.

The Home Office gave Auden their support but did little to ease the pressure he was under. Within Auden's own profession, support was given at the highest level and pressure was applied to military and political bodies in an effort to leave Auden free to do his job. What he really wanted was the freedom to tell the truth. Instead he was left to dispel rumours wherever he could without divulging any details of his findings, to answer all and sundry whilst adhering to the Official Secrets Act. The pressure must have been almost unbearable.

THE END